Underestimated
By Jettie Woodruff

This book is a work of fiction. References to real people, events, establishments, organizations, or locations are intended only to provide a sense of authenticity, and are used fictitiously. All other characters, dead or alive are a figment of my imagination and all incidents and dialogue, are drawn from the author's mind's eye and are not to be interpreted as real.

Warning! This is not your everyday fall in love romance. This book contains disturbing situations, strong language, graphic, sexual content, some forced, some not. If it's your happily ever after love story that you are looking for, you should probably move on. If you are up for the ride, stick around and it may just turn into a love story after all.

Dedication
To Syd for all of your feedback and support.
To Ms. C. Barr for the hours of perverted conversations, while this book was being transformed.
Only at the warehouse.

Chapter 1
Of all of the thirty-six alternatives, running away is best.

I couldn't hold my eyes open for one more second. I had just driven 2,954 miles, fifty-seven hours, not including the six hours that I tried to sleep at the Motel 6, *twice*. Thirty-four more miles, according to the robotic voice coming from the box stuck to the windshield of my not so new, used car.

The closer I got, the more my nerves began to stand on end. What the hell was I doing? Who does this? Who walks away from their life to start all over? Maybe walk isn't such a good choice of words. When I say all over, I truly mean all over. My entire existence had been nothing but an illusion.

My name is no longer Morgan Kelley. That one would take some getting used to. I spent many hours of my long drive going over the aspects of my new life with my invisible friend in the passenger seat. We actually had hours of conversations, okay, so they were one sided, but they were without a doubt, conversations. I'd even given my new friend a name and called him Slash, after the three-inch gash in the cheap vinyl seat.

Now, my name is Riley Murphy. I moved to Misty Bay, Maine, from Carson, Indiana, when my company downsized, and I lost my job as an advertising rep. The small two bedroom cottage was a gift from my late grandmother. "Wow, a small cottage in Misty Bay, population, 1,075." I interrupted my life studies when reality set in for the millionth time since I had left Las Vegas. I mean Indiana. "Dammit Morg... Shit, I mean Riley." I need to sleep. I just need sleep. I can't function. I know this. I have it all embedded in my brain. I'm going to be fine, and there is nobody from Misty Bay, Maine, looking for me. I had to stop. I couldn't repeat details of my new life out loud or to myself, one more time. Not if I intended to keep my sanity intact. It was already on the verge of toppling over.

"Turn right in one-point-seven miles," the robotic voice instructed. I turned right and was on a curvy blacktop road barely wide enough for two vehicles. The coast was absolutely breathtaking, and did wonders for my nerves. I reached over

2

and cranked the handle, rolling down the passenger side window. My nerves calmed when I heard the waves crashing onto the rock walls below me. I couldn't believe it. I was going to be living by the ocean. I could walk along the beach anytime I wanted, and I would too, I promised myself.

'Welcome to Misty Bay,' I finally read the homemade wooden sign, situated in the fresh spring, green leafed trees off the side of the road. I drove through the small town, looking out every window of the car. My head spun around until it wouldn't rotate any further. One bank, a post office, one grocery store, and one small library which looked like it would fit inside the one I used to go to in Las, I mean Indiana, at least ten times.

'Reminiscent,' I read as I pulled to the curb. This was where I'll be working. Me, working in a coffee shop slash, hippy store. I'd never had a job in my life. I felt a little whimsical thinking about it. I looked in the rearview mirror. I still had the bruise just below my right eye, but I had four days to get settled before I started work. It should be gone by then.

I waited for the school bus to pass and continued on my journey, excited to reach my destination, finally. "Turn right," the voice instructed again. I made a right and was on a one lane gravel road. It was a quaint little neighborhood, and an older gentleman waved as I passed him retrieving his mail. "Arriving at destination, on the right," I was informed. It wasn't what I was expecting at all. The cottage was sort of by the beach, and I hoped there was a strategy to get off the mountaintop to enjoy it. The aqua blue color of the house had to go. Who in their right mind would paint a house that color? It was the ugliest blue I'd ever seen. I actually had a sundress pretty close to that color. I wouldn't be wearing that, I decided when I got out of the car. It was the beginning of May and the temperature might have been sixty. When I left Las, I mean Indiana; it was ninety nine.

I opened the gate, just off the driveway. The picket fence was nice, and I liked the white, but would unquestionably be changing the color of the house. I walked up the small porch and unlocked the door, the door to my new home. "Wow," I said out loud to no one. The living room was open and led to

3

the small dining area. I walked across the hardwood floor to the other side. The French doors were great and led to a nice deck, although it was farther from the beach than I had hoped. Every wall that I could see was painted bright yellow. The kitchen wasn't bad and the appliances were updated and modern, but the bright paint was already giving me a migraine. The countertops were a dark gray. I thought they were some kind of fake marble, but I could work with that.

As I walked toward the side of the house, I peeked into the bathroom, and I was pleasantly surprised. I was happy to see a rather large, claw foot tub. Thankfully the walls were a pleasant, neutral, olive green color. I liked that room, and it only needed a good cleaning. The first bedroom would make a nice office. It was small but had a reasonable size window overlooking the ocean. I could even live with the light blue walls. The next room was bigger, but nothing like what I had in Indiana. I smiled to myself when I remembered that I was from Indiana and not Las Vegas. This room also had a marvelous view, overlooking pine trees and the Atlantic Ocean. The walls were a soft, subtle gray, and I loved it. One less thing to do. I noticed how rocky the yard was, and then it dawned on me; I would have to mow and take care of the yard myself. At least there was a small shed to keep a lawn mower. Lawnmower? I didn't know how to buy a lawnmower. Where do you even buy those things?

Okay, so maybe I didn't think this through that well. I had no bed. Where was I supposed to sleep? The only furniture left in the house was a table and four chairs. The table was one of those round, plastic, outdoor tables with a hole through the middle for an umbrella. The four plastic chairs didn't even match. One was green; one was white, and two were brown. No couch either this was just brilliant. I had the money, and had planned on buying new everything. That part I was looking forward to, however, it didn't help much at seven o'clock on a Thursday night. Food! I had no food either. I was so tired. I honestly didn't want to go back into town, although it would have taken me a full three minutes to drive. I decided to unload my car and at least get a much needed hot shower. No. I wouldn't be doing that either. Well I could, but I had no soap, shampoo, wash cloth, and not even a towel. I didn't even have a blanket to cover up with, let alone lie on.

I unloaded what clothes that I had. Nothing was mine, not even the ones I was wearing. Ms. K had made me change them and put on the ones that she got for me. I didn't even take any of the expensive items from Drew. Ms. K told me not to, afraid that if I pawned them, they might be traced. That was a chance I wasn't willing to take. I didn't even get the one framed picture of my Grandma Joyce, the only person who had ever cared about me or my well-being. The pictures of my life after Drew could have gone up in flames, and I wouldn't have cared.

After I had my clothes carried to the room that I would call mine, I dragged myself back out to the car. I remembered seeing a Dollar General Store in town. At least I could get a pillow, and a couple of blankets to sleep on. I desperately wanted some bathroom supplies, and I supposed that I should go to the grocery store.

I went to the Dollar store first that was my first mistake. By the time I had bought $212 worth of supplies, enough to get me through until I could go shopping the next day, the grocery store had closed. I bought a coffee pot and had no coffee for the next morning. My new adventurous beginning wasn't in accordance with how my mind had played it out… at all. What was I supposed to eat? I hadn't had anything since around noon, and wanted to put the miles behind me, and just get there already. Get there, to an ugly blue house, close to the beach, if you could get down the mountain. Get there to a house without a bed or food. Get there to a house that required me to wear sunglasses inside because the bright yellow paint hurt my eyes.

I unloaded my new belongings, but I didn't put anything away in the bathroom. It seriously needed a good scrubbing. Why didn't I buy cleaning supplies at the Dollar store? At least I could have disinfected the tub. I used the cheap, strawberries, and cream shampoo and a new washcloth to clean the tub, and then filled it with hot sudsy water. It was sensational, and the tension that had begun to build again started to evaporate. I tried to think about my new life and how to make this house my home, but my mind kept drifting back to Drew. It had been four days since I had vanished from his life. I wondered about his reaction when he realized that I'd disappeared. What went through his mind when he dialed my cell phone? I didn't even know where it was. I wondered if anyone would answer it. I knew Drew was probably beyond irate, and I was sure that a few things had been broken during his discovery.

When I woke, the sun was pouring in through the window. My homemade bed must have been sufficient because I slept the whole night without waking once. I didn't waste time stretching and lingering around in bed the way I was used to. Instead, I got straight up, brushed my teeth, and pulled my long dark hair into a ponytail. I still had a difficult time looking in the mirror without doing a double take. My hair had been blonde for the past six years, and my natural brown, seemed distant and foreign now. My bruised cheekbone also looked better. You could barely see it once I applied the foundation.

I pulled on a pair of hand-me-down jeans and a sweatshirt. That was the part about Las, I mean Indiana that I was going to find the most difficult. It was May, and the weather was so extreme. I could handle it, had it been a bit different, but forty degrees different? Come on. Why didn't I get a choice? I surely would have chosen a warmer climate. How was I supposed to enjoy living by the beach with a continuous layer of goose bumps?

I ate breakfast at Millie's Diner. Millie waited on me, herself.

"Good morning, can I start you off with some coffee?" she asked.

"Yes, thank you, that would be great." I sat at the bar and thumbed through the newspaper.

"Here you go sweetie. Do you need a few minutes yet?" The friendlier than I was used to lady asked.

"No. I'm ready. Could I get gravy and biscuits and two slices of bacon?"

"You sure can, coming right up."

6

I read through the local paper, smiling at its size. It was a full four pages. The Vegas Sun was a dictionary compared to the Misty Bay Daily News. The front page contained articles about the events planned for the year's Summer Fest. There would be apple bobbing, greased pole climbing; cornhole tournaments, and a wood chopping competition. The list went on and on about the weekend-long celebration. Saturday night would be a no-kid's night, and the article described the street dancing and wine tasting events for adults only. I flipped the page and read about the new breast milk flavored coffee at 'Reminiscent.' Are you kidding me? Where the hell was I going to be working? Where the hell would you even get breast milk? I kept reading and learned the benefits of breast milk coffee. I would not be trying it. I was sure of that. Gross.

"Here you go honey," Millie said, setting my plate in front of me. It looked mouthwatering. Either that or I was so hungry, it would have looked mouthwatering had it been a plate of gravy and worms. It was delicious, and I ate it in record time. Millie probably thought I hadn't eaten in weeks. She refilled my coffee cup, and I thanked her. The diner was fairly empty of people; of course it was getting kind of late for breakfast.

Almost eleven o'clock, and I hadn't even started my long list of shopping yet, let alone the cleaning that needed to be done. I was, however, feeling a little less uneasy. I had plenty of time to do everything. It may not be finished in the next three days, but I would mostly be working days, so I would just have to work on projects in the evenings. I was going to need something to do in order to keep my mind from thinking too much anyway.

"Is there a furniture store around here?" I asked Millie when she slid me a small strawberry Danish.

"There's one over on Long Road. Is there something particular you are looking for?"

I took a bite of the cheese Danish. "Hmm, this is amazing," I told her as the warm contents of strawberry and cream cheese teased my taste buds. "I kind of need everything," I smiled up at her.

"You bought Clara Bliss's little cottage, didn't you?"

Clara Bliss? How was I supposed to answer that? No. I live in a house that my grandmother left for me. That was what I was supposed to say. That's what Ms. K told me to say. Who is Clara Bliss?

"Clara lived there up until about ten years or so ago." Millie started to explain. I breathed a sigh of relief. "She moved to Portland to be closer to her grandchildren. The house has sat empty for a good many years. You can thank her for the lovely colors," she winked, and it made me smile.

Sheew, I didn't have to explain anything.

"Where is Long Road? Do they have pretty much everything? Do they deliver?"

Millie laughed at my run-on sentence. I didn't mean to cut off her answer. I was just happy we weren't talking about my house anymore.

"Yes. You can get furniture for every room in the house, even curtains."

I was glad she mentioned curtains. I had neglected to add them to my long list.

"Thank you," I said, taking a ten dollar bill from my purse. I liked Millie, and I hoped we would become friends. She was probably twenty years or more, older than me, but nonetheless she was a very nice lady.

"Can I offer you some more advice?" she asked.

"Yes, of course."

"There is a place about fifteen miles from here called Potters. It's a warehouse full of housewares. I'm sure you could buy everything you need there, and they only sell American-made," she added, proud of that fact.

I took out a piece of paper. "Thank you, Millie. I will definitely go there. Do you know the address?"

Millie laughed a short laugh. "You don't need an address, sweetie. Turn right at the stop light and drive 'till you see a billboard on the left that says Potters. You can't miss it."

"Thank you. I better get going. I have a long day ahead of me." I smiled and left the ten dollars on the counter, leaving her a three a dollar tip.

"Come back this evening. Tonight is meatloaf Friday," she invited, and I left with a nod and a smile.

Returning tonight was out of the question, there was no way I was going to be able to make it back this evening... I had too much to do, but I would come back and have meatloaf on another Friday sometime. I hadn't had meatloaf since before my Grandma Joyce passed away.

I drove to the furniture store first. I couldn't believe the prices. I had twenty-five thousand dollars in pre-paid visa cards to buy everything that I needed, and I wasn't going to spend near what I thought I would. I was pleasantly surprised at the quality. The dining room table that I had picked out would have cost me probably five times as much back in Las, I mean Indiana. I ended up buying more than what was even on my list. I hadn't planned on buying an area rug, a desk, television or coffee and end tables. I got everything that I needed for a fraction of what I had planned on spending.

I was on cloud nine, up until it was time to pay that is. I was standing at the counter, and the older man asked for my last name.

Dammit. What is it? I was drawing a blank. I had the Riley part, but the last name just wasn't registering. I could feel my face becoming flush when I didn't answer right away. He stood in front of me, awkwardly wondering why I wasn't answering.

"Murphy," I almost yelled, when it finally came to me. He gave me a funny look and turned back to his computer screen.

I finished giving him my information, and we had delivery scheduled for the following day. One more night of sleeping on the floor, but I was okay with that. I would much rather clean in the empty rooms than try to clean around furniture, and at least I would have curtains over the windows.

Next stop was Potter's, and I spent more time there than I should have. I was so thankful that Millie had told me about it. The prices there too, surprised me, and I bought everything I needed, and then some. I found the cutest set of dishes and couldn't help thinking about the exquisite china back in

Indiana. Drew would have never eaten off plates like that. They were white, and although I hated the bright yellow walls in the house, the cute little yellow ducklings circling the plates and saucers were adorable. I wondered if I had bought everything that Drew would hate on purpose.

I was so excited. I could hardly contain myself. I had stolen, well not actually stolen; we were married. I had taken a microscopic amount of his money. Drew probably hadn't even figured that part out yet. I honestly didn't want anything of his. I would have walked away and slept on the floor for months had Ms. K not convinced me to take what was rightfully mine. Boy was I ever grateful that she did. Now that I think about it, she didn't really give me a choice in the matter. I was taking the money.

Buying a house was a little more difficult. It took me almost six months to embezzle the $80,000 that Drew would never find. I had added $15 and $18,000 to various overhead expenses for six straight months. The first couple of months I was paranoid, no, I was terrified that he was going to catch it, but he never did. Stupid bastard shouldn't have been so credulous. I knew exactly where the key to his office was. It was rather simple to add bits and pieces to his overhead, donate to a made-up worthy cause, and a delightful fat scholarship, sending me to the University of Misty Bay. I had actually found a couple of ways to change things a little to save him some money, without his knowing of course.

I counted. It took me nine trips to unload my overstuffed Honda Civic. I stacked everything in the corner of the living room and would move it as needed. It took up half the room, and once again I forgot to eat. I wondered if there was a pizza place that delivered. Why would it even matter? I didn't have a phone book, and the pre-paid phone that Ms. K had given me only had seven minutes left on it. Ms. K had already told me that we would end all contact once I had left *Indiana,* so I wasn't planning on using the minutes. I was supposed to pitch the phone out the window before I arrived.

All of a sudden, my heart dropped to my feet when there was a knock on the door. Nobody knows me here. Who would be looking for me here? What did they want? I was pulled from my frozen paranoia by the second knock.

Stop it, Morg, I mean Riley. I said quietly but out loud as I made my way to the door.

"Hi. I'm Lauren. I live in the uglier-than-your blue house, across the road," my new neighbor said, introducing herself.

I shook her hand. "Nice to meet you. I'm Riley, but everyone calls me Ry." I was smiling to myself when I remembered that aspect of my new life. I had forgotten to mention that to Millie earlier.

"Wow, it looks like you have your work cut out for you," she observed peeking around me.

I suddenly realized that I was being rude. "Come in," I offered. "I really don't have a seat to offer or anything to drink," I teased.

Lauren walked through the door. "Wow, the inside paint is worse than the outside," she stated, and I laughed. "I forgot how bright it was in here."

She must have been in here before.

"That will be altered tonight," I assured her.

"I have a friend who does construction if you want his number."

"Maybe for the outside, the inside has got to be done tonight. I have furniture coming by noon tomorrow," All of a sudden I comprehended how much I had to do and what little time I had to do it. I was happy to have a neighbor, and I thought Lauren, and I would become friends. I just didn't want to be her friend at that moment. I had too much to do.

"Well I won't keep you," she said, and I was glad.

The first thing I did was fill the mop bucket with hot sudsy lemony cleaner. I smiled. The yellow paint with the citrus, lemony smell made perfect companions.

It was almost four o'clock in the afternoon, and I really, really wanted to get the yellow painted over before my furniture came the next day. I had planned on painting the living room as soon as the walls were washed down, but decided to go ahead and wash the kitchen down as well. That way I could continue painting and get that done too.

The living room took fifty-seven minutes. Five o'clock. I was hungry. Why the hell did I keep forgetting about food? Oh yeah, because I am used to having meals prepared and waiting on me. That was another one that I would have to get used to.

The kitchen took longer than anticipated because of having to clean all of the cabinets. It was now almost seven. I was still hungry, and I sat on the floor leaned up against the glass door. The ugly plastic tables and chairs were already moved out to the deck. I was eating crumbs from the bottom of a two day old Cheetos bag when someone was at the door again.

Once again my heart sank. Why didn't I lock the door? Lauren didn't wait for me to answer and opened the door, causing me to freeze in a panic.

"Relax," she said, seeing my shocked paralyzed face and stiff posture.

I smiled when I noticed her carrying a large pizza and a six pack of beer. She had changed clothes and was now wearing old jeans with a pink checkered flannel shirt. Her strawberry blonde hair was pulled back and hiding underneath a tied bandana.

My mouth was already salivating. Pizza, just what I needed. Not so much the beer. I had never liked beer. I was more of a wine kind of girl. No. Wait a minute. I drank wine because that was what Drew drank. Have I ever had a beer? Yes. I did. I was thirteen, and some friends and I hid under a bridge, and I drank one. Did I like it? I didn't remember.

"You are my new best friend," I told Lauren, patting the wood floor next to me. I didn't mind wasting twenty minutes. I needed food, and pizza was just what the doctor ordered. That would definitely make me feel better, and I would probably work faster, having some nourishment and regenerated energy.

We sat side by side, leaned against the glass doors and shared a pizza. Lauren probably thought I was a pig. I think I swallowed the first piece whole. I did drink a beer, and I didn't mind it a bit. I wouldn't say that I loved it, but it was okay.

"Well, we better get busy," Lauren stated, closing the pizza box.

I looked at her with a little bit of confusion mixed with hope. "I am not going to let you help me paint," I insisted with my head tilted.

Please help me paint, please help me paint.

"The way I see it, you don't have a choice. I'm doing nothing but sitting at my house watching reruns of Greys Anatomy. Now where are the paint pans?" she asked, and I smiled, happy that she wasn't giving me a choice. There was one problem, however.

"Paint pans?" I asked. I hadn't bought paint pans. I just bought paint and brushes.

"You don't have any pans?" she asked. I shook my head.

"What about rollers?"

I shook my head again, and she laughed. "Come on. Let's take a walk."

She removed the opened lock from her shed door, took out the two pans with four rollers, and handed them to me. "Do you have any drop cloths?" she asked.

Where was my mind? I had forgotten everything. I'd never painted a day in my life. How was I supposed to know that you needed more than paint and brushes?

"Nope." I smiled.

I was so grateful for Lauren's help. I would never have finished with a paint brush. She trimmed while I rolled on the light gray paint. I liked the color so much in my new room that I decided to use it in the living room, as well.

"Do you have a radio?" Lauren asked.

I ran over to my list and jotted it down along with other things that I'd remembered throughout the day. Like a microwave. How could I forget that?

"I am going to run home and do number two and get us one," she announced. I laughed out loud at the number two comment. I actually laughed and it felt great. Could this truly be happening? Could I really pull this off and not be found? My thoughts were all over the place, and Lauren was back disrupting them ten minutes later.

"Everything come out okay?" I teased.

"Do you really want me to elaborate on that?" she provoked right back. I shook my head. Nope, don't need to hear that.

Lauren turned the radio to a country station. I hated country music. Brakes. Wait a minute. Drew hated country music. I had never actually listened to it. How could I hate it if I had never even listened to it?

"Where're you from?" Lauren asked as we painted and listened to something about somebody digging their keys into the side of somebody's souped-up four-wheel drive.

"Indiana," I remembered.

"What part? I have a cousin in Indiana."

And the questions began. "Carson," I answered with only that.

"What brought you to Misty Bay? I know you didn't come all the way here just to work with Starlight Scarlett in her weird little coffee shop."

"Now you're scaring me," I stated, hoping to get off topic.

She laughed. "You will absolutely love Starlight. She is as Bohemian as they come. I just know that you didn't move to this sectarian town for that purpose," she assumed.

"Are you calling this town a cult?"

"Are you going to avoid my question all night?" she retorted with her own question.

I smiled down at her from my step stool, which thank God she owned too. "I lost my job when they downsized, and my grandmother left me this house. I just decided it was time for a change." I lied, hitting it right on the money. I smiled inside, proud that I remembered until I saw the look on her face. She knew I was lying. She knew my grandmother didn't leave me this house.

"If we're going to be friends, you can't lie to me," she said, being exceedingly blunt. "My aunt owned this house up until last month. She owns mine too. That's why they are both ugly blue."

I walked down the step stool to face her. "Lauren, please don't ask me too many questions about my past. I am not running from the law or anything like that. I just need to keep a low profile," I tried to reassure her.

"Well, you need a better story," she said, as she turned and started painting again. "People around here know that my aunt has owned these two houses for years."

Thanks a lot, Ms. K. Nice investigating skills.

"I've got it," she stated matter-of-fact. I looked down at her with a peculiar stare. Why would she be so zealous about helping me? I didn't get it.

"How old are you?" she asked, again bluntly.

"I will be twenty five next month. Why?"

"Perfect," she alleged while I continued to look at her as if she had two heads. "We went to college together, and when you lost your job, I told you about my aunt's house, and you bought it," Lauren exclaimed excited. "You didn't tell anyone else the grandma story, did you?"

I shook my head.

I was happy that Lauren stopped asking questions, and we talked and talked while the room was being transformed into a whole new domicile. We painted the living room and kitchen with the light gray almost silver tone paint. The walls around the French doors and the front door were painted in a darker shade of gray, and I absolutely loved it. I tried to get Lauren to quit and go home just before midnight, but she wouldn't. I was glad she didn't.

She washed all of the new dishes and put them away while I hung curtains. The only thing left to do was clean the hardwood floors and wash down the two bedroom walls. I could do that the following morning. The furniture wouldn't arrive until around noon.

"I'm done." I stated. I couldn't do any more. My energy was gone, and my body was telling me that it had enough. "I can't thank you enough, Lauren." I couldn't. I never would have gotten that much done without her, let alone with limited tools.

"Yes, you can. You can thank me by going there and getting some clean clothes and coming home with me. I have an extra bed."

"I'm fine here, but thank you just the same."

"I insist. If I leave, you're going to continue to work, and I can tell that you are exhausted. Now move it."

I smiled at her. We just met, and she already knew my intentions. I was thinking that I could have the walls washed before I went to bed. "I'm going to grab a shower, and I'll be over."

"Promise me."

"I promise."

I didn't wonder anymore why Lauren had picked the house on the other side of the road, rather than the one by the ocean. Her house was quite a bit bigger. She decorated with modern décor. The walls were similar to mine and painted two-toned but with beige and chocolate brown. There was a black and white, female country music singer picture hanging behind the couch. I knew I'd seen the woman before, but couldn't recall her name.

"You play?" I asked, eyeing the guitar on the couch.

"Yeah, I mess around a little," she said, modestly.

She was dressed in flannel pants and a t-shirt just like me. She yawned and showed me to her spare bedroom. It was a queen sized bed with a fluffy green comforter. I couldn't wait to crawl into it.

I lay in bed and stared out at a branch blowing back and forth outside the window. I had a million and one thoughts going through my mind, and they wouldn't seem to settle. I thought about decorating my new house and making it my own. That thought led to the mansion that I had just fled. My whole house was the size of my suite there, but already it was more inviting than the ice cold castle. That thought led me to thoughts of Drew, and I bet that he had at least five private investigators looking for me.

Would he find me? Was there any way that he could trace my whereabouts? I wondered what my friend Jena had told him. She knew nothing. I made sure of it. She had no idea where I was either. I talked to her the night before I'd disappeared, and we even talked about the weekend charity event that we would attend, *tomorrow*. I wondered if Drew were sly enough to report me missing. I had made my intentions perfectly clear with my short, to the point, note, informing him that I hoped he rotted in hell. It was a good possibility that he never even found the note. I had typed in my e-reader. I told him not to try to find me, but I knew that was like pissing in the wind. Most likely he had everyone he knew working on it, and then some.

I thought I had covered my tracks well enough. I didn't talk to Ms. K, not even once, on my cell or the house phone. The only telephone that I ever used to call her was the pre-paid one she'd given me, and once from Drew's desk phone, but that was months ago. He made so many calls from that phone he would never put it together, not to mention I didn't even know Ms. K's name. All she ever told me was Ms. K.

Chapter 2

I woke later than I had wanted. There was so much to get done yet, and I was still in bed at almost nine. I wasn't sure what time the exhaustion finally won, and I fell asleep, but I did feel rested. I walked out to Lauren's living room, and it was empty. Her bedroom door was open, so I peeked in, that room was empty too. Maybe she had to work.

Walking down the hall and looking at the portraits down the left side of the wall, I knew that Lauren had a much better childhood than I had. There were several pictures of her and her sister; I assumed. They both had strawberry blonde hair and were built with the same short but not too short build. There were two other pictures of the girls and their parents. Looking at the graduation picture, I presumed that Lauren was the older of the two.

I slipped on my flip-flops and walked across the road to my own house. My own house, I said, smiling to myself. Panic struck again when I noticed my front door open. I relaxed almost immediately as I got closer. I could hear the country music playing.

As I walked down the hallway, I looked in the smaller bedroom, and it was empty, but the walls had been washed, curtains hung, and the wood floor shined. I laughed when I heard Lauren singing something about having friends in low places. She was singing in a deep voice, not her own. I grinned as I opened the door.

"What on earth are you doing?" I asked, seeing her on the floor with a bottle of Murphy's oil soap and a rag. The curtains were hung there too, and I loved them. The white curtains with a black, willow tree pattern accented the gray walls perfectly.

"Sorry, I hope you don't mind. I am used to getting up at four in the morning for work. I was up by five and didn't want to wake you."

"You should have woken me," I claimed. "What on earth do you do that you have to get up at four in the morning?"

"Lauren and Levi," she said. Like I knew what that meant.

"Uh?"

"Oh, sorry, I forgot. You're not from around here, Lauren and Levi in the morning. I'm a radio host."

"Really? You talk on the radio?" I asked, intrigued. "Now I know I have to go buy a radio."

"Yup, I work from five a.m. to one p.m."

"I bet its country too, right?" I smiled.

She didn't answer and only looked up with a smile. "I brought coffee over if you want a cup."

"I do, but I want you to stop this, and come and drink one with me."

We sat on the deck overlooking the ocean and drank our coffee. I was so glad that Lauren was my neighbor. I loved her already. I wondered why there was no man, or was there? I should probably wait until I know her a little better before I ask.

"Are you divorced yet?" Lauren asked, breaking my thoughts about her love life.

I looked at her with a pensive expression, holding my cup to my lips.

"Relax, will you already?" she requested. "You have a tan line around your finger."

I looked at my finger. Sure enough, she was right. I wondered if makeup would cover that for a few days or weeks. How long does it take to get rid of wedding ring evidence?

"I have never been married," I said with a warning look. She laughed.

"Yeah right, okay, Ms. Mystery, but let me inform you, I will eventually gain your trust and you will confess all of your deep dark secrets to me. Your skeletons will be bowing at my feet. "

I looked at her with a serious expression. "It's not that I don't trust you, Lauren."

"I'm joking, Riley"

I smiled at her. "How the hell am I supposed to get down to the beach from here?" I asked, wanting off the subject of me.

"There's a path. I'll show you, but right now we have floors to clean." She stood and patted my knee.

By eleven o'clock, we were finished. I couldn't sit still. I was noticeably hyper and wanted my delivery, *now.*

Lauren showed me the path to get to the beach. It was rather steep and rocky, but nothing that I couldn't handle. I should have my house all together tomorrow, and planned to venture down there and explore my new surroundings.

She never left me, and stayed until five in the evening until the last picture was hung on the wall. I loved it, and I loved her. My house was complete, and I only needed to go shopping for a few odds and ends that I had forgotten. Food! Yes. I needed to do that. If I forgot to get food one more day, I was going to turn myself into an insane asylum.

I hugged Lauren before she left and thanked her again.

"Mushy friends aren't my thing," she teased with a warning look. "You are more than welcome. Oh yeah, what's your cell number?" she asked, pulling hers from her back jeans pocket.

"I don't have one," I said, and she cocked her head.

"There is a Radio Shack next door to 'Reminiscent,' where you will be working. You should probably have a phone."

"I'm not sure I want one just yet. I think I should wait a while."

"Afraid of being found?" she asked. I wasn't about to answer that one. She left, shaking her head as she skipped across my yard. My yard, I smiled.

I showered and bounced off the walls as I entered my new living room. I couldn't wait to lie on the black comfy leather sofa and watch a movie. That was my plan for that Saturday night. I was going to the grocery store first, not about to get sidetracked or forget that again. Then I was going to rent a movie or two and come back, lie on the couch and eat spaghetti. I loved spaghetti and Drew hated it. The only time I would get it was when he took me to 'Trattoria da Cesare,' a famous Italian restaurant on Las Vegas Boulevard, I mean Carson Boulevard. I giggled to myself and felt like a giddy little teenager.

After a long day, I was home by eight, listening to country music on my new radio as I chopped the needed ingredients for my spaghetti. I wondered what Lauren was doing. I should invite her over for spaghetti, and wished I could call her. When I looked out the front door, there were no lights on in her house. She wasn't home. I to the back deck and gazed out at the moon over the ocean. For the first time in an awfully long time, I felt lighthearted, and I had a new sense of calm.

I would never again worry about what kind of mood Drew was in when he got home. I would never again worry about focusing on what I could do to improve myself so I didn't set him off. My focus was on me for the first time in my life. I clasped my hands together and pressed them to my lips, almost as if I were praying and thanking God for the courage to do what I had done, and to be where I was standing. I truly was grateful.

My new sense of being was shattered when I heard a loud knock on the door. Would I ever get used to this? Would I ever be able to breathe and not think it was someone there to get me?

I looked out and saw Lauren. She pushed herself through the doorway carrying a bag and busily talking as she removed its contents.

"So, I figured I might as well get this myself. It was pretty obvious that you were not going to," she said handing me a new cell phone. "You have to have a phone, Riley," she assured me.

"Lauren, I can't accept this." I tried to hand it back.

"Hmm, this looks good," she said, sticking her finger in my homemade sauce, ignoring me.

"Lauren!"

"Look, Riley. I don't know what your story is, and I am not going to pry. If you ever need to talk I am here, and you never have to worry about me saying anything to anyone. Even if you never tell me your story, you still need a phone. It's pretty clear that you're afraid of having a phone in your name, so I put it on my plan. I am not giving you anything. The phone was free to add a line, and you can pay me the monthly thirty-five dollar payment. Okay?"

How could I argue with that? Why was she so hell bent on being nice to me? Not that I was complaining, it just felt sort of superficial. No. Stop it, Morg, I mean, Ry, not everyone has a motive.

"Thank you, Lauren. Would you like to stay for supper?"

"No, but I want leftovers tomorrow. I kind of have a visitor that I need to get back to. I put my number in your phone already, in case you need anything. I'm leaving before you hug me again."

I laughed and watched her walk back to her house. There was a guy building a fire in the barbecue grill at the side of her house. I watched as he wrapped her in his arms and kissed her. I wondered who he was and if he were her boyfriend.

Finally, I sat down to enjoy my spaghetti and the movie 'Wanderlust' with Jennifer Aniston. I couldn't contain my nosiness and peeked through the crack in the curtains across the yard every now and then. I watched Lauren lead her friend into her house by the hand around eleven o'clock. She probably wouldn't tell me about him unless I asked. I wouldn't, I mean, it wasn't like I was sharing any part of my life with her.

I slept like a baby in my new bed but woke a little too early, thanks to Lauren. I reached for my new cell phone on the nightstand and read the new text.

"You up?"

"I am now," I answered.

"Make coffee, I'm on my way over."

Okay, I said out loud, forcing myself out of bed. I didn't even have time to finish peeing before she was knocked on my door.

"Good morning," she said, way too happy. I glanced at the clock, and it was only eight. I wasn't sure I liked her much anymore. She walked past me and started the coffee herself.

"I'm going to brush my teeth," I said and left her alone. When I returned she was in my refrigerator, retrieving the leftover spaghetti.

"Want some?"

"No. Help yourself." I sarcastically replied.

I sat on my new sofa, and she talked. Not about anything particular, she was just rattling on about this and that. While she warmed up my leftovers, I sleepily listened and wished I had slept another hour.

"What are you doing today?" she asked, pushing my feet off the couch so she could sit.

There is a chair right there.

"I want to walk down to the beach. Other than that, I guess I don't have any plans. Why?"

"I bowl on Sunday afternoon. Wanna come?" she asked, sucking spaghetti through her lips.

"No. I don't think so, but thanks."

"Come on, Riley, it's fun. I will introduce you to some of my friends."

"I will, Lauren, just not today."

"Okay," she replied, and I was glad that she didn't insist. I certainly wasn't up for meeting new people yet.

Clothes shopping was definitely on the agenda. I dressed in a pair of dark blue wind pants with two small white stripes, and a white cotton shirt, unbuttoned over the top of a red t-shirt. Yes, once I did dress worse than now, but I had gotten used to the designer clothes that were a vital part of my life the past six years. Somewhere in-between this and that would be good, I decided as I tied the also-used sneakers. I was ashamed of myself. I shook my head in disbelief of wearing someone else's shoes. There was a time in my life that my toes cramped, curled in the only shoes I had to wear, probably two sizes too small.

I started down the path, holding onto the boulders as I made my way to the beach. This was surely not what I had pictured when I thought about living by the beach. From what I had seen so far, there was no beach. I climbed and maneuvered my way through the sarsens. Some of the spaces between the rocks were barely wide enough to squeeze through. It was probably a good thing that I'd been required to keep in shape. Finally, I was in the clearing. I moaned a disgusted breath when I saw the large peak I'd seen from my deck. It didn't allow room for walking. The only way I would be able to walk north was to sprint while the tide gave maybe a foot of wet sand. I would do it, just not today. I chose instead to walk south. The beach was nice, and I was pleased to have found my new favorite place. In a distance I spotted a pirate ship. I knew it wasn't a real pirate ship, but with the many sails, it could have passed for one. The windjammer was moving away from the lighthouse on a peak in the distance.

A large rock seemed to appear in just the right place, and I sat on it and pulled my knees to my chest. The air was crisp, but the sun warmed my face, and felt invigorating as I contemplated living there. I closed my eyes and breathed in the sea air and the sun's heat into my lungs. I was here. I did it, and I would never look back. My meditation was interrupted when a friendly yellow lab barked and placed his paws on the rock where I was perched.

"Hello there," I said, petting him. I looked up to find his owner. There was an older gentleman walking toward me with a smile on his face and a crooked stick in one hand.

"Sorry about that," he said as he approached lifting his walking stick and poking it into the sand with every step. I noticed that he walked with a limp and assumed the stick was for support.

"Oh, it's okay. I think he just wanted to say hi," I said, sliding from the rock.

"I'm John Hunter. I live about a mile north of here," pointing to the peak with his stick.

"Hi, I'm Riley," I offered, omitting my last name. I forgot it again, but just for a second. "I live right up there," I pointed, kind of in the right direction. He didn't need to know which house. You live on the other side of the peak?" I asked, wondering how he got around it.

"Yup, you have about three hours of sand before the ocean takes it back. This hour and two more," he smiled.

"Thanks. I'll remember that." I bent to pick up a piece of sea glass that the sun had radiated on, catching my eye. I wiped it with my thumb, feeling the smooth surface.

"Purple," John said, admiring the sea glass, "extremely uncommon. May I?" he asked, reaching for my sea glass find.

I handed it over to him and asked, "Why is purple uncommon?"

"Well, believe it or not, it started out as clear glass, used in a variety of applications from beverage bottles, food containers, decorative tableware, door knobs, and more. It could have even come from an old car windshield," he explained and handed it back. "Wanna know something else?"

"Sure."

"A purple sea glass find is considered good luck. You should make a necklace or bracelet out of it."

Good luck? I could use that.

"Come on boy," he called to his wandering dog. "It was a pleasure to meet you, Ms. Riley," he nodded and went about his walk.

I spent two hours on the beach, looking for more sea glass. I didn't find any more. My stomach began to remind me that it needed feeding, and I walked back up the path. Going down was a lot easier than getting back up.

Lauren wasn't around again that day. I began to get a little antsy about starting my new job the next day. I made myself hot dogs and french fries for supper and felt a little sneaky about it. Drew would have never eaten a hot dog. I also watched reality TV, something else that Drew refused to watch. I seriously needed to stop doing things just because Drew would hate them, but it did make me feel as if I was twisting the knife just a little, which made me smile.

I had a hard time falling asleep, and when I finally did, I woke with a pounding heart and was sweating profusely. My dream was so real, and it took several minutes to calm myself down and convince my conscious mind that it wasn't real, and I was fine.

When I walked to the kitchen and got a drink of water, I still tried to forget the dream. It was early morning, and I watched Lauren leave for work. Rather than going back to bed like I needed to, I ran a hot tub of water and tried to relax. I really needed to stop thinking about Drew. I was not Morgan Kelley. I was Riley Murphy, and Drew Kelley would never hurt me again. This was my life. I was not Drew Kelley's wife. I had my own life, and I could now live it however I pleased.

I honestly did think I could just walk away and forget the past twenty-five years of my life. Needless to say, it wasn't working, not yet. Maybe I did need to seek counseling. Ms. K had suggested it. No. I don't need counseling. I just need to focus on my future and not my past. I could do this. I closed my eyes and breathed in the steam from the hot water, giving myself a much needed pep talk.

After I made coffee, I turned the radio station to Z-103. I sat on my new sofa and listened to Lauren and this guy, Levi. They actually made me laugh. They had a psychic on the show, and people were calling in to find out how old they would be when they died. I laughed out loud when one caller told the two how much she enjoyed their show. She explained that she only had one complaint, and as soon as she said it, Lauren hung up on her, saying their egos wouldn't handle complaints.

I was overly impressed with their morning show and was starting to like the country music they played. That was until they played a song by Shania Twain, 'Black eyes and blue tears,' something about no more excuses, no more crying in the corner, and no more bruises. As soon as the country singer wailed out begging, please no more, I jumped up and turned off the radio. It was just too close to home, and my scars were still too raw to cope with the words.

The search through the closet to find something to wear to work was stressful. What the hell do you wear to a coffee slash hippy store? How do the two even go together? I decided on a pair of dark jeans that didn't quite fit. They could have been a size smaller. I was definitely going shopping my next day off. I wore a plaid, green and white shirt and tucked it into my jeans, hoping maybe to use up some of the slack. I brushed out my shoulder length hair and pulled just the top back, leaving one strand to fall around my face.

I was nervous as I parked my car in the back alley where I was told to park. I saw the back door, but wondered if I should I use the front door my first day. I didn't have to decide when Starlight came out with a bag of trash.

"Good morning," she said with a happy smile.

Starlight wore a long flowing skirt with sandals and a sixties looking shirt with some sort of Indian design, and long flowing sleeves.

"Good morning," I smiled back.

Starlight shook my hand, and the first thing I noticed was the peace sign tattoo between her thumb and forefinger.

"Well, come on in," she exclaimed, and I followed her in.

The door opened to a storage room with boxes and boxes of I had no idea what. I looked in the room of the first door as we passed. It was an extremely messy office with stacks of papers everywhere. This could be a problem with my OCD. Everything had a place, and I couldn't even blame that one on Drew. Even when I lived at home growing up, the dump we occupied was as clean as the place would allow. Maybe I tried to make it better than what I knew it could ever be, but for some reason it had always stuck with me.

"You can throw your purse in here." Starlight stopped at the office door. "Just remember where you put it. Things seem to come up missing in here," she joked, and I raised my eyebrows.

I wonder why.

We walked out to the front, and there was a counter with a register and too much junk. Oh boy, I thought, wondering if I could handle the mess. The part of the store on the far side was supposed to be a coffee shop. Near the register was the hippy shop, or something. I hadn't quite figured out what she had going on in all of the chaos. There was everything you could

27

think of including a big glass bong displayed in a glass case. No wonder she was so happy.

"Go ahead, look around." Starlight gestured with her hand.

I noticed three older gentlemen at a table in front of the window, drinking coffee and arguing about what year some bridge was built. I thumbed through the shirts and pants rack and moved over to the shelves. Starlight had every kind of tea imaginable. There were shelves of little figurines, and I fell in love with a miniature little boy in jean overalls rolled up to his knees and holding two little puppies as they licked his cinched face.

"Would you like some coffee?" Starlight asked.

"Sure," I replied and hoped she wasn't going to offer me the breast milk.

I followed her to the coffee bar and was relieved when she asked me what my flavor was.

"French vanilla?" I said in more of a question, wondering if she had it.

"The best," she answered, and she was right. It was the richest coffee I'd ever tasted.

I wondered why she would hire me to work there, after only seeing three customers stopping in for coffee after three hours. I didn't think she could have that much business to pay me. I got my answer around three o'clock when she decided to show me how to order the teas and coffees.

"Come on," she said and I followed her to her confusing office. "We only have a week to get you up to speed before I leave."

"Leave?"

"Yeah, I am flying to Australia for a few weeks. I usually just close the place up, but my usual patrons are getting pretty tired of me closing up and leaving. Don't worry, you'll be fine. The truck comes in on Tuesday. I will show you how to keep the coffee machines going. Saturday mornings are pretty crazy in here, but the good news is, you only have to ring them up. They get their own coffee. Phyllis brings pastries from her bakery on Saturdays, and Millie brings the best deli sandwiches ever on Wednesday afternoons. That empty cold case by the counter is where you will put them. We always sell out of them or pretty close to it anyway."

"If the pastries and deli sandwiches do so well, why don't you sell them every day?" I asked, curious.

"Nah, that's too much work, besides I don't want people hanging out here every day," she teased.

I did like Starlight, and Lauren was right, the lady was as Bohemian as you could get. I don't think the devil could have pissed her off.

◇◇()◇◇

I was slowly beginning to relax and fall deeply in love with my new life. I would almost say I had a delightful routine going. Wake up and laugh to the Lauren and Levi show in the morning, laugh some more with Starlight during the day, drink too much coffee, eat dinner with Lauren, and walk on the beach. By the end of the week I knew everything that I needed to know to keep the shop up and running, not that any monkey couldn't learn it, but still. I liked my job other than the fact that it needed a good cleaning. I planned to talk to Starlight about that on her last day with me. I didn't want to step on her toes, but come on, I didn't know how in the world she kept her books up with the mess in the office.

It was well into the afternoon when I finally worked up the nerve to ask.

"Starlight, I was wondering if it would be okay if I do some cleaning and organizing while you were away," I asked, really fast. I always had a problem with asking for things, even growing up. It was worse when I was with Drew. He always made me earn it one way or another. Why was my heart beating so fast? It wasn't like I asked to remodel the place or anything. The worse thing that could happen was she would say no.

"Honey, you do whatever you want to do here. I don't plan to spend much time here, now that I have you. You're going to be running the joint, so make it your home."

I smiled, relieved and relaxed.

Friday was the busiest day I'd seen since I had started. I sold some of the clothing articles to some high school girls and a few of the Indian figurines to a tourist. The coffee had to be replenished throughout the day, and we opened up one of the boxes in the back and restocked the shelves with figurines.

"Where do you get these?" I asked Starlight, unwrapping a family of picnicking figurines.

"I go to this trade show in Las Vegas twice a year. I will take you some time. It's the coolest thing ever."

My heart sped up at the mention of Las Vegas. I wouldn't go anywhere near that trade show.

"How do you get the things here?" I asked.

"They ship it to me after the show."

"There isn't a website to just order them?"

Starlight shrugged her shoulders as she continued to unpack the little knickknacks. "Maybe, but the trade show is too much fun for that." She smiled.

Starlight showed me where to find the petty cash, once she remembered where it was herself. She explained that I could use anything from the storeroom that I wanted and to replenish the shelves with whatever I wanted. I was looking forward to getting my hands on the rat race.

Lauren and I ate the meatloaf special for supper at Millie's, and it reminded me of my Grandma Joyce's. We chose the warm apple pie for dessert and then I let her talk me into going to the town bar. I had never been to a bar in my life. I'd been to elaborate restaurants and fancy clubs, but never to a bar. I didn't want to go to a bar. I just wanted to go home to my little house, sit on my deck and gaze at the beautiful sky overlooking the ocean.

"Come on, please," she begged.

I acquiesced, against my will. Why not? I had done things against my will my entire life, at least Lauren had my best interest at heart, sort of.

It was just a small bar with an old wooden floor, but the place was hopping, and packed to the gills. There was a band playing on the right side with an area cleared for dancing. A nice looking guy waved us over, and we sat at the table with him. Our table was directly in front of the guy singing something about a long black train.

"This is Joel, Riley," Lauren introduced the guy and then he kissed her.

I wondered if this was the same guy who had spent the night with her the previous weekend. Another guy joined us, and she introduced him as Levi. It was nice to put a face with the voice. A waitress brought us beers. I took my wallet from my purse and Levi put his hand over mine.

"You are offending me, put that away," he demanded.

I jerked my hand away, not realizing that I did it with so much conviction.

"Whoa," he stated, putting both hands in the air.

"Sorry," I said and noticed the puzzled look on Lauren's face. "Thank you," I said and turned my attention to the singer on stage.

Can someone say... Idiot?

I focused my attention on the stage, not knowing how to act around people. I felt like such an outsider, and didn't know what I should or shouldn't say. Lauren and the two men did all of the talking, and although they tried to include me, it was awkward. I was never allowed to speak when I went out with Drew. He was afraid I would embarrass him or me, so I played the pretty obedient wife and stood by his side. I noticeably shook my head, trying to rid the thoughts of those memories.

Lauren stood and insisted that I follow her to the bathroom. There was only one stall in the bathroom, and we waited outside the door for it to be unoccupied.

"What's your deal, girlfriend?"

I feigned ignorance. "What do you mean?"

"Haven't you seen Levi staring at you? He likes you, and you haven't even noticed. You're off in some other time."

I groaned. I didn't want Levi to look at me. I didn't want Levi to like me. I didn't want Levi to do anything. I wasn't interested in Levi. "I just don't think I like being here very much, Lauren. I've never been to a bar."

"You're joking." She opened the door and pulled me in with her.

Lauren dropped her pants and immodestly used the toilet, holding herself up from sitting on the seat.

"I think I am going to take off. I have to open the shop in the morning for the first time by myself."

"Ry, it's only nine o'clock. You're just going to go home and sit by yourself."

"I'm okay with that," I assured her, trying not to look at her squatted on the toilet. I was okay with that. I was used to spending my time alone.

"You can't tell me that you don't think Levi is cute."

"Lauren, please don't try to fix me up with anyone. I don't want anyone, okay?" I pleaded.

"Okay. If you really want to go, I will get a ride with Joel."

"So, are you going to tell me about Joel? Was he your company last weekend?" I asked, not wanting to talk about me and my hang-ups with men.

"I guess we are monogamous. He works on the oil rigs all week and is only home on the weekends, the best kind of man to have," she added, teasing.

I didn't go back to the table with Lauren. She gave me an easy out, and I took it. She gave me her keys, and I drove her jalopy of a car back to her house. I thought my ninety-three Honda was bad that thing was running on one cylinder.

The porch light wasn't on, because I hadn't known that I was going to be out past dark. I walked across the road to my house, and my heart began to beat in rapid thumps *again*. I hated being frightened all the time.

"There is nothing in there, Morgan," I said out loud and then shook my head at calling myself Morgan. I unlocked the door and pushed it, standing on the porch, peering in. I reached my arm around to the side and flipped on the light without entering. I shook my head again at how silly it seemed.

I lay in my comfortable bed and stared up at the ceiling. Would I ever be normal again, wait, have I even ever been

32

normal? What exactly defined normal? My mind drifted to my childhood, and that too, I was sure was as anomalous as imaginable. My Grandma Joyce probably had been the most usual person during that time of my life. There were a few things that she had told me that were probably not the healthiest things to tell a little girl.

Memories of sitting on the front porch of her one room cabin and listening to the stories of her childhood and living through the hard times on the mountain flooded into my head. She always told me that no matter how bad I thought that I had it, somebody else always had it worse. I wasn't sure that was possible, but then again, I'm sure it was. I could have been born a lot worse off than I was, I suppose.

I thought about little Justin, although I surely he's wasn't so little anymore. He had been put into foster care almost seven years ago. He would be twelve years old this summer. I hoped he was adopted and had a good life. I hated the thought of him being strewn about from foster home to foster home. I hated my mother for so long for leaving us and forcing him to live that life, then again my dad could have kept it from happening if he wanted to. I couldn't imagine choosing alcohol over my son. My mother, I could almost forgive. I said almost. I still hated her for not taking us with her, even though I understood her running away from her life of hell.

The Appalachian Mountains was where I was raised, in a small town in West Virginia where poverty was real, and still exists to this day. I was raised to believe that you grew up, signed up for welfare, and had lots of babies, so you could get more welfare and more food stamps. That was normal. After moving to Las Vegas and living the life of luxury, which became my normal. Now, well, now this was normal.

I finally drifted off to sleep, thinking about the two bedroom trailer, and the home from birth until my eighteenth birthday. The dream was so real this time, not that I didn't say that every time I woke in a panic, but this one was worse.

In the dream, I was huddled up to the only heat source in the house. The wood stove was barely throwing off any heat. I tried to bring some wood in, but it was frozen, and my fingers weren't strong enough to pull any of the pieces apart. It was late, and my dad wasn't home from the bar yet. Justin was no longer there, so I had to be at least seventeen. I sat with a blanket leaned against the stove with my back. The metal was barely warm, and I knew that it would be completely burned out within the hour.

It was the first time that my dad ever hit me, besides being whipped by his belt. The very first time was when he came home in a drunken stupor after my mom had left us. I guess it was my responsibility to fill her shoes. I heard the old truck pull into the drive, and I ran to my room, wrapped in my blanket. He started yelling as soon as he opened the door and realized the fire was almost out.

"Morgan! Get your stupid ass out here."

I didn't move. I hoped that he thought that I was asleep and just leave me alone. He didn't.

"If you're not out here by the time I count to three, I am going to beat you to a pulp."

Although I knew he was going to do it anyway, whether I went then or ten minutes later, so I walked out. He slapped me across the face, not giving me time to explain that I had tried to bring wood in. I could handle the slaps in the face. I would have chosen them over the sound of his leather belt being pulled from the loops, any day.

The events happened a long time ago, but I felt the burning stings on the backs of my legs and back when I woke, out of breath and panting like an overheated dog. I grasped the nightgown at my chest, and squeezed the material in a tight fist, trying to tell my heart that it was okay, and I was safe in my own home, in Maine. I brushed the damp hair from my forehead and got out of bed. It was too early to be awake, and I knew I needed to sleep, but I couldn't. I was too freaked out. I made a cup of hot tea. Starlight had given it to me the day before when she had told me that I looked tired. She said that it was a relaxing tea and would help me sleep. I dozed back to sleep on the sofa, wrapped in the fuzzy warm blanket from the back of the couch. I woke to the sound of my alarm going off in my room.

I yawned, still tired as I drove the short trip into town. I parked my car in the back and unlocked the door. No sooner had I gotten the first coffee machine brewing when I jumped, startled at the tap on the door. I breathed a sigh of relief when I saw the town sheriff, smiling at the door. Then I remembered Starlight told me that he hung out there on Saturday mornings.

"Good morning," he said, stepping in as I unlocked the door for him, "Didn't mean to startle you."

"Good morning," I returned, and continued to get the five machines up and running. "I guess I am not quite as fast as Starlight," I said as he sat at one of the small tables.

"Actually, I'm a little early this morning. You're fine," he assured me.

Phyllis showed up with the pastries next.

"Morning, Sheriff," she spoke, placing the goodies on the counter.

"Good morning, Phyllis. Please tell me you brought those little raspberry filled Danishes today."

"You're in luck, I did," she smiled.

Phyllis didn't stick around and had to go open her own little shop.

"Coffee is ready," I said to the sheriff, not turning to look at him.

I walked behind the counter with my own cup of coffee, and he poured himself a cup.

"My name is Dawson, by the way," he said stirring the cream into his coffee.

I snickered a little on accident.

His eyebrows rose as he looked at me. I felt my face blush from embarrassment.

"What?" he asked, and my face became even redder. I was sure of it.

"I'm Riley," I said, trying to smooth over my dreadful outburst.

"Nice to meet you, Riley. Why are you laughing at me?"

I couldn't help but laugh again. "I wasn't laughing at you, but I was just thinking how much your name fits your job

35

description. You know, sheriff named Dawson, in a small town."

He laughed too and sat down with his pastry and coffee.

"So what brings you to this small town, Riley?" he asked, and I didn't want to answer questions for a cop. I hated intimidating men, not that all men weren't intimidating to me, just some more so than others, and a uniformed man with a gun was one of the others.

"I'm not sure I have figured that out myself yet, sheriff," I said, and busied myself wiping down the counter in front of me.

I wished someone else would come in, preferably the same sex as me.

He snorted. "You can call me Dawson," he said, and I blushed again. What the hell is wrong with me?

I only smiled and pretended to be busy. He read his paper, and I was happy to see the three older men who seemed to drink coffee faster than I could make it, come in for their morning cup of Joe. I knew them by name because Starlight had told me, and although they were all exceptionally friendly, they never really spoke to me. I think that is why I liked them so much.

My nerves were getting the best of me when another group of men came in, pouring coffee and eating the pastries. How the hell was I supposed to remember who ate what, and how much to charge each of the five construction workers? I was now alone with nine men, and for absolutely no reason I felt extremely uneasy.

I was never so happy in my life to see Lauren come bouncing in. She got a cup of coffee and sat on a stool behind the counter with me.

"I almost commented on you being up so early, but I forgot that you rise with the chickens every morning."

She licked the strawberry filling from her pastry. "I have always gotten up with the chickens. My dad used to deliver the newspaper, and I was forced to get out of bed at five in the morning to learn some responsibility."

I laughed. "How did that work out for you?"

"Well, I suck at managing money, and tend to do things on a whim without thinking them through, but I did inherit his inability to sleep once the sun came up."

I left Lauren to replenish the one coffee machine that the men seemed to like the best. Of course, it was the plain old black coffee without any flavoring.

"What are you doing after work?" Lauren asked.

Oh, no. I am not going to any more bars with you.

"I am going clothes shopping for some clothes."

"Really? Where you going?"

"I'm not sure. I was hoping there was something more around here than Dollar General Store."

"There isn't. We have to go into Blain for that. They have a really nice mall. I'll go with you."

I laughed at her audacity but was really quite envious of it.

Chapter 3

By noon, the coffee shop had cleared out, and I found myself bored. I was anxious to get started with the much needed organization of the store, but decided to wait until Monday to tackle it. Customers were still coming in, and I was busier than any previous day.

Lauren and I went to a much bigger town and shopped. I realized going from store to store that I had never, in my life, shopped for myself. When I was growing up, I wore hand-me-downs and things from the local church or Salvation Army. After Drew and I married, my shopping was done for me, and I never got to pick anything out for myself.

I felt extremely joyful when I picked out new socks. I'd spent the last six years in pantyhose or thigh high stockings. I wasn't allowed to wear socks. They weren't attractive enough. I was even excited about the cute little cotton panties. If I were allowed to wear panties with Drew they had to be sexy, lacy thongs that I hated.

I stood in front of the rack with my hand on the underwear with tiny pink flowers as my mind once again drifted back in time.

Thank God, Lauren pulled my thoughts away rather quickly when she noticed I was off in another land again.

"Maybe if you talk about it, it might help," she said, touching my hand and bringing me back to the present.

I shook my head. "Sorry, I'm fine," I lied to her and myself.

"I'm going to carry my bags in and I will be over with some beer," Lauren said, once we were in my driveway.

As I took the tags from my five new outfits, I ran my hand across the leather of my new hiking boots. I thought they would support my ankles better when I climbed down the rocky terrain to the beach. I would have rather it been a flip-flop kind of beach, but it wasn't, and I was starting to like it just fine the way it was. I sat on my rock and watched the waves crash against the rocks for at least an hour every evening. My new friend, John, was often there, and he and his dog always stopped to visit.

Lauren and I sat out on my deck and listened to country music and drank a six pack of beer.

"Levi asked me for your number," Lauren said, propping her feet up to the adjacent chair.

"Don't you dare," I scolded.

"Don't you want to start dating? I mean you have to be getting frustrated by now."

"I am not the least bit frustrated," I lied, but didn't truly know that I was lying until that moment. Maybe that would help, maybe I did need some relief, but I didn't need Levi or any other man to take care of it. I was perfectly capable of it myself.

"How long were you married," she nosily continued.

I closed my eyes and took a deep breath. "Six years."

"Wow. What did you do, get married when you were eighteen?"

I didn't have to answer that question or any others. Her cell phone rang, and it was Joel telling her he was at her house, wanting to know where she was.

"Gotta go, duty calls," she joked.

I sat on the deck and stared off into the moonlit ocean. I dumped my warm beer over the side railing and heated a nice cup of Starlight's relaxing tea instead. I wrapped myself up in a fuzzy blanket and listened to the waves as they collided with the boulders below. This along with my tea was just what I needed to unwind. It didn't last long when my mind reflected on Lauren's comment about getting married when I was eighteen.

Drew was there to claim me on my eighteenth birthday. I thought about the weeks before my birthday, and how much the anticipation burned my soul. I couldn't believe what I was hearing that night as I lay in my thin walled bedroom and listened to the nice looking man who offered my father twenty-five thousand dollars to marry me.

I didn't even know who he was. I saw him once. He came to our worn out school and did a seminar after donating five thousand dollars. I remembered sitting right in front of him and listening to him talk about success and getting out of our situations and how valuable our educations were for our future. I admired him.

I shook my head at how infatuated I was with him that day. He was so cute and dressed like nothing I'd ever seen before. He actually inspired me. I no longer wanted to stay in that poverty stricken town. I wanted out. I wanted to wear fancy clothes, and drive expensive cars.

He sat beside me on the bottom bleacher once the gym had cleared out. I was in no hurry to go home and often hung around the school to keep from it.

"You're a very pretty girl," he said, and my faced turned the darkest shade of red possible.

"Thanks," I said with my head down. How could he say that I was pretty? I was wearing Goodwill clothes, and my sneakers were laceless. My hair was too long and straggly looking, and I didn't own any makeup. My dad would never have ever let me wear it anyway. He didn't want me to be a whore like my mom.

I should have run that day. I should have started walking and never looked back.

"You should look at me when I am talking to you," he said, and I looked up. I had to. I was already afraid of him, and I didn't even know his name.

"I'm Drew," he said.

"I'm Morgan," I replied and looked down and then right back up.

He laughed, and I didn't think I'd ever seen such perfect teeth in my life.

"I am going to marry you, Morgan," he said. I remember choking on my own saliva.

I got up and walked out of the gym, listening to him laugh as I did.

Why would he say that? Why would someone like him want to marry someone like me?

I went to bed that night thinking about Drew, and living the life of luxury. I fell asleep dreaming of the perfect life with the man with the perfect teeth. That dream soon turned into a nightmare when I swore I heard him in my house talking to my father. It was late, very late, and the thin walls did nothing to conceal the private conversation.

I could tell by my dad's slurring words that he was drunk. I lay on the mattress on my floor, trying to stop my racing heart.

"So you're telling me that you want to marry my daughter, and you're willing to pay me twenty-five thousand dollars to do so?" I couldn't believe what I was hearing. I wasn't property. He couldn't sell me. I knew he was going to punch him in the face and tell him to get the hell out of his house.

"That's right, Mr. Willow, but there is one condition that is non-negotiable."

"What?" my father asked.

"She has to be pure. If she's not, I don't want her."

"You mean a virgin?"

"Yes, that is exactly what I mean."

"Well I can guarantee that she is, or she better damn well be anyway, but I didn't say she was for sale."

"And what are you going to do with her when she turns eighteen? You know that you are going to lose her welfare and food stamps."

"I didn't say she wasn't for sale either, did I?"

What? This couldn't be happening. You don't sell people. This wasn't some third world country. This was America. Things like that don't happen here.

"Whatcha want a girl like her for anyway? I betcha you could have any girl you wanted."

"Oh, I could, but it's time for me to settle down."

"And no other girls will marry you?"

"Oh, I have plenty of women who would love to marry me. I am not interested in spoiled little rich girls. I want a pure girl who can be trained to be the kind of wife I want."

Trained? What the hell does that mean?

"Fifty thousand," my dad spat out.

"Thank you for your time, Mr. Willow," he stood to leave, and I was praying that my dad let him.

"Thirty thousand," he retorted, and I couldn't believe what was going on.

"You've got yourself a deal," he said. I was sure they were shaking on it.

The next three weeks were pure hell. My dad drove me to school every day and picked me up, insuring that I stayed pure. He didn't go out drinking for three weeks and wouldn't even let me go out after graduation. We attended the ceremony, stopped at the liquor store and went home to our dumpy little trailer. That was the night that he told me my plans to marry a rich man who was going to take care of me. He tried to make it sound like I was going to be living the life of luxury, and he was doing it for my own good. He forgot to mention that he was also receiving thirty thousand dollars for selling me.

I would like to say that my eighteenth birthday was the worst day of my life, but I had many worse days of my life.

Drew was there at eight o'clock in the morning to claim me. I had gotten sick so many times during the night, hyperventilating and dry heaving for hours.

He had two men with him. One carried a leather bag, sort of like an old timey doctor's bag. I stayed in my room, rocking back and forth on my mattress, willing this not to be happening.

My dad yelled for me, and I couldn't move. I sat on the mattress staring at the door with my heart in my stomach. He opened the door and the man carrying the bag came in with Drew.

"This nice man is going to exam you a little Morgan," my dad explained.

Exam me? What the fuck?

My dad stepped out, and Drew closed the door behind him.

"I need you to undress from the waist down," the man said, and I was in panic mode. I wasn't about to take my jeans off in front of either one of them, let alone let him touch me.

I looked at Drew, and he stood in his fancy suit and tie, smirking.

"Why?" I managed to ask.

"We just want to make sure that you are not damaged."

"I'm not," I all but yelled.

"Take your pants off, Morgan," Drew said with dark eyes that scared the hell out of me.

I didn't know what to do. This was going to happen whether I wanted it to or not.

After not moving and staring at the two of them in shock, Drew finally squatted to my face and put both of his hands on my knees. "We have a plane waiting on us, Morgan," he smiled.

"I don't want to go with you," I claimed.

He grabbed both my ankles and pulled me flat on my back. I could only stare in total shock. He unbuttoned my jeans and slid them off with my panties in one swift move. I crossed my ankles and covered myself with my hands.

"Spread your legs, Morgan." Drew spoke while the doctor or whatever he was removed a light and some sort of silver tool.

I couldn't even cry. I didn't know what emotions were transpiring as I lay there and trembled.

"Now!" he demanded.

I slowly opened my legs and squeezed my eyes shut. I didn't know which one of them was even touching me. I thought that Drew had been the one who pulled my knees up, exposing my very personal sex. I jumped when I felt the instrument penetrate me and then felt the warmth from the light between my legs.

"Her Hymen is fully intact," the man examining me said, pulling the tool from my vagina. I jumped again.

He stepped out leaving me alone with Drew.

"Get dressed, we have to go," he said, and that was when the tears started.

This was really happening. My dad was really going to let this man take me. Drew squatted down to me again and placed his hands on my bare knees after pulling me back to a sitting position.

"No tears, Morgan. I am doing you the biggest favor of your life. You are going to live like a queen and all you have to do to earn it is listen to me. Now get dressed. We are leaving," he demanded with a clenched jaw and a look that frightened me to the core. He moved my knees apart and looked down. I quickly snapped them back together. He snickered.

I dressed quickly and pulled on my sneakers.

My dad never said a word as I was led from the trailer. He was too busy counting the dollar bills and anticipating his night at the bar.

I rode in the back seat with Drew, and the two other men sat up front. We drove in silence other than Drew talking business on his phone and getting mad because of the poor reception. We were driven for almost two hours, and I wondered where we were going. Where was I going to live? He said we had a plane to catch, but we kept driving and driving.

Finally, we arrived at a small airport and Drew led me by my elbow to the private jet.

I looked around, wondering if I could run, knowing that I couldn't.

"Bring us back some refreshments once we are in the air," Drew told the man who hadn't examined me. I would soon learn that this man was around a lot.

I was now nervous about flying. I had never been on a plane. Hell, I had never been out of the mountains.

Drew directed me to the leather seat and told me to put my seatbelt on. The white leather was the softest thing I had ever felt in my life, and although I was scared shitless about my future, I couldn't help but to be a little excited about the flight.

Drew sat beside me and buckled in, as well. Once we were up in the air, I looked out the small window and was in awe of gliding through the clouds. He touched my hair and smiled at me. I flinched and pulled away.

"Where are we going?" I asked.

"Las Vegas," he answered.

"Las Vegas?" I asked.

"Did you not hear me the first time?" he snidely remarked.

I didn't know how to respond. He obviously expected some other reply, but I didn't know what it was, so I didn't say anything. I stared out the window, wondering what lay ahead.

I wasn't a dummy. I knew the distance between West Virginia and Las Vegas. I couldn't believe that I was going that many miles from the only home I'd ever known. Would I ever see my brother again? How would my mom ever find me? My dad could rot in hell. I didn't care if I ever saw him again.

The man brought two glasses of wine along with some cheese and crackers. Drew handed me a glass of wine, and I sipped it. I didn't like it and thought it was bitter and sweet. Of course, I drank it, and the cheese and crackers helped settle my stomach. I had never tasted such rich cheese in my life. If I did eat cheese, it was the wrapped imitation kind without much flavor at all.

I was brought back to my current life as I sipped on the now empty cup of tea. It was a lot easier to tell myself that I was going to move here and never think about my previous twenty-five years than it was to actually do it. Maybe I should seek counseling. No. No. I just need to occupy my mind and stop thinking about the past. I liked my job. I loved Lauren, and the house was perfect for me. I even loved the rough terrain beach.

I woke in a panic once again, too early. I sat up and calmed my speeding heart. I was getting used to talking myself down. I thought about the dream and wondered why it always went back to my childhood. I got up and looked out the window. The moon was full, a misty halo circling it. I could see Justin screaming for me not to let the social worker take him. He was so little and scared. All I could do was watch them take him. They didn't take me because the lady explained that nobody would want a seventeen year old girl and that I was old enough to take care of myself. She promised that I could see him, but every time I called, she had a different excuse why I couldn't.

Even though I should have gone back to bed, I showered first. I pulled on my new cotton panties and fuzzy socks. I checked myself out in the full length mirror, hanging on the back of the bedroom door. My jeans fit much better than the ones I'd brought with me. I wore one of the new shirts as well, and that too looked good on me. It fit snug and hugged my body in all the right places. I pulled a white button-up shirt over top. I knew I should have worn my old clothes. I was going to get dirty. I was sure of it.

As I parked next to the curb of the coffee shop, I didn't have to worry about taking any parking spaces since the shop was closed on Sundays. I made one pot of coffee for myself and looked around. Where do I begin? I was sure the place had never had a good cleaning, and after a week, my OCD couldn't take it a second longer. I knew I could rearrange things to make better use of the space. It was a decent sized store and was just going to take more manpower than just me. Maybe I could talk Lauren into helping. I decided I would start at the very front and work my way back. I needed to work on the front while the store was closed.

I poured a cup of the delicious coffee and started on the windows. Wow. These things have never been cleaned. I cleaned the windowsills first, using three buckets of water to rid the wood from the dust and grime. Starlight definitely wasn't the cleaning type. After cleaning the wood trim, I decided that I should clean the walls, as well. I was sure they had never had a good scrubbing either.

The sun was just coming up, and I was almost finished with the front wall. I was astounded at the difference between the front wall and the side walls. They weren't tan after all. They were very unique pale yellow. I liked it. I was just finishing up with the window cleaner on the door when I heard a tap on the glass. I peeked down from the chair that I had been using for a ladder and hopped down.

"Kind of early for criminals eh, sheriff?" I asked, opening the door for Dawson.

"Or late," he replied, stepping in, "and I told you, call me Dawson."

"What can I do for you?" I asked, not wanting to stop my task at hand. I was making good time, and I wanted to keep at it.

"I just got off the night shift and saw the lights on here. What on earth are you doing here this time of morning?"

I shrugged my shoulders. "Couldn't sleep, I have had this on my mind since I started working here, so I decided to get up and get it done."

"Wow," he said turning to the clean storefront.

"I know. Isn't it nice?"

"It's amazing," he said, not believing the difference. "You have a cup of coffee?" he asked, walking to the pot and not giving me time to answer.

No. I don't. I want you to leave. I don't have time for entertaining.

"Sure, help yourself."

I didn't stop to chat or entertain. I emptied my mop bucket again and started on the next wall, hoping he took the hint. He didn't. He sat at the table and watched.

"You know coffee has caffeine. I would think after working the night shift you would want to go home and sleep," I tried.

"Are you trying to get rid of me?"

Yes. That is exactly what I am trying to do.

"No, not at all, but if you stick around too long, I might put you to work."

"Let me go home and change, and I would be happy to help you."

I was speechless for a moment. I was joking. I didn't think he would take me up on it.

I laughed. "Thanks, but I'm okay. You should get some sleep."

"I actually won't go to bed until tonight. I am on days during the week, and if I sleep, I will be all messed up and won't be able to sleep tonight."

"Thanks for the offer, but I couldn't ask you to help me."

"I don't think you asked Riley. I think I offered."

Now what the hell was I supposed to do? I could use some muscles to help me move the shelves, and I would really like to move the cash register counter closer to the door.

"You'll get dishpan hands."

"I'm a bachelor. I am used to dishpan hands."

Great, just what I need, a bachelor.

I turned to look at him, trying to think of something to say. I noticed how handsome he was and how nice he looked in uniform. He had a military cut, and I could tell that he was very well built. He was wearing a five o'clock shadow and had the bluest eyes I'd ever seen. I wondered if they were contacts.

What the hell is wrong with you, Morgan? You are not getting involved with a man. Forget it.

I broke our gaze and turned back to wiping the wall. I still hadn't said anything, and had no idea what to say. I had never in my life said no to a man. I wasn't *trained* that way.

"It's settled. I'll see you in an hour."

Dawson left, and I sank to the floor. I didn't want him to help. I didn't want him around. I jumped when my cell phone started singing something about having a girl's night out. I knew it was Lauren. Every time she came around she changed the ringtone on my phone.

"Where the hell are you? I was going to come over and eat your leftovers."

"At the shop cleaning, you can go over and eat my leftovers if you come here and hang out with me so that I don't have to be alone with the sheriff."

"Why is the sheriff there?"

"He saw the lights on and stopped to make sure everything was okay. He saw what I was doing and has now gone home to change so that he can come back and help me."

"Are you kidding me, Ry? That man doesn't have an interest in women. He hasn't dated since his wife left him."

"When was that?" I asked for unknown reasons.

"Um, let's see. I have been here for almost two years, and I think she left about a year before that so I'd say three years or so."

I almost asked why she left and then remembered that I didn't care.

"Please come here. I don't want to be alone with him."

"Fine, I will be there in a little bit, but I don't understand you. Let me get Dawson Bade alone."

"Well, I will gladly go to the back of the line so that you can do that."

"Yeah right, I have asked that man out three times now. My ego won't take any more than that."

I was dreading the day ahead with Dawson. I didn't mind Lauren and was glad that she was coming, but I really, really, really didn't want Dawson to be there.

Lauren showed up first, and Dawson arrived ten minutes later. Lauren and I were talking about how handsome he was, or she was anyway. I was trying my best not to notice. That worked until he showed up in jeans and a nice fitting t-shirt.

Oh, my God. Stop it, Riley.

I was pleasantly surprised at how much fun we had. We all worked and talked. I was relieved that I didn't have to answer any personal questions. I didn't really have anything to talk about, but commented on the things that Dawson and Lauren talked about. We managed to get all of the walls washed down and after Lauren, and I moved all of the things from the shelves we all turned them. After three tries, I had them the way I wanted them. I was proud of myself. I had a really hard time telling them that I didn't like it the way we moved it the first time, and the second time was even worse. Thank God Dawson picked up on it.

"You don't like it, do you?" he asked, looking at me staring at the shelves.

I looked over to him, and our eyes did that uncomfortable locking thing again.

"Not really," I smiled and turned my eyes quickly back to the shelves.

We worked until after four and stopped when our pizza arrived. We all sat at the same table, and I looked around at our work. I couldn't believe we got so much done. I just wished we would have gotten the wood floors cleaned. After moving the shelves, there was a noticeable difference in the two-toned wooden floor. The walls were spectacular, and I planned to talk to Lauren about her friend in the construction business painting the ceilings. The register by the door was a lot nicer too. You could actually engage in conversation with the customers, rather than being in the back of the store.

I hope Starlight isn't mad about changing everything.

"Earth to Riley," Dawson said snapping his fingers.

"What? Sorry. I was just thinking about what to do next."

"I'm leaving," Lauren abruptly said, afraid that I was going to start another project at that time.

"I didn't mean now," I said, giving her a look of, don't leave me alone with him.

It didn't work.

"I will see you at home. I need a shower," and she was out the door. I knew she was leaving me on purpose and wanted me to be alone with Dawson.

"You should probably leave and get some sleep too," I said to Dawson, standing up to clean up our paper plates.

"Yeah, you wore me out today too. I should sleep like a baby."

The mention of sleep made me apprehensive about going to bed. I wasn't sleeping much lately and hated waking and remembering my nightmares.

"You can go. I'm not far behind you. Thanks for your help today. I greatly appreciate it."

Dawson stood and sucked the noisy soda through the ice of his cup. "Don't mention it. It was fun. I would love to see the look on Starlight's face when she walks in this door."

"I just hope she's not mad. I mean she did tell me to do whatever I wanted, but I'm not sure that meant to remodel the whole place," I smiled.

"She will love it. I'll see you later."

Please stop smiling at me like that.

"Okay. Thanks again for your help."

I didn't leave and worked until after nine. I was hoping that getting myself good and exhausted would cause me to fall into a deep sleep and not be tormented by my dreams.

It worked, and I slept sounder and healthier than I had since I left Drew.

I felt rehabilitated and improved as I unlocked the back door to the store on Monday morning. The three locals showed up just as the last pot of coffee had run through. All three of the older men made a big deal about how clean the place was. I felt very comfortable with them for the first time, and had no problem talking and laughing with the men as they drank their morning coffees.

I was rearranging some clothes on the rack toward the back of the store when I heard the one man that they called Tom.

"Good morning, Sheriff. What brings you out and about on a Monday?" he asked, knowing that he was usually only there on Saturday mornings.

"Morning, Tom, Jake, Luke. Just thought I would stop in and see what the fuss about the new look was all about."

I smiled, amused that he didn't mention doing half the work.

I was looking right at him still carrying the smile when he looked around, looking for me, I was sure.

He smiled when he saw me. "Morning, Riley."

"Good morning, Sheriff," I said and nervously moved my eyes away from his.

That wasn't the only day that Dawson showed up. He was there every morning after that. I tried not to let things be awkward between us. I also made little comments about not being interested in romance or dating, hoping that he got the hint.

My week was going well. I had managed to get the entire front of the store reorganized and looking like a new place. I worked late into the night, mostly because it did wear me out and I slept better.

The next project was the office, and I had to keep telling myself that the store had been just as bad, but the outcome was well worth the work. I planned to start on it as soon as I locked up on Friday. I was on the phone with Starlight wanting to know how things were going when Dawson walked in.

What the hell is he doing here?

He only smiled and took the last little bit of coffee from the pot.

I finished up my conversation with Starlight after telling her that things were going great and not to worry and have a good time.

I started rinsing the pots and cleaning up when Levi walked in, as well.

"Hello," I said, surprised that he was there. I had only seen him in there once since I had started work.

"Hey, Riley. How are you?"

"Good, Levi, and you?" I asked as I continued to clean up.

Levi and Dawson exchanged greetings, and Levi turned his attention back to me.

"Ms. Riley, would you like to accompany me to dinner tonight?" he asked, and my mouth dropped.

No, I wouldn't.

"Thanks for the offer, Levi, but I am not leaving here for a while. I need to get some things done in the office, and I can't really do it until I close the store."

"How about I bring us food here?"

Now what the hell do I say? Just be blunt and tell him Ry.

"Levi, I appreciate the offer, but I'm really not interested. Okay?" I watched his reaction, hoping he understood that I wasn't going to date him.

"Okay, but just so you know, I don't give up easily."

Great.

"I'll see you around." He nodded to the sheriff and was gone.

"Turning down Levi Straits uh?" Dawson said with some sort of stupid sexy grin that made me crazy.

"Yes. I guess so."

"Why?"

None of your business.

I shrugged my shoulders. "Not interested in men," I said matter-of-fact.

He looked at me with narrowed eyes. "Were you married before moving here?"

"Yes," I said with only that and continued to clean up the coffee bar.

"How long?"

I looked at him, hoping he could read my face and take the hint that I didn't want to talk about my past with him. "Six years," I replied.

"Was it ruthless or mutual?"

Okay, now I am getting a little annoyed.

"Mutual," I lied. "What are you doing here?" I bluntly asked.

He snickered. "I was going to ask you out to dinner, but now I am afraid to."

"I would say no anyway."

"I didn't ask you out on a date. Just because you are not the same sex as me, doesn't mean that we can't be friends, does it?"

"We are friends, but I still don't think dinner is a good idea."

"Why? You do eat, don't you?"

I snickered that time. "Yeah. I eat, but I wasn't lying about tackling the office tonight."

"How about you give the makeover a break and go out to eat with me. Not on a date, just as friends. You've been in here from daylight to dark all week. Take a break."

Say no Riley, say no.

"Fine, I need to go home and shower."

"Me too, you didn't think that I was going to take you out in this, did you?" he asked, looking down at his uniform.

"You're not taking me out. We are going to get food, something we both need."

He laughed. "I'll pick you up at your house in an hour."

My house!?!

"Okay, see ya in a little while."

I groaned as soon as he was out the door. Why can't I just learn to say no? Why was that such a challenge for me?

Because you were never allowed to say no, that's why, but you can now you coward.

Chapter 4

Dawson picked me up in his pickup truck. He got out and opened the door for me. I was chastising myself as soon as I saw him in his jeans, button up shirt and brown leather loafers. I reprimanded myself again when I breathed in his cologne.

"You look very nice," he commented, and I gave him a look.

"This is not a date remember?" I said but was smiling on the inside.

He playfully put his hands in the air and laughed. "I am sorry, but it's really hard not to notice how nice your ass looks in those jeans."

How many shades of red are there?

"You are definitely not allowed to say stuff like that."

He laughed and closed my door.

"Where are we going?" I asked.

"Put your seatbelt on, we're going into Marshall and eat ribs at Hogly Wogley's."

"I was going to put my seatbelt on, sheriff," I said, and he laughed.

We were talking about the coffee shop while we drove through the little town. When we passed the bar where Lauren had taken me, Dawson pulled into the parking lot. I wondered what he was doing, and then I saw.

"Stay in the truck," he said and got out.

I rolled down the window so I could listen. He grabbed a guy off another guy who was punching him in the face. He jerked him to his feet and stood between the two men.

"What the hell are you doing, Mike?" he asked, holding him by the chest.

"He started it. Tell him to keep his mouth shut about shit he doesn't know anything about," the guy yelled, angrily, pointing his finger at his opponent.

"Tim, what's this all about?"

"Dude, I didn't mean to piss you off. I didn't know Chuck was your boss."

Dawson facilitated the conversation and in no time had the two men calmed down.

"Are we done here?" he asked them. They both said yes.

"Good, shake hands and go drink a beer. No drinking and driving," he warned and left with the two guys walking back inside as friends.

I looked up to the crowd that had gathered out front and saw Levi staring right at me.

Oh, how nice.

He gave me a nod, and I did the same.

"Sorry about that," Dawson said as we backed up.

"It's okay, but you just got me in trouble. Levi was there."

"And you care?"

"No, not necessarily, but I did blow him off, remember?"

"Trust me, Riley, Levi Straits is not going home alone tonight."

Well, I'm glad I did shoot him down then.

We ate the best and messiest ribs I had ever tasted in my life. There was nothing elegant about them at all. I couldn't help but think about Drew eating something that messy. He would have had his little servant there picking the meat off the bone for him.

I had a good time with Dawson, and we talked and laughed about nothing at all. That too made me think about Drew. I had never in the six years that I was married to him, laughed with him. Yes, I am sure that I faked many laughs, but this was different. Dawson was just a charming, funny guy, and so much fun to be around.

Dawson had no sooner dropped me off when Lauren walked uninvited through my front door.

"Why didn't you tell me you were going out with Dawson?" she spouted.

"I didn't know that I was."

"Levi called me. He said you blew him off to go for Dawson."

"He wanted to take me on a date. Dawson and I are just friends."

"Do you really believe that, Ry?"

"What?" I asked surprised, "that we are just friends?"

"Yes."

"Of course I believe it. There was nothing romantic about it."

"Yeah okay, whatever."

"There wasn't, and I am not dating Dawson, Levi or anyone else. Now stop it."

"Let's go to the bar."

"Um, no. I am staying home."

"Come on, Ry. Don't make me go by myself."

"I just saw Joel on your porch. You're not going alone. You little conniver."

"But I don't want you to sit here alone."

"I like being alone. I am going to change and veg out on the couch. I'm tired. I worked harder than I am used to this week."

"Fine, party pooper, I'll talk to you later."

I did veg out on the couch and dozed off by ten. It was the first night in almost a week that I dreamed, and again I was taken back in time to being a little girl. My mom had just gotten home from her shift at the truck stop. I was twelve, and Justin was just a tiny baby, maybe two or three months old. He was sick and burning up with a fever. I was trying to give him a bottle and rock him and do everything that a twelve year old child would know to get him to stop.

My mom took him from me and was mad because I let him get sick. I was crying and trying to explain that I had told my dad to stop and tell her that he was sick on his way to the bar, but she wouldn't listen and slapped me across the face for back-talking her.

That was the first time I was ever alone. She took him to the hospital, and they kept him for three days. I knew he was in the hospital because my dad came home long enough to shower and leave again for his weekend bar routine. He never came home the rest of that night, and my mom never did either. It was the dead of winter, and I couldn't keep the only heat source burning. It was freezing in the trailer, and there was no food in the cabinets or freezer. I ate a bag of microwave popcorn the first night and dry cereal for the next two days. I was afraid that nobody was ever coming back, and by the third day I was hungry, scared and freezing.

My parents came home together with Justin, and again I was in trouble because the fire was out. It was so cold in the old trailer that there was ice on the inside of the windows. My dad bent me over his legs on the sofa, no, he didn't bend me over, he threw me over his legs. My mom stood there and watched him hit me over and over until she finally told him that was enough.

I woke up to Justin crying in my room a few hours later. I waited for my mom to come and get him, but she didn't come. I left him crying in my room while I heated a bottle. I hated my parents and neither one of them deserved me or Justin. I could hear the bed creaking and both my parents moaning and going at it in the next room. I put Justin in bed with me after changing his diaper and covered us both up.

I didn't wake panicked or scared with this dream. I felt pain and neglect and my heart ached for Justin, hoping that he was doing well. I wanted to go there and find him, just to make sure for myself, but I didn't dare. I knew that Drew had somebody staked out there, waiting to see me. I wiped the single tear from my eye and got up. I didn't have to open the shop for another two hours, but got dressed and went anyway. I would rather have been working then sitting there alone with my thoughts.

Before I knew it, I had been in my new dwellings for a month. I was hanging out with Dawson quite often, and he hung around the shop drinking more coffee than normal. The store looked sensational, and the office was actually a productive working space now. I filed everything in the empty filing cabinets that were buried with boxes and boxes of stuff that I was sure Starlight didn't even know she had. I used some of the petty cash and Dawson built shelves in the storeroom for me. I had everything organized and on shelves. I found some really funky things in the storeroom and continued to make the dining room more customer friendly. There was a box that I was sure Starlight got for that purpose that had yellow and white checkered tablecloths. I brought out three booths that were also buried in the back, and Dawson screwed them to the floor for me in front of the glass windows. I brought out three more tables and covered them all with the tablecloths.

I also found a whole stack of beautiful Indian paintings that needed to be on display. They were beautiful. The first day that I had hung them on the hooks that Dawson hung for me, I sold three of them. I hung some unique dream catchers which were also selling like crazy. I found the company that made them and ordered another box in all shapes and sizes.

Lauren and Dawson helped two Sundays in a row, scrubbing and re-staining the wood floors. I couldn't wait for Starlight to get back to see her new store. I also hoped that she wasn't going to be mad at all of the changes that I took upon myself to do.

A young girl from the next town stopped in one day and had just opened up a cookie and cupcake store and wanted to know if I would be interested in placing an order. I told her that I would order once and see how they went and if they did okay, I would order more. They did more than okay, and she was bringing fresh orders daily. The display case that Dawson got from the back room was perfect, and I even had room for Phyllis's Saturday morning doughnuts in the case. I took orders for the cookies, cupcakes, and pastries from the case. I hated the way it was before and people could just finger whatever. I felt much better about taking the food out with my plastic gloved hand.

Dawson was there, as normal, earlier than he needed to be on Saturday morning. I was frantically cleaning and making sure everything was perfect for Starlight. I was a nervous wreck and hoped that she was okay with all of the changes.

"Will you get over here and sit down," Dawson pleaded. "I know Starlight. She is going to love it."

I got a cup of coffee and sat at the booth in front of the window with him, patiently waiting and wishing that she would get there already.

"You want to go eat some ribs tonight?" Dawson asked as we waited.

"Hmm, maybe," I replied.

"Maybe?"

"Well it's six o'clock in the morning. I can't think about supper until I have breakfast and lunch."

Dawson laughed. "Okay, let me know after lunch."

I ran to the back room when I heard the door unlock, knowing that it was Starlight. She came in with huge eyes, and her hand covered her mouth. Dawson followed me back, wanting to see her reaction, as well.

"Oh, my God, Riley, did you do all of this," she asked in awe of the neatly organized storeroom that you could actually see the floor, and it was clean.

"Well, I had some help," I answered, smiling at Dawson. "I would have never have been able to do it all myself."

"You haven't seen anything yet, Starlight. This girl is a working machine. Welcome home," Dawson added.

"I don't think I am home. This is not the store that I left."

She walked down the hall and opened the office door and gasped. I had hung pictures on the walls; the desk was clear, except for the computer and a folder in a medal slot with an order for some psychedelic flip-flops that I wanted to purchase for the store. It was now pretty warm out, and with more tourists coming in the store, I knew they would sell.

Starlight couldn't believe what she was seeing. She opened the drawers and filing cabinet with the wisely placed tabs and a tangible system. She couldn't seem to close her mouth. She continued and walked into both the men's and women's restrooms. They too were transformed into delicately decorated rooms. Both rooms had an Indian theme and the décor all came from things that I had found in the storeroom, except for the paint. We did paint those two rooms because they desperately needed it. The rust colored paint with the Indian design looked almost urban.

"Riley, I am speechless," she exclaimed.

"So you're not mad?"

"Mad? No way. I am in shock that you did this."

"Keep walking," Dawson said. I gasped when I felt him place his hand on the small of my back. I knew it was just a friendly gesture, but it made me feel like, like, I don't know, like maybe I liked it.

I thought Starlight was going to have a heart attack when she finally made it to the front. She took note of every little detail, not missing a thing, and commenting on every little alteration.

She loved the new look and thought that my design was magnificent. She thought we had painted there too, and couldn't believe it when I told her that we only scrubbed the walls. I told her that I had wanted to get the ceilings painted as well, but didn't want to use all of her petty cash.

"I will get the ceilings painted for you," she almost demanded. She walked around the new counter and slid the deli case open just in time for Phyllis to bring in the Saturday morning doughnuts.

"Oh, I better get the coffee going," I said, forgetting the time after getting wrapped up in showing Starlight everything.

"Oh no, you don't. You've done enough. I've got it," Starlight demanded, taking a bite of an oatmeal cookie. "I love the cookie idea, and I love you, Riley Murphy," she stated. Dawson and I smiled at each other.

Dawson didn't hang out as long as he normally did, and Starlight was truly amazed at the traffic that came in and out all day. We didn't get to close until an hour later than normal and then stayed another hour restocking the sold merchandise.

"Riley, I don't know if we can keep up at this rate," she said as she replenished the tie-dye shirts on the rack.

I smiled at her, and she shook her head. "Let me guess, you already have it covered?"

"I do," I said. "I sent for a catalogue from this company out of Oregon. They have the coolest stuff ever," I explained, disappearing into the office to retrieve it.

Starlight followed me, and we sat across from each other at the desk while she turned each page. I had corner pages folded of the things that I thought would be nice for the store and she circled a few things, as well.

My cell phone rang, and I answered the call from Dawson.

"Are we eating ribs or not? I'm starving."

"I forgot all about it, Dawson. You go ahead. I think I am going home and making homemade pizza."

"You made me wait until eight o'clock at night and didn't call me. I'm coming over for homemade pizza," he demanded, and I laughed.

I wasn't nervous around him anymore and wasn't worried about anything happening between us. We had been hanging out for a month, and he had never even tried to kiss me.

"Okay, I have to stop at the store and then I am headed that way."

"Sheriff Dawson, uh?" Starlight smiled.

"No, we're just friends. There is nothing romantic between Dawson and me."

"Why not? Dawson is a great guy."

"I just got out of one mess. I am not interested in another one. No thank you. I will see you Monday," I said, taking my purse from the hook.

"No, you won't. You take the day off, take a couple of them if you want. You deserve it."

"I really would rather be here, Starlight," I admitted, not wanting to be home alone with my thoughts.

"Well, only if you want to be. Thank you so much for all of this, Riley. I couldn't have asked you to do half of what you did."

"I'm just glad you like it."

"I love it. Have a good night."

It was almost nine before I got the pizza in the oven. Dawson came, and I told him to chill out while I grabbed a shower. I didn't care that he was there, and I was putting on comfortable clothes, done with the whole impressing somebody else situation. I put on a baggy, comfortable t-shirt and a pair of soft flannel pants. I figured we would end up sitting on the deck, and although the days were fairly hot, the evening ocean air was brisk.

"I brought a couple of movies," Dawson said as I entered wrapping my hair in a ponytail.

Lauren was there and sitting on the sofa.

"Hey, what are you doing? I figured you would be with Joel tonight," I said when I saw her.

"I am. Dawson answered your phone and said you were making homemade pizza."

I laughed. I don't think the girl ever cooked. She just came to my house and helped herself.

The three of us sat out on the deck and ate pizza and drank beer. I tried to tell Lauren to invite Joel over to my house, but they wanted to go to the bar because they had a band. She tried to get us to come with them, and I refused. She didn't push it. Turning her down for offers to hang out in the bar was starting to catch on, and she didn't badger me about it as much.

She drank two beers, ate two slices of pizza and left to meet Joel.

Dawson and I stayed out on the deck and I consumed more alcohol than I should have. I could feel it, and knew that was my limit when I stumbled a little on the way to the bathroom.

"Comedy romance or action romance?" Dawson asked, holding up the two DVD's.

Romance? Awesome.

"I don't care. You pick."

We sat on separate ends of the couch, and he picked a comedy romance with Sandra Bullock. I had already seen the movie but didn't tell him and watched it anyway. The wedding part took me back to my wedding day, and I stared blankly at the TV.

***

I was looking out the small jet window when I knew we were descending. I saw one runway and knew that we were going to land there. I remembered my heart beating too fast and I was trying to talk myself out of a full blown panic attack. The jet landed and a black limousine picked us up.

"Good evening, sir," the man dressed in a black suit nodded to Drew, opening the door for us. I didn't know where the other two men from the plane had gone, but they didn't get into the car with us.

Drew talked on his phone the entire time we were in the limo, but it wasn't a long drive. Fifteen minutes later, we pulled up to the mansion of a house. Later I had found out that the runway belonged to him, it was his own private one, and was on the property of the estate. I couldn't believe what I was seeing. We drove through two stone pillars with the numbers 41293. I remembered repeating the number over and over in my head, just in case somebody cared and needed to come and rescue me. I wondered why the gate read, Callaway Estates, but assumed he had purchased it from the Callaways or something.

I could barely keep my mouth shut when a lady answered the door and let us into the house. She was maybe in her mid-thirties or so. She smiled at me and could probably tell how scared I was. Drew was still talking to someone on the phone, telling whoever it was that he couldn't drop the price and if they wanted it, the price was thirty-five thousand and to take it or leave it.

Wow, what could he be selling for thirty- five thousand dollars? No wonder he lived here.

Drew held my elbow and led me to his office where two other men waited for us. He walked around and sat in the oversized leather chair. I stood awkwardly at the door. The one guy was the one who had traveled with him to retrieve me. I wondered how he got there before us and why he hadn't ridden in the limousine with us.

"Let's get this over with. I have a plane to catch." he told one of the men.

"You sign here," the same man in an expensive suit said, sliding the paper to him.

All three men turned to look at me, and I didn't know what I was supposed to do.

"Come on, Morgan, I don't have all day," Drew said. I was still puzzled.

He got up and pulled me by the arm to his desk when I didn't move. He grabbed my hand and shoved the pen in it.

"Sign!" he almost yelled, poking hard at the X where my name was already printed.

My hand started to tremble when I saw the top of the paper that said Secretary of the State, Nevada, and then it said certificate of marriage.

What! This was my wedding? I couldn't believe it. What was his motive? Why was he doing this?

"Sign the Goddamn X, Morgan!" he yelled, and I could feel the tears forming in my eyes. I didn't want to sign. I didn't want to marry Drew Kelley.

He grabbed my hand and scribbled my name with his.

"Witness it, Derik," he demanded and the other man signed as well.

I was speechless. What the hell was going on? I was just forced to marry someone against my will. A very rich someone who didn't care about the law, or that we had just gotten married illegally, I was sure.

"That isn't real," I stated boldly. "You have to have a county clerk or a judge or preacher or justice of the peace," I was rattling on and on nervously. Drew laughed.

"Don't worry, Mrs. Kelley. Ronald is a judge. It's legal. Somebody get her the fuck out of here," he said, and the lady that met us at the door came to retrieve me.

"I will show you to your quarters, Mrs. Kelley."

"I am not Mrs. Kelley. Stop calling me that," I demanded. She shushed me.

"That is what I am ordered to call you. Please don't make it difficult for me. I am just trying to do my job."

"But don't you even care that I don't want to be here? I don't want to be his wife. I don't even want to be in the same state as him. I hate him already."

The lady shushed me again. "Everything you say Mrs. Kelley is heard by Mr. Kelley," she whispered.

Great so now I am going to be spied on too.

"Do you have a name?" I asked.

"Rebecca," she answered, moving me right along.

She opened the double doors, and I couldn't help but suck in a deep breath at the beauty of the room, my room. It was absolutely gorgeous. The king size bed was bigger than my whole bedroom in the trailer. I never saw Drew again that night or for the next seven nights. Rebecca explained to me that he had to fly to Africa on business, and he would talk to me when he returned. I hoped he didn't return, and his plane went down in the African rain forest, and he was eaten by a lion.

Rebecca showed me around, and I gasped again at the bathroom. She told me to get cleaned up and to come back to the kitchen after I was bathed. She explained that she had a few things sent for me but not much, and I would have a fitting the following day for more clothes.

A fitting?

I showered with shower heads hitting every part of my body. I had to admit even though I was scared shitless, wondering why the hell a good looking, rich man would want to marry me, I couldn't help but be just a little excited. The shower gel scent was outlandish and left my skin feeling soft and smooth.

I put on the pantsuit that was left for me on my luxurious bed, it was so pretty and soft, it made me want to do my hair and put on makeup. I didn't of course. I didn't have anything to do that with, *yet*.

Looking for Rebecca, I wanted to open every door that I passed to find her. I passed another younger girl who didn't speak or look at me. She was carrying a stack of towels, and I assumed she too worked for Drew.

I didn't sit at the massive table in the dining room. I sat in the kitchen at the table that was still at least three times bigger than my wobbly table back home. I had the best meal I had ever had in my life. I had heard of shrimp scampi from the magazines that I used to get from the library and always looked at the recipes wishing that I could try some of them.

I actually went to bed with a smile. I had the biggest flat screen TV that you could possibly buy. I stayed up so late watching all of the channels. We had a TV back home, but it was an old console one, and we didn't have cable. We had an antenna and only got two channels. You had to beat the side of it every so often to make the lines stop rolling up. I was so comfortable in the massive plush bed with satin designer sheets. I couldn't believe that I was there. I think it was around two in the morning when I finally turned off the television and dozed off.

I had slept until almost eleven before Rebecca finally came into wake me.

"Mrs. Kelley, it's time to wake up. You have an appointment at noon," she said.

I remember thinking that it must have been a dream. I felt so good in the bed, and the silk nightgown felt elegant against my skin. I didn't want to wake up. I liked the dream.

"Mrs. Kelley," Rebecca called again, waking me from my dream that wasn't a dream after all. "You have to get up and get something to eat. You have an appointment soon."

"Appointment for what?" I asked sleepily. "Where am I going?"

"You have an appointment here to have your hair and nails done, and they are doing your fitting so that you can get more clothes."

This is not real. This doesn't happen in real life.

I went to put on the same pantsuit from the night before, but it was gone and a new light pink pants and jacket were in its place. It was the softest material I had touched in my life. I looked at the tag, and it said 100% cashmere. I didn't want to put on the stockings or the shoes. I loved the feel of a plush carpet under my feet, but I did wear them. I had a feeling bare feet weren't quite acceptable around there.

I had fruit and coffee for breakfast. I was eighteen and had never tasted coffee in my life. It was divine with just a hint of vanilla.

"What does Drew do, Rebecca?" I asked, curious about his business.

"That is a subject for you and Mr. Kelley," she replied. I had a feeling that she was pretty loyal to Drew, and I wouldn't be getting any information from her.

My hair was long and hung past my waist. I wasn't upset at all about cutting it. I had wanted it cut for a long time. I had even tried to cut some of the length off myself, but the only scissors that I could find in the trailer were too dull to cut one strand. I was not as happy about dying it. I liked my brown hair and wasn't crazy about being a blonde.

"You can cut it, but I will decline the blonde," I said.

Rebecca bent down to my ear sitting in the chair. "Mr. Kelley wants your hair lightened. Don't be difficult, please," she pleaded.

I let them do my hair. I let them do my nails and a pedicure that felt wonderful. I loved being pampered and couldn't believe that I had three people sucking up and kissing my ass the way they were. However when it came to the bikini wax I had no part of it. My hair was down there for a reason, and nobody was waxing it off, let alone one of these strangers, especially the guy. I threw a fit for ten minutes, refusing to lie on the table. Rebecca pulled me out to the hall and pointed to three men.

"Mrs. Kelley, I am ordered to have you forcefully held down by those three men if you refuse to cooperate. I don't want to do that, and it's not in your best interest either. Please just let them do their job. You are done after that, and can do whatever you want."

"Rebecca, why do I have to do that? I don't want my vagina waxed."

"I am afraid it's going to happen whether you want it to or not."

I couldn't believe that I was laying on top of that table getting a bikini wax. I didn't want the guy in there but lost that fight too. He was there explaining that he was going to brush something on me, sort of like Anbesol for toothaches. He said that it would help with the pain.

Pain? Really? This truly wasn't real life.

I closed my eyes in embarrassment and humiliation while my pubic hair was being ripped from my body. I didn't even protest when the guy lifted my right knee and rubbed warm wax on my left lip. I knew I would just be fighting a losing battle. I did scream however, when he swiftly pulled it off. He did the same with my right leg and then rolled me to my side, making sure I was clean all the way back to my other hole. I had never been so humiliated in my life, and they acted like it was no big deal. I assumed that it probably wasn't, and I certainly wasn't the first girl that they had given a bikini wax.

Rebecca told me that I could shower and that I was done for the day. She said that my supper should be about ready and to come into the kitchen when I was ready.

I decided to bathe in the oversized tub and hissed a little when the hot water reached my recently stripped sex. I slid my hand down, and the only patch of hair was a neatly trimmed line running straight down the middle. I touched the smoothness of my lips and actually liked the feel of it.

I stood naked in front of the full length mirror. I didn't look like the same girl. My hair was cut just below my shoulders and tapered around my face. The highlights and the blonde made me look older than I was. I wondered if that were the purpose of going blonde. I moved my eyes down my curves and once again touched my naked sex. I knew that this was another one of Drew's demands, and got a little nervous when I thought about him wanting to have sex with me. I knew it was inevitable and that it was just a matter of time. Why else would he demand that I be a virgin or want me naked down there? Any idiot could figure that out.

Later that night, once I was in my bed for the night, my phone rang beside my bed. I didn't know whether or not I should answer it. Was it my phone or was it ringing throughout the house?

"Hello," I finally answered.

"Hello, you are even more beautiful now," the voice said, and I knew that it was Drew.

"How do you know how I look?" I asked, looking around the room for a camera.

"I can see you in every room of my house, my dear."

"Every room?" I asked, thinking about touching myself in front of the mirror. He laughed.

"Yes, my love, every room, but for future references, you're not allowed to touch yourself."

"Go to hell. I'll do what I want, when I want," I scolded. Who did he think he was?

He laughed again. "I assure you, Mrs. Kelley, you won't, and I wouldn't advise you to speak to me like that forthcoming."

"Why?" I said boldly. He was in Africa, although I knew that I wouldn't have spoken to him like that had he been standing in front of me.

"Because you will be punished for outbursts like that."

"And how do plan to punish me?" I asked, but was already in half of a panic attack.

"I am sure you will soon find out. I will see you in a few days, Mrs. Kelley," he said and hung up.

***

"Riley!" Dawson called. I was sure that it wasn't the first time he had called my name.

I turned to look at him.

"One of these days you're going to have to tell me where it is you go when you zone out like that."

I hadn't even noticed the credits rolling up the screen.

"Sorry," I said and shut the television off. I looked at the clock and knew that he should be leaving soon. It was the weekend. He worked the night shift, and had to go home to change.

I picked up our beer bottles and carried them to the kitchen. I turned around, and Dawson was right there. He didn't give me time to speak, or protest when he backed me up to the sink and kissed me.

Dammit, Dawson. Why did you have to go and mess up a good thing?

I parted my lips just a little, and his tongue darted in and entwined with mine. I hadn't even realized that I had moaned in his mouth until I heard it with my own ears. It was most certainly my moan. His hands went up my sides and around my back pulling me closer to him, and I didn't have the power to make him stop.

Really vagina? You traitor.

It was a good thing that he stopped because I was ready to rip my clothes off right there on the kitchen floor.

"Jesus, Ry," he whispered to my lips.

"What the hell did you do, sheriff?"

"I don't know, but I liked it," he said, kissing me softly again and then pulling away.

"You better get out of here," I whispered back to his lips, willing myself not to shove my tongue down his throat again.

"Yes, I better," he agreed and kissed me again, and again, and again. He finally pulled away, and I followed him to the door, locking up behind him.

What the fuck was that?

I cleaned up the kitchen and crawled into bed, flipped on the television and dialed Lauren.

"What's wrong," she answered alarmed.

"Dawson freaking kissed me," I blurted out.

"He did? How was it?"

"I don't know yet, confusing I guess."

"Ry, you should have known that it was going to happen. I mean you two do spend a lot of time together."

"I am not ready for that, Lauren."

"Forget that. Life is too short to wait around. I have to go, Ry. I'm getting ready to sing. I will be over in the morning."

"Okay, break a leg. I'll see you tomorrow."

Chapter 5

I lay there for a long time, thinking about Dawson, and of course it led to Drew. I thought about the first time that he and I did anything. He was gone for seven days, and I had just started getting used to being in the exquisite house, and having servants doing everything for me. They did everything from fixing my hair to picking out my clothes. I even had delicious meals prepared three times a day. I had full access to every room in the house and the pool outside. My favorite thing to do was ride around the property alone in one of the four golf carts.

You don't know how many times I scoped the place out, thinking about running away on my little golf cart. Of course, I was always too scared to try it, and knew that the battery would be dead before I ever even got off of his property. I didn't know how much land he had, but I was sure it was a lot.

It was later in the evening, and I had already retired to my room for the night. I didn't even think about it when I saw the fresh clean nightgown and panties on my bed. I was starting to get used to having my clothes laid out every morning and every night. I grabbed the panties and left the nightgown on the bed.

I walked out of the bathroom with a towel wrapped around me and Drew was sitting on my bed. I jumped and pulled the towel tighter around my naked body.

"What are you doing in here?" I asked.

"Now, is that any way to greet your husband after he's been gone for a week?" he asked with a smirk.

"You could have stayed gone for a month, and I wouldn't have cared."

He stood up and was in my face in a split second. "Where are your manners? Mrs. Kelley."

"I ain't got none," I yelled back.

"I don't have any," he corrected my hick language, "now, say it again."

"Fuck you!" I said through my gritted teeth.

That was the first time he hit me. The back of his hand went right across my right cheekbone, and I almost landed on the floor.

"That will be the last time you ever say anything like that to me. Do you understand?" he asked as I held my throbbing face.

I didn't answer and willed my tears to stay put.

"Answer me!" he said raising his voice.

"Yes!" I yelled right back.

"Yes, Drew, and try to say it a little nicer this time."

"Yes, Drew," I said quietly. I had to. I was afraid he would hit me again.

"Good girl. Now come here. He sat back down on my bed."

I didn't know what to do. I didn't want to go to him. What did he want? Why did I have to go to him… on my bed?!

"I said to come here, Morgan," he warned. I slowly took the five steps to him, counting every one and stopping when I thought it was close enough.

"Closer," he demanded with a hungry look in his eyes.

My knees were shaking as I walked. He ran both his hands down my still damp arms, and then moved my right arm away from holding the towel closed. He pulled it apart and let if fall to the floor.

"Oh my, my, you have got to be the hottest little thing I've ever seen," he said as his eyes went right to my vagina. I was so glad that I had taken the panties with me, and was somewhat covered. I should have known that I wasn't going to keep them for long.

He pulled the front of my panties out and only looked, at first.

"I love this," he said and touched the thin line of hair leading to my sex.

I gasped from his touch and stepped back with one foot. He stood up and walked behind me. He kissed the back of my neck, and his hands explored my stomach and ribs. I could smell his cologne and closed my eyes at what was transpiring, and having no say in it, what so ever.

His lips trailed my neck and shoulders and then his fingers found my nipple. I almost moaned when he teased it between his thumb and finger. I felt the sensations electrify from my nipple all the way to my groin.

Stupid vagina.

He slowly moved in front of me and kissed me. I didn't kiss him back and kept my lips pressed firmly together.

"Open your mouth," he ordered to my lips.

I parted them slightly, but it was enough for him to gain access and take my mouth with his tongue. I tried my best not to kiss him back or touch him, but my body was betraying me, and strange emotions took over.

I didn't think my heart could beat any faster, not until he pulled away from my lips and dropped to the floor in front of me. He slowly moved my panties down my legs and had to tell me to pick up my feet so he could remove them. He sat back on his feet and stared at my sex.

"I love this," he said and moved his fingers between my legs. I gasped from his touch, and he snickered a little. He hadn't touched between my folds yet, and only, gently ran his fingers on my smooth lips.

"Do you want me to touch you, Morgan?" he rasped.

Yes, please, touch me. Now!

"No," I spouted out in a hateful tone.

And he snorted again. "I think you do," he said and took his thumb and forefinger and opened me up, still not touching me. I was afraid that he could see the throbbing that was begging for attention.

He stood back up and kissed me lightly, circled me, and kissed my neck again. I was begging myself with everything in me to keep it together. He might be able to make me do what he wanted, but he couldn't make me enjoy it. I tried to tell myself that I wasn't enjoying it, and I didn't want him to touch me, but I was quickly losing the battle.

Stupid fucker probably has a little dick that he can't even get up. Why else would he have to buy a wife?

Holy shit… maybe not.

He thrust his hips into my naked backside, and I could feel his not so small erection.

"Lay down on the bed, Morgan," he whispered in my ear. He walked me forward when I didn't move.

Was I supposed to lie on my stomach? I didn't know what he wanted me to do, so I did nothing, nothing except notice my heart beating out of my chest, and the dull pain on my cheekbone. He turned me around and moved me back so that I had to sit. He wasn't modest at all and didn't care that his dick was right in front of me. He grabbed himself and made a hissing sound as he moved it, trying to get some relief in the now too tight dress slacks.

He picked up both my legs, willing me to lay back. I scooted back on my elbows, not wanting to be exposed to him. He had the most lustful, crazed look in his eyes as he engrossed in my naked body beneath him. He slid both his hands up my legs and to the edges of my vagina. He still didn't touch me where I felt I needed touched.

"Spread your legs," he said as he grabbed himself again.

"I don't want to," I said weakly.

"But you are going to, so you should take heed in my warning and listen to me now."

I was afraid of the warning he spoke of, and slowly raised both of my legs. He hissed again as he stared at my extremely open sex. He took both of his thumbs and opened me more. I closed my eyes, trying to shut out the humiliation.

"You're very wet, your pussy wants to be touched, doesn't it, Morgan?"

Yes… Yes it does, like now.

"No," I said through my rapid breaths.

"I am not touching you until you tell me to."

Great.

He continued to tease my outer folds, but wouldn't go anywhere close to my inner core. He would get close, very close, and after what seemed like hours that I was sure were only minutes, I twisted my hips, hoping his fingers would slip and find my throbbing nub, but he stopped moving altogether.

"Do you want me to touch you now?"

"Yes," I said in a panting breath and noticed the winning, smirk on his face. I wanted to kick it right off him, but I wanted him to touch me more.

He turned his hand, palm side up, and ran his middle finger from my opening up to my clit. I squirmed beneath his fingers, and closed my eyes, trying not to moan. He never slid his fingers inside of me like I was hoping he would, and focused on my slippery juices, massaging the slipperiness into my clit. He placed his thumb on the throbbing sensation, circling it with just the right amount of pressure. I knew I was going to explode, and my hips moved with him. I was almost there, so close to the crest when he slowed his pace and pressure.

"Do you want to come, Morgan?" he asked, towering over me.

I did want to come, and I wanted to come right that second. I knew I was going to have to play his game, and he wasn't going to do anything without me telling him.

"Yes," I whispered.

He picked up his speed and pressure again. Just when I was right there, ready to be relieved, he abruptly stopped. My eyes opened, and he pulled me up, pushing me down to kneel in front of him.

"You can come when you learn to listen and watch your mouth."

I started to panic again when he undid his belt and freed himself. He placed the head right on my tightly, squeezed lips.

"Open your mouth, Morgan."

"Uh-uh," I moaned as he moved his head from one side of my lips to the other, applying his pre-come to my lips like lipstick. He continued this, enjoying it, I was sure until he wanted in my mouth.

"Open your mouth, Morgan," he demanded again, but I still wasn't doing it. No way was he was putting that thing in my mouth.

He brought his hand up and rubbed my already bruised cheek, and then plugged off my only source of breathing with his fingers. I still didn't care. I would pass out before I opened my mouth for his dick. That only lasted for about a minute and my survival instincts betrayed me, causing me to gasp for air. I tried to do it quickly, but he was faster and shoved himself inside my mouth with a gratifying moan.

"Oh fuck yeah," he muttered, sliding in and out of my mouth. He held my head by the top of my hair and thrust in and out of me, sometimes causing my gag reflex to engage. He moved rapidly, and when I felt the pulsating and knew he was about to come in my mouth, I swiftly jerked away from him. He continued to stroke himself and held my nose again.

"Awe, open up, baby," he moaned, close to release.

No way fuck you, dude.

Again, the stupid survival instinct kicked in, and I was forced to take a breath, allowing him access again, but this time he held my jaw open with his fingers. He pulled out again and stroked himself ferociously on my lips, and just like that he was spewing out, moaning as his eyes, watched the show. He managed to get his head in just enough to insure that I did get it in my mouth and then smeared the rest of it around, moistening my lips with his come. Every time I tried to push it out of my mouth with my tongue he used his head and pushed it back. I finally swallowed what was in my mouth just to get it out.

He picked up the towel that I had around me, wiped himself off, and put himself away. He tossed me a towel, and I instantly spit into it, wiping as much of him away as I could. He squatted to me on the floor and ran his middle finger up my glistening wet folds again and whispered to my lips.

"You're not allowed to touch yourself," he said, quietly. He dialed a number from the phone by my bed.

"Mrs. Kelley is going to need an ice pack," he said and left me confused and frustrated.

Rebecca brought me an ice pack and whispered close to my ear.

"Save yourself from this, Mrs. Kelley, just do as you're told."

***

I didn't even realize that I was masturbating myself when my cell phone rang, breaking me from my past with Drew. I didn't take my hand from inside my panties when I answered Dawson's call.

"Hello," I said, realizing that my breathing was a little erratic.

"Hi, you okay?"

"Yes, why?" I asked confused for a second.

"You just sound like you were running or something."

I slowed the pace of my fingers, knowing exactly what was causing my overexerted breathing.

"I'm fine, just went to bed."

"I just wanted to make sure you were okay after what happened."

"You mean, you kissing me?"

Dawson laughed. "Yeah that."

I snickered a little too. "I'm fine, but I would advise you to keep your distance from me, sheriff. I'm kind of fucked up in the head, and it's probably something you don't want to deal with."

"What does that mean, Ry?"

"Nothing that I can talk to you about."

"You can't, or you won't?"

"Both."

"You can talk to me, Riley. You're not going to scare me away."

"Hmm, you don't know what you are saying. Trust me."

"Tell me."

"I'll talk to you tomorrow, Dawson," I said, not so much that I didn't want to talk to him, but I had another project manifesting, and I was dying to finish it.

"Good night, Ry."

"Night, Sheriff."

I continued to please myself and was moaning in pleasure moments later.

That night I actually slept without bad dreams. Maybe release was what I needed.

I woke to Lauren yelling from my kitchen too early the next morning.

"I'm eating the pizza," she called.

Why the hell did I give her a key?

I brushed my teeth and met her in the kitchen, still feeling tired. I knew I could have slept for at least another two hours when I saw that it was only seven in the morning.

"I want a new friend, one that can sleep in," I pouted, sitting at the table.

Lauren brought me a cup of coffee. She had been there longer than I thought. She kissed me on the cheek from behind.

"You love me, and you know it."

I groaned. "Yeah, yeah," I said, sipping the coffee.

Lauren hung around, watching television for a couple of hours. She decided she had to go when Dawson showed up, unannounced.

"Call me later," she said and bounced her happy ass across the yard.

"That girl is way over ardent," Dawson said, walking in. He had been home and showered and replaced his uniform with jeans and a t-shirt.

Dawson and I spent the entire day together. He didn't mention our kiss, nor did he kiss me all day. We walked along the beach, and he reached for my hand, entwining our fingers. I thought about Drew touching me, and could only remember a few times that he had ever held my hand, and it was just for show for his dinner parties.

Dawson left around ten, tired from working the night shift. I actually didn't want him to leave. I wanted more than a kiss that he left me with. I needed more. I was so used to the sex that Drew and I shared for six years. I had a more of a difficult time not having it than I thought I would.

I again went to bed and pleased myself, thinking about Drew. I hated him. I never loved him, and here I was miles away, fantasizing about sex with him.

***

Our second sex encounter had come the very next morning, or I should say his sex encounter. I was being punished. He wasn't about to let me have any pleasure.

He came into my room the next morning carrying his laptop. I was still sleeping when he sat on the side of the bed. I jumped to a sitting position.

"I thought I made it clear that you weren't allowed to touch yourself, Morgan," he said, running the back of his hand down my cheek.

I flinched and pulled away from his touch. "I didn't," I lied. I thought that he wouldn't be able to notice if he were watching. I had lain on my stomach and used the weight of my body to control the movement of my arm.

He turned the laptop so that we could both see it. You couldn't tell that I was doing anything, not until my hips thrust into my fingers. The look on my face as I came was undeniable, and the soft moan, that was abundantly clear, made it impossible to deny.

I looked up into his dark eyes, and he wore the same smirk. "You know that I am going to punish you for this, don't you?"

I didn't answer.

He moved my covers back and told me to get up.

I listened, afraid not to.

He raised my nightgown and rubbed my silky panties, covering my butt. He pulled them down just below my cheeks and rubbed soft and gentle.

"I am going to spank you, Morgan," he rasped.

What the fuck?

My eyes darted quickly to his, and I hated the constant smirk he wore.

"Bend over my lap," he said, pushing himself back on the bed a little.

My heart began to pick up instantly. I was afraid not to listen just as much as I was afraid to listen.

He pulled my arm, and I was over his lap, resting my top half on the bed. At first he just rubbed my backside and then I felt three very quick slaps that promptly stung. He rubbed my butt again, causing satisfying relief before repeating his steps three more times. The fourth time while he rubbed away the pain, I tensed, waiting for the next swat. He didn't hit me again, and instead ran his hand up the folds of my vagina.

Oh, sweet pleasure.

"Your pussy is wet. You like getting spanked, don't you, Morgan?"

I didn't know if it was a question that I was supposed to answer or if it was for his benefit only. I didn't reply.

"You need to answer me when I ask you a question," he demanded.

How the hell do I answer that?

"Yes," I almost moaned as his fingers teased my throbbing clit. I wondered how long he was going to keep me bent over his lap, and then his hands spread my ass cheeks, exposing my anus. I flinched when he ran my slick juices from the front all the way back to my sphincter, massaging the muscle around the opening. I could tell that he was holding me open with one hand as his fingers went back for more lubrication. I came off his lap when I felt his finger trying to penetrate the opening of my anus.

"What the hell are you doing?" I yelled angrily and took my second blow to the same bruised cheek. I didn't even have time to regain my composure when I found myself across the bed on my stomach. He held my right arm on my back, bent with just enough pressure to cause pain and keep me from moving. When I tried, he pushed it higher, and I quit trying to get away from him.

I heard him unzip his pants with his free hand. He ran his dick up and down my folds, and I was scared out of my mind. Surely he wasn't about to do what I thought he was about to do. He was, and he did. I felt him push inside of my anus, and I squirmed, trying to get away again. He pushed my arm higher, and the pain shot all the way around my shoulder blade as I called out.

"Okay, okay," I yelled, forgetting about the invasion going on below due to the fact that I thought he was going to break my arm.

"Are you done fighting?" he asked, shoving my arm one more time.

"Ouch, yes," I screamed, and was instantly relieved when he let it go.

"Are you going to touch yourself again?" he asked, rubbing himself all over my liquids.

"No," I promised, and I meant it.

"Roll over and bring your legs up," he demanded.

I rolled to my back and watched him roll a condom down his shaft, and rub himself down with lubricant from a small bottle.

"Hold your legs up," he said again. "I want you to see what is going on so that you know I mean business when I tell you something."

I slowly pulled my knees to my chest, humiliated, knowing where he was planning on sticking his dick. Why was he so worried about me being a virgin if he wasn't even going to use it?

"Spread your legs," he said when I tried to keep them together. I did what I was told as he pulled me closer to the edge of the bed.

He had to bend a little and I felt him slide into me. I squeezed my eyes tightly closed.

"Open your eyes," he demanded and I felt him move in a little more. "Stop flexing your muscle, just relax and let me slide in."

That was easier said than done. It hurt. It hurt like hell, and I thought he was going to rip me apart. He was finally all the way in and started moving slowly, in and out of my ass. He brought his thumb to my clit and circled. The pain in my rectum had eased up, and it was almost pleasurable as he rubbed me with just the right amount of pressure. I wondered if he was going to let me finish, and hoped like hell that he did.

I was so close and thought that he was going to let me finish when he stopped giving my sensitive nub the pleasure that it needed. He pumped in and out of me frantically.

"I am going to pull out of you, and you are going to swallow me," he said looking down at me.

I didn't reply. He pumped faster, and all of a sudden pulled out and slid the condom off. He pulled me up and pushed me to my knees.

"Open your mouth," he said, breathing heavy and stroking himself.

I closed my eyes and opened my mouth, knowing it was in my best interest to do what he said.

"Good girl. Open your eyes," he said as he slid his dick into my mouth.

I was hoping that he was going to be quick, and he was ready, but he wasn't and he had fucked my mouth for at least ten minutes before I felt the pulsating down his shaft. I had a plan. I was going to take it all the way in and let it go straight down the back of my throat so that I didn't have to taste him. He had other plans, and as soon as the first stream was expelled, he pulled out and came on my lips, moving only his head in and out of my mouth.

***

Ecstasy was easy, as I moaned into my pillow, and then lay in bed feeling like a horrible, broken person because I had just gotten off for the second night in a row, thinking about Drew and his sick twisted sex rituals. I *was* fucked up in the head, and I didn't want to be. I wanted to have a normal life for once in my life. I wanted the house, the job, the good friends, and the man that loved me, but I was beginning to realize that it wasn't going to be possible for me. My whole life had been fucked up, and I didn't know what the hell I was thinking when I thought that I could just walk away from all of it and never look back.

I was glad to get back to work and spend my day with Starlight and my happy customers. Starlight couldn't believe the traffic in and out all day, or the coffee and cookies that we had gone through. I sold two pictures, and three dream catchers, along with several articles of clothing to a few tourists. Starlight was amazed at the foot traffic that we had for a Monday, and when I showed her the new system for closing up, doing an actual inventory, and accounting for every penny, she was overly impressed.

The week was good, and I saw Dawson every day and sometimes in the evenings. He was off on Friday, and we ate barbecued ribs and saw a movie. He kissed me and touched me a lot more that night than he had before, and it was really starting to get to me. I had been pleasing myself, pretty much every night for the past two weeks, but it wasn't enough and I needed more.

"Come in," I whispered to his lips in the car.

"That is probably not the best idea, Ry," he said, knowing what was going to happen if he did.

"Yes it is," I said, kissing him and forcing my tongue in his mouth.

"Ry?"

"I need you to fuck me."

Shit, I didn't want to say it like that.

His eyes opened wide, shocked at my outburst. He opened the door and came around to my side.

"I want to take you to bed, Ry," he spoke with me as I leaned against the door in front of him. "But I don't want it to be like that."

I snorted, "I warned you that I wasn't normal."

"You need to talk to me about it."

"I don't want to talk about it, Dawson."

I would never want anyone to know my background let alone being married to a man who didn't love me at all for six years. I was messed up, and there was nothing that Dawson or anyone else could do to fix me. I took his hand and pulled him toward the door.

I found myself in a terribly awkward position when he followed me to my room. I slowly undressed in front of him and stared at him with hungry eyes. I wasn't sure what I was supposed to do. I had a feeling that laying down and spreading my legs wasn't right. I didn't think that he was the type to tower over me and make me tell him what to do to me. Drew always stayed dressed until he was ready to take me. Was that what all men did?

What the hell am I supposed to do?

Finally, Dawson walked to me standing naked in front of him.

"Are you sure about this?" he asked.

"Yes," I said and kissed him. I needed the thoughts to stop. I needed him to take control and step by step tell me how to react to him.

I raised his shirt, and he slipped it off, toeing off his shoes. He pulled the covers back and I crawled in. I watched him take his jeans off and come to me. My eyes rolled back as I felt his fingers slide between my wet folds. I couldn't help the moan or the thrusting of my hips into his fingers. My mind was once again taken back in time. I tried my best to control it and keep it right there with Dawson, but I lost, and the control was once again given to Drew.

***

I hadn't seen Drew in over a month. He left for a long business trip after his introduction to my anus. I had fallen into a routine and liked living in the mansion and having servants and Rebecca waiting on me hand and foot. I loved the pool, although I waited until late evenings to swim because the Las Vegas heat was too unbearable during the day. I went for my daily ride around the property every morning and watched more television and movies than I ever had in my life. I spent two hours each day with Leo. He was there to teach me how to speak the proper English, lose the thick southern accent and acquired slang. Drew thought that it was unattractive, and I didn't mind it and liked learning. I had never had a teacher who took an interest in me. I only did what I needed to do in school. Most of the kids around there didn't even graduate. I probably only made it because it meant that nine months of each year, I could get away from my house and my family.

A doctor came and gave me a shot of something that Rebecca had explained was for birth control. Two weeks after that Drew came home. I didn't know he was coming. It was almost nine at night, and I just got out of the pool and entered the house as he entered the same room. His eyes scanned my body, and I pulled the towel over my midriff and breast, trying to cover my bikinied body.

"Move the towel," he demanded. I watched Rebecca scurry from the room.

It was the first night he slept with me the entire night. He directed me to get cleaned up and ready for bed, telling me that he would see me in a few minutes. I took a hot shower, and he was waiting for me when I entered the bedroom.

"You could have left the clothes off," he said, standing and coming to me. He slid the nightgown over my head, and smiled when he saw that I wasn't wearing panties. I hadn't done it for him. They were laying on the bed because I had dropped them when I picked up my night clothes. I wasn't going to explain that part to him though.

"You have been a very good girl. You haven't touched yourself at all."

"How do you know that? You weren't here." I asked, boldly.

"You are always on my laptop. It doesn't matter where I am. I was really hoping to spank you," he said as he kissed the corner of my mouth.

Jesus, vagina, chill out.

I didn't speak. I could already feel myself becoming wet and swollen in anticipation.

"Do you like touching yourself?"

I moved my eyes to his and shrugged one shoulder.

"Did you touch yourself in your little dumpy trailer back home?"

I nodded.

"Speak up or I am going to have to spank you."

"Sometimes," I answered.

"Show me," he said.

You have got to be kidding me.

I didn't move, not knowing what I was supposed to do.

He moved me to the little sofa in the sitting area and I sat down. "Pull your legs up," he said and I did. He moved my feet out further; exposing me all that he could, and then ran his fingers right through the middle of my sex.

"You're always so fucking wet," he slid the desk chair right in front of me. "Show me how you please yourself."

I rubbed my fingers between my legs, embarrassed, sliding my essences up to my clit. I watched as he too grabbed his erection and stroked it through the dress pants.

"Don't come until I tell you to," he said, not taking his eyes from my penetrating fingers.

How the hell am I supposed to pull that off?

I was careful not to rub too firmly, not wanting to find out the consequences if I had an orgasm. I started to squirm after I watched him take his rock hard penis in his hand and stroke himself. I needed to come, and it was starting to be inevitable. It was going to happen. I stopped my fingers from moving when I knew it was almost too late.

"Don't stop," Drew demanded.

"Drew I have to. You told me not to come."

"I still don't want you to come yet. Keep rubbing it," he demanded. He took his thumb and pulled my right lip out, exposing me more.

My head dropped; my eyes closed, and I moaned. I was spent and couldn't control it a second longer. Drew didn't say anything as I rubbed my shuddering clitoris, coming down from my long awaited high.

When I opened my eyes to look at him, he was wearing that stupid smirk, and I knew that he was glad that I messed up.

"You didn't listen, Morgan," he spoke.

"I tried," I pleaded my case.

"I don't think that you did. I think that you wanted me to spank you."

I shook my head back and forth, but if I were being honest with myself my clit had already started to throb again at the thought of being bent over his lap.

"Bend over in front of me," he demanded.

I slid down the front of the sofa and bent in front of him. He rubbed my bottom and then spread me further open with his hands. He slapped my right butt cheek and then rubbed away the sting. He did this several times, all while keeping my cheeks as open as he could with one hand. His feet went between my legs moving them further away from each other.

"Bring your hands back and open yourself for me," he requested.

What the hell?

I did as I was told and spread my ass cheeks with my hands. He ran his fingers up my wet folds and to my anus. I wanted to moan, but didn't dare. I didn't know if I were allowed to do that.

"You want my finger in here, don't you?" he asked as he traced my entrance.

Fuck no...

"Yes," I answered with the answer that I knew he wanted.

I heard him laugh a little. "Tell me what you want."

Oh God.

"I want you to put your finger in my ass," I replied, with my eyes already tightly closed, waiting for the intrusion.

"Relax your muscles," he demanded as I felt his finger trying to gain access.

How the hell am I supposed to do that? You have your stupid finger in there.

I lay there totally exposed and under Drew's control, thrusting his finger in and out of my rectum. It wasn't bad after a bit, and I was just waiting for it to be over. He moved his erect penis to my clit and began pushing and circling, causing a building deep in my core to initiate. I moaned and pressed myself back toward him, wanting more compression on my swollen essence.

"Don't come," he whispered into my hair.

What the fuck?

Thank God he had other plans for me, and eased up.

"Are you ready to have your pussy fucked?"

Do I have a choice?

"Yes," I again said what I knew I was supposed to say.

"Tell me."

Really dude? Your hang-ups are starting to give me whiplash.

"I want you to fuck my pussy, Drew."

"Go to your bed and spread your legs."

I couldn't help but moan a little when he withdrew his finger from my anus. I did what I was told and lay across my bed, spread eagle as I watched him undress. My heart had started to pound out of my chest at the anticipation. I was trying to talk myself calm, reminding myself that it couldn't hurt any worse than the imposition on my butt.

He walked toward me and grabbed both my legs, pulling me closer to the edge.

"You ready for my dick to be in your pussy?" he asked, not looking at me, but only my wide-open sex.

"Yes," I answered in a deep breath.

I screamed and backed up at least a foot when he wasn't gentle at all. I felt the give and the pain that came with the forced diffusion that was almost excruciating. He didn't care and pulled my legs back toward him. He didn't have to tell me not to come. I didn't want to come. I just wanted him to hurry up and spew out so that he would get off of me and leave my room. He took no compassion whatsoever as he pounded in and out of me. Finally, when I could tell that he was getting close, I started to relax. He pulled me up and to the floor, and I knew that I was expected to take him in my mouth.

My mouth remained open. I didn't even try to keep it shut. I didn't turn away, and I didn't try to take him in the back of my throat. I knew what I was supposed to do, and I parted my lips, awaiting his flow. He must have lost the drive because he didn't come right away, and pushed me back to the bed. He entered me again, thrusting frantically in and out of me and did the same thing when he was ready. I dropped to my knees and took his essence into my mouth as he rubbed it around my lips and tongue with the head of his dick.

"Go clean up," he demanded.

I went to the bathroom and dropped to the floor and cried. I knew he would see it on camera the next day, but I couldn't help it. I felt so violated and used. Once I had regained my composure and cleaned up the blood I went back to my bed, ready to sleep and be rid of him until the next time.

He was in my bed, and I stopped dead in my tracks. I didn't want him there. He patted the other side of the bed, and I got in. I stayed on the far side of the king size bed, and he never touched me. We slept in the same bed, worlds apart. He did wake me early before leaving for work and made me have sex with him again. He again did the same thing, as he seemed to always do. As soon as he was close, he pulled himself to his knees and released in my mouth. Once again, I wasn't allowed to come.

Chapter 6

"Riley!"

I didn't realize that Dawson was not on the bed with me anymore. Nor did I comprehend that I was touching myself or crying.

I sat up in one frantic motion. He sat on the edge of the bed and stared at me with an expression of revulsion.

"Are you okay?"

"What did I say?" I asked, but wasn't sure I wanted to know. I was more humiliated than I may have been in my life.

"It doesn't matter," he tried.

"It does matter, Dawson. Please tell me what I said."

He ran his fingers through his short hair, and I had to coax him again to tell me.

"You wanted me to spank you. You wanted me to stick my finger in your ass, and you said you needed me to fuck your pussy," he told me the things that I would say to Drew, unable to look at me while he did.

"I warned you. I told you I was fucked up," I knew that he was seconds away from storming out of my house and my life, which was fine by me. I should have known a normal relationship wasn't plausible for me.

"Why, Ry?"

I rolled over and lay back down, facing away from him. "You're off the hook, Dawson. You can go."

He kissed my hair. I was surprised when I felt him snuggle up to me and wrap me in his arms.

"I don't want to be off the hook. You invited me to spend the night."

I smiled, not used to the affection, but relished being in his arms. He never tried to finish what I had started and we fell asleep in each other's arms. I woke at the beginning of a nightmare, glad that I roused before I said anything else that would make him think I was crazy, not that I wasn't. I slid out of bed and walked out to the kitchen and onto the deck.

I didn't hear him walk behind me because I had left the door open. I am not sure what I was thinking at the time or even if I was thinking. As soon as he spoke, asking me if I was okay, I jumped startled. I turned to look at him and could only see his black silhouette in the night. I covered my face with my arm as he stepped closer to me.

"Ry?" he quietly said, stopping in his tracks.

I moved my arm and breathed a sigh of relief when I realized where I was or who he was.

"I'm sorry, Dawson," I spoke.

He held me in his arms, and I wanted to cry. Nobody had ever held me. Nobody had ever cared. I didn't know how to be with someone who cared.

"What the hell happened to you?" he asked, rubbing my back in a comforting fashion.

I couldn't tell him anything. I couldn't tell him how I was raised in the poorest parts of West Virginia by two parents that never should have had kids. I couldn't tell him that my dad had sold me to a rich, twisted sex pervert. I could never tell him anything about my past.

"Let's go back to bed," I said, pulling away from him, taking his hand to follow me.

He pulled me close to him and I lay in his arms. I felt soothed and calm nestled close to his chest. I had never lain in Drew's arms like that. If he did spend the night in my bed, it was because he planned on taking care of his sick needs again before morning. I had never stayed in his bed at all and only had sex in his bed a handful of times.
***

The dream that I woke from earlier in the night returned. I was back in the trailer, and it was once again winter. My mom was working the night shift at the truck stop. My dad was, of course, at the bar. I was fifteen and Justin was three. I told him to sit on the couch and not move while I went out to get wood. He decided that he wanted to help and opened the wood burner door with his bare hand. I dropped the armful of wood and ran into the house to his terrified screams. The skin on his hand dripped off onto the floor. I didn't know what to do. We didn't have a phone, and the only place I knew to go was about half a mile down the road to my Grandma Joyce's. I was afraid to go there too. She was sick, and my dad warned me to leave her alone and not bug her.

I picked him up and ran his little hand under cold water. He screamed to the top of his lungs. The only kind of salve that I could find was Vaseline that I had found beside my parent's bed. I rubbed the greasy ointment on his hand and wrapped the burn with a torn white sheet. I didn't know much, but I knew enough to know that he needed to go to the doctor.

We were sitting on the couch when both my parents came home together, drunk. I was rocking him back and forth as he slept in my arms sucking in short puffs of air from all the crying.

"I thought you had to work," I scolded my mother. I was there taking care of her kid while she was out getting drunk.

"What happened to him?" she asked, ignoring my statement.

"He touched the wood burner," I said.

"Stupid kid," my dad said and grabbed the container of Vaseline from the stand. "We might need this," he said, pulling my mom back toward their room, laughing.

"He needs to go to the doctor," I yelled.

"I'm sure he's fine. I'll look at it tomorrow," my mother said without care one about her son hurting.

I carried Justin to bed with me and held his little body close as he whimpered the entire night.
***

Dawson sat up in bed. "I'm sorry, baby. I'm sorry, Justin," I called over and over.

"Riley," Dawson said, softly, four times before I hysterically sat up in bed.

"Shhhh," he said, pulling me back into his arms. "You're okay, you're right here with me," he whispered into my hair. He pulled me tight, wishing I would tell him what I had lived through, or anything that told him why I was like this.

"Who's Justin?" he asked, kissing the back of my head.

"My little brother," I answered, sadly with a heavy heart.

"Where is he?"

I shrugged. "I don't know."

"How old is Justin," Dawson asked, trying to keep me talking.

"He was only five the last time that I saw him, but he is twelve now."

"Why haven't you been able to see him?"

"Children's services took him away," I replied, gloomily.

"In West Virginia?"

I sat up and looked at him.

"I didn't say anything about West Virginia," I demanded.

"You said it in your sleep. Come here. I am not your enemy, Ry."

I lay back down, and was glad that he stopped with the questions.

What else did I say?

We dozed off for the third time that night. I was sound asleep when Dawson woke me by kissing my sleeping lips. I always slept the best in the morning. My nights seemed to be full of demons that kept me awake until the exhaustion took over early in the morning.

"Good morning, beautiful," he said, and I had to smile. Him calling me beautiful had an entirely different meaning behind it than when I heard it from Drew. When Drew gave me compliments it was always in the bedroom, usually when he was close to shooting his load.

"You mean I didn't scare you away last night?" I asked as he kissed my lips again.

"Not a chance," he smiled.

Things were going extremely well. I couldn't believe that my new life was working out. I may have just pulled off the biggest disappearing act in history. Dawson continued to come around, and we spent a lot of time together. He spent the night on several occasions, but neither of us tried to take that next step. He did a lot of comforting during my long nights when he was there, and tried to get me to talk to him. I didn't, and didn't plan on ever revealing my dark skeletons to him or anyone else.

Summer Fest was extremely busy at the shop. I was happy that we were closing at four rather than six, and were planning to join in the festivities. Lauren was singing on stage, and she and Levi were DJing for the street fair later that evening.

Dawson stopped by in uniform around three. I thought he seemed preoccupied but assumed he probably had a pretty busy day himself with all of the commotion going on in town. He told me that he was going to go home and change, and he'd meet me back there. I told him I was going home to get a shower and change as well, and I would just find him in the streets somewhere.

I dressed in a long skirt and tank top with psychedelic sandals that I had ordered from one of our suppliers. For once, I wore my hair down and was excited to spend the evening with Dawson, Lauren, Star, Joel, and even Levi.

Dawson was already there, wearing khaki shorts with a nice red shirt and brown leather flip-flops. He stood from the picnic table and kissed my cheek.

"You look very pretty," he offered, causing me to smile. He always made me smile.

I was in such a happy mood and laughed at Starlight being the center of attention, dancing in the street all by herself. She had tried to get everyone to join her, and when nobody would, she went alone. It was only a matter of time before more and more people joined her, all waiting for someone else to do it first. Lauren and Levi were hilarious on stage and argued back and forth about funny issues. I was laughing at them talking about how Lauren steals his food at work when I looked across the table to Dawson. He was staring intently at me with a serious expression.

"Are you okay? You have been kind of out of it all day," I asked.

"Yeah, I'm fine. Do you want to dance?" he asked. I smiled and gave him a peculiar look.

"I am not sure I can dance to this music," I admitted. I could dance. I loved my dance classes in Las Vegas. I just didn't think that ballroom dancing would correspond with the country music.

"You need to dance the waltz or something?" he teased.

"Something like that," I laughed.

I wondered what he was doing when he walked up to Levi and whispered in his ear. Levi smiled and nodded his head. Dawson came back with a smile and took my hand.

"What are you doing, sheriff?" I asked, taking his hand.

He didn't reply, and Levi came across the speakers, saying he had a request for some ballroom dancing. Some song called the Tennessee Waltz started playing, and I laughed.

"That was as close as he had," Dawson smiled down at me.

It was close enough to a slow song that would allow me to be in his arms as we danced across the blacktop dance floor.

"You seem to be a little distracted today," I said, looking up to him.

"I guess, I kind of am, but we'll talk about it later," he smiled down at me and kissed the end of my nose.

"Talk about what?" I asked curious as to what could be on his mind.

"We'll talk about it later," he smiled a reassuring smile.

We sat at the table and watched the people dancing. I too was distracted, wondering what Dawson wanted to talk about. I stared blankly toward the dancers as my mind wandered back to Drew and my own dancing coach.
***

Drew wanted me to learn to dance so whenever he thought I was ready to be in public and wouldn't embarrass him I would be able to dance as gracefully as him. I worked with

Jaymas Wellington, a retired Broadway star. I was on my third week with him, and we were in the open end of the gym. I didn't know that Drew had returned. He'd been gone for nearly three weeks.

Jaymas and I were doing a spin and were laughing and really doing more goofing off than anything. I liked him a lot, probably more than I should have. It was nice to have someone to talk to. We didn't talk about anything personal. I knew everything I said could be heard by Drew anytime he wanted. I had just slid down Jaymas's body after the spin, and we were both laughing when I lost my balance and fell to the floor. We stopped dead in our tracks when Drew entered with a look of pure anger.

"Leave!" he demanded through gritted teeth to Jaymas.

Jaymas left, telling me that he would see me later. He didn't see me later, and I never saw him again. Drew walked up to me and took me in his arms and started dancing with me around the floor.

"You like flirting with other men?"

"I wasn't flirting with anyone," I demanded.

"That's not how I saw it. It looked to me like you were enjoying being in another man's arms."

"We were dancing. You're the one who made me take lessons," I reminded him.

"Do you like him rubbing his dick all over you?"

"You're impossible," I demanded and took the blow to the same cheek that he seemed to always go for. He grabbed my arm and dragged me out of the gym. I looked at Rebecca as I was being forced into his office. She gave me a warm encouraging smile, but it wasn't reassuring to me. In the five months I'd lived there, I had only been in Drew's office once and that was on our wedding day. I wasn't allowed in that room, and it was kept locked unless he was in there.

"Get out!" Drew said to the two guys with folders and some sort of brochures in their hands.

"Drew, you have to make a decision on this ad," Derik argued.

"That one," he demanded, pulling one of the pamphlets from his hand without looking at it.

Drew locked the door, and I was scared, more than I ever had been with him. He was angry, and I didn't know what he was going to do to me. Suddenly, that day was the beginning of my allowed office visits.

"Take your clothes off," he demanded, and then yelled, "NOW!" when I hesitated.

I removed my practice shorts and shirt as he watched with crossed arms. He nodded when I didn't move, beckoning me to take off my bra and panties, as well.

"You know that I am about to beat your ass like I never have, don't you?"

"Why?" I asked. I hadn't done anything wrong.

He was in my face in a split second. "You do not ask the questions, got it?" he asked, squeezing my nipple so hard that it burned.

"Bend over my desk," he demanded. I did. I had to. I panicked when I heard the belt being pulled through his belt loops. It reminded me of when my dad used to whip me with his belt, and I remembered how bad it hurt.

I couldn't hold still after the first crack across my bare cheeks. It hurt way worse than I remembered from my dad. He shoved me back to the desk and delivered four more blows before he finally quit, only because his desk phone wouldn't stop ringing.

He pulled me to him and bent me over the other side while he talked business with someone on the other end. I was sobbing, and although I knew there was no blood, it sure as hell felt like it. He rubbed the inflamed welts on my ass, and it was soothing as he sat in his chair, conversing as if I wasn't bent bare butt over his desk.

I flinched a little when I felt him slide his finger into my vagina. He swatted me lightly across my backside with a warning. I didn't understand my body, at all. How could I go from sobbing to wanting to press into him deeper? I could tell that I was building and so could he. He put the phone to his chest and bent to my ear.

"Don't you dare come," he demanded through gritted teeth.

He was going to make sure I came. No matter how hard I tried to think about everything else, his penetrating fingers on my clit were causing me to lose control. I was hoping I could get off and hide it. If I closed my eyes and didn't move, maybe he wouldn't realize that I had come. I tried my best to control my breathing and uncontrollably let go. His fingers stilled inside of me, and I knew he could feel my quivering orgasm. I could see the smirk on his face without even looking at him.

I didn't move as he removed his hand from my body and walked to a locked cabinet. I heard him cutting plastic or something and messing around with something as he continued to demand whoever he was talking to, to fly to Chicago and take care of the matter himself. I tried to turn my eyes enough to see what he was doing, but I couldn't tell.

He finally hung up the phone and told me to stand up. He was holding the biggest dildo that I had ever seen. Well, I had never really seen any, just the ones that I had seen in my dad's magazines. He took my hand and wrapped it around the massive shaft. My fingers barely reached around its girth.

"You didn't listen again, Morgan," he smirked.

I wanted to ask him how I was supposed to listen when he was trying his damnedest to make me come, but I didn't. I knew I wasn't allowed to ask the questions.

"What are you going to do with that?" I couldn't help it. I had to ask. I had a right to know; after all I knew it was going to be used on me.

"Oh I'm not going to do anything with it," he assured me. I watched as he lubed it up and slid it up and down in my hand. He pulled a small table in front of his chair and sat down, placing the large tool on the table in front of him.

"Have a seat, Mrs. Kelley," he smirked.

You have got to be kidding me. Was this guy serious?

I could only stare from him to the object that he was holding in place with his hand.

"Turn around, Morgan," he demanded. I did. He was going to make me do it, and I knew it could either be the easy way or the hard way, not that either would have been the easiest in my book.

I was hoping that it was going in my vagina, but of course he had other plans and when I squatted he moved it to the hole that I was dreading. I felt him open my ass cheeks as my weight held it in an upright position.

"Awe, yeah baby, take it all," he said in a lustful hiss.

"I can't," I begged. I was sure that I didn't even have the head in yet.

"Just sit back a little more," he coached and I felt it go in a little more as I did.

Once I was uncomfortably sitting on the table, he came around to the front of me and stood with his front right in my face. He crossed his arms and waited. I knew what he wanted. I just didn't know if I was going to be able to handle it with what was going on in my behind. He jolted his hips toward me once, telling me what to do.

I unbuttoned his dress pants and freed his erection right into my mouth.

"Rock back and forth," he coached.

I couldn't do that either. It was all I could do to be still. He moved my shoulders with his hands willing me to listen. I did, and he brought his fingers to my clit. Between his fingers and the pressure from the foreign object in my ass, I felt another orgasm building, and hoped that he was going to let me finish.

"Do you want come?" he asked, and I nodded with a moan.

He moved his hand around to my behind and pulled out of my mouth. He kept the object right where he wanted it and told me to lie on his desk. I did. He placed my legs on his shoulders as he moved into me. Every time he thrust, he pushed the foreign entity in and out, as well. He moved my legs and spread me as far as he could, holding down on both legs until I felt the pull in my groin. I was spent and couldn't take it much longer. He had only asked me if I wanted to come, he didn't say that I could. It didn't matter because as soon as he started circling my clitoris with his thumb, I couldn't control it and

called out in ecstasy. This was the first time that we had sex, and he released deep inside of me instead of in my mouth.
***

I jumped, startled when Dawson touched my arm with a cold bottle of root beer, pulling me from my thoughts.

"Sorry," he apologized, not realizing that I was lost again. "You okay?" he asked. I wondered what expressions came across my face when I traveled back in time.

I smiled and took his hand. "Yes, but I am ready to get out of here."

"Really? It's only eight o'clock. Summer Fest runs all night long."

"You haven't been here with me all night," I accused, and he smiled, not denying it.

"Do you want to stay at my house tonight?" he asked.

I had stayed there a couple of times already, but for some reason, whatever he needed to discuss with me had me a little apprehensive and I wanted to be home.

Lauren and Starlight both threw a fit when I went to tell them goodbye. I lied and told them that I didn't feel well. Dawson followed me home.

I was unlocking my door when he got out of his truck with a manila envelope.

I put water on to boil while Dawson sat on the couch, slipped out of his shoes and dropped the envelope to the table.

What the hell was going on?

I brought us both a cup of tea and sat beside him, eyeing the envelope.

"You have to talk to me, sheriff. I can't stand it a second longer."

He took a deep breath, looking nervous as hell.

"Ry, I don't want you to think that I am out to get you in any way," he started.

"Dawson, you're starting to scare me," I admitted, and my heart was beating at a more rapid pace than it should have been.

"I wanted to do this to surprise you, I didn't know that I was going to find out what I did," he explained. I was scared shitless. I was sure he knew who I was. Would he call Drew? Would he send me back to Las Vegas?

"What the hell are you talking about, Dawson?"

He handed me the envelope, and I opened it, pulling out its contents.

My heart instantly dropped to my stomach. I couldn't believe what I was seeing. I looked over at Dawson and couldn't speak. I didn't know what to say. I turned my attention back to the photographs. I would have known those dimples anywhere. It was Justin, and he was so handsome. He looked so happy. I flipped to the next photo. He was dressed in a baseball uniform and was standing on the pitcher's mound.

"Where did you get these, Dawson?" I asked, touching my beautiful little brother's face.

"Remember when I said I had to go out of town for a family matter last weekend?"

I nodded.

"I met with the social worker who managed his case."

"Why?" I asked, not understanding.

"I wanted to see if he was still in foster care. If he was, I was going to somehow get him back with you. He's not, Ry. He's in a good home with a family that loves him very much. He does well in school and plays four different sports."

"Where is he?" I asked, staring down at his image in front of me.

"He lives in a very prestigious part of Las Vegas."

My head snapped, uncontrollably to him, but I played it off fairly well. What the hell would he be doing in Las Vegas? Who had him? How does a rich family in Las Vegas even know about a little boy in the welfare system from West Virginia? I would never know. I was too chicken to do any investigating on my own. I was too afraid of somebody finding me because of it. No. I would let it go. I had to. He was in a loving home and looked happy. That was all that mattered.

I didn't realize how much I loved and missed him until I saw what a handsome young man he had become. My heart ached for him. I still had a million questions. I didn't understand how Dawson found him. What did he know about me? I answered myself when I flipped to the report obtained from the social worker. It had Justin Michael Willow at the top of the page. I read through the report on how we lived; our trailer that should have been condemned, how there was no food in the house, and how they had left a seventeen year old sister, Morgan Willow, behind.

I turned to Dawson. He knew my name. He knew where I grew up. What else did he know?

"You were out playing private investigator?" I asked, not believing him.

"No, Ry. I was not. I told you. I wanted to find your brother for you. You talk about him in your sleep... a lot. I knew that you told me your maiden name was Murphy, and that was where I hit my roadblock. There wasn't a Justin Murphy in the system anywhere in West Virginia. You were scolding him one night in your sleep and called out Justin Michael Willow. It was simple after that. I don't know how you went from Morgan Willow to Riley Murphy. I need some answers from you that I can't get, and you won't tell me.

"Did you go to my home town?" I asked. My heart was ready to explode.

"Yes," I know how you lived, and it breaks my heart, Ry. I don't blame you for leaving there, but you need to tell me why the name change. Why is your past such a secret? I found five Riley Murphy's in the whole country. One was a seven year old girl, two of them were men; one was killed in an automobile accident, and one was an eighty-three year old woman who lived in a nursing home. You don't exist. You disappeared on your eighteenth birthday as Morgan Willow and hadn't been heard from since. What is going on, Ry?"

I ignored his probing questions. I was too freaked out.

"I can't believe you did this, Dawson. You have no idea what you've done."

I stood and paced the floor. My instincts went right to the window. If he did this last week, chances were Drew had already found me. He would have used Justin from the start, hoping that I would try and contact him. Dawson had just led him right to me.

"I can't stay here," I said and turned back to Dawson.

"What the hell are you talking about, Riley?"

I was in panic mode. I didn't want to speak, afraid that my house was wired with cameras and bugs. I didn't want to go to his house because his house was probably wired too. I walked out to the deck, breathing crazy breaths, trying to get air into my collapsed lungs.

Dawson followed me out. "Riley, please tell me what is going on. I didn't mean to upset you. I only wanted you to know that your little brother was more than fine, healthy and happy. Tell me what has you so freaked out."

"You shouldn't have gone there. He is going to find me. He will kill me."

"Who is going to find you? Nobody is going to kill you."

"You don't know him, Dawson. You ruined everything. You just led him right to me by going there. I assure you he followed your trail right back here."

"Who!? For God's sake, Riley?"

I looked at him with tears in my eyes but didn't speak.

"Are you afraid of Drew?" he asked.

I nodded, not sure how much I was willing to disclose. I didn't even freak out about how he knew his name. I already knew that one of my many nightmares had unveiled the information.

"Who is he, Ry?"

"I can't, Dawson. I do have to leave. I can't stay here."

"Nobody is looking for you here," he tried, but I wasn't buying it. I couldn't.

He took his phone from his pocket which was probably bugged too. He dialed a number as waited and listened.

"Hi, this is the Dawson Bade. I spoke to you last week about an adoption."

I listened to the one sided conversation as he talked.

"I need to know if anyone else knows about me being there or the information that you gave me."

"Yes."

"I see."

"Thank you. That would be great."

Dawson said goodbye and I looked at him waiting for something, anything to ease my mind.

"I am the only one she has ever given any information to. There was an attorney there for some big company five months ago asking for information. The guy flashed five hundred dollars for any information about anyone asking about Justin Willow. She told the guy to go to hell and had him escorted out. Nobody has been back until me, and she promised that she would not tell anyone that she gave me what she did. She said she could get into a lot of trouble for sharing it with me. She only did it because she knew you were his sister, and I told her how much it haunted you, not knowing where he was.

"Do you really think nobody knows you were there?" I asked, feeling just a little better.

"Yes, Ry. I do."

I breathed a deep long breath, and Dawson wrapped me in his arms. I wrapped my arms around his waist and rested my head on his chest. He kissed the top of my head and squeezed me tighter.

"You have to talk to me, Ry."

I looked up to him, and he kissed my lips softly.

"I'm scared, Dawson," I admitted. I couldn't tell him who I was or where I came from. I needed him in my life, and I didn't want him to leave me.

"You're safe with me. I'm not going to let anything happen to you, Ry," he promised, and I truly wanted to believe him.

Dawson made love to me for the first time that night, and it was like nothing I had ever experienced. It was hard for me at first. I wasn't sure how I was supposed to act, and I wasn't used to having someone put my needs first. He was so gentle and loving toward me, and my emotions were on overload.

He kissed me passionately, something else I wasn't used to. We were standing in my bedroom, and when he moved his hands up my shirt, I thought it was the most comforting thing I had ever felt in my life. His hands were gentle and warm on my back and sides. I was trying to be with him in the moment. I really was, but I felt almost like I was doing something wrong. When he moved his lips down my neck, kissing and sucking seductively on my neck, I found myself leaving him.

I opened my eyes and caught myself looking around for the camera. I just knew that Drew was watching me with Dawson. What I didn't know was that Dawson was more in tune with me than I was myself.

"Stay with me," he whispered just below my ear. His warm breath quickly brought me back to him.

What the hell was I supposed to do? I knew that laying spread eagle on my bed for him wasn't what he wanted, but what did he want? I didn't know how to be in a relationship, not a real one anyway. I didn't know how to make love. I knew how to do what I was told and please my man. Dawson wasn't interested in me pleasing him. He wanted to please me.

I was terrified. I didn't know if I was supposed to touch him or wait for him to tell me what to do. Yes, I know. A twenty-five year old woman should know these things. I didn't. I swear I didn't. I didn't have a clue. How could I? I never had an orgasm until I was sixteen. I was afraid to, and that went back years to my fucked up life.

My dad had come into the bathroom once when I was seven. Seven, for God's sake. I didn't know what I was doing then either. I was bent over curiously, looking at myself sitting on the toilet. He came unglued. He whipped me so hard, and demanded that I wasn't going to be a slut like my mother. I didn't even know what a slut was. He had told me that he would know if I touched myself because my fingers would start turning black. He would make me show him my fingers every so often after that. I remembered how I would freak out if the toilet paper ripped and I accidentally touched myself. I would wash my hands over and over, afraid that they really would turn black.

My grandmother had set in stone when she told me too that my fingers would turn black. I never found out the truth until I was over sixteen years old. We were at my aunt's house one evening, and she and my other aunt were laughing and joking about my grandmother telling them the same thing when they were little girls.

"Where'd you go, Ry?" Dawson asked once again, pulling me from my thoughts.

"Seven."

"Uh?" he asked, backing away briefly.

I didn't answer. I kissed him instead, trying to make myself focus on him.

He sensed every part of my trepidation and would stop and kiss me lightly until I was calm and was back with him and not Drew. I didn't talk to him about Drew that night, and was not ready to share that part of my life just yet. I didn't know if I ever would.

After a couple of weeks of looking at every new face that came into the shop as if they were there to spy on me, constantly staring out my windows at night for a strange car, and jumping at every little noise, I started to relax. I began to realize that nobody was looking for me, and nobody was taking me back to that place.

I had been in Misty Bay for almost nine months. My life was good. I had good friends, and was madly in love with my sheriff. Yes. Me. In love. It made me as giddy as a bunch of teenaged girls at a slumber party. I loved my job and my boss, Starlight. We had grown the shop into a lively and striving business.

The months passed, and I happily settled into my life. I still had hang ups, but the dreams of a crying, starving and cold Justin were replaced with happy ones of him playing baseball and sitting at a table with a real family. The nightmares of Drew still haunted my sleep, and I was grateful for Dawson, who woke with me and soothed me back to reality.

One morning I opened the shop and Starlight was already there, sitting at her desk in her office. She was wearing the biggest smile ever.

"Good morning," I said, depositing my purse on its rightful hook.

"Guess where you and I are going?" she asked, holding an envelope in her hand.

"Where?" I asked.

"Vegas, baby," she exclaimed, pulling two plane tickets from the envelope.

Like hell, I am…

"Why?" I asked as my heart plummeted to the bottom of my stomach.

"Remember I told you about the trade show they have there. You have done so much with this place, and I want you to come with me. I wouldn't feel right going without you."

"We can't just close the shop," I tried, knowing it wouldn't work. I knew she just wanted to reward me for my charitable work, but I didn't want to go anywhere near Las Vegas.

"Yes we can. It's for four days, and we would only really be closing for three. We will fly out after closing on Thursday, close up on Friday, Saturday, and Monday, and be back for business on Tuesday."

"When?" I asked. Chances were Drew wouldn't even be home, but that didn't mean that I wouldn't be recognized. I had no idea what he'd told people. Was I supposed to be missing? Did he tell them that I left him? I had no desire to go to Las Vegas. I had never even typed so much as the word Las Vegas in a search engine. I was tempted a few times, curious as to whether or not he was looking for me or what was being said, but I didn't. I was afraid he could somehow find out what I had searched, like he did when I was there.

"Next month, and don't you try to get out of it either. We'll have a blast, and we could use a couple new vendors."

"Why wouldn't you want to go to Vegas?" Dawson asked later that evening as we both made spaghetti in my kitchen.

I still hadn't disclosed any more information than I had to, and he still didn't know that Drew was there. I knew it was crazy, sort of. Las Vegas was populated with almost two million people, but I still didn't want to go. I didn't want to disappoint Starlight either.

"Because I can't stand the thought of being away from you for four whole days," I replied, it wasn't a lie. We spent every waking moment that we weren't working, together. He had even stopped working the night shift on the weekends after he discovered that I was scared out of my wits, worrying that someone would for me.

He kissed me. "Have I told you that I loved you today?" he asked.

"Maybe, but you can tell me again if you want," I replied, kissing him back.

My mind drifted back to Drew a lot that night. Even while standing there in the kitchen, chopping onions, I thought about Dawson telling me that he loved me several times a day.
***

Drew never once told me he loved me, not in six years. The closest time that I did was late one night when he just got home from someplace that I didn't know. I never asked. I wasn't allowed to know because it didn't concern me. The one time that I did ask, he had told me that my business was to please him, and that was it.

I was already in my bed asleep when he crawled in beside me. It was the only time I could ever remember him being somewhat gentle with me. He kissed me a lot. He hardly ever kissed me when we had sex, but that night he kissed me deep and passionate. He didn't ask me to do anything and caressed me like he never had.

He didn't tell me not to come, and when I was ready he was ready with me. He stared down at me attentively when we were finished, and brushed my cheek with the back of his hand. I kissed him softly and spoke.

"I could have loved you," I said, and I could have.

"This isn't about love," he said, got off of me and left me there alone with my thoughts and fears.

The following morning he was back to being Drew, and demanded that I sit naked in his office, spread eagle on his sofa while he worked. I had to give him a blowjob under his desk while he did a video conference, and endure one of his spankings because he had masturbated me to orgasm and had told me not to come. I spent seven hours in his office that day, and he wouldn't even let me dress when Rebecca brought in our lunch. He said she had seen me naked before and I sat there humiliated, waiting for her to leave.

After lunch, he decided that the sofa was too far away and made me sit on his desk with one foot on the floor and one on his desk. He worked the mouse on his computer, made phone calls, and even did a conference call about margin in a store in, Los Angeles, all while I sat there and let him penetrate me first with his fingers than an ink pen, a letter opener, and when he would get bored he would go back to his job for a while. He would just nonchalantly pick something up, anything that he could push in and out of me while I sat quietly, letting him do what he wanted, waiting for the time that he would tell me that I could go.
***

My first dream that night was about Justin. He was around a year old. It was the middle of summer and extremely hot. He was sleeping beside me on my mattress on the floor. I had the windows rolled out and kept him covered with a sheet so the mosquitos wouldn't eat him during the night. I was awakened when my parents came home fighting. They always fought. I knew my dad hit my mom and could tell that she crashed into the table. She never backed down though. She always gave it right back to him.

Justin had sat up, scared, and I rubbed his back and hummed a soothing tune, letting him know that I was there, and he was okay. I listened to my dad scream at my mom and call her a slut and a whore and how no other man would do what he was doing and raise some other man's kid. I knew after they came and took Justin away from me that day. That was why it was so easy for my dad to let him go. He had a different dad than I did, but I didn't understand when or how. I remembered when Justin was born and how happy my dad was that he was a boy.
***

I sat up in bed with tears in my eyes, missing my little lost brother. I did do a lot better, and the dreams were less frequent. Finding out that he had a nice home and parents who adored him, made it easier, but they still crept up every now and then. I looked over at Dawson. I hadn't awakened him. Normally, I would wake to him holding and caressing me, talking to me calmly, and letting me know that he was there. I was safe there with him and wrapped in his arms. I touched his cheek with my hand. I was so blessed to have him. Any other man would have probably deemed me crazy and got the hell away from me as fast as he could. Dawson didn't. He was always right there, and for the life of me I didn't know why. He turned and kissed my wrist.

"You okay?" he asked with closed eyes. I lay back down as he pulled me close to him.

Chapter 7

I dreamed about Drew more and more. He was haunting me, consuming my sleep, and I knew that it was the Las Vegas trip that weighed heavy on my mind. I was so thankful for Dawson, being there to talk me down every time I woke up panicked.

Three days before the trip was the worst. I went to bed with Dawson, and the dread and anticipation of being in Las Vegas were nerve-wracking. I fell right to sleep after he had fixed me a cup of Starlight's famous relaxing tea.

***

It was the first time ever that Drew took me out in public. He had a benefit banquet and a lot of well-to-do people were going to be there. He had someone come and do my hair, bought me a beautiful evening gown. My makeup and nails were done professionally, as well. I met him in the foyer, and I actually felt a little something for him. He looked so handsome in his tuxedo and his mouth noticeably dropped when he saw me. My hair was up with soft dangling curls. I wore a beautiful, open back dress that was black with a low cut front, showing just the right amount of cleavage. The dress was long and slit clear up my right side. The material hugged my curves perfectly and the three inch stilettos with the strap delicately wrapping my ankles, tied it all together.

That was the first time that I knew for sure what Drew did for a living, and why he was so rich. He took my hand and opened the door for me. I felt happy and was glad to get out of the house, of course he coached me the whole way. I knew what I was allowed to say and what I wasn't, which was pretty much nothing. Smile and look pretty that was my job.

We pulled into a fairly empty parking garage, and I wondered what we were doing there. It didn't look like a place for a banquet; however, the building was breathtaking. I had been to downtown Las Vegas a few times, but not in the evening when the lights seemed magical.

"What are we doing, Drew?" I asked, wondering whether I should or not.

"I am taking you to one of my stores," he replied as the driver pulled right up to the elevator doors.

I wanted to ask him what kind of store, but I had a pretty good idea. I had heard him on the phone enough to pick up bits and pieces.

The ride was in a very impressive elevator. The back wall was mirrored. White, soft leather benches covered the other two sides. My breath caught in my throat when the doors opened to the sixteenth floor.

We were standing in the most exquisite jewelry store I had ever seen. Well, I had never seen one, but still. The white marble floors gleamed, and the massive amounts of lit display cases with sparkling diamonds were breathtaking. I knew that Drew worked in diamonds, but I wasn't expecting that, at all. The lighted sign above the store read, 'Callaway Jewels.' I had seen the commercials a million times and never knew. I knew that this was not his only store, and the commercials advertised the twelve others throughout the country along with three in Europe.

"Drew?" I said, questioning what I was doing there. A man in a white tuxedo reached for my hand.

"You need to go pick out your wedding rings. I can't take you to a party as my wife without rings." He actually smiled happily at me.

"I need your help," I assured him.

"Why?" he asked annoyed.

"How do I know what to get? How much money should I spend? I don't know how to do this, Drew. Come with me, please," I begged.

He laughed. "Don't worry about the money. Pick out what you want. I have to make a call. Carson is here to help you."

I took the man's white gloved hand, and he led me to the lit case of rings.

"You can pick anything from this case," he instructed.

I didn't want to pick from that case. I knew that I was being shown the most expensive pieces in the store. They were all so beautiful, and I had a hard time deciding. I wanted them all. I only remembered owning one ring in my entire life. My grandma Joyce had ordered it from Avon for me. I felt bad for leaving it behind when I was taken away from my home. I didn't wear it much because it had left a black ring around my finger when I did, but I cherished it because it was a gift from my grandma.

I chose a stunning, six-carat shimmering pink diamond ring, complete with three baguette white diamonds set in platinum and rose gold. I stared at the ring constantly as we drove to our destination. Drew noticed my joy and commented.

"You like that?" he asked.

"I love it. It's the most beautiful thing I have ever owned. Can I ask how much it's worth?" I asked. None of the prices were on any of the rings, and I was sure that elegant jewelry stores like his didn't place the price on their jewels.

"Thirty five thousand," he replied. I gasped.

Holy Shit....

I thought that I did exceptionally well at the banquet. I stayed close by Drew, and mostly only smiled when he introduced me to his acquaintances. I wouldn't have called them friends. I was sure that Drew wasn't capable of having a friend. Even the guy, Derik that seemed to be his sidekick and was with him all the time seemed to be annoyed with him more than anything.

Drew was more attentive to me that night than he ever had been. His hand constantly rested on the small of my back, and he held my hand. I was sure that it was all for show, but nonetheless it did make me feel special for a little while.

It was obvious that I was envied by the women standing around watching as Drew waltzed me across the dance floor. I was flattered when he raised his eyebrows at my flawless, elegant ballroom dancing.

I did what I was told to do. I stood by his side with my glass of wine and looked pretty.

I noticed a man in a wheelchair who constantly stared at us. He looked sick and was being escorted by a much younger lady who I was sure was his nurse or caretaker. I turned to Drew, just in case the guy could read lips.

"Drew, why does that man keep staring at me?" I asked. "Who is he?"

"Don't worry about it," he said with a tone that told me that he didn't want me to know, or it was none of my business.

I let it go, but shortly after, the man was wheeled over to us. I had never seen Drew suck up to anyone before. He was kissing this man's ass like nothing I had ever seen.

"This is my beautiful wife, Morgan," he said, introducing me, but failed to disclose the name of the man in the wheelchair.

He took my hand and ran his hand over my pink diamond. "I'm Randal Callaway," he said, not letting go of my hand.

I felt uncomfortable and wondered about the name again. Our home said Callaway estates. The jewelry store said Callaway Jewels, and his name was Callaway. Maybe Drew really didn't own any of it. Maybe he was a relative. Maybe he was just the CEO. I wished that I could ask Drew about the name, but knew that he would tell me that it didn't concern me.

"Leave us, Drew," the man said looking up, finally letting go of my hand.

"I am not sure that is such a good idea, sir. Morgan isn't used to being around this many people. She's a little uncomfortable," Drew tried.

"Walk away, son," the man demanded with a stern expression, and just like a little whipped pup, Drew retreated with his tail between his legs. I was in awe that somebody actually put the narcissist ass in his place.

"Sit with me," the man said, taking my hand again and leading me to an elegant set of chairs in a corner.

I sat, and he held both my hands in his. I was confused and wanted to know who he was. I didn't ask. Drew was giving me a death stare, and I wasn't about to say anything without being asked first.

"How do you like the estate?" he asked.

"I love it there." I replied. I did love the estate. I just wished I didn't have to share it with Drew. I wanted to ask him why his name was on the stone wall, so bad, but didn't dare.

"Good. So you are happy?"

Fuck no...

"Very," I lied.

"You have no idea how happy that makes me, Morgan," he smiled. "Is there anything that you need?" he asked, and again I was confused as to why he cared. He acted as though he knew me or something.

"No, sir, Drew gives me more than I need," I explained. I did have everything that I needed, minus the essential emotional care.

I mostly listened, and he talked, knowing that Drew was staring daggers at me. I didn't know what I was supposed to do. Did he want me to refuse to talk to the man? I didn't even know what his interest in me was, let alone who the hell he was. He gave me a card and explained that his cell phone number was on there and to call him if I ever needed anything.

I thanked him, and his caretaker wheeled him away.

Drew was angry, and I could tell. We left shortly after that. He tapped his foot nervously on the floorboard of the limousine.

"Did I do something wrong?" I finally asked. He turned and angrily glared at me.

"You are joking, right?" he asked.

What the fuck...?

"I thought that I did everything that you asked me to do. What did I do?" I asked, and had a feeling that it had something to do with Mr. Callaway.

"What did he say to you?" He asked with an angry tone.

I shrugged my shoulders. "Not much of anything. He admired my ring, asked me if I was happy, if I had everything that I needed, and he gave me his card and said that if I ever needed anything that I could call him anytime. Who is he, Drew?"

Drew put his hand out, and I knew that he wanted the card. I unsnapped my little handbag and handed to him. He wadded it up in his hand and tossed it to the floor. He held his hand out again, and I didn't know what he wanted. I didn't have anything else. Did he want me to take his hand?

"What?" I asked.

"The rings," he said.

Fucking dick head…

I should have known that it was just for show, but a little part of me wanted to believe that he wanted me and that the rings were a symbol of that. I slid the rings from my finger, and he dropped them in his shirt pocket. He still didn't tell me who the man was, and I was a little taken aback at how he seemed to cower to the older man.

The driver didn't drive us home, and we went to the penthouse in downtown Las Vegas. I knew that it wasn't going to be a pleasant romantic evening, and I was in for a night of hell. That was an understatement. I froze as he led me to the bedroom. The bed was draped with a red velvet cover and had black straps with soft red collars at all four posts. There was a table with different sex toys laid out, and I knew they were all for me.

"The next time somebody asks me to leave you alone with them, and you hear me say that I don't think that it's a good idea, you need to agree and ask me to stay," he said in a low warning tone as he circled me and kissed my bare chest.

"You should have clarified that before we got there. I didn't know what I was supposed to say. I don't even know who the guy is," I tried to explain and took an angry blow from the back of his hand.

"Don't be so stupid," he accused. "Don't you ever talk to someone without my presence again. Do you understand, Morgan?"

"Yes, Drew," I answered, holding my face.

"My father is none of your fucking business. Nothing I do is any of your business. Do I make myself perfectly clear?"

Father?

"Yes, Drew," I answered again. He seemed to think that I gave a half of an ounce about what he did. I didn't, and I didn't want to know him, his father, or what he did. I just wanted out of that room, and was terrified that he was going to hurt me.

"Take your clothes off and lay on the bed," he demanded and left the room.

The first thing that I did was walk to the glass doors. I didn't care that I was somewhere high in the sky. I would jump. It would have been better than living and being married to that monster. The doors were locked and wouldn't budge, of course. That was my luck. I didn't know how much time I had before he came back, so I did the only thing that could do. I undressed and lay on the bed, close to the edge with my feet crossed, trying to cover my naked body as long as he would allow it.

He returned a few minutes later with a drink in his hand. "Hmm," he moaned, staring at my naked body. He caressed my breast and pinched my nipple.

"Do you want spanked first or would you rather I fuck your pussy?" he asked, gesturing his hand along the table of tools that he would use on me. The sick bastard was going to make me decide. He was going to do both, so it didn't really matter in my book.

"Spank me," I answered.

"You like it when I spank you, don't you, Morgan?" he asked as he ran his fingers up my sex, sipping his drink.

Stupid, deserter, vagina.

"Answer me," he demanded, lifting my leg so that he could get a better view.

"Yes. Drew," I answered in a whisper.

He pulled an ice cube from his drink and held it over me. "Spread your legs. You like spreading your legs, that's why your pussy is always so wet. Did you know that, Morgan? Did you know that you get so wet because you love the things I do to you?" he asked. I flinched a little at the ice-cold droplet of water on my clit as I pulled both of my legs higher.

I hated what he did, but was he right? Was that why I always got so wet when he did the things that he did? Maybe I was as sick as him.

I could feel the bed becoming wet as the water droplets ran from my clit to my opening, and onto the bed. I was almost numb from the cold by the time the ice cube was gone. Drew sat his cup down, and my heart started to beat a little faster, anticipating what was about to come.

He undressed and sat on the side of the bed. He was already harder than iron, and it stood at attention when he scooted back, making room for me on his lap. He looked over at me and moved his hand, letting me know what I needed to do.

I pulled myself up and lay across his lap. I could feel his shaft on my hip as he thrust it into me a little, needing the contact. He rubbed his hand over my bottom a couple of times and moaned.

"You may be a stupid hillbilly and not good for much, but sure am glad I have you around for this," he said, and I grimaced at the first blow to my bare cheeks. He spanked me more and longer than he ever had, and I was beginning to wonder if he was ever going to stop. I could feel his welted handprints on my ass, and I didn't think it could sting any more than it was.

Finally, he was bored with that and told me to get up. He laid long ways on the bed, and I stood there awkwardly waiting for his orders on what I was to do next.

"Lie down with your mouth level to my dick," he ordered as he rolled to his side.

I did as I was told, and he put his leg over my head and guided himself into my mouth. He instructed me not to move my head and to just keep my mouth open while he fucked it. We were both lying on our sides, and I gagged more than once as he held my head down with his leg and thrust in and out of my mouth with lustful moans. I was beginning to wonder if he was ever going to tire of invading my mouth when he finally pulled out and rolled me to my back.

"Scoot up," he demanded. He stroked himself while he waited for me to get into position. He fastened my hands to the post and then my legs, which he didn't leave for very long because he said that I wasn't spread enough that way. He positioned my legs where he wanted them and demanded that I not move.

I wasn't sure what the first object that he took from the table was. I had never seen anything like it. It was a long thin metal rod with a wired loop on the end. I watched as he turned the knob on the bottom of it and touched the small loop on his finger. He jumped when it came in contact with his finger, and he turned the knob again.

Oh, fuck.

He ran his fingers into my wet folds, and I writhed beneath his fingers, wanting release. He spread me open with his fingers, revealing as much as my swollen crux that he could. He brought the rod closer to me, and I held my breath waiting for what I knew was going to be some sort of shocking volt. He brought it to my sex in a slow, leisurely motion and held it centimeters away from my clit, wanting me to suffer the expectancy. He moved his hand over my waist and held me down with his forearm, still spreading me with his two fingers.

It was unquestionably some sort of electrical shock and the most painful yet pleasurable feeling I had ever felt. I tried to jump back, but he held my hips with his arm. I moaned and writhed beneath him. The orgasm was almost instant, and the shock brought me right to peak, and then stopped. After only three torturous contacts, I couldn't take it, and was begging for him to let me come. He didn't, of course, and I spent the next ten minutes being brought to ecstasy only to have it pulled away over and over again.

Drew finally placed the tool back on the table. He ran his fingers across my lips and asked me if I wanted to come.

No, I would rather you just torture me for hours.

"Yes," I moaned.

He slapped me between my legs with several quick smacks as he stroked himself. I could have come that way too, but I knew he wouldn't let me.

"You were a bad girl tonight. I am not sure I should let you come, but I am," he added, touching my lips again. He moved up and straddled my face. I didn't try to protest, and willingly opened my mouth as he once again darted in and out of my mouth, making the most lustful sounds that he could muster. I knew he was close, and he would come rather quickly. I was right.

"Stick your tongue out, Morgan," he rasped, frantically stroking himself on my tongue and lips. "Aw fuck yeah," he moaned as his essence released in bouts onto my tongue and down my throat as he made sure none was wasted or spilled out, using the head of his shaft to push it back in.

"Suck me clean," he demanded, going back into my mouth.

Once he was licked and sucked cleaned, he moved off me, and retrieved another device from the table. All I could do was watch and wonder what the hell was next. He again restrained my ankles and pulled my knees, strapping them to my restrained hands. He then took a black rod with straps on each end and some sort of silicone, rubbery thing right in the middle. I watched as he strapped the rod to my legs and then turned the smaller rubber rod. He adjusted the bar going from one leg to the other and explained that he had some work to do and would be back in later. He turned on the object, and it did a full turn only brushing my sex once every spin.

Son of a bitch…

It didn't hurt at all and felt incredible. It slowly slid all the up my slippery slit, but it wouldn't rest in one place long enough to do anything. I tried to twist into it, trying as it rotated, to get enough pressure to come. I had never in my life wanted anything as bad as I wanted to come at that moment. I felt like I was ready to pass out when Drew finally returned, I don't even know how much later.

He turned off the device and removed the rod. He touched my dripping juices, massaging it into me. I noticed that he was already at half-staff again as he rubbed me. I couldn't help but twist into his fingers, begging for release.

"Please, Drew," I begged and was actually crying from the painful sensations in my body.
***

"Riley," I heard my name and somewhat woke up enough to see that I was no longer with Drew, and Dawson was in my bed.

"Dawson, I need to come, please," I begged, still panting from my nightmare with Drew.

"Ry?" he said, trying to figure out whether or not I was coherent or still back in time.

I was not with Drew, nor was I coherent. It was all still fresh and raw, and I did need sexually stimulated right that moment. I knew what I was doing. I knew that I begged him to spank me, and to give it to me in the ass, and to put his dick in my mouth.

Dawson straddled my waist and held down on both of my shoulders, looking me straight in the eyes.

"I am not doing any of those things to you, Riley. You are not that person, and I am never going to treat you like you are. You don't deserve that and I refuse to be that person for you."

That was the most unbelievable orgasm of my life that night. I am not sure whether it was because I was so sexually frustrated or if it was the way that Dawson handled me. Dawson made slow passionate love to me, kissing me deeply and whispering that he loved me to my lips, over and over. When I would lose myself and venture back to Drew, he would stop until I was back, right there with him. When I came, it was mind blowing over the top, and I called out and writhed beneath him in much needed pleasure.

"Why do you put up with me?" I asked, nestled to his chest.

"Because I love you. Go to sleep," he said to the back of my hair with a tone that I wasn't used to hearing.

Dawson was up and sitting at the table with an almost angry expression when I woke to join him the next morning.

I poured a cup of coffee and sat with him.

"Good morning," I said, trying to read his mood.

"I need answers, Ry," he commanded.

"What are you talking about, sheriff?" I asked with a smile, trying to lighten his mood.

"I am talking about these nightmares that you have. They are either about your little brother or about sex. I want to know what happened to you. I want to know who Drew is."

I looked down. I wasn't going to answer either of those questions. I was too embarrassed to tell him what I had done or where I came from. I would never explain how Drew bought and paid for me to be his sex slave. I couldn't, and if that meant it would send him running for the hills, then so be it.

"Riley, please talk to me," he pleaded.

"I can't, Dawson," I said, quietly looking up to him, hoping that he understood. He didn't. He took a deep breath and got up.

"How about you call me when you can," he said, angry.

"Fuck you. I have been threatened enough in my life. I am not going to be threatened by you," I spouted off before even thinking.

He walked back to me after sliding on his shoes. "Baby, I am not threatening you. I am just at my wit's end with you. Why won't you talk to me and let me help you?"

"You can't help me, Dawson," I sadly said and kept my eyes down. He kissed the top of my head and retreated with a heavy sigh.

I drove to work and knew that I had to break it off with Dawson. I was never going to trust him or anyone else. I was never going to let him in as far as he wanted, and I was always going to be fucked up. There was nothing I could do about that and I didn't want to hurt him. It was best that I let him go. I hated myself as I unlocked the door to the shop, wishing that I have never started anything with Dawson. Lauren and I were doing just fine without adding Dawson to the picture.

Starlight talked excitedly about Las Vegas and her friends that she couldn't wait for me to meet. She could tell I wasn't really there, nor was I paying much attention. My mind was on Dawson and my terrified state about going to Las Vegas. I should have just told her no. That would have been nice, had I ever been allowed to say no. I might have done just that. I couldn't go there. What the hell was I thinking?

I ignored three calls from Dawson, and when he stopped by in the afternoon, I kept busy with a couple who was looking at the aromatherapy oils, explaining the difference. Dawson was on duty and couldn't hang around, waiting on me.

He texted a while later and asked me if I wasn't speaking to him. I texted him back and told him honestly that no; I was not talking, and wanted to end things with him. I thanked him for being so patient with me and explained that I didn't expect him to hang around waiting for me to miraculously be normal. I told him that it wasn't going to happen and that he should move on.

"Don't you dare do this, Ry. I love you. I'm not going anywhere," he texted right back.

"Dawson, just stop. I don't want you. Please understand that." I shut my phone off and poured myself a cup of coffee.

"Get out of here," Starlight said as I stared off into space.

"Excuse me?" I asked, not sure I heard her correctly.

"Your mind has been somewhere else all day. Go home and relax. I can handle things here," she said and didn't give me time to object. She held my elbow and walked me toward the back.

I didn't object. My mind *was* somewhere else, and it was in Las Vegas. I didn't want to go there, at all.

As I drove out of the back alley and onto the road, I saw Dawson in his police cruiser through my rearview mirror. He was riding close behind and flashed his headlights at me. I knew he wanted me to pull over, but I didn't. I knew he wouldn't follow me all the way home; however, the chances of him showing up at my door once his shift was over were pretty high. He turned on his red and blue lights. I blew out a puff of unbelievable air.

I still ignored him and when I didn't pull over, he turned on the siren. I ignored that too and turned down the road toward my house. He pulled up beside me on the narrow road with lights and siren, waving me to pull over.

"What? Are you going to give me a ticket?" I asked my rearview mirror.

I finally decided that I should abide by the law and pulled over, angry that he was stopping me for no reason other than I wasn't talking to him. It pissed me off that he was using his authority to control me. I had dealt with enough of that in my life, and I'd be damned if I was going to deal with it from him.

I didn't even roll down my window. I opened the door and got out. I wasn't about to be compliant with him. Before I could even speak, he slammed his car door and pointed back to his car.

"That is a God damned police car. I am a God damn police officer. If I instruct you to stop, you'd better damn well pull over," he yelled.

I yelled right back. "Fine. If you're going to pull me over, you better God damn have a reason to do so."

"You are not pushing me away, Ry," he demanded.

I crossed my arms and snorted.

"Please, don't push me away," he calmed and ran both hands down my crossed arms.

"Dawson, what is wrong with you? You don't want me," I assured him.

"I do want you, Riley. You don't want me to want you."

"Why? I think you have seen enough to know how fucked I am."

"I don't think you are fucked up at all. I think you have been through something horrific, and I would do anything to make it better for you."

"Why? I don't understand you. You are very good looking, funny, caring and compassionate. You could have any girl that you wanted. Why me?"

"I don't want any girl, Ry. I want you. Why is that so hard for you to understand?"

"Do you like being awakened two and three times a night by my stupid hang-ups? Dawson, I was practically begging you to do sick perverted things to me last night. Don't you find that a little disturbing?"

"I find it a lot disturbing, and it breaks my heart because I know that somebody did those things to you, and you won't talk to me about it."

"I can't, Dawson. I relive it enough. I don't want you to know that part of me."

"Ry, I hear things that you say. I see you crying in your sleep. I know you were abused. I know you are hiding from someone named Drew. Don't you think that I could understand a little better if you would talk to me?"

I didn't know what to say. I had given the man every opportunity in the world to run and run as fast as he could, but he wasn't running. He was there as he had been since the day I met him.

"I'm afraid to, Dawson."

He looked at his watch and kissed me. I have two more hours. I am going to bring supper over, and you and I are going to talk about Drew," he demanded.

"Dawson," I tried, but he cut me off with a kiss.

"Get out of here before I write you a ticket," he teased and kissed me again.

I called Lauren and woke her from her afternoon nap. She woke me all the time, so I didn't care. She came over, and I wanted her to stick around. I didn't want to be alone with Dawson, although I knew that she would leave, and I would eventually be forced to talk to him. She stayed and ate the fried chicken that Dawson brought and then yawned around eight, saying she was going to bed and was tired after getting her belly full.

I cleaned up, and Dawson stared, waiting for me to start. I didn't start anything. I didn't even know what to say to him.

"Talk to me, Ry," he finally said.

I gave him a warm smile and took a deep breath. "Can I take a bath first?"

"Yes, but we are having this conversation," he assured me.

I filled the tub with an extremely hot tub full of bubbles. I sank down and closed my eyes, wondering what the hell I was supposed to say to him. I opened my eyes when he dropped the lid on the toilet and joined me.

"You don't have to tell me anything you're not comfortable talking about," he began. "I will ask the questions, and all you have to do is answer, okay?" he asked.

Oh boy. Here we go…

I nodded.

"Who is Drew?" was the first question.

"My husband," I answered.

"Your ex-husband?"

I shook my head.

"You're still married, Ry?" he asked, shocked.

"Yeah, I guess I am."

He stood up and ran his hands through his short hair.

"Why didn't you tell me? You said you were divorced."

"I would be if it were possible. Riley Murphy isn't married. Morgan is married," I replied, omitting the last name.

"Ry, you can't just run away and change your name. That doesn't make you not married."

I knew this was a crummy idea. I knew he wouldn't understand. I stood up and dried off, and he stepped out. We went to bed, and both sat up under the covers while our conversation continued.

"Why did you marry him, Ry?" Dawson continued with his investigation.

"I am not sure how much I should tell you, Dawson," I admitted.

"Tell me everything," he required.

I took a deep breath and he reached for my hand. I snuggled up in his arm. It was easier for me to talk to him without looking at him.

"I didn't want to marry him. I didn't even know him. He paid my father thirty thousand dollars for me. He came to our trailer on my eighteenth birthday to claim me. He is a very rich, powerful man."

Dawson abruptly moved from the bed and paced the bedroom floor. I only watched while he regained his composure.

"He bought you?" he asked in disbelief.

"Yes."

"Ry, that is as illegal as you can get. I will have that bastard incarcerated so fast his head will spin."

"Dawson. No. You can't do that. Promise me you won't go anywhere near him let alone try anything at all. You don't know what you are dealing with. He will come for me."

"You can't hide, looking over your shoulder your entire life."

Oh yes I can...

He sat back down and pulled me back to him, not wanting me to shut down and stop talking.

"Keep talking," he said and kissed my fingertips.

"I can't. You keep asking the questions. It's easier that way."

"I need to know what he did to you, Ry. Did he hit you?"

"Yes, often," I admitted.

"Why?"

"Because he is crazy, I don't know why. I tried to be whom he wanted me to be, but he always found something to punish me for. He got off on it."

"He hit you to punish you?"

"No, he usually only did that when I mouthed off something that he didn't like."

"How did he punish you?" Dawson asked, and I knew that he already knew the answer to his question and just needed to hear it from me.

"He used sex to punish me or so he said. He did it because he is a sick bastard who got off on it."

"What did he do, Ry?"

"Dawson, you really don't want the details. He did everything imaginable; unimaginable would be a better term," I decided.

"I need to know, Riley. Just think about one time that he punished you. Why were you being punished? Walk me through it. Help me understand."

I took a deep breath and thought about it. Maybe if I told him he would finally realize that I was too broken to fix. I contemplated a time that I had been punished. I had no idea it was going to be so real for me to talk about it. The dreams were part of my subconscious. It was inevitable for them to be so real. Talking about it wide awake was a different story altogether.

"One afternoon when he was home, he was in his office, and I wanted to ask him if I could go somewhere."

"You had to ask permission to go somewhere?" he asked, running his finger up and down my arm.

"Yes. When I was growing up, I used to go to the local library for some solace, especially after they took Justin away. I tapped on his door, and he told me to come in. I was afraid to interrupt him because I wasn't allowed in his office."

"Drew, I was wondering if it would be okay if I went to the library here," I asked.

"Why?" he asked annoyed.

"I like to read, and I like spending time in the library," I answered.

"No. Not yet. I will let you know when you deserve that privilege."

"He dismissed me, and I left disappointed. I lived in an eight thousand square foot house, and had plenty to do, but I just needed out," I explained.

Dawson didn't speak and continued to listen.

Chapter 8

"That night after I had retired to my room…"

"You didn't share a room," he interrupted.

"No, I never slept in his room, but he did stay in mine on occasion, but not often. Anyway, he sent someone out to buy me an e-reader. That was when they were fairly new, and all that you could really do is read on them. He brought it to me and told me that he had already downloaded enough books to keep me busy for quite some time."

"Did he know what you liked to read?"

I blew out a puff of air. "He didn't care, but just wait, it gets better. First I had to do things to get the e-reader."

"Like what," Dawson wanted to know. He wanted details, and wasn't letting me maneuver around them.

"Well that particular night was actually mild. He made me undress and bend over his lap so that he could spank me for coming into his office."

I felt Dawson tense beneath me, but he didn't stop me as I let my mind drift back in time, once again.

"You know you're not allowed in my office without me telling you to be there, don't you?"

"Yes, Drew."

"And you also know that I am going to spank you now, right?"

"Yes, Drew."

I didn't even wait for him to tell me what to do next. I slid out of my panties and my nightshirt and lay across the bed and his lap. He rubbed my ass a couple of times as he always did and began his ritual. He slapped me hard and then rubbed the sting away, purposely moving between my legs as he did. I could feel his erection on my hip, and he would ever so often, pull me toward it to so that he could grind into me. I tried to make myself not get wet. I would think about any and everything under the sun except for the orgasm that I wasn't going to be allowed to have.

Once he was finished with his routine he told me to lay down and spread my legs. I did of course, and he rubbed my conspiring juices into me.

"You want it up the ass don't you?" he asked, knowing that I would say yes, regardless of my true answer.

"Yes," I whispered, and he flipped me to my stomach, roughly.

"Get on your knees," he demanded and I did.

I felt his head touch my entrance.

"You want it, you take it," he said, wanting me to push back into him.

I slowly moved back, trying to relax and press his erection into me.

"Aw, yeah, baby, take me in your ass," he said. He always said perverted things to me which should have repulsed me, but didn't. It made me wetter, and I wanted him even more. I knew that it was a mind game and a way for him to control me even more, knowing that he would be the only one to acquire any pleasure.

"Move me in and out now," he demanded once I had him buried inside of me.

I did as I was told and rocked back and forth on his dick. I was fine until he brought his fingers around and started circling my clitoris.

"Drew," I begged.

"No. You were a bad girl. You came into my office. You are not coming," he assured me as he tried even harder to bring me to bliss.

I clenched the comforter in both fists, willing myself not to come. I counted to one hundred by twos and then did it backwards. I wasn't going to give him the pleasure of knowing that I failed, *again.*

He finally gave up and pulled out of me. He lay down and told me to straddle him. I did, and he helped guide me over his shaft. I knew he only did it because he wanted to see the struggle on my face as he masturbated me to orgasm.

"Fuck my dick with your ass," he said as his fingers frantically rubbed my throbbing nub. "Harder," he demanded when I wasn't moving fast enough for him.

"Drew, I can't," I begged for him to let me orgasm.

"You don't want to disobey me Morgan," he warned as he rubbed even harder.

He clicked his tongue and shook his head as I quivered above him, uncontrollably letting go.

"You just insist on defying me, don't you?" he asked, and moved me off him.

He got up, went into my bathroom and cleaned himself up. He walked out still wearing his erection and clicked his tongue again as he left my room. I knew he would be right back. I just didn't know what he'd bring back.

He returned with a new toy with two ends. I knew that both of my orifices would be taking it. One end was fairly good sized and the other had knobs all the way down. He waved it at me, telling me to lie down and take my position. I did what I knew he wanted, and lay down, pulling my knees up and opened. He guided the new object into my vagina first and then moved the knobby twin into my ass. He then turned the knob, causing a light vibration that I knew was going to make me come again. He massaged my clit with his thumb and then made me suck my essences from it. He continued this for a few minutes while he moved the foreign object in and out of me.

I was glad that he left my aching core to stroke himself off. The faster he stroked, the faster he moved the two sided dildo in and out of me. I was hoping that he was going to come soon so that I didn't have to disobey him again.

All of a sudden he moved up to me and shoved himself deep into my throat and then pulled out. He jerked himself, telling me to open my mouth. I did, and he let go as I swallowed him once again. He always made me lick and suck him clean, and then he removed the toy.

I hadn't seen the other one that he had brought in. He turned it on and told me to lie down on top of the covers. I did, and he placed it inside of me with just enough vibration for me to want more. He gave me the e-reader, and told me not to come and not to touch myself or the new vibrator. He said that he would be watching, and I wasn't to move until he came back to remove it.

Well at least I could read and take my mind off of it. That was not going to happen either. Every book that he had downloaded was erotic. It was just one more way to get me to submit to his every need. He wanted me to read the stories about having a master and the way I should be submitting to him.

The very first short story made me feel blessed that I had Drew and not the monster that tied, gagged, and did everything imaginable to his captive. Although I was glad that I wasn't the girl in the cold dungeon, and I did have the luxuries and spectacular food, reading about the sex was torturous. I bucked my hips, hoping that it wasn't enough for him to notice, needing contact from anything. I didn't know if I was allowed to stop reading, but I couldn't read about this guy doing the things that he was doing to this girl much longer.

I wanted the vibrator out of me. I wanted to come, and I knew that I wasn't going to be allowed. I didn't think he was ever going to come back. It was after one in the morning. I wanted to sleep, but couldn't. There was no way I could fall asleep as long as I had the constant vibration inside of me. I wondered how long the batteries would last, and finally turned off the e-reader. I closed my eyes and tried to think about anything but my sopping wet pussy, begging to for pleasure.

Drew finally came to remove the object, and I thought I was going to come just by him sliding it out.

"You're very wet Morgan," he said, rubbing my juices with his fingers.

Fucking idiot… Really?

By no surprise, Drew didn't let me come, and left me with the smirk that I hated. I finally did stop thinking about it and fell asleep.

He had to go out of town the next day, and made sure that I knew that he would be watching. He explained that he expected to see me reading every night. I picked up the e-reader that night, thinking I would read his stupid smut for thirty minutes or so, and then watch television. I ended up reading until I couldn't take it any longer. He had the cable turned off in my room so I had nothing to do, but read.

"Did you eventually get to go to the library?" Dawson asked, sensing that I needed to stop talking about the sex.

I nodded, being pulled from my thoughts. "Yes, but I was always escorted by his right hand man, Derik. I wasn't allowed to use the computers, and was only allowed to check out one book at a time because he wanted me to read what he downloaded for me."

"Wow, Ry. I don't even know what to say. How did you end up leaving him?"

I thought about it for a second and I didn't want to talk anymore. I needed him to treat me the way that Drew did, and I needed him right that second. "Dawson, I need to save that for another time. I need you to do things to me right now."

Dawson knew exactly what I was talking about. "Ry?" he spoke, not sure really what to say.

"Please, Dawson," I begged. I was used to begging. I didn't care what he thought. I needed the attention in my throbbing core.

"Riley, this can't turn you on," he said, sounding a little taken aback.

"I told you that I was fucked up, and yes it can. What do you think?" I asked, taking his hand and sliding it between my legs. "You can't tell me that it didn't turn you on as well."

"Oh yes, I can. I am not turned on in the least by what that bastard did to you."

He kissed me deep and passionate as his fingers continued to please me.

"You turn me on. Touching you turns me on," he whispered to my lips.

"Dawson I need you to be somebody else right now. I need you to be controlling and do the things that I just told you about," I practically begged, thrusting my hips into his fingers as I lay back.

"No. Ry. I am going to make love to you, and I am going to try like hell to please you. I am never going to keep you from it, and I am never going to treat you like that."

I groaned. It was what I needed. I didn't want him to make love to me. I wanted him to use and abuse me. It's what I knew. It was what was consuming my mind. I wanted to be spanked. I wanted him to make me swallow him. I needed him to forcefully invade my ass.

"Please Dawson," I begged as he removed my panties and his own clothes.

He came to me and kissed me again. "Close your eyes baby," he whispered on my lips, and I did.

He gently caressed my arms and shoulders, massaging me all the way to my fingertips. I moaned when I felt his lips on my breast as he gently kissed and sucked each one of them, continuing to move down my body. He massaged both of my legs all the way to my feet. I didn't realize how tense I was, and the sore pressure points on my feet were magically erased by his strong hands.

By the time he was back to my lips, I had calmed, and quit frantically thinking about what I needed him to do and let him take control. He was going to anyway; my begging had no influence on him. He kissed me deeply, and I moaned in his mouth as he moved between my legs. He made slow, passionate love to me; when he sensed I was leaving him for Drew, he would stop, make me open my eyes and look at him, telling me that he loved me before he would move again. That seemed to become routine for us. I was glad he didn't do as I begged him to do. I knew that so many men would have jumped at the chance to treat me like I felt I deserved, but not Dawson. Dawson truly did love me, and I loved him.

I lay in his arms that night feeling like I had never felt in my life. I knew I craved the things that Drew did to me because it was the only time I was touched. I never grew up with loving parents. Drew surely never made me feel loved, but his touch was something I needed emotionally. Dawson's touch was different from anything I had ever experienced.

"Thank you," I said, looking up at him as he kissed the tip of my nose. He knew what I was thanking him for, and I truly was grateful that he hadn't given in to my dark requests.

"You're welcome. Is he still in Indiana?" He asked, and I already knew what he was thinking.

"Yes, and you promise me that you're not going to do anything. I just want to forget him Dawson, please don't try to do anything." I knew that he was a cop and could find out fairly easy that he was in Las Vegas and not Indiana, but I thought it would at least throw him off track. And I wasn't about to give him a last name.

"Ry, don't you want to see that prick rot in prison? He bought you. You were forced to marry him, and I am sure that too was not a legal wedding."

"It wasn't, but I want you to let it go. It was a legal document because a judge did it. I signed all of the papers myself. Please don't do anything, Dawson. I am begging you."

"A judge did it?" he asked, disbelieving his own ears. "What else did you sign?"

"I'm not even sure. I signed the marriage license and then something else that was about ten pages. He just flipped it to the back page, and I signed it. I'm sure it was a prenuptial agreement, not that he was ever going to let me leave him anyway."

"Why would you sign something without reading it first?"

"Dawson, I was barely eighteen. My dad had just sold me to a man that I didn't know. I did what I had to do to survive."

"You're going to be okay, Riley. I promise," he said, and I smiled. Dawson took a deep breath and kissed the top of my head.

I didn't dream about anything that night. I fell asleep in Dawson's arms feeling safe and content. I had promised myself before I had come to the little tourist town that I would never reveal any of my skeletons to anyone there, but I was glad that I had. I was glad that Dawson knew where I had come from and still wanted me. It felt good to tell someone.

We landed at the McCarran airport just before noon. I was still a nervous wreck, afraid that someone would recognize me. I wasn't sure who I was worried about. I never did get out much. It wasn't like I was someone famous. Drew had his own private plane. He didn't fly out of McCarran. I still wasn't sure what was said about my disappearance or if he just told people that I had left him.

I wore dark sunglasses and a ridiculously large sun hat. Las Vegas was a very public city and it was fairly easy for anyone to blend in. I didn't relax until we were in our hotel, miles away from Drew's home. He would never come to this side of town. I enjoyed dinner with Starlight, her sister Sunny, and all three of her hippy friends who were just as unconventional and carefree as Starlight. I loved them all. We had so much fun. I think all of us had a little too much of something called purple Martians.

Dawson called to check on me just before we turned in for the night. Starlight moaned in the bed next to me, regretting the number of deep purple drinks that she had consumed.

"Was that Star?"

I laughed. "Yeah, she may have had one too many drinks downstairs."

"I miss you. You should come home now," Dawson teased.

I looked over to Starlight, not wanting to say anything in front of her. "I'm sure you will be fine for a couple of days," I said, playing it safe.

"Will you?"

I knew what Dawson was asking. He had been in my bed every night for three full months. He was there to calm my nights, hold me, and tell me that I was there with him, and Drew was nowhere around.

I took a deep breath. "Yeah, I'm good. I'm hoping the alcohol will help."

It didn't. I was afraid to go to sleep at all, afraid that Starlight would deem me a lunatic and fire me or something. I lay awake purposely trying to tire out my subconscious mind. Maybe if I was beyond exhausted, I wouldn't dream. I did finally let the fatigue take over sometime around three in the morning. I may had been okay had I kept my mind on Dawson back in Maine, but I didn't. I lay on my side watching Starlight's breathing moving up and down under her covers.

It reminded me of Drew on the few occasions he stayed in my room. I would stay as far away from him as I could, staring at him breathe just like Star was doing. I waited for it. I wanted him to fall asleep. I would rather not to be in bed with me, but when his breathing changed, I knew he was asleep.

That was the first night that I didn't remember what I dreamed. I knew that it must have been bad though. I woke to Star on the side of my bed shaking me and yelling my name.

I startled her as much as she startled me when I screamed and jumped to the top corner of the bed. My hair was drenched from sweat and my damp nightshirt stuck to my body. My breathing was erratic, and I was sucking in air that wasn't available.

"Jesus, Riley." Starlight exclaimed with wide eyes.

"I'm sorry," I apologized once I realized where I was.

I got up and went to the bathroom. I splashed cold water on my face and the back of my neck.

I hung out in the small hotel bathroom as long as I could, hoping that she would go back to sleep. She didn't. She had a smile, a cup of water and two little pills waiting on me.

"Here, take these. It'll help," she said warmly.

"What is it?" I asked, taking the pills. I didn't really care what they were. I would take anything if it would help. Her relaxing tea sure the hell didn't work. It helped me fall asleep but didn't keep me asleep.

"Just Melatonin. It's all natural, and will help regulate your sleep and your wake cycle."

I already knew that the two little pills were all natural. Starlight wouldn't dare put anything with chemicals in her body.

"Do you want to talk about it?" she smiled.

Of course, I didn't want to talk to her about how fucked up I was. "What did I say?" I asked. That's what I wanted to know. I wanted to know how much I said. I wondered if the alcohol kept me from remembering what I had dreamt. I always knew what I dreamed about. They were too real not to remember.

"I'm not really sure what you were saying. It was mostly muffled. Are you okay now?"

She lied. I nodded and lay down.

I did sleep the rest of the night or morning I should say. I finally dozed back off, freaked out about what I had said and wondering about this dream.

I woke. Starlight was in the shower, and I heard the two little dings from her cell phone. I sat up and nosily slid open her screen on the night stand between our beds.

It was from Dawson.

"Sorry, was on phone. Is she okay, now?" It read.

I couldn't help it. I had to see what she had said to him. I could still hear the shower running, so I had time. I went to the first message so that I could read the conversation in order.

"Dawson… What the hell? You need to give me some answers about Riley."

"What do you mean?"

"I think that is a dumb question, and you already know what I mean. She woke up screaming, drenched in sweat during the night, and the things that she was saying were horrific. Don't tell me you sleep with her every night and don't know what I am talking about."

"I know what you're talking about, but I promised her that I would keep it to myself. I can't Star."

That made me feel good. He was being loyal to me.

"I think she needs help, Dawson."

"She does, but she won't get it."

"If it's the money, I would gladly help her out."

"It's not. She doesn't want anyone to know where she came from. Please just let it go. I am afraid that she'll run, and I don't want her to do that. I love her."

That made me smile again.

"We're here for two more nights. What do I do?"

"You can do what I do. Hold her and kiss her beautiful lips and tell her that you love her, lol,"

I smiled again.

"You're an ass. This isn't funny. I'm a little blown away here."

"Relax Star, she's fine. If she does it again tonight just talk her down. She's not going to do anything crazy if that's what you're worried about."

"I'm worried about her."

That was the last message and I quickly laid her phone down and crawled back into bed when I heard the shower shut off.

I stretched and pretended that I just woke up.

"Good morning, hungry?" Star asked with her carefree smile.

"Yeah, I could eat, but I need a shower."

"Go. Get a shower. We have a busy day. I can't wait until you see these vendors today. It's epic."

I smiled at her enthusiasm for the hippy festival.

"Star, I'm really sorry about last night."

I don't know why I felt the need to apologize to her. I just didn't want to ruin what I had going on, although the thought had crossed my mind to run away and start over again somewhere, neglecting the relationship and friends. I would be safer the next time. I knew what I could and couldn't do, and having people in my life who wanted to get close wouldn't be an option. But the truth is I couldn't imagine not having Dawson, Star and Lauren in my life.

"Honey, you don't have to be sorry for anything. Just tell me if there is anything that I can do to help. I owe you so much already."

I looked at her puzzled. I owed her everything. I didn't understand.

"Why would you owe me anything?"

"You are joking, right? You turned my money pit dive into a thriving, profitable business. I would have never done that. It was just something to occupy my time. I never dreamed that it could be what it is now. I owe you for that."

"You don't owe me anything. I think that I love that place more than you do."

"I owe you breakfast and one hell of a fun day, so go get your skinny little butt ready."

I was glad that Star was letting go of my night. I would just have to make sure I didn't sleep that night.

We had to take two cabs because there were six of us. I rode with Starlight and Sunny and couldn't help but laugh at the two sisters. They were talking about how the fortune teller once told them that they both would marry and have three girls each. Star was said to have two marriages in her life. She didn't have any. She had an illegitimate daughter. Of course, her name was part of the universe as well, Moon Beam Straights. She went by Moonie.

I could feel my heart begin to beat faster when we got close to the jewelry store. I knew that the chances of Drew being there were slim to none. I had heard enough of his business calls to know that he was rarely in any of his stores. That's what he had Derik for. Derik did all of his dirty work.

I think I stopped breathing. I don't know how I even saw him. There were so many people on the sidewalk, but I did. He was pacing with one finger in his ear and his cell phone to the other one. It was Derik for sure, in his expensive, elaborate suit and tie. He never looked up and kept his eyes down. I knew without knowing that Drew was on the other end of the phone.

"Riley?" I heard Starlight call my name. I was sure that it wasn't the first time.

"Sorry, did you say something?" I asked a stupid question.

"Not anything important. I was just telling you about all of the coffee vendors that will be set up here."

I couldn't believe all the cars and people that were at this expo. I would have never dreamed that so many people were into the retro hippy craze. I was happy to see that we were some place where you wouldn't find Drew or his sidekick, Derik. We had to walk a mile because our cab driver refused to go any farther into the multitude of traffic. I didn't mind. I proudly wore my dark sunglasses and my oversized sun hat.

Starlight and I both had ordered a new outfit for the special day. I wore a brown and green tie dye Mudmee wrap skirt and a brown hippy style fringed leather vest with a pair of water buffalo sandals. Starlight wore a patchwork sundress and the same sandals as me.

We spent the entire day at the swap meet. We did eventually go our separate ways. There was way too much to see in five days, let alone two, and we wanted to acquire some new and exciting merchants. The storeroom had quickly started to get cleared out from our robust sales over the past few months. Starlight went for the coffees, teas, aroma oils and scented candles. I spent my time with Sunny and we hit up all of the clothing, novelty items, and pictures. I definitely wanted more of the artwork. They seemed to be one of the hottest items for the tourists we attracted.

It was after seven before we finally made it back to the hotel. I was hot, tired and excited all at the same time. Starlight went to the shower, and I called Dawson.

"I was beginning to think you forgot me," he answered. I could sense the smile on his face.

"Never, how are you?"

"Lonely. I'm not used to sleeping alone anymore. I didn't sleep much."

"I think you are lying to me. You probably slept like a baby without me there to wake you during the night."

"I promise I didn't. I would much rather have you here waking me. I kept throwing my arm over you, and you weren't there."

I laughed. I missed him. I really missed him. The only person who I had ever missed in my life was Justin. I didn't even miss my mother although I often wondered where she was.

"I have to say that I missed you last night too." I didn't say why. He knew why.

"How was your expo?"

"It was amazing, Daw. You should have seen the people at this thing. I talked to a guy who came here all the way from Florence, Italy. He flew here just for the meet."

"He wasn't cute was he?"

I laughed at his jealousy. "No. I promise. He wasn't cute. We have twenty-four new catalogs to go through."

"You didn't buy anything to have shipped back home?"

"No. Star wanted to, but I talked her out of it. It'll be much cheaper to order and have it sent direct from the wholesalers than to have it shipped from here."

"Have I told you how much I loved you today?"

"No. I haven't talked to you today, silly."

"I love you more than the stars, the sun, the moon, the ocean, the air…"

I laughed before I cut him off. "Okay. I get it, and I love you too, but Star just got out of the shower, and I desperately need it."

"So you don't love me as much as a shower."

"I do, just not right at the moment. Do you have any idea how hot it is in Las Vegas in July?"

"Nope. Never been there. How hot?"

"It was a hundred and five today. That is ridiculously hot, and I have enough sweat on me to water a house plant."

"Ewe. That's kind of gross. You'd better go shower. I love you."

"I love you too, Dawson."

Starlight and I spent our evening looking at the many products and dog-earing pages of the catalogs. We didn't eat any supper. We had both eaten so much at the meet that neither of us was hungry.

I crawled into bed first, and Starlight gave me two of the little pills. I took them with a smile, hoping I didn't wake her with one of my episodes.

"Where did you grow up?" Starlight asked as we both lay down in our side by side beds.

How much should I tell her? Should I lie and say that I grew up in Indiana? It wasn't that I didn't trust her. I was just afraid. Afraid of what, I wasn't sure.

"Pennsylvania." I lied. It was somewhat in the same vicinity.

"Do you have any siblings?"

I didn't want to have this conversation. I had an awesome day, and I wanted to fall asleep thinking about all the neat things that we would soon have in the shop.

"I have a brother," I said, yawning a fake yawn, hoping she took the hint.

She didn't.

"How long were you married?"

Did I tell her that I had been married? I didn't remember telling her that. I was afraid to lie. Did Lauren or Dawson tell her that I had been married?"

"Six years," I told the truth.

"Ry, I'm here if you need to talk," Star said, sensing my apprehension.

"I'm fine. I would rather let the past stay in the past."

"Okay, but just so you know, I'm a pretty good listener and an even better secret keeper," she smiled.

I did dream that night. Maybe it was her asking about my upbringing, but for the first time I dreamt about my mother. At least I didn't wake up screaming bloody murder, and I didn't think that I had talked in my sleep.

***

I should have known that morning that something was up. My mom never told me to come to the truck stop and eat after school. I wasn't allowed to be in there. She couldn't flirt with all of the truckers if I was there, and she sure wasn't going to use her tip money to buy me supper. I didn't have that kind of mother. I had a mother whom I knew didn't stay loyal to my dad, not that he ever did either.

I cautiously wandered into the dive and sat at the bar with my mom. She wasn't working at all, and she wasn't wearing her ugly green polo uniform shirt. She patted the red plastic barstool beside of her.

"Order anything you want," she offered.

I did. I ordered a chocolate milk shake, a cheeseburger, and fries. I felt guilty for eating the food and even more so for the milk shake. I knew Justin would have loved to have had a milk shake.

"I'm not coming home tonight, Morgan," my mom explained while I ate my glorious meal.

"Where you going?" I asked around the cheeseburger in my mouth.

"I am moving away from here. I can't stay with your dad anymore. It's not healthy for any of us."

"We're taking Justin too, aren't we?" I asked, not understanding what she was trying to say.

"I need you to stay and take care of Justin for me."

"You're not taking us with you?"

"I can't, Morgan. Someday you'll understand. I promise."

I turned when I heard the well-dressed man clear his throat beside her.

"I have to go, Morgan. You take care of your brother for a while for me, okay?"

"Just for awhile? And then you're coming for us?"

"I won't be coming for you, but you will be eighteen soon. You'll leave this place too."

She didn't hug me, didn't kiss me, and only patted my knee.

"I love you. Finish your food and head home before your dad gets home."

That was how my mother said goodbye.

***

I did sleep well, other than that haunting dream about my mother leaving her children to be with some man, obviously with more money than my dad had. I felt strange about the dream. I couldn't pinpoint exactly what it was, but it was almost like a clue for some odd reason.

We spent the next day at the expo again. Star's all-natural sleeping aid helped once again. I was too happy to have nightmares about my past. We had such a great day that it made it almost impossible.

◇◇()◇◇

I could not wait for the plane to land. I even asked the stewardess if she could tell the pilot to speed up a little. I missed Dawson so much, and couldn't wait to see him. I don't know what my hurry was. We landed at eleven in the morning. I wouldn't see him until he got off work at four.

I couldn't wait. As soon as Star dropped me off at my door, I tossed my belongings inside the door and headed back into town.

"You have a really hard job," I said, seeing him looking oh so fine in his uniform with his feet propped up on his desk. He almost knocked over his cup of coffee when he abruptly sat up with a smile. I loved that smile.

"Welp, guess I better go catch me some bad guys," his Deputy Matt decided, excusing himself.

Dawson had me in his arms in a split second.

"Don't you ever leave me like that again," he demanded, kissing me. I mean really kissing me. My arousal went from zero to eighty in two-point-seven seconds.

I was panting. His hands seemed to be magical, causing sensations to places that he wasn't even touching.

He let me go rather quickly.

"Your house or mine?" he asked, retrieving his cell phone.

I didn't have time to answer before he was on the phone with Matt, telling him to get back there because he was taking the rest of the day off.

Dawson drove his car, and I followed him to his house and had to laugh when he accidentally hit the siren on his cruiser trying to get out of the car.

I was twenty-five years old, and it was the first time ever in my life that I felt passion. I wanted Dawson more at that moment than I ever wanted anything in my life. It was also the first time that Drew stayed out of our sex life. It was the first time that Dawson had ever gone down on me, actually it was the first time that anyone had gone down on me. Wow. That's a lot of firsts. Drew wasn't into pleasing me. He was into pleasing himself.

Dawson walked me backwards toward his bedroom, never letting the contact of our lips break. He had my long flowing sundress around my hips and was thumbing off my panties. I didn't take any of my clothes off except for the panties. He backed me up until the bed stopped me and I pulled myself back with my elbows. After he pulled my shirt above my breasts, I watched him hastily undress himself. He raised my knees and kissed my stomach while his hands caressed the satin on my bra. I wasn't used to that either. Drew just demanded that I spread my legs, and I did it. Dawson moved down and kissed me on the inside of my right thigh.

I thought I was going to come off the bed when he slid his finger into me. These were all new and foreign feelings for me. I didn't know it could be this way. My emotions were instantly halted when I felt his tongue next. It scared me at first, but he sensed it and softly laid his hand on my stomach forcing me to stay with him, promptly bringing me back to him and not Drew.

Never in my life had I felt anything like that. I came. I came hard and called out in loud, totally unbelievable agony. I hadn't had time to regain my composure when Dawson came to me. He kissed me, another first. I never dreamed that tasting myself on his lips could have been so sensual. He rolled me over, and I took over the driving. My long skirt covered us, and he kept his hands under it, caressing and pulling my hips to him. My hands ran up his sexy as hell chest. I loved the hair on his chest. Drew had a bare chest, not that I ever touched it or anything.

I came twice. The second time wasn't as intense as when he had brought me there with his mouth, but none the less, I did, and it was incredible. Dawson was right there with me and rolled me over. He frantically took me sending us both over the edge.

We both kind of laughed at our hungriness for each other.

"Damn, I love you," he said, kissing my lips.

I was glad that Dawson loved me. I loved him, and couldn't imagine not having him in my life.

Chapter 9

I was doing well, and I was so proud of myself. I slept every night in Dawson's arms, and my nightmares were becoming a thing of the past. My thoughts of Drew grew few and far between. I did it. I was happy in my small town practically living with my sheriff. I loved calling him my sheriff. I think he secretly liked it too, although he did tell me more than once that he had a name. It was usually followed by a kiss.

The shop couldn't have been better. There was no such thing as a slow day anymore. I did, however, have to keep on Starlight some. Her lack of organization and my OCD sometimes clashed, but we handled it out of fun.

I turned twenty-six on October 2nd, well not really; Riley turned twenty-six on October 2nd. Morgan had turned twenty-six in June. I was never so happy in my life. It was almost surreal. I had run away from Morgan Willow, leaving her in the hills of West Virginia, and Morgan Kelley was dead in Las Vegas. I never wanted either Morgan back. I loved being Riley Murphy.

I thought that Dawson was taking me out for my birthday. I showered and was ready to go when he picked me up at my house. I had on a new pair of jeans that fit me well, and a new flowing embroidered Kurta that I had ordered from one of the hippy catalogues. It was white with brown embroidered Indian design around the sleeves and waist. I wore brown leather dingo boots with my jeans tucked inside. I looked cute. The mirror behind my door said so.

"Happy birthday. I don't want to take you out anymore," Dawson decided, kissing me.

He told me happy birthday at least ten times already, not counting the multiple texts that I received throughout the day. I loved his compliments. I didn't always love them, and it took some getting used to, but I finally learned to accept them with a smile.

"Feed me and I may let you spend the night," I teased.

I read the text from Starlight just as we pulled out of my drive.

"Star wants to know if you will stop by and hang some kind of hooks for her," I said, looking at Dawson.

"I guess we have time," he replied.

We parked on the front street, and held my hand as we went inside.

I should have known something was up. Star never said anything about any hooks before.

He held the door for me, and the whole place was decorated with balloons and banners.

Lauren, Levi, Matt, Star and several of our regulars were there. I couldn't believe it. I almost cried. I was twenty-six and was having my first birthday party... ever.

"You guys," was all that I could think of to say. I was in shock.

Starlight handed me a blue drink on ice with a cute little umbrella.

"What is it?" I asked, eyeing the neon blue drink.

"Sex in the driveway," Lauren was the one to say with a smile.

Dawson and I exchanged a private glance, both of us were thinking the same thing. A couple of months back we had gone out with Lauren and Joel to celebrate her birthday. We never made it inside and jumped in the back seat and had sex. We woke up just after daylight, both still naked. The paper boy had come and left the paper on the door. Needless to say, he had to walk right past the car to leave the paper.

We ate pizza and drank the sex in the driveway drinks.

I couldn't believe the presents. I had never gotten presents like this for my birthday. I did usually get one gift. When I was real little it would be like a Slinky or one of those plastic Barbies that seemed to always get their faced smashed in, and you could never push it back out. I would get cheap jewelry when I was older. I never got a birthday present from Drew. Hell, he probably didn't even know when my birthday was. Rebecca always got me something though. It too was usually earrings or a bracelet.

Even the patrons bought me gifts. Nothing extravagant. I got the cutest little key chain from my beach friend, John. It was a piece of sea glass. He explained that it meant happiness. I was very happy. Lauren bought me a Miranda Lambert CD. I opened all of my gifts and Dawson had saved his for last. When I turned to see where he was, he knelt on one knee in front of me.

Oh, God...

I didn't freak the way I would have expected. I could only feel how much I was loved, and was beyond grateful for my friends and of course Dawson.

He smiled and opened the black velvet box.

"Will you marry me, Riley?" he asked.

"Of course I will marry you," I smiled. I didn't need to think about it. I knew what I wanted. I wanted my sheriff.

He slipped the diamond on my finger and kissed me while my friends hooted and hollered.

I was well on my way to being drunk from the blue drinks I'd been consuming for the past three hours by the time we left.

Dawson stayed at my house, and it was the best night of my life. I couldn't believe that I was going to become Mrs. Dawson Bade. We were planning a May 1st wedding, and I wanted it all. I never had a church wedding, the white gown or anyone who cared about me at my last wedding. I didn't want anything lavish or anything, just a small church wedding with my friends.

Dawson made slow passionate love to me that night, and I don't think I could have been happier had my life depended on it. I'm not sure if it was because of all of the excitement, the fact that I was going to marry Dawson or the ring that I proudly wore on my finger, but I did dream that night. It was bad.
***

It was the third time that Drew had given me my wedding set back. We were meeting some very prominent clients for dinner at a fancy high-rise restaurant. He coached me to keep my mouth shut and to only speak if he spoke. He would answer any questions directed toward me.

I was almost sick from the affection he was showing me. He held my hand, kissed me several times and called me baby. He never called me baby unless it was when he was close to coming. He made sure that he kept my hand in his on the table, showing off my thirty-five thousand dollar wedding set; I was sure. He was trying to get his prospects to be envious of my expensive set, or at least her anyway.

After a couple of drinks, I needed to go to the bathroom. I didn't dare just excuse myself without asking first. I almost puked when I leaned into Drew and whispered in his ear. He nodded and smiled the fakest smile I had ever seen.

"I love you too, sweetheart," he said with the nod, giving me permission.

"Excuse me," I said politely, laying my fancy cloth napkin on the table.

"Oh, I'll go with you," the beautiful diamond ring prospect announced.

My eyes instantly looked to Drew. He didn't like it. He didn't like it one bit.

I tried to get back to the table as quickly as possible, but Ms. Chatter Box wanted to talk, and thought she needed my opinion on which of the three engagement rings I liked best. Of course, I said the most expensive one, talking it up like nothing else.

We were gone for at least ten minutes. Our entrees were being placed around the table.

Drew was livid. It was written all over his face. His clenched jaw may not have been noticeable to his guests, but it was exceedingly obvious to me. The young lady did end up picking the one that I had suggested. I was sure that Drew wouldn't want to hear about how I talked it up though.

As soon as we were in the back seat of the limousine he practically ripped the rings from my finger.

"What the fuck did you tell her?" he asked.

"I didn't tell her anything, Drew. She was only asking my advice about the rings. I swear. I never said anything that I shouldn't have."

He ran his hands through his hair, angrily. I was scared. I knew he was mad, and I knew that I was going to be the one he took it out on. I just wasn't sure how.

He grabbed me by my hair and threw me over his lap. I didn't have to worry about the panties. I was no longer allowed to wear them when he was home. He raised my party dress and cracked me on the ass more times than he ever had. He didn't even rub the sting out between the blows. All I could think about was whether or not Derik could hear what was going on from the driver's seat of the limo, not that he didn't know what was going on. He had to know. He was around almost as much as Rebecca. I didn't cry. I had stopped that a long time ago. It didn't do any good anyway. Drew had no compassion.

Drew kept me bare assed over his lap the whole ride home, even after he thought I had enough of his assault on my ass. Once Derik parked the car back in the extravagant garage Drew threw me off of him.

"Don't move!" he demanded, getting out.

I didn't. I was too scared to move. I heard him tell Derik to keep me out there until he cooled off and called him.

Derik scared me. I had never spoken to him before. I couldn't believe that Drew was going to leave me with him. Wasn't he afraid that I would talk? Of course not, I was sure that Derik knew more than anyone, he was there when he forced my signature on his stupid marriage license. He probably knew more than I did. Maybe I could talk to Derik. Maybe he would help me get out of here. I stopped that notion very quickly. I wasn't getting out of there. That was my life, and I wouldn't take the chance on Derik telling him that I tried to get him to help me.

I didn't even need to think about that. It wasn't at all what Derik planned. He opened the back door and sat across from me. I didn't like the smirk on his face, and I was all of a sudden afraid of him. I had reason.

He pulled my knees apart and raised my dress more. I swiftly put my knees back together, only to have them forced apart again.

"What are you doing? Drew is going to see you through the cameras," I pleaded. I wondered then if I was more afraid of Derik or of Drew. He would make this my fault. He always did.

"There are no cameras in this car or this garage. I have waited for this opportunity for almost two years," he said as he slid to his knees in front of me. I wanted to object, but how could I? He had more power over me than I had over myself. If I screamed, Drew might come out. I didn't want that either.

He moved his fingers into me and all I could do was stare out the dark window while he rapidly and vehemently thrashed his middle and forefinger in and out of me. I didn't get aroused. I didn't want to come. I was too terrified to even think about it. Not of him as much as Drew. I just knew he was going to sling the door open at any second.

Derik must have been worried too. He was in a hurry, and it showed. He took himself out and moved into me with a hiss. Now I was freaked out. Drew would know. I was sure of it. He didn't speak, and only made sexual grunting and moaning noises. He had one thing on his mind, and that was getting off. In me!

Or not.

"I'm going to pull out, and you are going to swallow me. I don't want to leave any evidence for Drew. Do you understand?"

Fuck no…

He grabbed my hair and pulled when I didn't answer. "Do you understand me?" he asked again, and I tried to nod.

He pumped faster and harder, and I knew that he was getting ready to come. He stood as much as he could. I wouldn't open my mouth and turned my head. It didn't work. He grabbed my head forced his dick into my mouth, pumping just as rapidly there.

"Oh, yeah fuck," he moaned as he invaded my mouth just before he spewed out. I was happy that he didn't do it like

Drew did and make sure that I had to taste him. I was able to swallow all of him without any dripping out of my mouth.

He kissed my lips. The bastard had the nerve to kiss me.

He put himself away and got out of the car without one word. I supposed he didn't need to say a word. He knew that I would never mention it. I sat in the car waiting and anticipating what Drew had in store for me next, for over an hour.

When I was finally escorted back into the house, I never saw Drew. I went to my suite and bathed away his idiotic sidekick. Drew came in and sat on the toilet while I bathed. He didn't speak, and only sat there glaring at me. I got out of the tub, mostly to get the rest of the night started so that it would be over. He hit me right across the same cheekbone that he always seemed to aim for. When I stood back up, he did it again.
***

"Riley!" I heard Dawson calling my name over and over.

I jumped and covered my face to stop the next blow.

"You're okay. I'm right here, baby," he said, trying to soothe me back to reality.

"Dawson?" I wept, needing to make sure that I was with him.

"Shhhh, I've got you, Ry," he said, trying to calm me.

"I didn't tell her anything. I swear."

Dawson sat up and turned the lamp on, trying to get me coherent enough to realize that I was safe with him.

I crawled into his arms, and he embraced me. I couldn't for the life of me figure out why he wanted me. Would it always be this way? Would I always be the broken one?

"Tell me about your dream," he requested, holding me tight and placing soft kisses to my forehead.

"It wasn't a dream. It was a nightmare."

"Tell me about it."

"I did. I told him every last detail, and then some. I never got to finish my dream before Dawson woke me up. I told him about how after he dragged me from the bathroom he made me squat on a rather large dildo that he had lubed up for me. I wasn't allowed to sit on it. I had to hold myself up while he sat on the bed and watched. When my legs finally gave out, and I plopped on the bed he removed the foreign object and replaced it with himself.

Once he was spent, he picked up the phone and called Rebecca. It was almost two in the morning. I couldn't believe that he expected her to be at his beck and call whenever he wanted her.

"Morgan's going to need an ice pack," he said, but I wasn't sure why he cared about my black eye. He didn't care when he was giving it to me.

I started to get under the blankets to cover myself before she came in.

"Did I tell you to move?" he asked. I froze.

"Lay down," he demanded.

I lay down and crossed my ankles.

"Spread your legs. You want to humiliate me? I'll show you humiliation."

I was mortified, enough so that a tear did escape from the corner of my right eye when I heard a tap on the door. I lay there spread eagle while Rebecca brought me the ice pack. She only looked at my face and smiled a warm smile as she placed it on my eye. I flinched from the pain.

"Riley. Please tell me that was only a nightmare and didn't really happen," Dawson begged, but he knew. Now he not only wanted to kill Drew he added Derik to his hit list too.

"It did happen, Dawson, and so much more. I am never going to be whole."

"What's his last name?"

"You know that I'm not going to tell you that. I don't want you to do anything. Please," I pleaded.

"Don't you want that son of a bitch to pay for what he did to you?"

"No. I just want to forget that he ever existed."

"Is he a good looking man?"

I rose up to give him a stressed look. "What the hell does that have to do with anything?"

"I'm just trying to figure out why, if he is so rich and powerful, why he would come to a poor town in West Virginia to marry you?"

I relaxed and lay back to his chest. "He is very handsome. I've asked myself that same question a million times."

I finally dozed back off. Dawson never let go of me.

When I woke, Dawson was still holding me. He was never still in bed when I woke up. He was an early riser too, not quite as bad as Lauren, but he was still normally up before me.

I looked up, and he was wide awake, staring pitiful glares through me. He opened his hand palm side up, and I placed mine in his. He kissed me on top of the head as I lay back to his chest.

"What are you thinking about?" I asked. I knew what he was thinking about, and I wished I would have kept my past in the past and not shared my horrific nightmare.

"You," he quietly said, kissing me again.

"About how pathetic I am?"

"Not at all, I was thinking about how much I love you, and how I wish I could take all of this away from you."

I snorted. Nobody could take it away. Drew had taken it all, and although I hated to admit it. He still controlled me. It wasn't as much as when I first left. It seemed like every time that I was happy, and things were going exceptionally well for me was when he decided to haunt me. Why? I didn't know. I guess the subconscious is just one of those mysteries that you just never figure out.

"Why did your wife leave you, Dawson?" I asked for some reason. I never asked about his past. I guess it was just another one of my hang-ups. I was never allowed to ask questions, and it was always no concern of mine.

He snorted next. I assumed he was thinking about how crazy I was.

"I met her at the police academy. I knew I wanted to stay here and take over once my father retired. She was from Chicago and couldn't get used to the small town. She needed more action than Misty Bay could give her."

"Your wife was a cop too?" I asked. I never knew that. I had seen a picture in his house once of a graduating class, and I assumed one of the two females was her, but had no idea that she was an officer. I was shocked that Lauren never mentioned it. Not that she was much on gossip, but she would answer my questions. I guess I never asked.

"Yes, she was a cop or *is*, I should say. She went back home to Chicago after one year here. Her dad was also a cop, so she knew there was more action than writing parking tickets in some small hick town."

"I like this small hick town," I smiled up at him. He carried a heavy heart. I could see it in his eyes.

"I need for you to talk to me, Ry."

"I'm not telling you who he is, Dawson," I assured him.

"Then don't, but I need some answers."

I took a deep breath. I owed it to him. There was nothing that I could tell him that would scare him away. If he were going to run, he would have done it before now.

"What do you want to know?" I asked, turning back to lie on his chest. It was easier not to look at him when I talked about my past. I didn't want to see the disgust on his face.

"How did you spend your days there?"

"Most days were good. He traveled a lot, so I spent most of my time either alone or with Rebecca."

"Tell me about Rebecca. She knew. She knew that you were there against your will. Why didn't she help you?"

"Rebecca helped me in more ways than you could ever know. I don't know that I would have survived without her."

"How old was Rebecca?"

I'm not sure why that mattered, but I answered. "She was probably in her mid-thirties when I first got there."

"And she was just the help there?"

"She was more than the help. Her only job was to take care of me."

"What do you mean take care of you? What did she do?"

"Hmm, a little bit of everything I guess. She made my appointments for my hair, dress fittings for his stupid dinners, made sure that I had my birth control shots. She cooked for me too, but I think that was because she liked to do it. I remember her always being close by. I used to ride around the property on one of the golf carts, and sometimes I would see her in a distance checking to see where I was."

"Were you able to talk to her?"

"Not much. Every room in that house had cameras, and he could hear everything that was said. Sometimes she would ride with me on the cart, and we would talk, but she was always afraid to say anything."

"Why would she work for a man like that?"

"Rebecca and I came from the same side of the tracks. She grew up very poor and never had much. She was waitressing in a diner in some small town when Drew approached her about working for him. I don't think she really knew what she was getting into, and I think she too was afraid of him. She had a five year contract to take care of me. He gave her, her own suite, took care of all of her needs, and once her contract was up, she was paid half a million dollars for her time. I guess Drew thought that five years would be enough time to train me."

"So she too was weak. What a coward. So she left before you?"

"No, she signed another one year contract. I think she was afraid to leave me. She was the one who came and put me back together when he decided to come home pissed off and take it out on me. But she was leaving shortly after I left. I hope she did," I added.

"How often were you…"

"Punished, you can say it," I said, finishing his sentence.

"You were a grown woman. You shouldn't have been punished."

I ignored that part. "It depends. Sometimes I would go months without any encounters. He would come home and do his thing with me and leave me alone. Other times, mostly when I had to go out with him," I added. "I always said something or looked at someone or something that he made sure that I was going to be punished for."

"And this Derik prick, did he leave you alone?"

I snorted. "No. Once I was trusted enough to go out and shop or go to the library, Derik had to be the one to go with me. He always made sure that he took a back way home, but I did become friends with his wife Jena and was occasionally allowed to go out to a show or to eat with her."

"You couldn't talk to her?"

"And tell her what, Dawson? Hey, your husband has sex with me, and I am living in this mansion with everything that a woman could want with this good looking rich guy against my will. We didn't talk about personal things, well I didn't anyway. She did. I used to be absolutely repulsed when she would giddily tell me about their sex life."

I almost felt bad thinking about it. I said, almost. I did start to somewhat enjoy sex with Derik. Not that I liked him or anything. I hated the slime ball, but at least he would let me finish. He loved for me to come and tried to make sure that I did every time, unlike Drew who used it to torture or punish me when I did.

"So you were getting raped by not only Drew but his business partner as well."

He didn't say it like a question. He knew what it was.

"Not for long with Derik. I got up enough nerve one night and told Drew that I thought Rebecca should go along the next time I was going to the library. I told him that I didn't think it looked good to be running around the city with him so much alone. The bastard agreed. He made sure that Rebecca was with me from that point on."

Our deep conversation was interrupted by none other than my annoying neighbor.

"I'm making coffee. You guys going to sleep all day?" Lauren called from the kitchen.

We both laughed.

"Why don't you have any leftovers in here?" she asked as I made my way out to meet her.

"We had pizza at the shop last night, remember?"

"Yeah, but what happened to that lasagna?"

"You ate that yesterday."

"Great, now I'm going to starve," she pouted.

"Or you could go home and cook. Hey, I know. How about you cook once and let me come over and eat your leftovers?"

Lauren laughed. "Nah, I kind of hate that idea. What are you guys doing today? Wanna go hang out at the mall?"

"No. We're staying in today," Dawson said, joining us. I knew then that our conversation wasn't over.

"You guys are pathetic. You act like you're forty or something," she stated.

"I am forty," Dawson said. I laughed. He wasn't forty. He was only thirty.

I made us all breakfast and noticed how Dawson kept staring at me. It wasn't his sexy "I want you" stare. It was more of trying to determine whether or not I was okay, kind of stare. I wasn't okay, and was beginning to wonder if I ever would be. Some days I did think I was okay, and couldn't be better. Other days, like that day, I questioned it.

I smiled a warm smile at him. He returned it.

After Lauren left, we got dressed and walked down the path to the beach. It was chilly but not too bad for October in Maine. Dawson held my hand as we walked. He was quiet, and I didn't quite know what to say. We spoke to John, out for his daily walk with his dog, and then sat in the sand. The sand was warm from the sun. It felt nice, therapeutic.

"I want to know how you got here, Ry."

I knew it was just a matter of time before the questions continued. I picked up a handful of warm sand and let it funnel through the bottom of my hand. I looked up at him, and he leaned in and kissed me.

"Please talk to me," he begged. "I think maybe getting it off your chest will help."

"It doesn't help, Daw. It makes me relive it."

"I need to know, Ry."

"Because you need to decide whether or not you should marry me?" It wasn't actually a question. I was just stating a fact.

"I am marrying you, Riley Murphy. I love you. But we have been together for over a year, and I know that there is so much that you haven't disclosed. Why won't you tell me?"

"Why did I ever get involved with a cop? I should have gone out with Levi. He probably wouldn't care about my past. But no. I had to go fall in love with someone with investigating training."

"Investigating training?" Dawson said lightheartedly with a smile. I smiled back. I couldn't help it. He was just too darn cute.

I took a deep breath. "What do you want to know?"

"I want to know everything, but right now I just want you to tell me how you left. What made you decide to leave?"

"Remember that I told you that Rebecca started to go everywhere with Derik and me?"

"Mm hmm."

"Well, after a few times. Derik stopped stalking me in the library. He was pissed that he couldn't get me alone anymore, and pretty much pretended that I didn't exist."

"Did Derik always drive you?"

"Mostly, I think he was the only one that Drew trusted. Drew gave me a cell phone so he could track my whereabouts and call when he wanted."

"Did you drive?"

I snorted. "No. I did get my driver's license when I turned twenty-one. I'm not sure why. I was never allowed to leave without Derik, Rebecca and sometimes Jena, but if I were with Jena, either Derik or Drew himself followed."

"And Rebecca?" he asked.

"We were in the library right after Drew had agreed to keep her on for one more year. I was looking for a book that I had been waiting to come out. It was the third in a series."

I smiled, when I noticed that Dawson wasn't the least bit interested in the book that I had been so excited about.

"Anyway, I looked up, and Rebecca was giving me some sort of a strange look. We were never close, like in talking about anything personal. We talked, but she would mostly just listen. I think she was afraid of what Drew would hear."

"What, Rebecca," I asked.

"You need to leave, Morgan," she stated, and for some reason I knew that she wasn't talking about leaving the library. I feigned ignorance anyway.

"I have twenty more minutes," I stated.

"You need to leave Drew, Morgan. I am going to help you. We have nine months to get you out of there, and I will be gone. I don't think I would ever forgive myself if I left and didn't at least try. I may end up dead, but at least I would die without a guilty conscious."

"Rebecca, you know that I can't just leave. I can't even leave the house without a babysitter. I have nowhere to go. I wouldn't go back to where I came from. He would just find me."

"We are going to figure it out. I promise Morgan."

I kept looking at Dawson, trying to read his face. Every time that I did, he leaned in and kissed me.

"So, how did you two scheme up your disappearance?"

"We never talked about it again for a month. Drew had beaten me pretty good one evening, and the next day she brought it up again while she brought me food."

"Why did he beat you up?"

"I thought you wanted to know how I got out."

"I want to know it all," he insisted.

I turned my gaze back to the little mountain that I'd been forming from funneling sand through my hand.

"It was time for another event and I had to go," I started with a heavy sigh. I hated Drew's events, dinner parties, and prospect meetings. I knew what it meant. I was never going to make it through one of his engagements without messing up. He knew it. He thrived on it. He knew that we would come home, and he would play his sick games with me. That was really the only time that he raised a hand to me. It was inevitable. I would screw up somehow.

"I was having my hair and makeup done when he came in to check on my progress. He was rushing me, or the stylists, I guess. For some reason I felt that I wasn't intended to go to this particular event. I overheard him telling someone that I wasn't feeling well, and I wasn't going to be able to make it. He then went on to suck up to whoever was insisting that I be there."

"I'm actually looking forward to this night," he whispered close to my ear, holding his hand around my throat while he glared at me through the mirror with a warning.

I listened to the normal lecture in the back of the limo. Don't talk to anyone, but Jena. Don't look at anyone, don't answer questions, and the most important one of all that night. I was in no way allowed to talk to Mr. Callaway alone, and if he asked, I was to tell him that I'd rather my husband stay. I wondered who Mr. Callaway was. I knew that Drew said that he was his father. I wasn't sure that I believed him. He called him Mr. Callaway. Why would anyone call their father by Mr.? Even for a fucked up family like that, it seemed off to me. This would be at least a dozen times that I would have the pleasure of being beaten because he insisted every time that I talk to him in private. Drew never helped. He walked away with his tail between his legs.

Jena never showed only Derik. He said that she had come down with something and wasn't feeling well. I really wanted Jena to be there.

I saw Mr. Callaway being pushed around in his wheelchair. Drew looked over and told me not to look at him.

What the fuck?

I turned my gaze away from him. I knew that I was going to be in trouble regardless, so I asked.

"What's wrong with him, Drew?"

He shot me a death glare. "Don't ask questions that don't pertain to you. That's one," he warned, holding up one finger. One what, I didn't know. It could mean anything with him.

My dress had an open back and Drew kept his hand there. It made me sick that he made all of these people think what a wonderful husband he was. He never kissed me unless it was in public around people he was trying to impress.

Mr. Callaway of course made his way over to me. I couldn't figure out what his interest was in me. Why had he always insisted that I be pulled to the side with him?

"Leave us Drew," he boldly stated as soon as he was wheeled by his caretaker to us.

"With all due respect, Mr. Callaway, I would like for Drew to stay," I tried. I did want him to stay. This guy was just going to ask about my happiness like he cared about my wellbeing.

"Nonsense, leave!" he demanded. Drew walked away. I looked past Mr. Callaway and Drew held up two fingers. I almost rolled my eyes at him, but caught myself, knowing that I would get the third finger.

Mr. Callaway gently took my hand, beckoning me to sit. "You look absolutely gorgeous, as always."

"Thank you, sir."

"How are you doing? I missed you last month for our grand opening."

I had no idea what he was talking about. Drew didn't tell me things that pertained to his business.

"Drew said you weren't feeling well. Is everything okay?"

No. You old moron, I am married to a monster. I don't feel so well at all.

"Yes. I'm fine. Thank you for asking. It was just a little bug," I lied.

"How is Drew treating you? Everything okay at home?"

What the hell? Who the hell are you, and why do you care?

"Yes, everything is wonderful."

I had no idea what this guy's deal was, but for some reason he felt the need to go on and on about his son. Michael. I mean, I'm not cold hearted or anything. I did have compassion for the guy losing his only son. I just couldn't understand why he felt the need to tell me, especially with my obstinate husband glaring scalpels at me.

Chapter 10

"What was the party for?" Dawson interrupted when I got silent, thinking about the party.

"I don't know, some software launch or something," I lied. I wasn't about to tell him Drew owned fifteen different jewelry stores throughout the country. It wouldn't be hard to pinpoint the Callaway name to them now that I had volunteered the old man's name. It was better that he thought he was some kind of a software developer from Indiana. Maybe someday I would tell him, but not yet. I couldn't take the chance. I knew Dawson would go after him, and probably end up dead.

"Why didn't he want you to be alone with this man?"

I shrugged my shoulders. "I don't know. I still don't know. I never did figure out what his interest was in me. Drew had told me the first time that I met him that his father was none of my business, but I'm not so sure if the guy was truly his dad."

"Did you ever meet any of his family?"

"No. I don't even know if he had family, other than Mr. Callaway."

"What happened after the party?"

"Let's go up to the house, and save that for another time," I tried.

He pulled me toward him causing me to knock over my sand creation with my foot. He kissed the corner of my mouth and then whispered.

"I love you, Riley, and that was a real nice try," he smiled.

I leaned my back to his side, and he put his arm around me.

"We left almost immediately after Mr. Callaway was wheeled away. Drew didn't say a word all the way home. He did put his hand out for my rings once again which I always handed over to him."

"Where are you going?" Drew asked once we were inside.

"To change?" I said in a question, asking for permission.

"Uh-uh, go to the gym. I want you to watch."

I knew he was talking about the mirrored wall, but I asked anyway. "Watch what?"

That was the first blow to my face that night, and the blood from my lip ran down my sky blue dress.

"That!" he demanded and shoved me toward the gym.

I looked around the gym puzzled. The room was empty. The weight bench, the elliptical, the treadmill, it was all gone. Other than the one padded bench, and the small refrigerator in the corner where bottles of water were kept, the room was empty, and I didn't understand why. I took a towel from a rack in the gym and dabbed it on my already swollen lip, glad that it was still there.

At the sound of the doorknob, I jumped, but it hadn't turned. I heard it lock. I walked over to it and sure enough; I was locked in. I didn't understand that either. All Drew had to do was tell me to stay in there, and I would have. It was just another one of his mind games.

I stood there for probably ten minutes waiting for I didn't know what. I just knew that his plan *wasn't* to lock me in that room and leave me alone. I took a deep breath and walked to the far wall. I slid down the wall and sat on the shiny hardwood flooring.

"Stand up!" I heard him say through an intercom that I didn't know was there.

Okay. Here we go with the head games.

I stood up but stayed leaning against the wall.

"Walk to the middle of the room and stand in front of the mirror. You need to see what a stupid bitch you are."

I wanted to yell, fuck you. It was a very strong urge, but I didn't do it. I walked to the middle of the room and stood in front of the mirror like a proper little submissive.

It must have been fifteen minutes before he spoke again, and that was because I spoke first.

"Can I take off my heels?" I asked to the empty room.

"Did I say you could take off your heels?"

I rolled my eyes and didn't answer. My feet were killing me and my lower calves were starting to ache.

"You can take off the dress," he said.

I didn't want to take off the dress. I wanted to take off the damn shoes. The dress was the only thing that I had on. It was cut low so I couldn't wear a bra with it, and of course I wasn't allowed to wear panties. I did as he requested and slid the dress from my shoulders, and down to the floor.

"Turn around," I heard him say from wherever the hell he was.

I turned half a turn, and he told me to keep going. I turned some more and when I stopped he told me to keep turning.

What the fuck.

I was standing naked in the middle of the room wearing three inch stilettos, and he wanted me to play ring around the fucking rosy. I managed to play his stupid game for about fifteen minutes, and I couldn't do it anymore. My legs felt like jello, and were going to give out. That's exactly what happened. My ankle twisted, and I went down. I sat on the floor and grabbed my ankle. It hurt so badly. I thought for sure it was broken.

Drew laughed. I slid the heel from my foot and flung it across the room. I didn't know where the cameras were, but that was what I was aiming for.

"You shouldn't have done that," he warned.

I couldn't help it. I had enough. My ankle hurt. My legs felt like they were going to fall off from prancing around like some idiot for him, and my tongue wouldn't stay away from my swollen lip.

"Fuck you!" I yelled. I hadn't said anything remotely close to that since my first week there.

He didn't say anything. I knew that he would be bursting through the door at any second. I didn't care. I was pissed.

He didn't come, and all of a sudden the room went pitch black. That made me supremely happy. The bastard couldn't see me anymore. I removed the other shoe. My ankle still hurt, but I knew that it wasn't broken. The lights stayed off for maybe twenty minutes. I slammed my eyes shut all of a sudden at the bright light while my eyes tried to adjust to the abrupt brightness.

"Move to the middle of the room," I heard him say.

I started to stand and then-stopped. I didn't care because it hurt to stand on my ankle.

"Crawl."

I did as he said, and crawled like an animal back to the center. I sat in the middle of the room waiting for instructions. He didn't send any more, and my heart sank when I heard the door being unlocked.

I knew I was in for a night of hell as soon as I saw the look in his eyes and the bag that he carried, at least until he got off anyway.

He stood right in front of me and looked down.

"What did you say to him?" he asked in an angry tone.

"Nothing," I said, taking my second blow to my face

"You're a liar. What did you say?"

"He only asked if I were happy and how I was doing. I told him yes that I was happy, and I was doing fine."

He grabbed my hair and pulled his face close to mine. "What did I tell you before we went there?"

"I tried not to talk to him without you. You're the coward who walked away."

I didn't mean to say the last part out loud. It just came out, and I knew that I would pay for it.

"Stand up," he demanded.

I stood, and he turned me sideways so that he could get a nice long stroke when he brought his hand to my bare ass. It hurt. It hurt like a son of a bitch, but I wasn't going to let him know that. He made sure that we were facing the mirror so that I could watch.

"You've been here five years. Are you ever going to learn to do what you're told?"

Should I tell him to go to hell now or later?

"I don't know what you want. Nothing I could do would ever make you happy."

I took another welt from his hand on that one.

"Did I tell you to talk?"

"Yeah, kind of, you did ask me a question," I smartly said. What was wrong with me? I never defied Drew nor did I smart off to him.

Third crack to my naked ass.

"Sit," he demanded.

I did, and he made me turn toward the mirror. He stood behind me and reached into his bag of goodies. It wasn't anything new, and I had been introduced to that vibrator before.

He turned it on high power and ran around my collarbone and to my nipple while he watched our reflection in the mirror.

"Do you think you're going to come, Morgan?" He whispered in my ear. I could smell the whiskey on his breath.

Well that's a stupid question.

"No."

"And why not?" he asked, teasing my nipple with the vibration. "Keep your eyes on the mirror," he demanded when I turned away.

"Because, I was a bad girl."

Fucking asshole.

I was twenty-four and had to tell him that I was a bad girl. I hated him. I could have shot him in the head and never felt bad about it. I could have spit on him while he bled out and died.

"Spread your legs, bad girl."

I did as I was told, and he moved the vibration between my legs. He pulled my hands back so that I could lean back more and hold myself up. I tried not to moan as he slid the vibrator up my already wet folds.

Stupid vagina, always taking his side.

"Does that feel good, bad girl?"

It was a trick question. I didn't answer.

Drew moved around and sat in front of me, spreading me as far as my legs would allow. He rubbed the hard plastic vibrator down to my anus, and I knew exactly where it was going to end up.

"Open your eyes," he demanded when I felt the vibrator penetrate my opening.

He slid it in slowly, enjoying the show as his free hand massaged my wet core. I was okay with that. I was used to being violated there. It was the next device that he pulled from his bag that I despised. I almost stopped breathing when he pulled out the rod that would send an electrical current through all of my female parts, bring me to an almost immediate orgasm, and then stop. I hated that stupid thing and would have loved to shove it up his ass.

He smiled broadly when he saw the look on my face. He moved the vibrator in and out of my ass a few times, torturing me with the rod in his hand. I just wished he would hurry up and get it over with, but that was too easy. He got off on seeing the distress written all over my face.

"This hurts my knees. Move onto the bench," he demanded.

Poor fucking baby.

I didn't mind the bench. The floor was rather hard. I limped when I put pressure on my sore ankle. Drew sat at the end of the bench and put both my feet on the tops of his legs. The vibrator was slowly moved back to where Drew wanted it. He brought the wand to my clit, and I jumped. He laughed. It wasn't turned on.

Dickhead.

He pressed his thumb inside of me while he moved the vibrator in and out of me. I wanted to come, oh, how I wanted to come. He continued his toying with me and then stood to remove his clothes. He moved to the top of me and stroked himself on my lips a little, before telling me to open my mouth. He fucked my mouth until he was close. I wished he would have just finished so that I could be finished. He wasn't about to do that. He wanted to play.

He moved back below me, straddling the bench and placing my feet back on his legs.

"I want to see if I can feel this too," he said, pulling me toward his erection, sliding into me. He hissed as he pulled my hips in and out of him a couple of times, but stopped. I knew he was getting close, and if he would just allow some friction to his shaft we could be done with his charade.

He laughed again when I tensed as he turned on the rod that was going to drive me insane. It truly was a torturing rod, and no matter how hard you tried, you couldn't come with it.

Drew pushed himself deep inside of me, and I held my breath as he brought the tip of the rod to my core. He did it in slow motion, rubbing it in as much as he could. He split me more with his thumb and forefinger and watched my face as he quickly touched my clit. I called out in pleasuring pain. He rubbed me with his thumb, spread me again with his fingers, and repeated the process.

"I don't feel any current, but you tighten around my cock like crazy."

Glad you're enjoying it, fuckface.

I didn't know how much more I was going to be able to take. I wanted nothing more out of life than to be released at that moment. I don't know why thirteen, but that is how many times I had to endure the torturing rod. He probably wasn't even counting, but that was the magic number when he got bored. I breathed a sigh of relief when he laid it on the floor.

"Roll over," he demanded, pulling the other object from my rectum.

I lay on the skinny bench, and he moved my hands back wanting me to spread myself for his entrance.

"Turn your head," he demanded, wanting me to watch. I did, not removing my hands from behind me, and he pushed my hair from my eyes. I watched and felt the drip from the cool gel.

"Keep your eyes opened," he demanded when I tightened them after feeling him penetrate my opening. He frantically pumped in and out of my ass, and I knew it was just a matter of time before he let go. He didn't. He pulled out and told me to get up.

I got up, and he lay on the bench with his hands above his head. He stared up at me like I was stupid or something. He bucked his hips, and I didn't know whether he wanted me to sit on him or give him a blowjob. He jumped up and hit me right across my right eye.

"Sit down!" he screamed and lay back down.

He moaned as I took him in and out of my ass for a few minutes, and finally, he released.

He stood and dressed as I caught a glimpse of my battered face in the mirror. He left, locking the door behind him.

Great.

It was just a matter of time before the room went black again. I used the opportunity to release myself. I knew I only needed a minute and hoped the lights didn't come back on before I was done. They didn't, and although I didn't want to stay in the empty room, I wasn't frustrated anymore.

I was squirming in the warm sand after talking about it with Dawson. I needed relief.

"He kept you in the room all night?" Dawson asked.

"Yes. Can we go up to the house now?"

"You still haven't told me how you got out."

I leaned over and kissed him. "Daw, I can't right now. I need for you to take me up to the house and back to bed."

"Talking about it makes you want to have sex, doesn't it?"

"I don't know if it makes me want to have sex, but it definitely makes me frustrated."

What Dawson did next took me by surprise. He took off his jacket and laid it across my lap.

"Lay back," he whispered to my lips.

"What are you doing?" I asked, already listening.

"Taking care of you, so you'll keep talking to me."

I looked around at the empty beach. John would be walking back soon, but as soon as I felt him unbutton my jeans and slide down the zipper, I didn't care.

"Damn, you do need this," Dawson agreed, feeling how wet I was.

It was quick. I don't know if it even took five minutes. I softly moaned, and Dawson kissed me, really kissed me.

"I love you," he said on my lips.

"Hmmm, I love you too," I replied, still trying to come down from what had just happened.

"Okay, you spent the night in the room," Dawson said, getting right back to what I didn't want to talk about anymore.

"Three nights. The only light that I saw for three days was when I opened the little refrigerator. It almost blinded me every time I reached in for water or the veggies and fruit that he had left for me. He knew he was locking me in that room before we ever went to that stupid party. By the time I got out of there I was ready to go crazy. I think that was the whole point."

I stopped there, and although I wasn't happy about the house fire in town, coming across Dawson's hand held scanner, I was happy that he had to leave for a while. That was enough for one day.

Dawson was gone for around three hours. I had a nice supper made when he got back.

"Hmm, something smells heavenly," he said, wrapping his arms around my waist and kissing the side of my neck in the kitchen.

"Cube steak, mashed potatoes, gravy, corn, and rolls," I described as I turned to him. "And you smell like smoke. Is everyone okay?"

"Yeah, everyone was fine. The house is pretty much history though. Do I have time for a shower?"

"Yes, I'll set the table."

I was just getting our two plates down from the cabinet when Lauren came in.

"I swear I can smell your cooking from inside my house," she said, sitting at the table.

I laughed and grabbed another plate. She would just be at my house later looking for food. I figured she may as well join us, not that she wasn't going to anyway.

"Do you ever eat at home?" Dawson asked, coming to join us.

"Not really. Why would I?" she asked, and the bad part was, she was dead serious.

She did stay and help clean up and was then left.

Dawson and I settled into the sofa to watch Sunday night football. I had never watched football until that fall. It was one of my favorite pastimes with him. We had our favorite teams and mine was the 49ers. His was Green Bay. I loved for him to sit and explain the plays to me while I cuddled up with him on the couch. I had never felt so safe and secure before him, and I cherished the feel of his arms strongly around me.

I was glad for the distraction and was really hoping that he didn't bring up Drew again that night. I knew that he wasn't going to drop it for good, but I was eager to let it go for a night.

"Take your sweats off," he requested, pulling the blanket from the back of the couch.

"What are you going to do, Sherriff?" I asked in a flirty tone as he lifted me out of them himself.

He didn't answer. "Roll over," he requested.

He didn't do what I was expecting at all, and massaged me from my neck to my feet. I don't think I have ever felt anything so relaxing in my life. His strong hands felt amazing as he rubbed the tension right out of me. I'm sure I moaned more than once.

"Roll over," he said again. This time with a more raspy sensual tone.

Hold your horses vagina.

I was instantly aroused when he slowly and seductively slid my panties over my hips. He ran his hand down my chest and my stomach. I swear his hands were magical. Not really. I knew I felt this way with him because he loved me, and he wanted me to feel just what I was feeling.

Dawson made slow love to me and stared down at me with the most emotional eyes ever. I was sure he could see my battered soul. That's how deep he was into me.

"I love you, Riley," he whispered as he pressed himself in and out of me.

"Hmm, I love you too, Daw," I was spent. I tried to wait on him, but I couldn't. I moaned a soft physical moan and let go.

Once I was coherent enough after the amazing orgasm, I opened my eyes and looked up at him.

He bent and kissed me softly. "I love pleasing you," he smiled. I was happy that he loved it. I loved that he loved it.

We lay on the sofa naked, tangled in each other, and finished watching the game. He got up and took my hand after turning off the television. We again lay naked engrossed in each other.

"Do you want to talk?" he whispered in the dark.

"That's a rhetorical question," I stated, and he snickered.

"You don't have to talk anymore tonight," he said, stressing the word tonight, meaning that I *was* going to talk.

I didn't have any recurring nightmares that night. I was actually surprised that I didn't with all the reminiscing that Dawson insisted on.

We spent the next few nights at Dawson's house because he just couldn't wait for one more day to start a fire in his fireplace. It was cozy, and I loved sitting in front of it wrapped in his arms. I loved making love in front of it even more. He hadn't asked me about my past anymore, and I sure as hell wasn't going to bring it up.

We went to bed fairly early one night while at his house, and I have no idea what triggered it. I was happy and in love, not thinking about Drew at all. I did have a nightmare, and woke up panting and gasping for air, with Dawson holding me tight.

"You're okay. I've got you," he whispered over and over as I came to my senses.

"Dawson?"

"Shhhh, I'm right here, Ry."

I realized that he really was there, and instantly relaxed.

"Do you want to talk about it?" he asked, kissing my head.

"No. Just don't let me go."

I never did tell Dawson about my dream that night, but I did come to the conclusion that he only asked about my past when I woke him in a panic. That was my new goal in life. Don't have a nightmare and Dawson wouldn't ask about where I had come from. That dream too was very real, although it had nothing at all to do with my life with Drew. It was about

Dawson. Derik had shot him in the head right in front of me while Drew dragged me by my hair to the awaiting limousine. It haunted me for days. I would never forgive myself if something happened to him because of me. I didn't think that I could live without him. He was too much a part of me, and I loved him more than anything in life.

I started taking three instead of two of Starlight's all natural sleep aids. It helped. I slept sound without being haunted from my past. It had been almost a month since I had woken trembling, and scared.

Dawson and I, Lauren and Levi all got together at Star's for Thanksgiving. We had a lot of fun yelling at the television for our favorite football teams. Star was an awesome cook, and I think everyone ate more than their fair share. We didn't leave Star's until almost midnight, and I went home with Dawson, only because neither of us wanted to be woken by my annoying neighbor who we both loved dearly. We just wanted to sleep in.

We went right to bed and for some reason Dawson decided that I needed to talk again. I was extremely annoyed with him. We had a great day and had just made beautiful love together, and he wanted to go and ruin it.

"You still haven't told me how you got away from Drew," he said with a soft kiss. I was glad that it was dark, and he couldn't see me roll my eyes.

I rolled over to my side, and he snuggled up to my back.

"I'm too tired for that." I wasn't tired at all. I just didn't want to end a perfect day that way.

"You can't avoid it forever, Ry."

"I could if you shut up about it."

"But, you know I'm not going to."

I sat up. I was pissed. I didn't know where it was coming from because I didn't have that emotion. I was never allowed to have that emotion. I didn't care. If he wanted to do this then that's what we were going to do.

"Fine, Dawson. What would you like to know? Would you like to hear more about how fucked up my sex life was or were you thinking more along the lines of when he beat the shit out of me?" I asked, angrily.

"Riley, uh-uh, we're not doing this. I'm sorry. I didn't mean to upset you."

Dammit all the way to hell. Why did he have to be so good to me?

"I'm sorry," I apologized, and he pulled me to him.

We lay quietly for a long time. The only noise was a dog barking down the street somewhere, and his occasional kiss to my head every now and then.

***

"Rebecca came into my room once I was allowed out of the gym," I began, and I felt Dawson hold me a little tighter. "I didn't feel well. My face was pretty busted up, and my ankle was black and blue. She got close enough when she set my supper on the nightstand so that she couldn't be heard through Drew's security system, and whispered.

"I have a plan."

I looked at her, and she looked back with eyes that told me not to speak. She winked and left me with a little bit of hope.

A week later Derik drove us to the library and for some reason followed us in. I assumed it was because Drew had told him to.

That didn't stop Rebecca. She got a magazine and pretended to point and talk about an article.

"You need to take some of his money," she started.

I looked at her with a "you're crazy" expression, and she gave me a look to turn back to the book.

I glanced back to the magazine. "How the hell do you propose that I do that?"

"I know where he keeps the key to his office. We'll wait until he is out of town and go in."

"And do what?"

"I have been in that office numerous times. We can get on his computer. We'll open a fake account, and you can start moving some money."

"You're nuts. What the hell am I supposed to do with it once I have it?"

"I have been talking to a lady who is going to help you get a new identity."

I looked up at her again, and she tapped the page and pretended to laugh, knowing that Derik was watching us.

"He'll find me, Rebecca," I assured her.

"Not with a new identity and a move someplace in the middle of nowhere."

I looked up to her again, but this time she didn't point at the magazine. She smiled a warm; it'll be okay, smile.

"I'm scared," I admitted.

"You are scared every time you see that bastard come home. Would you rather be scared with him or without him?"

I thought about what she was suggesting nonstop. I tried all evening to read the book that I had gotten from the library, but my mind kept going to her plan. Could I really just disappear and become someone else? The thought of it caused a flood of adrenaline. I wondered where I would live, what my new name would be, about having my own car, a job. I could have a job and not be forced to stay home all the time.

I jumped when Derik and Drew walked into the living room, arguing about losing a big account. I closed my book and started to leave them alone.

"Don't move," Drew demanded with a pointed finger in my direction. He never looked at me and kept going with the conversation. I listened closer. Maybe I should start paying more attention. If I were somehow going to steal his money, I should probably know a little more about it.

"It's not dead yet, Drew, just calm down," Derik said, sucking up to him.

"He's looking at a two hundred thousand dollar cushion cut diamond with two trapezoid cut diamonds on the sides totaling 1.63 ctw. I have nothing of that magnitude."

"I'll find something," Derik promised. I hated him.

"You better hope you do," Drew threatened. "Get out of here, I need to relieve some stress," he demanded. I was about to be his stress relief.

Drew walked over and closed the pocket doors behind him. He sat on the couch and took my book.

"John Grisham? Didn't he make a movie?"

Yeah, a bunch, asshole.

"Yes, a few."

Drew pulled my back to his chest and handed me the book. "Read it to me," he demanded, spreading my legs.

Why? You're too ignorant to understand it anyway.

"Read it to you?" I asked.

"Morgan," he warned. "You know that I hate it when you repeat stupid questions. Yes, start from the beginning and read it," he demanded.

It was an older book, but I had never read it before, but always wanted to. I was only allowed to check one a week out, and I wasn't allowed to download anything on my Kindle. He took care of the books that I was to read on it. All of a sudden I was happy to be reading The Rain Maker to him. I would have hated to read the smut from my Kindle to him. I was thankful that he never thought about it.

Drew sat up a little and removed his shirt, and then slid to the far end of the couch. He patted the sofa between his legs and I slid in. I hated being nestled into his bare chest. There was nothing sexy about it at all. I don't mean him. He was sexy as hell, but only on the outside.

I started from the beginning as he pulled my sundress over my legs and caressed the inside of my leg. I swear if I could disown my vagina I would have. I had no idea what I was reading. The closer his fingers came to my sex that I was sure was already wet, the harder it was for me to read. I stopped when his fingers slid up me.

"Keep reading."

Fuck...

I knew my breathing was becoming erratic, and I didn't even know if I was reading in order. I could have been reading the same sentence over and over and wouldn't have known it. My eyes closed briefly when he applied a soft circular motion to my bullet.

"You're all wet, Morgan," he whispered into my hair.

You think?

I don't know if it was guilt from the light bruising still on my face or what it was, but Drew was a lot more attentive that night than normal. I was trying my damnedest to focus on what I was reading and not the way his fingers were antagonizing me.

"Come for me," he requested, picking up speed.

I was afraid that it was a trick. I kept reading.

He moved from behind me to in front of me, spreading my legs on each side of him. I squirmed into his fingers as he slid his middle finger inside of me while his thumb tortured my clit.

"Keep reading," he said when I stopped.

He did let me come, but it wasn't easy. I wasn't allowed to stop reading, not even when I was breaking and spiraling from my reached ecstasy.

Drew stood and removed his dress pants and told me once again to keep reading when I stopped. He lifted my legs to my chest. I knew he wasn't paying one bit of attention to what I was reading. It was nothing but a mind game. I stopped reading again when he came between my legs on his knees and entered me. Again, he reminded me that I was to keep reading.

I didn't want to read. I wanted to come again, and I knew that the chances of my being allowed to do that were slim to none. Drew moved in and out of me while his thumb circled my core, and I tried my best to focus on the words in front of me.

Chapter 11

"Okay. Stop talking about the sex, and get to the part where you left," Dawson interrupted.

"I am getting to that part," I replied, but didn't want to get to any more parts. I wanted to have an orgasm.

"No. You're not. You are going to stop any second now and tell me that you need for me to take care of you."

Shit...

"I kind of like that idea better than talking," I admitted, trying to be sexy. I wondered if I could take control. Could I lead him rather than him always leading me? I would have never tried it with Drew. I knew from the bottom of my heart that Dawson would never hurt me, physically or emotionally. Not intentionally anyway. I decided to try. Hey, I was already miles away from my comfort zone anyway, might as well add another milestone.

I straddled him leaning against the headboard, and his hands went to my hips, grasping the satin material in his hands. Okay. Maybe I should have thought about it for a few days before I acted on it. I didn't know what to do next, and I felt self-conscious, and ashamed of myself for some reason.

Dawson sensed it. I swear the man could read my thoughts.

"You can start by kissing me." He smiled as if he knew my struggles.

I did kiss him, and his hands ran up my back and sides, lifting the material as they traveled. I moaned in his mouth and ground into him. He rolled me over, and I was glad. I wasn't ready to take the lead. I had wanted to give him a blowjob for months now, but he wouldn't ask for it or better yet demand it. That's what I needed him to do, but he would never do it. That, I was sure of, although I had a feeling he would enjoy it. I was somewhat of an expert at it. I knew that it wasn't going to be that night. I couldn't work up the nerve to do it.

Dawson towered over me, kissing and whispering how beautiful I was, how much he loved me, and how much he loved making love to me. I loved him too, but at that given moment I just needed a fire put out.

"Tell me what you need, Ry," Dawson's warm words spilled out just below my ear.

I didn't know how to respond. I knew he wasn't saying it like Drew had when he would make me tell him to fuck my pussy or tell him that I wanted him in my mouth, or sick shit like that. It was more attentive toward me, but I still didn't know what I wanted. Well, I knew what I wanted I just knew that I couldn't say it out loud.

"Touch me."

What? Where the hell did that come from?

Dawson slid his hand down my body and across the silk of my panties. I moaned and thrust my hips into him. I knew I was wet, and he could feel it through the cloth, but I didn't care. I wanted to take them off anyway. He moved his fingers around the elastic on my right leg and I felt faint. Holy mother of Pearl, did he feel good. He slid me out of my panties and continued his task. I finally worked up the nerve to release him from his own constricting jeans, and moved my hands between us. I didn't break the contact of our lips. I needed that distraction.

I worked my hand up and down him while his continued pleasing me, beneath him. It was a small step, but I felt proud. I wished I could get enough nerve to tell him to do that thing that he did so well with his tongue and mouth, but I would surely die of embarrassment.

"What are you thinking right this second?" he whispered to my lips.

"I don't know, Dawson," I panted with a heavy breath.

"Yes. You do. Tell me what you need, Ry?"

"I can't. I just need for you to do it."

"I can't read your mind."

"I beg to differ. You're always reading my mind."

"And I think I know what you want, but you have to tell me. I want you to be open with me, and I want to give you your every desire."

We kissed some more, and I was hoping he was done with that request.

"Tell me, Riley."

"I want you to go down on me."

There. I said it.

I meant to say that he was already doing everything right, but for some reason those words just fell right out of my mouth.

"That's my girl," he smiled with one more kiss as he made his way ever so torturing down my body.

We both moaned at precisely the same time. Drew could have never made me feel like that. The orgasms weren't even the same. Orgasms with Drew were just that, an orgasm. With Dawson they were a mixture of emotions, love, sensations, feelings, senses and affection, all tangled up in one.

As soon as I felt Dawson sensually slide his finger into me, I let go, clenching the sheet and arching my back from the release.

Dawson made his way back to my lips and then moved to my side.

Um...What are you doing?

I was puzzled briefly as he pulled me close and whispered that he loved me.

"I love you too, but don't you have something to finish?" I bluntly asked. We hadn't had sex yet.

"You did finish. I'm sure of it," he smiled.

"You didn't."

"I don't need to. This wasn't about me."

"Bullshit, Dawson. You have a hard on."

Dawson laughed at my boldness. "I wasn't planning on taking care of me. I want you to know that I will always take care of you without asking for something in return."

"Okay. That's just great," I said, feeling my anger evolving.

"What, Ry?"

"You. You're not a God damn shrink. Stop trying to fix me. That's the stupidest thing I have ever heard of. Why couldn't you have just made love to me? Why do you have to go and investigate everything?"

"You're mad because I am trying to show you that I am here for you?"

I blew out a puff of air and dropped back to the bed. It was over. I didn't want to have sex anymore anyway, and if he brought up one thing about finishing my story, I swore, I would punch him.

He didn't. He never said another word. He snuggled next to me and wrapped his arm around my waist. I presumed he didn't know what to say. I didn't know what to say. I just knew that I was tired of the constant Dr. Phil attitude. It was driving me crazy.

◇◇()◇◇

"You okay?" Starlight asked as I dropped the refill of the Styrofoam cups for the second time.

I wasn't okay. I had a horrible headache, and just wanted to go home to my couch alone. I didn't want Dawson there, and just wanted to be alone. I knew he planned on coming there. We hadn't spent a night apart in months, but I needed a break. I needed to breathe without him up my ass.

"Yeah, I'm fine, just fighting a headache is all."

Starlight walked over to the shelf and looked through the different teas. She filled my peace mug with hot water and seeped the teabag.

"Drink this. It's lemon balm; it'll help. I have some good news for you, well maybe. I hope it's good news anyway."

Star stopped talking when a tourist couple came to pay for their novelty items, coffee and Danishes. I thanked them after ringing them up and turned back to Star.

"Drink," she said first, wanting me to drink the herbal tea. "I just got the schedule for the next swap meet. We're going to Vegas, baby," she said excited.

I was actually excited this time. We had such a great time when we went the last time, once I relaxed and knew that I wasn't going to run into Drew, that is. I thought that Dawson and I needed a break.

"When?" I asked.

"March."

Great, that was almost four months away, a whole winter.

"I can't wait," I said, trying to sound excited. She talked on and on about it, and was going to make hotel reservations right away to insure we got closer to the expo this time.

"Why don't you go on home? I'll close up."

I looked at the clock, and it was almost three. I knew she wouldn't be overwhelmed with customers, so I took her up on her offer and left, stopping at the grocery store on my way.

"Hi," I answered my cell phone.

"Hey, you still mad at me?"

"I'm not mad at you, Dawson."

"I'm sorry, Ry. I didn't mean anything by it."

"It's fine, Daw."

"Where are you?" he asked, when he heard a car horn blow, figuring that I wasn't at the shop.

"On my way home, I left early."

"Why? You okay?"

I rolled my eyes. I loved that he cared about me. I loved that he loved me, but his constant badgering was almost more than I could take. I couldn't forget my past because he wasn't about to let me. If he wasn't continuously asking me if I was okay, he wanted to talk about it, or rather for me to talk about it.

"Just a little headache, I'm going to go home and take a nap."

"Okay. I'll bring supper home."

"Dawson, can I just be alone tonight?" Why did I just ask him permission to be alone? I was a twenty-six year old woman. I didn't need his permission.

"Please don't push me away, Riley."

"I'm not, Dawson. I am still going to marry you, and I still love you. I just need some alone time."

"I love you."

"I love you too. I'll talk to you later."

I put the few groceries away and lay on my couch. I didn't really have a headache anymore, but I was feeling a bit of, I don't know, self-pity, maybe. I dozed off and slept for all of twenty minutes before Lauren's key unlocked my door, and she let herself in.

"Ry?" she called.

I raised my hand for her to see that I was on the couch.

She bounced around and sat in the chair.

"Watcha doing?"

Really?

"I was trying to take a nap," I stated the obvious, sitting up.

"Are you sick?"

"No. Tired."

"What are you doing for supper?"

"Do you think about anything but food?"

"Yeah. Sex," she smiled.

I smiled too. "What are you doing tonight? Let's order Chinese and have a girl's night."

"I don't think Dawson is going to fit in," she teased.

"He's not invited," I replied.

"Uh oh, did you guys have a fight?"

"No. Not really. I just told him that I wanted to be alone tonight. I feel like he is suffocating me."

"Did you talk to him about it?"

"No. I am tired of talking about it," I said, not talking about the same thing that she was talking about.

Lauren and I wrapped ourselves in warm fuzzy blankets and sat on the back deck with a twelve pack of beer. It was just what I needed. The November sky was dark and cloudy, kind of like my mood, but laughing about silly stuff with Lauren pulled me right away from my self-absorption. We only made it outside for about an hour and were freezing. We ordered Chinese around seven. Lauren flirted with the poor delivery boy something fierce. I couldn't help but laugh at her.

She didn't stay long after that. She woke too early, and it was getting close to her bedtime. I found myself alone and dammit if I didn't miss my sheriff. I was surprised that he hadn't called, but I was sure that he was trying to give me my space.

I showered and cuddled up on the couch as I flipped on the television. I channel surfed for a while, never landing on one certain show. I took a deep breath, giving in and dialed Dawson.

"Feel better?" he asked on the first ring. I smiled. I loved him so much, and then wished that I hadn't been such a prune. He would have been right there with me had I not decided to go all dark on him.

"Yes, and I am sorry."

"What are you sorry for?"

"I don't know. For being such a pain, I guess."

"You're not a pain, Ry. I love you just the way you are."

I snorted. He shouldn't love me. He shouldn't love me at all. He should have run the other way as soon as we met.

"Well, I feel like a real idiot now."

"Why?"

"Because, I am going to bed alone."

"I will be there in twenty minutes," he said. I could see his smile through the phone.

"You will?"

"Unless you don't want me to."

"I want you to."

◇◇()◇◇

I almost missed Las Vegas after enduring winter in Maine. It was freezing, and I was tired of being indoors. Dawson and I spent a lot of time looking at wedding magazines and planning our little wedding, and I freaking loved it.

The week after New Year's, I had gotten out of the shop later than usual. Star was off visiting her daughter, Moonie in Australia. I wanted to go with her. I was sure she was warmer than I was. I locked the back door and scraped the ice from my windshield.

Nine degrees? Really?

I cranked the ignition and my old car didn't like the winter either. It wasn't starting.

I did the only thing I knew to do. I called Dawson.

"Hi, baby. You on your way? I've got a pot of chili, homemade bread, and a warm cozy fire waiting for you.

"That sounds amazing, but my car won't start."

"What's it doing?"

"This," I answered and cranked the key again, holding the phone for him to hear.

"Hmm, sounds like the battery. Go back inside where it's warm. I'll be there in ten minutes."

I did as I was told and watched out the front glass, waiting for Dawson.

I leaned in and kissed him as soon as I got into the warm car. "Thank you."

"You're welcome. I called Charlie. He's going to come over in the morning and take a look at it for you."

"You're my hero," I teased. He was my hero. I didn't know where I would be without him. I didn't even like to think about it.

I think Dawson could have won a cook off contest with his chili. It was the best chili I had ever tasted, and my Grandma Joyce made some pretty good chili. I was so full. I couldn't eat another bite. I tried to get him to let me clean up, but he refused and made me go soak in a hot tub while he did it.

We sat in front of the fireplace and made out like a couple of teenagers. Dawson hadn't asked about my escape since we had gotten into the argument on Thanksgiving. It had been weighing on my mind though. I wasn't having the nightmares and Drew didn't haunt me in my sleep. It wasn't that. I just felt like it was something that was important to Dawson, something that he wanted me to share with him. I felt like I owed it to him. He had been there for me so many times, including that night when my car decided to break down on the coldest day of the year.

"Dawson?" I softly spoke, pulling away from his lips.

"Riley?" He mimicked my tone. I smiled.

I turned my back and snuggled up to his chest. It was easier for me to talk when I didn't have to look at him. He opened his hand, and I placed mine in his.

"You ask the questions," I suggested. He knew what I was talking about.

"Are you sure, Ry?"

"Yes. I'm sure."

"Um, okay. You're here, so I presume you did get into his office. Tell me how that came about."

I was silent for a bit as I thought about that night. It was the dead of summer and extremely hot out. I hadn't even been in the pool because the water wasn't refreshing at all. It felt like bath water, and the air outside was so thick. Drew had come into my room after getting home late and drunk.

"I'm not going to go into the details about that because I will stop and want you to have sex with me," I told Dawson.

"That's okay. I have a pretty good idea how it went, and the truth be known, I hate to hear about the things that he did to you," Dawson said, kissing my head.

"He didn't leave my bed that night. He stayed all night and until noon the next day. He never did that. He held me in his arms, and we watched television together while he did things to me, daring me to come. I did of course, and had to spend an hour episode of Criminal Minds over his lap. He watched the show and would bring his hand in contact with my bare butt when I least expected it. Finally, after he was bored with his game and got off in my mouth, he got up. He gave me my cell phone and told me that he was going out of town that night."

"He kept your phone?"

"Yes, unless he was leaving or I was out, and then I was allowed to have it."

***

Drew disappeared into his office, and I went into the kitchen with Rebecca. She gave me a look, knowing that I had been tied up entertaining Drew all day.

"How much flour does that recipe say?" she asked, nodding to the laptop on the bar.

I walked over to the bar and pulled my feet under me and leaned on the counter. I looked up to her as soon as I saw the quick note on the laptop.

"We have your identity. We need to start acting now."

I read and quickly closed it out when I caught a glimpse of Drew coming. Rebecca was smart and did have a recipe pulled up for some kind of cake she was making.

"What are you doing in here?" Drew angrily asked. I was sure he'd seen me in one of his cameras. He walked up to the laptop and looked at the recipe. He dropped the window to see what was behind it. There was nothing but the mountain wallpaper.

"I was just reading off this recipe for Rebecca. She's going to teach me to cook."

"Why. You don't need to know how to cook."

"Because I have nothing else to do, and it's like a hundred degrees outside."

"I don't like you on the computer. You know that," he said. I was glad that he didn't tell me that Rebecca couldn't teach me to cook.

"It's only a recipe, Drew."

He looked right to Rebecca. "I don't have a problem with it if you don't mind me blocking your internet," he said to her.

She shrugged her shoulders. "I don't care. That recipe is not on the internet. It's from one of many cookbooks that I have downloaded. I don't need to be online to access them."

Drew turned the laptop away from me so that I couldn't see the password that he put in to block all internet access. He really was a stupid son of a bitch. I knew all his passwords. I had sat on his desk while he did what he wanted with me so many times it was pathetic. I knew as soon as he put it in he had typed, all my love with no spaces. I often wondered what it meant. I knew that it wasn't about me. He never in the almost six years that I was there hinted anything about love. He turned the computer back to me and left without another word.

I wished that Rebecca had said more about her plan, but that was all the note had said. We would be alone that night because Drew would be gone.

***

"Wait," Dawson said, interrupting my story again.

"What?" I asked, entwining my fingers with his.

"He left you and Rebecca alone?"

"Yeah, all the time. Why?"

"Why didn't you both just leave?"

"It wasn't that easy, Dawson. I wouldn't have done that anyway. Rebecca had stayed with me and took care of me for almost six years. For one thing, she needed her money when she left. I didn't want her to be associated with me leaving him at all. Not to mention he could log on to his laptop anywhere in the world and go right to the cameras. Every room in the house had cameras. He had called me several times, and asked me things like how was your bath, your snack, your swim. Once, he called to warn me that I was in trouble for going too far in the golf cart. He couldn't hear me when I drove the cart around, but he could see where I went."

I snickered a little. "That was when I called him every name in the book."

"How did you get into his office with all the cameras? Didn't he have one outside of his office?

"Yes he did, and Rebecca was an expert criminal. She really thought things through. I didn't know how in the world she expected us to get in there. I was scared shitless"

I was sitting on the sofa after taking a bath, reading when all of the lights in the house went off. I didn't know where Rebecca was, and wondered what was going on. My cell phone rang, and I answered it right away, seeing that it was Drew.

***

"What the hell is going on there?" he angrily asked.

"I'm not sure. All of the lights just went off."

Rebecca called from the kitchen. "Power's out."

"Rebecca said the power must be out." No sooner did I say that, the lights were back on.

"They're back on," I said.

"Don't hang up until I see for myself," he demanded.

I waited, and it took three minutes for the cameras to reset so that he could see me. I just knew Rebecca was behind it.

Drew hung up without another word. I went back to my book, wishing that I could talk to Rebecca without him hearing. What the hell was she up to?

Another thirty minutes or so went by when the lights mysteriously went out again, and this time Drew called Rebecca. I listened to the one sided conversation from the kitchen. Rebecca told him that she already called the power company. She did... about ten times. She too knew Drew, and knew that he would call them too. She wanted the power company to tell him that they had several calls already.

I was so confused when I finally turned in. I never talked to Rebecca again, and the power had only been out a short time again.

I was sound asleep when Rebecca quickly came into my room. I jumped when I felt the tickle of something soft. It was pitch black again, and the light that usually cast a soft, dim light through my window was out too.

"Hurry. We don't have much time."

"Rebecca, what the hell are you doing?"

"We're going into Drew's office. The lights are going to come back on any minute. Get up!"

I got up, and she moved the pillows under the cover and placed the blonde wig on my pillow. My heart was beating a million miles a minute. She was going to get us both killed.

We had just gotten the door closed when the lights came back on. "How the hell are you turning the lights on and off?" I wanted to know.

She ran right to the computer and moved the mouse, bringing the sleeping computer to life. "Ms. K is taking care of it. I didn't ask questions. I just know how long we have. What's the password to log on?" she asked, sitting in his chair.

I couldn't think. I had seen him put in that password a hundred times, and it wasn't coming to me.

"Come on, Morgan!" Rebecca pleaded.

"Ten karat 4," I yelled in a loud whisper. I didn't know why I was whispering. I knew that the office had no cameras.

I watched while Rebecca pulled up different accounts. When she finally found the one that she was looking for, I stopped her and told her not to take it from that one because he would miss it. I told her to pull up the one in Florence because that was the one he was least involved in. She did, and of course it was password protected. I went through all of the passwords that I could think of, and it was finally the last one that I could remember.

"What the hell are you doing? You can't move that much money," I said when I watched her move seventeen thousand dollars into Lisa Fitzgerald's account.

"I already did," she said hitting 'approve transaction.'

"Who the hell is Lisa Fitzgerald?" I asked.

"Nobody. If he traces it back, he will hit a brick wall," she said logging off.

She ran back to my room and took the blonde hair with her. Five minutes later the power was miraculously restored. I pretended to move a little when the light from outside came into my window.

I freaked a little when my cell phone rang.

Fuck...

I didn't answer right away and feigned sleep. I looked around the room dazed and groggy, trying to put on a good show for Drew. I sat up and reached my phone.

"Why the fuck, aren't you answering your phone?" he yelled.

"I did answer," I said. I didn't know that he called while I was in his office.

"I called you three times."

"I'm sorry. I didn't hear it. Rebecca gave me something for a headache earlier. She said it was Tylenol pm. I must not have heard it. Did you want something? What time is it?" I was proud of the quick sleeping aid response.

"Why the hell does the power keep going out there?"

"Was it out again?" I asked, feigning ignorance.

"Forget it, go back to bed," he said and hung up.

I laid the phone down and pretended to go right back to being sound asleep. I was far from it though. My mind reeled like mad. Rebecca was going to get us both killed. What the hell was she up to? This couldn't possibly work. Could it? The excitement that we may just get away with it made me think about a life. A real life without Drew. Where would I live? Would I have neighbors? I wondered if I would ever be able to be with another man. Probably not, not for a long time anyway. What kind of job could I get? I'd never had a job in my life, other than babysitting my little brother and my cousins back home.

I lay awake, not moving for hours thinking about being free from Drew. I kept my eyes closed and didn't move, afraid Drew was watching me, wherever he was. I knew I would endure some of his tedious crap when he got back, but I didn't care at the moment. I was too excited.

When Drew arrived back home three days later, I was terrified. I tried to hide it as best I could, but I just knew he found the missing money. I was reading a book in a chaise lounge by the pool when he opened the door and told me to follow him into his office. It was fairly early, not even noon yet. My heart sank. He knew.

I got up and wrapped a towel around my body and followed him to his office. Rebecca winked a hang in there wink.

***

"Should I skip this part?" I stopped and looked back at Dawson, asking if he wanted me to skip the bad. He caught my cheek with his lips.

"No. I'm okay. You can continue," he replied, rubbing my arm.

I knew that I would be spending my day in Drew's office while he worked. Once I knew that he didn't know about the missing money, I relaxed and was glad to spend the day with him. I planned on paying more attention to his conversations and what was on the screen of his computer if I got that close.

***

"I called you four times the other night," Drew said, removing my towel. "What are the rules, Morgan?" he asked, running his fingers across the crook of my breast.

"I'm sorry. I didn't feel well that night. I answered as soon as I heard it."

"Are you making excuses, Morgan?" he asked, circling me and breathing his warm words on the back of my neck.

"No. I'm sorry. I should have answered on the first ring."

I could feel that he was already erect when he ground into my back.

"What should we do about your irresponsibility?"

Aw fuck...

I hated it when he made me tell him how he should punish me. I knew the drill. I was to de-pants myself and bend over his desk.

"I would love to spank your ass right now, but I have to be on a conference call in five minutes," Drew whispered into my hair, grinding himself in my backside.

He moved around and sat at his desk. I waited for instructions.

"Come around to this side," he requested. I listened and resumed my position over his desk.

He rubbed my naked ass as he dialed the number on his desk phone. My eyes went right to the folder on the desk. There were over forty thousand dollars donated to various charities last month alone. I was sure he didn't have a clue what half of them even were for. He just liked to keep the noble Callaway Jewels in the public eye.

I stayed bent over his desk while he talked to whomever on his phone. One of them was Derik I was sure.

"No, you can donate to one of them, but that's it. Make sure it is donated by my wife," I heard him say, and wondered why. Had I donated to these charities before? Neither he nor I was ever in the public eye; he made sure of that. I was never allowed to go anywhere except the library, and occasionally out to eat with Derik's wife Jena which I never wanted to do because I had to keep a little digital recorder attached to my cell phone. I was always afraid of saying something wrong. It was inevitable. It was always wrong in his eyes.

I remember having dinner with Jenna and Derik one evening while Drew was out of town. Jenna had gotten up and gone to the bathroom. I could see how Derik was looking at me, and just before he spoke I held up my cell phone showing him the tiny little chip stuck to the back of my phone. He abruptly closed his jaw.

When I felt an ink pen penetrating my rectum, I flinched. Drew opened a drawer in his desk, and I knew that he was lubing up the foreign object so that it would slide in. It did, and he moved it in and out of me as he continued to talk business. That was as bad as it got. I was pleasantly surprised. I was sure I would spend hours enduring his torture, but I didn't. I was also sure that it was for no other reason than he needed relief and had work to do. He didn't have time to play.

He stood, and I heard his zipper slide down, and then felt him slide into me, still holding the phone to his ear. He took me from behind slowly, stopping every so often when he needed to talk. He laid the phone on his desk when he was close and grabbed my hips and really went at it until he released.

Dawson sensed where I was. He could tell I was squirming a little.
***

"Keep talking," he said sliding his hand inside of my flannel pajama pants and the rim around my panties. I could tell that I was wet, and thought that I must be as sick as Drew. Who in their right mind would be turned on after talking about their sexual abuse? Dawson always tried to tell me that there was nothing wrong with me, and nobody could go through what I did and come out scar-less. I supposed that he was right. It was the only sex that I knew for six years. I never had anyone to be attentive with me until Dawson.

I continued to tell Dawson about my day spent naked in Drew's office, but getting a lot of beneficial information. I wasn't sure what I was even saying anymore. He was quickly bringing me to mind blowing orgasm with his fingers. I stopped talking and dropped my head to his chest as I called out and let go.

"You good?" he asked, kissing my hair. I could feel his erection on my back and was sure that he could use a little release himself, but knew that he wouldn't. I was talking, and that was more important than his sexual gratification.

"Yes. Thank you," I rasped. Dawson kept his hand down there and just held it still, cupping me as I continued to talk.

Chapter 12

Drew didn't leave again for six weeks after the first time that Rebecca and I broke into his office. I had no clue where or how long he would be gone. I knew it would be overnight because he took a bag. Rebecca and I had talked a couple of weeks before, and I told her how, when the power had gone out the last time, that Drew made me stay on the phone until the cameras reset. I knew we had three minutes. Our plan was for her to go to the basement and quickly trip the breaker, giving me just enough time to run into his office before the cameras reset, and pray to God that he didn't notice until they were back on.

He must have been away from his computer. He never called because he couldn't see me. I had a story made up that I was in Rebecca's room if he called. I knew that I wasn't allowed in her room, but I was going to tell him that she wasn't feeling well and that I had gone to check on her. I didn't have to worry about it, and once I donated fifteen thousand dollars to the new bank account for my newfound charity. I tapped on the floor. I couldn't text or call because I was afraid that Drew would find out. The lights blinked and I ran to the sofa and back to the show that I may or may not have been watching.

I don't think I've ever had that much adrenaline forcefully pumping through my body in my life.

He was only gone for a couple of days that time and again when he had returned I thought for sure that he knew. I just knew that he had found out about the missing money. He didn't mention it, and when he came out of his office later in the afternoon, I asked him if I could have Rebecca take me to the library. I wasn't about to knock on his door and ask, so I just waited for him to come out.

He ran his finger down my arm with some sort of seductive look. "Do you need me to download some more books on your e-reader?"

"No. I have plenty on there. I would rather go to the library and get out of here for a little while."

"Were you a good girl while I was gone?" he asked, brushing his thumb over my nipple. I knew that he would be paying me a visit later.

Fuck you…

"It's kind of difficult not to be. I'm not allowed off this property."

"You can go to the library. I have work to do anyway, but I expect payment later. Do you understand?"

"Yes, and thank you."

Drew stuck the little chip on the back of my phone so he could plug it into his computer when I got back. I was hoping that I could pump information from Rebecca, but it wasn't going to be in the vehicle. I held up my phone in the car so that she knew not to say anything.

She instead talked about recipes and a show that we both had watched on television the night before.

Rebecca asked the librarian for some paper. I grabbed the first book that I saw.

"June 2nd," Rebecca wrote and passed the note to me.

"Three months?"

"Yes. Ms. K is working on your new residence now. The money that you have rightfully taken over the last couple of months has been withdrawn and has made a nice down payment on your new house."

"My new house? I'm going to be a homeowner?" I wrote really fast, trying to contain my excitement. "Where?"

"She wouldn't tell me. She said that you didn't need to know that part yet."

"Do you trust this Ms. K? How do you know that she isn't taking the money, and we will never hear from her again? How do you even know someone that does this?"

"She's not stealing your money. She is good, real good. You will disappear from here and be untraceable. Do you remember on the news about three years ago when Constance Simmons disappeared? She is safe, living a beautiful life."

"Constance Simmons, that senator's wife?"

Rebecca nodded. I did remember that story. Her husband was all over the news. I actually felt bad for him. He seemed so sincere and loyal to his missing wife.

"How do you know Ms. K? I asked again. Rebecca had been at the mansion as long as I had. I mean she did leave when Drew was home sometimes, usually when he wanted the house to himself with me.

"Lots and lots of red tape. I had to go through nine people before I finally got to talk to her. Three months, Morgan!!!"

We were only in the library for fifteen minutes when Drew sent a text to my phone.

"Time is up."

Dickhead...

What the hell did I check out of the library? I sat naked in Drew's office reading about some sort of little creatures getting into people's houses through drain pipes while Drew worked and played with me, of course. I usually checked out autobiographies. I loved to read about other people's lives, it helped me to step out of my own for awhile. I wouldn't step out of it with that book. I couldn't even read it.

That was a good office visit. I lay bent over Drew's desk while he played with me, using different objects. He held the phone with his shoulder, and I watched him click on different views of the house. I paid close attention as he clicked on different windows, hitting stop camera, when he hit stop camera whatever image was up, froze on the screen. That was very useful information. We could stop the camera during the night when I needed to get into the office. It would look like I was sound asleep, without using pillows and would allow me more time in Drew's office.

***

I stopped talking when Dawson removed his hand from between my legs and slid from beneath me.

Dammit...

"I have to pee. I'll be right back," he said.

"Let's go to bed," I suggested, "instead."

"Are you done talking?" he asked, sounding disappointed.

I smiled. "No. I would rather tell you now so that we don't have to do it again later."

He smiled back. "I'll meet you in bed."

"You know what I still don't get?" Dawson asked, sliding into bed with me.

"What?"

"I still can't figure out, why you? I mean how would he even know about you?"

"The only logical exclamation that I have been able to come up with is, when he came to our school and donated all of that money. He donated to a lot of things, including me," I smiled a devious smile to myself, proud of the fact that he bought me my house. "The only thing that I can come up with is he wanted someone who wouldn't be missed, someone that their drunken father would sell. I don't think he is into the whole romance thing, and he just wanted someone he could control and not have to worry about a family getting in his way. He didn't have time for a real relationship, not that he ever wanted one. You know what does baffle me though?"

"What's that?" Dawson asked, pulling me into the arms that I loved holding me.

"You located Justin in Las Vegas...." I suddenly stopped. I couldn't go there with Dawson. He still thought that I was from Indiana. I almost spit out that I didn't understand how Justin and I both could end up in Las Vegas.

"Yeah?" he questioned.

"I don't know, it just seems so far away. How did someone from Las Vegas come to adopt my little brother all the way from West Virginia?"

"Hmm, I don't know. I would imagine that people adopt kids from all over the country."

"I guess," I replied. I was letting that one go right that second.

"So you and Rebecca snuck into his office and moved money? He never got suspicious? I mean that seems like an awful lot of money to move without his knowing? What did you say he did again?"

I didn't...

"I'm not exactly sure. I know it has something to do with software," I lied. If he were going to go digging, he was going to need a mighty big shovel. "Yeah, we pretty much just snuck into his office, moved money and got the hell out of there."

"Tell me about the day that you finally left."

"I left a month earlier than we had originally planned. I couldn't take the chance on staying another month. I was in the kitchen eating lunch with Rebecca when Drew came in being way too happy and cheery for Drew.

***

"I thought you were going to the library?" he asked, taking a bite of my sandwich.

"We are, right after lunch," I answered.

"I have a surprise that is going to keep you very busy, right here at home," he chanted.

I looked over to Rebecca standing on the other side of the counter.

"Do you mind?" he asked, and she disappeared.

"What?" I asked, wondering what in the world could keep me busy at home.

"A baby."

I almost choked on my own tongue. "I don't want a baby," I stated.

"Doesn't matter what you want, does it, Morgan?" he said with a smirk and a tilted head. "You're done getting your shots. I will have you barefoot and pregnant in a month," he smiled, taking another bite of my sandwich.

Now what? I couldn't let him get me pregnant. I would be terrified of the monster that he could produce. There was no way he was injecting me with that poison. I started doing some calculating in my head. I was supposed to have a shot in about a week. How much time do I have after my last dose before I could get pregnant?"

"I think Derik needs to drive today," Drew stated, got up, kissed me on my shocked cheek, and disappeared. Was he afraid that I would try and run after that bomb?

Rebecca followed me to the nonfiction section of the library after our silent ride to the library.

"Tell me already," she demanded in a quiet whisper as we pretended to look through the books.

"He's not letting me get my next shot. He wants to get me pregnant," I whispered, and turned to see Derik sitting at a small table looking right down the row at us. He had an annoyed look on his face and looked down at his Rolodex and then back to me. I knew he didn't want to be there, and was telling me to hurry.

"He what?!?"

"Shh," I warned.

I picked up a book and flipped open the cover. It was called 'Once in a house,' and was about a woman held against her will, forced to marry, and bare the children of a prince in England. I really wanted to read that book, but I didn't dare. I knew that Drew would throw a royal fit about it. Instead, I chose a book of short stories from Ernest Hemingway.

Drew was out of town for almost three weeks the next time. I asked Rebecca every day about a new plan and always got the same answer. Apparently whoever Ms. K was didn't work like that. She couldn't get hold of her and had to wait for an unknown number to send a text. She had tried to text the numbers from before, but never got a response.

Finally, on the day before Drew's return she got a message. 'Send last donation to Sulton Flux Bank,' it read with the account information.

Rebecca quickly texted back and told her what Drew had planned for me, not knowing how much time she had with the new unknown number.

"Wait for instructions," was the only reply back.

We made our very last transaction that night. Rebecca took care of the lights, briefly causing the cameras to reset. I quickly went to the cameras on Drew's computer and froze my sleeping body on the one facing my bed. My fingers trembled something fierce and my heart beat a million and one miles a minute. I had never taken that much money at one time. I was terrified that he was going to get an alert or something. He would know that forty thousand dollars had just come out of six different accounts. I quickly hit submit on the very last transaction and stomped on the floor for Rebecca to get the lights and get me the hell out of there.

I don't think I slept a wink that night. I was so nervous for Drew to come home. I wished I had known when he was coming. It could be any second or days.

Drew did know about my last transaction. He frantically spent hours on the phone that morning when he got home, trying to get someone, anyone to tell him what happened to his money, and who authorized forty thousand dollars of his money to go toward a remodel of an animal shelter.

That was the last day Drew had ever hit me. I didn't know at the time that it would be the last time. I was sitting in his office, naked of course. It seemed like that was when he wanted me there, when he was stressed, but this stress was over me. He just hadn't figured that part out, and I silently prayed that he didn't.

I thought after his toying with me and finally releasing his frustration in my ass that he calmed down some.

"Is it okay if I go to the library?" I submissively asked.

"For what?" he asked annoyed.

What do you think asshole?...

"Probably to get a book and get out of this house," I didn't mean for it to come out so smart, but it did and I felt the back of his hand come in contact with the same cheekbone that had taken his blow so many times.

"You can go to the library when you can learn some respect. Get the fuck out of my office," he demanded with a thick voice.

I lightly shook my head, letting Rebecca know that he wasn't going to allow me to go that day. I wanted out of there so bad. I needed to tell her that he was looking for the money.

I was silently eating lunch in the kitchen later in the afternoon when Drew came in. I could feel the black eye and the puffiness just below it.

"That looks pretty good, make me one and bring it to my office," he said talking to Rebecca and looking at my food.

"Sure," Rebecca replied, nicely.

"You can take her to the library after that if you want" he stated.

Yes...

"Is Derik available to take her today? I was going to go take a nap. I'm not feeling the best today."

I couldn't help it. My head just snapped right toward her with a look of vengeance. I couldn't believe she was going to send me away with Derik, knowing what he would do.

Derik never spoke in the car. I made sure to show him my little chip that would be placed in Drew's computer when I got back. I hoped that would scare him off, and he wouldn't try anything. It didn't. He smiled a devious grin and turned on the radio.

"You've got fifteen minutes," he warned, opening the library door for me.

I was scared shitless. I knew that Derik was going to do what Drew had already done that morning to me. I went right to the nonfiction row and had to look around a dumpy lady who just stood there in front of the section that I wanted.

"Go to the bathroom, first stall," she said and disappeared.

I of course had to ask permission from Derik.

"I need to go to the bathroom," I whispered. He followed.

I opened the first stall door to a dark blue duffel bag waiting for me on the floor. I quickly opened it and read the short note.

"Change into these clothes, immediately, walk out the front door and get into the waiting cab."

This was well thought out. I stuck a piece of the bubble gum in my mouth and started chewing to soften it up. I sprayed the cheap perfume that I was sure Derik would catch a whiff of, and pulled on the long black wig. I was glad that my hair was up and didn't have to waste time on the hair with the provided hair tie.

"What the hell is this?" I wondered, pulling out a thin sleeve of some sort. I pulled it on, and it literally looked like I had a tattooed sleeve from my fingers to my shoulder. I quickly undressed placing my expensive pantsuit in the bag. The jeans were old, ratty, and way too big. I put on a flannel shirt with the cut off sleeves and topped if off with nerd glasses and work boots. My heart was going crazy. If this didn't work, I knew I would be spending the rest of my life eating carrot sticks and apples, locked in the gym.

I threw the duffel bag over my shoulder and left with a bubble in my mouth. I didn't know whether I was supposed to take the duffel bag or not, so I did. Derik was waiting right outside; arms crossed leaning against the wall to the left. I didn't look at him but could see him out of the corner of my eye. I knew I had seconds when I heard his knuckles knock on the bathroom door, telling me to hurry.

There were two yellow cabs parked right out front. I panicked. I didn't know which one to take. I just knew that Derik was going to grab me from behind at any second. I couldn't even open one of the cab doors and ask if they were going to I didn't know where.

I stood in a frozen state, not knowing what to do. I almost jumped out of my skin when someone grabbed my elbow and shoved me toward the first car. They opened the back door for me, and I got in. I didn't even look to see who it was. I did turn around once we were in traffic. There were a lot of people on the sidewalk. I didn't see Derik anywhere.

It took forty five minutes for my heart to regulate, and the nerves to settle throughout my body, and then it started all over. The driver handed me a manila envelope, chocked full of information and ID's.

"What's this?"

No answer. He wasn't going to discuss anything with me. I opened the flap and pulled out the prepaid phone as the driver pulled off the side of the road, and I was quickly rushed into another vehicle parked right behind us.

"Thank you," I said to the driver who only nodded. I didn't know what I was thanking him for. I didn't even know how much he knew.

"I need your cell phone," my new driver said before I exited the cab. I handed him my new prepaid cell phone.

"Not that one," he stated, and I fished Drew's phone from the pocket on the side of the duffel bag. He handed it to the cab driver and ushered me on my way. I had never thought about being tracked, and the panic started all over again. I was sure he was tracking me.

I jumped again when the new phone rang in my hand.

"Hello," I cautiously answered.

"Are you doing okay?" the unidentified voice asked.

I hadn't even noticed I wasn't breathing until that moment. I inhaled deeply.

"Yeah, I think so. This was just so unexpected. Are you Ms. K?" I asked.

"Yes, I am. It's always best that you don't know what is happening. You have full instructions in the envelope. I will call you later. Don't answer any calls from that phone unless it is this number, understand?"

"Yes, thank you Mrs. K."

"You're welcome. Relax, it's over. You're going to be fine."

It's over?

That was the first time I had realized that I was on the run. I was away from Drew, but still had no idea where I was going. I pulled out the contents of the package and began to find out who I was and where I was going.

At first I was Lisa Fitzgerald, and when my new driver, who also didn't talk to me, pulled to the front curb of the first of six banks where I would withdraw money, it started to become real. I was nervous as hell there too. I just knew that Drew was onto me, and I would be escorted to the office by bank security where I would be held until he arrived for me. He didn't come, and I walked out with a seven thousand dollar prepaid Visa card, one of many that I would accumulate during the journey.

Everything started to sink in when I was driven to the last bank by my fourth driver. This was really planned out, and I had no idea. I had gone into six different banks, with six different identities and was carrying over twenty-five thousand dollars in prepaid cards. The majority of the money had been withdrawn for the purchase of my new home. I still didn't even know where I was going. I had been in four different vehicles, but at the stop of every bank it became easier for me to walk in, withdraw my money and leave. I never removed the black wig until my last driver pulled into the parking garage hours after my escape. I knew we were in Freemont, Nebraska, but that was it. I had never been out of West Virginia until I was sold to Drew Kelley almost six years prior.

We parked beside an older white Honda Civic, and I had no idea what was going on.

"This is it, good luck to you, I need the envelope and your phone now," my last driver said, holding out his hand and wishing me luck. Those were the only words that my chauffeur had spoken to me the entire three hour trip.

He pulled the keys from the package and handed them to me with a smile. Where the hell was I supposed to go? The contents of my package only had information about the banks and my identities. I didn't know where I was supposed to go in this car.

I got in the older car, and the black SUV pulled away and left me alone. There was another package on the passenger seat, along with a brown leather purse. I sat there forever trying to pull myself together. I was scared. I didn't know what was out there. I had lived in a bubble my entire life. Could I really do this? It was a little too late for that. I was there. If I went back now, Drew would kill me for sure. I had been gone for over three hours. I was sure that he was beside himself.

I noticed the little black GPS stuck right in the middle of the windshield, took a deep breath, and opened the new packet of information. There was another phone and papers, clipped together. I rummaged through the purse and smiled a little.

Lipstick, mascara, fingernail clippers, tiny little mirror, and a wallet. I opened the wallet to my new identity. Riley Murphy, 1712 Long Gate Road, Misty Bay, Maine. Was this where I was going? Did Ms. K expect me to drive clear across the United States in this car? I pulled out my driver's license and wondered who had taken the picture. I knew that it was taken at the library even with the blue background. I was wearing the same outfit that I had worn there not too long before. I had a credit card, insurance card, a social security card, and a registration to the car, all with my new name. I must be Riley Murphy, and that would be the last name that I would have from my multiple identities.

I turned on the GPS, and it was already set for my destination. I was nervous about driving. I hadn't really driven much, but I did just fine and was out of that city and on to the next. I actually turned on the radio and felt myself relax. I was free. I couldn't believe it.

At that moment that I realized that I never got the chance to thank Rebecca. I would never see her again, and I owed her so much. I wondered if Drew would make her leave. I assumed that he would. She was kept there to babysit me. He didn't need her anymore. I hoped that he wasn't too hard on her. I knew he would try to get information out of her. I was glad that she didn't know anything.

My new phone rang after a couple of hours of driving. It was Ms. K, telling me that the rest of my trip would be left up to me. I had already figured as much. She told me not to get off track and to go where the GPS took me. It was already set for food and the hotels that I would check into. She told me that she would call the next day and not to answer the phone unless it was that number again.

I was scared that first night in the hotel. I should have just kept driving. I didn't sleep a wink, waiting for the door to burst open and find Drew or Derik. I took a shower and pulled on the clothes that had been sent with me. The duffel bag with my designer pantsuit was left in the second escape car, and this was what I had to work with. Three pairs of jeans, a couple of sweatshirts, new panties, socks, a few shirts, and a box of

brown hair dye. I was happy to see that. I hadn't seen my natural brown hair since the first week I was at Drew's house.
***

I hadn't realized that I talked for so long until I looked at the clock. It was almost midnight and Dawson, and I both had to get up for work the following day. I looked up at him, and he smiled, kissing my lips.

"And that was almost two years ago," I said kissing him back.

"I'm glad you're Riley Murphy," he said as we both slid down into the bed.

"Me too," I agreed, snuggling my back to his front.

I lay in Dawson's arm contemplating where I had been and where I was now. I was by no means looking for love when I ran from Drew, but that was exactly what I found. I couldn't imagine loving anyone as much as I loved Dawson Bade. I had never felt the security that I felt with him, and I knew that he truly did love me. Who else would have loved someone as messed up as me? I wasn't always going to be screwed up. I was getting stronger and better every day, thanks to Starlight, Lauren, and my sheriff.

I had to open the shop earlier the next day because Dawson had to drop me off. I didn't mind, and I was happy to ride the short drive with my hand in his. I kissed him, and he waited until I unlocked the front door and was inside before waving and pulling out.

It was fairly slow that day. I wasn't surprised. I wouldn't have gone out in that cold either if I didn't have to. Dawson came in around one and brought me a hot roast beef sandwich and a bowl of broccoli cheese soup from Millie's. He ate with me, and we sat at the table in an empty shop, right in front of the window.

"Charlie thinks you need a starter," Dawson said as we ate.

"Is he going to get it fixed today?"

"No. He said it would probably be a couple of days before he could get to it. He's coming to tow it later on today.

What? You don't like being escorted to work in my cruiser?" Dawson teased.

"I love it," I smiled. "I've been thinking about something, Daw," I said.

"What's that?"

"Where are we going to live once we are married?"

"I don't know. Where do you want to live?"

"Well, your house is bigger, but mine is closer to the ocean, and I kind of like being close to Lauren."

"You have got to be joking. That girl is a pain in my ass. You know she is only your friend because you feed her, don't you?"

"She is a pain in the ass," I agreed, "but you still have to love her."

"You have to love her. I don't. I have to go, Ry. I'll come and get you at six."

"Call me when you get off. If it's this slow, I might just close up an hour early."

Dawson kissed me goodbye, and I cleaned up our lunch trash.

◇◇()◇◇

I didn't think we would ever make it through the long Maine winter. I pretty much lived at Dawson's for the entire winter. He was in love with his fireplace, and my house was not equipped with one. March wasn't warm, but at least it wasn't freezing either. I was not looking forward to the trip to Las Vegas again, even though I was when Star had first told me about it. The closer it got, the more and more I hated the idea. I hated the idea of being away from Dawson for four days, and although I knew I was being silly; I still feared running into Drew or someone seeing me. I didn't know who. I never got to know anyone there except for Jena, and now that I had Star and Lauren, I knew that Jena and I were never truly friends. Not like what I had with Star and Lauren anyway.

I was looking forward to the hot weather. That part was exciting. I was anxious to wear shorts, a skirt, and short sleeves, anything but the winter coat that had become attached to me over the past few months.

Starlight left almost two weeks before our scheduled trip. Her daughter Moonie would be accompanying us on the trip and Star was going there first and flying out with her. I was picking up a rental car and would meet them the same day in our shared hotel room. We did need to visit vendors and find some new merchandise for the shop. Tourist season in Misty Bay was right around the corner, and if we were as busy as the previous summer, we would need all the merchandise that we could get.

On Saturday night, Dawson, Lauren, Joel, and I built a fire outside, roasted hot dogs and drank a few beers. It was cold outside, but the heat from the fire made it comfortable. We were having a good time when my cell phone rang with an unidentified number. It was Star's daughter Moonie, letting me know that her mother had broken her ankle and was having surgery as we spoke. She wanted to inform me that they weren't going to make the trip to Vegas. Star still wanted me to go and said that her two friends Wendy and Marsha, whom I had met the last time, along with her sister, Sunny would still be there. I was disappointed. I was looking forward to my weekend with Star and Moonie.

"You should just go with me, Dawson," I suggested after hanging up with Moonie.

"Yeah, well, had I known Star was going to break her leg a week before you were leaving, I would have. It's too late for me to get vacation now."

"Lauren?" I looked to my friend for help.

"Sorry, I'm in the same boat," she replied. "I need more than a week to get vacation approved too."

"Joel?" I joked.

"Sure, why not," he teased.

I was a little apprehensive about going alone although I wouldn't actually be alone. I would have Marsha and Wendy, and Sunny would be my roommate. I knew I would have a blast with the free spirit. She was a lot like Star.

Chapter 13

Dawson drove me to the airport on Thursday morning.

"I told you the last time that you did this that I didn't like it," he said, sitting in an airport chair beside me while I waited for my flight to start boarding.

"I told you to come with me," I countered, just as we heard my flight called.

He carried my bag as far as they would let him.

"I love you. I'll call you during my layover in Chicago," I said, holding him tightly around his neck.

"I'll be waiting. Hurry back to me. I love you."

I settled into the window seat and stared out the tiny window, reflecting on where I was. I never met Ms. K in my life, but I owed her my life. I hated to think about living with Drew, having his baby, and never having a life of my own. I felt safer and secure in Misty Bay than I ever had, and of course I was madly in love with my sheriff.

I did call Dawson and talked to him the whole forty-five minute layover in Chicago, and then again when I was safely in my hotel room in Vegas. I walked down to the dining room around seven with Marsha, Sunny, and Wendy for supper. Star's sister returned to my room with me. I loved Sunny almost as much as Star. She painted my finger and toenails with a neon green polish with black tips. It wasn't my style at all, but I laughed and told her that I loved it.

The swap meet was just as epic as I remembered it from the last time, and there were even more vendors. I knew I would be paying for extra weight on the way home. It was only the first day, and I had seven catalogues of the neatest novelty items ever.

We went out for supper that night and had a blast once again. We had walked to the restaurant, and Sunny and Marsha had gotten a little intoxicated. Wendy and I told them both several times to quiet down as we walked back to our rooms.

The next day was just as much fun. I found a vendor of old-time candies and thought that it would make a perfect fit for the shop, and of course grabbed one of his catalogues. There were candy cigarettes, those necklaces that you had to bite the candy off, wax lips, and every flavor of jelly beans imaginable. I crinkled my nose at the thought of sardine flavored jelly beans, but knew they would sell, just because they were different.

The four of us went out for supper again at the same restaurant. I was the one who drank a little too much that time, but I didn't care. I was having the time of my life, and I don't think I have ever laughed so much.

I said goodbye to Sunny, Marsha and Wendy and headed to the airport with the rental car the following morning. Sunny and Wendy were staying another night. They wanted to catch one of the shows before heading home the next day. Marsha was flying out the same evening. I couldn't wait to get home and see Dawson. It was crazy how much I missed him. If someone had told me two years prior that I could be in love with someone the way I was with him, I would have deemed them crazy.

I parked the rental car in the designated space. I called Dawson just before boarding and told him that I would see him in eight hours. I had another layover in Chicago for an hour, but I was fine with it. I would be going to bed in his arms that night. That was all that I cared about. I told him that I loved him and was getting ready to board when I realized that I had the keys to the rental in my hand.

"How much time do I have?" I asked the lady at the gate.

I told her that I would be right back. I had ten minutes to board. I wished that I would have just taken the keys and sent them in the mail.

I rushed out to the parking lot to deposit the keys in the glove box of the car, where I should have left them. I was just crossing the crosswalk and like an idiot, turned when I heard someone yell.

"Morgan?"

I knew it was Derik before I ever turned my head.

Fuck...

What the hell was I supposed to do now? I panicked and sprinted to the rental car, started it and backed out of the parking space, trying to get out of there in the ridiculous traffic. I would catch the next flight. I knew they would track down every name on that plane if I had gotten on it. I wasn't chancing that. Every thought possible was going through my mind. What if he caught me? What would Drew do to me? I couldn't go back there, and for the first time since I had met Dawson, I wished I would have given him his name or even mine before I became Riley Murphy. He had no way to find me. He thought that I was on a plane heading toward Chicago.

I kept a close eye on my rear view mirror. Derik was one car behind me. I could see him on his cell phone and knew exactly whom he was talking to. I could hear Drew's voice on the other end, telling him not to lose me. I felt like my world was crashing in on me. Everything that I had worked so hard for, for the past two years was hanging by a thread, all because I was stupid. I should have never chanced being there in the first place.

I was finally out of the airport traffic and into even more traffic darting in and out of lanes, trying to lose him. I had no idea where I was or where I was going. I wanted to call Dawson. I had to call Dawson. He had to be able to find me if I was caught. I reached into my purse to retrieve my phone and looked up just in time to keep from hitting the stopped bus. My purse and all of its contents landed on the passenger floor.

This couldn't be happening. It was like one of those movies that kept you on the edge of your seat, waiting to see what happened. I went around the bus, and Derik was now right behind me. I shot back in front of the bus and took the next street to the right. I kept darting in and out of traffic, up and down different streets with Derik right on my tail.

I finally got out of the city enough to get some speed, still passing cars, illegally. I didn't care. I would have loved for the cops to see me and stop me. They didn't, and I was left to fend for myself. I was a few cars ahead of him when I came up on a sports car with the top down, full of young girls. They were yelling and having the time of their life, but they were driving too slowly. I knew I shouldn't try it. I couldn't see if anything was coming from the little knoll.

Everything moved in slow motion. I darted around the sports car, and I was right. I shouldn't have done it. Neither I nor the city bus driver had time to react before my car was under his bumper. I don't remember much after that. I could vaguely recall sirens, voices and the sound of a saw. I was hot. I was so hot, and I could smell smoke. Was the car on fire? Was I being cut out of the car? I didn't know. I was drifting away. I felt my body becoming lighter and lighter as I floated into the dark.

I'm sorry, Dawson...

<><.>()<><>

I didn't know how long I had been there. I coughed and didn't like the tube in my throat. The lights were bright, and I was confused. I gagged on the tube inserted into my throat as I tried to move my head.

The tube was being pulled out. That was why it was gagging me. I managed to get my eyes opened and saw a doctor, a nurse, and a man that looked familiar, but I just couldn't put my finger on who he was just yet.

"Mrs. Kelley, can you hear me?" the doctor asked.

Mrs. Kelley? Mrs. Kelley? I repeated over in my head unable to speak. That didn't sound right. Was that my name?

I let my eyes close again and drifted back into the darkness. I don't think I was out very long. I think the doctor had continued to call my name or somebody's name. None of it made any since. I had no recollection of anything.

"Mrs. Kelley, can you tell me your name?" the doctor spoke.

I looked at the man who felt familiar, and he looked worried. Was he worried about me? Who was he?

"Where am I?" I asked.

"You're in the hospital, baby," the man who seemed to know me said. I pulled my hand away from him. I didn't know who he was.

"What's wrong with me?"

"You were in a bad car accident, but you're going to be okay," the man that thought he knew me replied.

"How long have I been here?"

"We have had you in an induced coma for five weeks now. You suffered a ruptured spleen, broken pelvis and serious head injury. Your brain was swollen severely, so we put you into an induced coma so it could recover."

"Five weeks?" I asked. I wasn't sure why it mattered. I couldn't even remember my name.

"Mrs. Kelley, can you tell me what your name is?"

"Who are you?" I asked, turning to the man who seemed to care about me.

"It's me, Morgan, Drew. I'm your husband."

What the fuck??? I don't think so...

"I don't think that is right," I assured him.

"You might suffer some memory loss from your head injury, but I am highly optimistic that you will have a full recovery. Memory loss is a common side-effect of serious head injuries. It is highly likely it will return in time," the doctor explained.

I drifted back off. That was enough. I couldn't take anymore. Maybe the next time I woke it would be over. Maybe it was just a bad dream. Yeah, that's what it was. I will wake to my real life the next time.

I think I was out for a long time. The room was dark, and the same man that was there earlier was sitting in the chair. He jumped up when he saw that I was awake.

"Hey," he softly spoke. I pulled my hand out of his again. It took every bit of strength that I had. My arm felt so heavy.

"You should leave. I don't know who you are," I demanded.

"I'm your husband, Morgan. We've been married for almost eight years."

"I don't believe you."

He got my purse and showed me my Nevada driver's license. The picture looked familiar but was it me? That didn't prove anything.

Every time I woke this man was sitting there. Why wouldn't he leave?

I don't know how many more days I was there drifting in and out of consciousness, but every time I woke this man was there. He was there when I was moved to a rehabilitation center, as well.

I was starting to come around and was awake more and more. This guy who claimed to be my husband was always there, always telling me how much he missed me being home with him.

Evidently I had just gotten home when I had my accident. Apparently I had been studying English Literature in France, and hadn't even made it home yet or so I was told. I didn't remember being in France either. I was scared, and I felt like my whole life had been erased. Why couldn't I remember something? Anything? It was so frustrating. I felt a massive void, and despite the things this Drew character had begun telling me about my past, it was all alien. He said that we were getting ready to start a family; we lived in a beautiful mansion and that I loved books. It all sounded so superficial, and for some reason I didn't believe him.

Each morning, I'd wake up hoping it would be the day everything would come flooding back. It was frightening and frustrating because each day was as strange as the one before. No matter how hard I tried, I had absolutely no idea who Drew was or how much we meant to one another. He seemed to care about me a lot more than I cared about him. He was always there.

I did start seeing less of him because he said that he had to work. I didn't care if he went to work. I didn't want him there. He still came every night, but sometimes it was a few days between his visits because he had to go out of town. He could have stayed out of town.

I spent three weeks in the rehabilitation center learning to walk and regaining my strength. Had I known that the doctor was going to release me to that man I would have contrived being injured longer.

"Where are my parents?" I had asked when the doctor talked to me about going home.

"Honey, both your parents are gone," Drew explained.

"Gone where?" I wanted to know. I knew that I was only twenty-six. My Nevada driver's license said so. Why didn't I have parents?"

"Your dad passed away a few years back, and you never really knew your mom. She left when you were just a little girl?" Drew explained. He sounded sincere. I guess I didn't have a reason not to believe him.

"What about brothers or sisters? Don't I have any family?"

"Not really, Morgan. You and I were getting ready to start our own family, remember?"

No, you fucking idiot, I don't remember.

Someone else with a familiar face picked us up from the hospital. I was wheeled out, and Drew helped me into the back seat. I was doing much better and could walk on my own, but moving into the car hurt.

Drew sat right beside me in the back seat. I wished that he would move over, and every time he tried to take my hand, I pulled it away. It just didn't feel right to me.

I know that my eyes had to be wide open when we pulled into the long drive with a security gate. I read the sign above the gate.

'Callaway Estates.'

Wow, was this where I lived? None of it looked familiar. The house was a mansion. I mean big enough to get lost in. This didn't seem right either. I didn't think that I had really lived there at all.

"What the fuck is he doing here, Derik?" Drew asked the driver, and then looked to me like he was afraid of scaring me or something.

"I don't know, but I'm sure he has a right to be here whenever he wants," the driver stated, and I wondered what that meant. Whom were they talking about?

I saw the frail older man in a wheelchair waiting. Was he waiting for me? I didn't know him either. There were three nurses with him. Was he sick?

Drew helped me out of the car, and the older gentleman pushed the joystick on his chair and came to me.

"How are you, Morgan?" he asked with a warm smile, reaching for my hand.

"I wish I remembered," I smiled down at him. My hand in his didn't feel like it did when Drew held it. This man felt genuine.

"We'll help you with that. I've hired the two best nurses in the state of Nevada. They will make sure you get better," he assured me.

"I'm very sorry. I know that I am supposed to know who you are, but I honestly don't," I explained.

"That's not important right now. My name is Randal. Let's get you better before we worry about that, uh?"

I smiled with a nod. He turned his chair and pretty much demanded Drew's attention.

"I've got Terri and Melissa set up in the north wing. They will see to Morgan's needs. I want her taken care of, and that's an order. Do you understand?" he asked Drew.

"Yes sir. I will be sure of it," Drew said, bowing down to the man. I wondered who he was and why Drew was so intimidated by him.

Randal Callaway didn't come into the house with us and left with the third nurse.

I stood immobile once we were inside. Drew dismissed the two women and turned to me.

"Do you remember this place, Morgan?" he asked, staring very intently at me, probably trying to read my face and figure out whether or not I did.

"I'm sorry," I apologized. I didn't remember. I didn't remember at all, and nothing about the magnificent home did anything to jog my memory.

"That's okay. It'll come," he smiled, and I heard the Derik guy snort.

"I kind of wanted to talk to you about something," I said to Drew.

He dismissed Derik, and held my elbow while we walked into the living area.

"I'll be right back," he said.

He did come right back and sat beside me on the sofa.

"What is it, Morgan?" he asked, turning his legs toward mine. I moved. I didn't want his legs touching mine.

"I know that we are married, and all, but I really think I need to sleep alone for a while. This is all like very new to me, and I am having a hard time figuring out where I fit in."

Drew smiled as a lady brought in two cups of hot tea. I didn't recognize her either.

"It's okay, Morgan. I have already moved your things to a nice suite upstairs. I thought you might feel that way."

I smiled. "Thank you, but is there a bathroom up there. I realized as soon as I had asked that it was a stupid question. Of course, there were bathrooms up there. The house was amazing."

"Yes, there is one in your suite," he smiled.

I sipped the warm tea, but really didn't want it. I just wanted to lie down.

"Do you mind if I go there now? I'm a little tired."

"Not at all, you rest, and I will have some food brought up to you when you wake up."

"Thank you."

I held the rail going up the stairs and Drew walked beside me, holding my arm. I wondered why he put me in a room upstairs. He knew that I had a broken pelvis.

When I got to the top of the stairs, I stopped. There were so many rooms, all with closed doors. Drew didn't help me figure out which one I should go into.

"Do you mind helping me out here a little?" I asked. It came out sort of cold.

"You don't remember which one is your room?"

I looked at him oddly. "My room? I thought that you moved my things in here after my accident."

"I did, I was just trying to help your memory along."

How was confusing me going to help me get my memory back?

He opened the door, and I looked around. That room did feel maybe a little familiar, but I wasn't sure if it was a good feeling. I almost felt like I was going to have a panic attack being in there, but didn't know why.

"I'll leave you to rest. If you need anything, just pick up that phone and hit one. It goes right to my office" Drew smiled.

"Thank you," I smiled back.

I walked around looking at the room. It appeared that he had taken all of my things from our shared room and brought them to that room. A jewelry box sat on the vanity, and I opened it to find some beautiful pieces. I entered the walk-in closet, and none of the expensive clothes were ringing a bell. I ran my hand across the fashions and walked to the back of the enormous closet. I had more shoes than any one person could wear in a lifetime. I was rich. I was really, really rich. Okay. Maybe Drew was the rich one, but none the less.

I walked into the bathroom and was happy to see the jet tub that was calling my name. I started the hot water, and walked back to the bedroom to find comfortable clothes that weren't so fancy. There were none. I had expensive nighties, not a cotton t-shirt in sight. I opened the underwear drawer and frowned, pulling out something that I thought was supposed to be panties, but I wasn't honestly sure. What was the point in wearing them?

That just wasn't going to work. I wanted comfortable flannel pants, underwear that covered my ass, and a soft cotton t-shirt.

I walked over to the phone and hit the number one.

"Is something wrong?" Drew asked.

"Yeah, kind of," I stopped talking when I heard my voice coming from his end of the phone. How was that possible?

"What's wrong, Morgan?"

"Are you sure these are my clothes?" I asked. I didn't hear my voice on the other end that time and blew it off as another side effect of my brain injury.

"Yes, I am very sure that those are your clothes."

"Well, I would like some comfortable sweats or flannels, some normal panties, and maybe some socks. Didn't I wear socks?" I asked.

"Not very often, you wore pantyhose mostly. I will send someone out to get you a few things."

"Thanks, do I have a laptop?" I asked.

Drew didn't speak. He kind of acted like that took him off guard for a second.

"You did have, it was in the car when you wrecked it."

"Well, do you think that I could get another one?"

"Not yet. The doctor is afraid that too much eye movement will cause seizures. You have a television. You can watch that awhile if you want."

"I don't want to watch television. I want to do some research on my head injury. I would kind of like to know what I am up against, maybe find some stories from other survivors."

"I'll tell you what. You get a bath and rest awhile, and you can come down to my office and use mine. Okay?"

"Why would I take a bath?" I asked. Why would he say that?

"Is that not what I hear in the background?" he asked. I relaxed.

"Oh, yeah, I guess it is. Sorry."

The hot water felt amazing, and the jet streams were hitting sore spots that I didn't know that I had. I think I was dozing off a little when I heard someone in my room.

"Hello," I called out.

"It's just me, Terri," the one female called. "Can I come in?" she asked.

"Sure," I replied, covering myself as much as I could.

"Mr. Kelley said that you were requesting some more comfortable clothes while you recovered. Mellissa went out to get you some things. I brought you some lunch," she added.

"Thank you," I replied. She smiled and left me to get out. The only problem was. I couldn't get out. Every time I tried to pull myself up, the pain was unbearable and shot from my pelvis all the way down my right leg. Why the hell did I get in there?

"Terri!" I called out with no response. She was gone. Great, how long was I going to have to stay in there until someone came back?

I tried a couple more times with no avail. I couldn't lift myself out. I wanted to cry. I felt so helpless, so alone, so lost, and now I needed something for the pain. If I ever got out the bathtub.

I heard Drew call out next.

"Morgan," he tapped on the door.

Great. I didn't want him to be the one to come and rescue me.

"Can you go and get Terri for me?" I called out, not wanting his help.

"Why? Is something wrong?"

"No, I just need help getting out of the tub."

He didn't wait for a reply. He opened the door and was smiling at me.

"I can help you out, Morgan. We slept together for almost eight years. I've seen you naked before."

I took a deep breath. I supposed he was right, and I was being obtuse. I smiled and nodded.

He took my arm and helped me out of the tub. I quickly grabbed a towel to cover my front. He was looking at me with pure lust. I knew that's what it was. How could he look at me like that when I was hurt? I didn't like it. I didn't like it one bit.

"I'm good now. Thanks," I coolly said, wanting him to leave.

I didn't put on any of the clothing, and settled for the terrycloth robe hanging on the back of the door. I lifted the silver lid from my tray and actually felt a little hungry. I had turkey, mashed potatoes with gravy, corn and a roll. I sat on the edge of the bed and picked at it. I guess I wasn't as hungry as I initially thought. I pulled pieces of the roll off, dipping it into my potatoes and gravy as I looked around my room. I felt like crying. Nothing seemed right. I didn't feel rich, and certainly didn't feel like I belonged there. Why couldn't I remember who I was? I hated this, and only hoped that the doctor was right, and I would regain my history.

I covered my half eaten food and lay on the bed. I wiped a falling tear with my thumb. I didn't understand. I could remember the words to songs, but not how I knew them. I could remember whole books that I'd read, but not where or when I read them, and this place. I had absolutely no recollection of ever living there, at all.

After I slept for a couple of hours, I woke with a horrible headache, but was happy to see the freshly washed clothes folded and laying on my bed. I took two of the pain pills by my bed, went to the bathroom and pulled on the normal panties, a bra from the drawer, pink and green flannelled pants, and a simple white t-shirt.

I walked out and slowly descended the stairs. I felt every step as the pain shot up my pelvis and back. Why the hell would he put me on the second floor with a broken pelvic bone? I intended to ask him, along with a few other questions.

"Where is Drew?" I asked the lady who was chopping vegetables in the kitchen.

"I think he's in his office," the lady that I didn't recognize explained. I looked at her, and she read my mind. "It's the door straight across from the living room."

I opened the door to the office and Drew was on the phone. He looked up with instant anger.

What the hell?...

I slowly lowered myself to the settee across from his desk. He replaced the irritated expression with a smile, telling whoever he'd been talking to that he would have to call them back.

"Did you also forget how to knock," Drew asked, annoyed.

"I don't know. Did I always knock before I came into your office?"

"Yes, and I would appreciate you doing so in the future. I do conduct business in here. Is there something that I can do for you?" Drew asked with a smirk that made me want to slap off his face.

"Yeah, there is," I said, giving him attitude. Who the hell did he think he was? "Maybe you could show me some wedding or vacation pictures. Where did we meet? Did we always live in this house? Do I have any friends that I could talk to?"

"Must you walk around dressed like that?"

What?

I looked down at my comfortable attire. "Are you concerned with the help seeing me? Did I always dress in the fancy clothes upstairs to lounge around the house?"

"Yes. You did, and I would also appreciate you doing that as well from now on."

"You're surely not telling me how I should dress," I asked in disbelief. Was this guy for real? Did I really stay married to him for almost eight years? No wonder I was in another country.

Drew got up and came to me. He took my hand and smiled a warm smile. "I'm just trying to show you what your routine was before the accident. Dr. Tharp says that getting you back into your normal element should help with your memory. You never dressed this way, Morgan."

I pulled my hand away. "Can I use your computer now?" I asked. I knew he was just trying to help me regain my memory, but it was still frustrating as hell. I still couldn't believe that I dressed in the fashions that hung in my closet on a daily basis.

"Sure," he said, patted my leg and walked over to close out of what he had been doing.

I sat in Drew's chair and tapped traumatic brain injuries on the keyboard. I looked back at Drew who was watching me. "How is it that I know how to type on a keyboard, but I can't remember learning it?"

"I have faith. You're going to remember every little thing that you've ever done," he said with a cold face. I still couldn't believe that I was married to this man. I mean, shouldn't I feel something?

After about twenty minutes of reading things that Dr. Tharp had already told me, I leaned back, took an exasperated breath and rubbed my temples. My finger traced the L shaped scar from my injury, reminding me that I had no idea who I was.

Drew rubbed my shoulders from behind. Hmm, it felt good. I didn't realize how tense I was.

"Just give it some time, Morgan," Drew said.

"What about the pictures? Do we have any of those?" I asked, tilting my head for him to hit the crook of my neck with his magic hands.

"That's kind of your fault. I have told you and told you that you needed to print the hundreds of pictures on your digital camera. You never would. It burned in your car."

"What about our wedding pictures? Do we have those?"

"I wish you could remember this stuff. I feel like the bad guy here. You didn't want a wedding. We ran away and got married."

"How long did we know each other?"

Drew laughed, and I knew it was going to be bad. "We got married after spending three weekends together."

I turned to look at him dumbfounded. What the hell was wrong with me? Maybe I didn't want to remember who I was. She sounded pretty stupid.

Drew kissed the top of my head. "You were married to me for almost eight years. I think you would have left had we not been right for each other."

"I was away taking classes in France, how long was I there?"

"That was all you too. I didn't want you to go, but you insisted. You were there not quite two years, but came home often, and I would fly there to be with you when I could."

"Why is my purse the only thing that survived the crash?" I didn't understand that either. My camera, my laptop and all of my clothes had burned in the car, but my purse came out unharmed.

"It was on your lap. They assumed that you were digging for something in it. That's why you hit the bus. You weren't paying attention."

I still didn't understand it. I mean the scar above my eye along with the bigger one on the side of my head had to have bled. Why was my purse free of blood?

I sat up straight when I had an idea. I rested my fingers on the correct letters of the keyboard.

"Where did I grow up?" I asked. Maybe if I could find some pictures or my school or something it would jog my memory.

"I think that's enough for one day," Drew decided, spinning me away from the computer.

"Did I always let you decide what was best for me?" I asked, standing up. He didn't move. We were inches apart.

"Always," he whispered, and moved close to my lips.

I placed my hand on his muscular chest to stop him, although I have to admit I was staring right at his lips. "Drew, I don't think I am ready for you to kiss me," I said in a low tone.

He placed his hand over mine on his chest and smiled. "I'll see you at dinner," he replied and let me step around him.

"I want to see our bedroom, the one that we shared," I said, turning to him before leaving.

"Okay, but it's kind of empty right now. I moved my things into another room when I had yours moved. I couldn't stand the thought of you not being in our bed with me."

Well that was sweet. It made me feel guilty for being such a pain to him. I never once thought about how difficult this was for him. I smiled, and he walked out with me.

Nothing. I didn't recognize that room any more than any other one in the house. It was just another fancy room with expensive furnishings.

"Anything?" Drew asked, looking down at me.

I shook my head lightly.

"Don't worry about it. Maybe you should just stop trying to remember and let it come when it's ready."

"Maybe," I replied. "Drew why did you move my things to the second floor, knowing I have a broken pelvis."

"Awe, shit Morgan. I never thought about that. That was your favorite bedroom in the house. I just thought you would feel better being in there. You said it was the best view in the house. You used to go in there and read a lot." he explained with a sincere response.

I smiled. "It's okay. My therapist made me climb steps at the rehabilitation center. It's probably good for me."

"Do you want to go rest before dinner?" he asked, placing his hand on the small of my back as we closed our shared suite.

"I think so, but I would rather just lie on the couch, I think," I replied.

"The couch?"

I looked up to him. "I didn't do that either, right?"

He smiled. "No, but if you want to do that, I will close the doors and make sure that you are not disturbed."

"Thank you," I smiled. I didn't want to be in that room for some reason. It didn't feel like my favorite room in the house at all.

Drew brought me a pillow and a blanket. "Do you want the television on?" he asked.

"No, I don't think so. I kind of just want the quiet for a while," I answered, snuggling under the soft blanket. Drew kissed me just in front of my ear.

"Have a nice nap," he whispered hot words to my skin.

I drifted off staring at the beautiful portrait of Drew and me. I was wearing a beautiful evening gown, and he was in a tuxedo. We looked happy. He was smiling down at me as I stared up at him.

Chapter 14

Dawson never gave up looking for me, but I left him with very little to go on. He knew about my father selling me to a man named Drew. He knew that my name had been Morgan Willow. He knew that I had been in Indiana since then, and nothing more. He had gone to my father, and my father told him what I was sure he was to tell anyone looking for me. That I married a very nice man, and he hadn't seen me since.

My sheriff tried to use his law authority, but it didn't work. My father still said he didn't know anything. He did so much research trying to find someone that was in the software business by the name of Drew, nothing but a brick wall. He couldn't even find a marriage between Morgan Willow and Drew anyone. I'm sure trying to find wedding records with no last name was next to impossible, especially when you were looking in the wrong state.

Lauren and Star helped as much as they could, but came up with nothing. I didn't leave them much to go on. Dawson knew that Drew had me; he just couldn't find me. He assumed that he had found out about me somehow and had taken me from the layover in Chicago. He was at his wits end, and didn't know what else to do.

Our wedding day came and went, and he was still clueless, hurt, and alone. He was even beginning to think that I had left on my own accord, and the whole wedding thing scared me off. That was easier for him than thinking that I was back with Drew, and what he was doing to me.
***

The truth was; Drew never did anything. He was always the perfect gentleman. There were times when I questioned the looks he gave me when I would say things that he thought were out of line or when I would just burst into his office. But for the most part he was unusually attentive and caring toward me. I still didn't like his copilot Derik but didn't really have a reason.

I just didn't like him. He gave me the creeps when he was around, which was a lot.

I still defied Drew's wishes about wearing the designer clothes around the house. It just seemed so artificial to me, and I was more comfortable in my sweats and flannels. I did do some online shopping one afternoon with Drew peering over my shoulder. I heard a few groans when I ordered a few pairs of jeans, shorts, t-shirts and sneakers. Who didn't own a pair of sneakers? I related it to who I was before Drew, and although I may have dressed the way he wanted, to impress him at one time, I didn't want to do that. I wasn't going to do that.

I'd been back at the mansion with Drew for almost a month. The one nurse, Melissa, was gone, but Terri was still there and she and I had become pretty good friends. Drew didn't like that either and pointed it out to me one afternoon. Terri had just left for the day and wasn't spending the nights anymore. She came and did therapy with me and went home in the afternoon.

I really didn't need her anymore, but I started to go stir crazy being in the house all the time. No wonder I chose to go to school. I liked having Terri there to talk to. Drew didn't, and a week later, he explained that it really wasn't proper for me to associate with the help the way that I did, she was gone. I was furious. He could have at least told me that her assignment was up so I could say goodbye to her.

I still couldn't remember anything about anything. It was like my conscious mind was erased. I didn't dream about my past. Nothing became more familiar, and I began to wonder if I ever would.

Drew took me out shopping for a new dress for a dinner party that Mr. Callaway held on Saturday night. I came down to go, and he smiled. I had decided to appease him and leave the jeans in the closet. I wore a satin white top with no sleeves, tucked into a pair of designer black dress slacks with a large silver buckle. I was surprised by the heels. I thought for sure that I would hate them, but I wore them like a pro which was expected, I guessed. I did dress like that for a good many years, or so I was told anyway.

I tried on three different dresses in the expensive store while Drew gave his opinion. He didn't like the first two and told the two women who were making a tremendous fuss over me, no. They would leave and bring me something else. When I walked out in the short, flowing, black sequined dress he instantly said, "No way."

I spun around looking in the mirror. I thought that it made me look extremely sexy, and it made my legs look longer and my breasts look bigger.

"I'll take this one," I told the two ladies. They looked to Drew as if they were asking his permission.

What the fuck?

"Whatever Mrs. Kelley wants," he offered, surrendering with his hands in the air.

I smiled at him, and he smiled back. We were absolutely flirting.

He took me to a nice restaurant for dinner where we both continued to flirt. I even let him hold my hand on the way back to the car. I was sure we hadn't had sex in a while, and I was a woman after all. I couldn't help it that things were stirring that hadn't recently been stirred.

I said goodnight to Drew, and walked upstairs to my suite where I soaked in the glorious hot tub. I pulled on a pair of stretch shorts and a solid light pink shirt with a V-neck. I'm not sure why I did it, but I opened the nightstand drawer, and pulled out the e-reader.

Hmm, I thought, pulling myself up on the bed. I didn't turn down the cover. I had told Drew it was his fault that I walked around in sweats or flannels because he kept it so cold in there, he adjusted the temperature, and it was rather warm in my room.

I tried to power on the e-reader, but it was dead. I looked in the drawer for the charger and just got it plugged in when Drew was there. He took it out of my hand like he knew that I had it. I looked at him confused, not knowing what to say.

"You shouldn't read this yet, too much eye movement," he smiled.

"How did you know I even had it?" I asked with a bit more attitude than I meant to expose.

"I didn't know that you had it. I was just coming to ask you if you wanted to go for a walk around the property."

"Is that something that we used to do?" I asked, calming down from my accusations of I didn't know what.

"Yes, all the time, as soon as the sun was down."

"Sure," I replied with a smile. It was only ten o'clock, and I wasn't really tired anyway. It was obvious that he wasn't going to let me read, so I figured I may as well.

He shook his head, amused, when I put on the socks and sneakers.

"You stop it," I said, knowing what he was thinking. I was flirting. Yup, that was what I was doing.

Drew held my hand as we walked around the property. I let him, and although I couldn't remember being in love with him before. I could see myself falling in love with him all over again.

"What do you do exactly, Drew?" I asked.

"You mean for work?"

"Yeah, I mean you obviously do something that pays very well."

He snickered a little. "Diamonds, beautiful diamonds, I have fifteen stores and just purchased three more that were getting ready to go under. I have been patiently waiting for months for them to fail enough to swoop in and take the burden off their hands with an exceptionally low price."

"Did they want to sell?"

"No, but they didn't really have a choice. My stores were overpowering them."

"It's kind of sad," I decided out loud.

"That's business," he replied. He stopped me by pulling my hand. I spun right into his chest.

I was terrified to look up. I knew he wanted to kiss me. Did I want to kiss him? I wasn't sure, but I was about to find out. He lifted my chin with his hand and parted my lips with his tongue.

I pulled myself up on the tips of my toes to get closer to his lips. I did want to kiss him, and his kiss was shooting streams of fireworks right to my groin. I wrapped my arms around his neck, and he pulled me closer. He ran one hand up the back of my shirt, and the other one through my hair and to the back of my neck, of course I moaned into his mouth.

Drew kissed me like that in the dark night of the back yard for, I didn't know how long. I could feel his girth on my stomach. It made me moan again.

"Sleep in my bed tonight," he whispered, to my lips.

Was I ready for that? My vagina was telling me that I was. It wasn't like I had never had sex with the man for God's sake. What was I worried about?

I didn't answer and Drew led me back to the house by my hand. What the hell was wrong with me? Did I forget how to have sex too? I was sure I could keep up, but there was something that I just couldn't put a finger on that scared the hell out of me.

Drew led me right to his room and moved me to his bed. He slid off my sneakers and socks. He ran his hands up my bare legs and told me to lie back. I did, and he removed my shorts and panties. He pulled me back up and helped me out of my braless shirt. I couldn't breathe. He was moving too fast. I wasn't used to this and wasn't sure what to do. I didn't have to worry about it. Drew took control and instructively told me what to do.

All of a sudden I was scared. The look on his face instantly changed, and I was staring into the eyes of Satan.

"Spread your legs," he said with a tone I didn't like. I didn't do it.

I trembled when he did it himself. What was he doing? Why was he making me feel this way? Shouldn't he be holding me in his arms, telling me that he loved me, and it was okay?"

That was the first night that I caught a glimpse or a vision. I wasn't sure what the hell it was, but it scared the hell out of me.

Drew ran his fingers up my slippery folds. My eyes closed, and I felt faint.

"Do you want to come, Morgan?" he asked in a voice that was familiar. I just didn't know why it sounded familiar.

How the hell was I supposed to answer that? Of course, I wanted to come. I wanted to come the moment he touched me down there. He leaned on one elbow beneath me as his fingers did extraordinary things to me. I was so close. I was right there ready to climax when the image flashed through my mind. It was Drew. He hit me across the face with the back of his hand, and I heard his angry tone.

"I told you not to come," the voice echoed through my mind, and just like that it was gone.

It was enough though. It was enough to scare the living hell right out of me. I quickly sat up.

"What's wrong?" he asked, shocked as I grabbed my clothes and started pulling them on.

"I don't know what it is, something." I assured him.

He softly took me in his arms. "Morgan?" he said.

"Did you hit me, Drew?" I asked, looking up to him. I had to.

"What?" he asked like I was crazy. "No. I never hit you. Why would you ask something like that?"

"I just had a quick image of you hitting me."

"Baby, I'm sure it's just your mind playing tricks on you. Come back to bed with me."

"I can't," I admitted, pulling on my shorts. "I'm not ready for this."

I left him and headed back upstairs to my own safe room, but it didn't feel safe at all. I felt far from safe when I closed my door. I crawled into my bed and tried to relax. Why did I just see Drew hit me? It was so real. Was it my subconscious? Did he really hit me? I was probably just being over sensitive. It was probably nothing. I let my mind drift off to what was about to happen in his bed. I knew that I was still wet and more than ready as I recalled his fingers doing what they were doing.

Before I knew it, my own hands were inside of my panties, pleasing myself. It felt strange. I almost felt like he was watching me for some reason. I knew that it was crazy and was probably just in my overactive imagination.

"Stop," I heard Drew whisper right beside my bed.

I did stop. I inconspicuously tried to remove my hand without his knowing that it was there. How embarrassing was that? Did he know? Why was he telling me to stop?

I stared at him with wide eyes as he removed the covers and ran his hand up my leg. He didn't look at my face and again slid me out of my shorts. I was frozen. I couldn't move. Twice now I had been on the brink of orgasm. I wanted to stop him, but I didn't want to stop him. I wondered what the chances of him taking care of me and not making me have sex with him were.

I could tell that he was trying exceedingly hard to be attentive to me, but for some reason he was fighting something. I just couldn't figure out what it was. The expressions changed rapidly from patient and loving to vengeance and hate. What the hell was his problem? I didn't stop him again. I didn't have the control. I had a need that was dying to be filled.

He didn't let me come. Every time I would get close he would stop. I wanted to come so bad I could taste it. What the hell was his problem? The third time that I was close, and he knew it, he stopped again. He took my leg and twisted it over my body so that I was half on my stomach. I wanted to protest, but when I felt his fingers slide my juices from the front of me all the way to the back, I couldn't. I was aroused, scared, and exposed, and all I could do was lay there and let him have his way. I knew then that he was the leader in the bedroom. I just wasn't sure how I felt about it. I obviously liked it. I did marry him almost eight years before.

I wasn't sure how I felt again when I felt his finger penetrating my anus. I mean. I thought I liked it, but I didn't know if I was reacting out of fear or arousal. I grabbed the sheet and squeezed it into my fist as I felt him slide his finger into me. The other one had been dancing on my clit up until that time. He moved it and used his hand to spread me more as his finger penetrated me, slowly in and out. I would have to say that it felt better when his finger was massaging my clitoris, but I still didn't stop him. I couldn't.

I almost panicked when I heard his zipper being slid down. I wanted to protest and stop him, but I was afraid of him. Why would I be afraid of him?

I couldn't believe it. Our first time making love in who knew how long and he thought that he was going to put it in my ass? I don't think so.

That was exactly what he did and I let him. He brought his knees to the bed and spread me as much as he could. As soon as I felt his finger slide out I felt the head of him trying to enter me, I had to protest.

"Drew," I said, trying to stop him.

"Shhhh," he countered as he moved in a little more. "I'll let you come too, don't worry."

What? Why would I worry? That vision suddenly became so real.

"Give me your hand," he requested.

I reached my hand to his. I thought he wanted to hold it, to reassure me. He wanted me to hold myself open for him so that he could put his hands on the bed to the sides of me and move in and out of me more forcefully. This wasn't what I had in mind for our first time. He did hold true to his word. He moved into an upright position, pulling me with him and placed his thumb back to my core as he pulled me toward him. I called out in agonizing pleasure as he shoved deep into my ass and released his own satisfaction.

"God, I missed you," he whimpered, pulled himself out of me, kissed me on the head and left.

What the fuck?

What just happened here? I felt violated, hurt, confused, and dirty. I jumped in the shower and scrubbed every inch of him off of me. I didn't love that man. I could never love someone like him. Did I? No. No. I couldn't love him. It was impossible.

I spent the better part of the next day in my room, afraid to face him after what had happened the night before. He sent the cook up with a tray, and I ate in my room. I felt like I was sinking into a hole, some sort of depression. I sat in the chair by the window and stared out blankly trying to figure out where I belonged. I didn't feel it was there at all.

Around one in the afternoon, I heard a knock on my door. When I opened it, there was a lady carrying a bag. I had forgotten all about the dinner party I was attending with Drew. I didn't want to go. I wanted to go somewhere, but not there with him.

"I'm here to take care of your hair for the night. Are you ready?"

I didn't need anyone to take care of my hair. I could take care of it myself. Did Drew send her?

Of course, I let her in, and we moved to the vanity. She did my hair and makeup, taking almost two hours. My butt hurt so badly from sitting, and I squirmed trying to ease the discomfort.

I followed her to the door and then headed to Drew's office.

I was stoned stupid when I stood outside listening to the conversation between him and Derik.

"She's not your little slave anymore. I'm telling you; she is going to make trouble," I heard Derik say.

"Don't worry, my friend. I will have her back to knowing who her master is in no time flat."

I walked quickly past the door and into the kitchen with Marta, the cook.

"Can I get a cup of coffee?" I asked. My hair and makeup were done beautifully, and all I needed to do was pull on my dress. I didn't want to go anywhere with Drew. I felt sick. Slave? Master? What did that mean? Why can't I remember? I really need to remember. Something dreadful happened there. I could feel it.

I tried to tell Drew that I didn't feel well, and I should stay home, but he wouldn't hear of it. He was making me go, and all of my nerve to tell him no had disappeared with the slave and master remark.

I reluctantly went with him. Derik drove us, and I wondered what role he played in Drew's business. He always seemed to be around. I stared out the window and jumped when Drew took my hand and smiled at me.

"You okay?" he asked.

No. I wasn't okay.

"I'm fine," I smiled a weak smile.

We had to stop at one of his stores on the way to the party, and that did seem familiar. I looked straight ahead in a daze as I took in the jewelry store.

"I've been here before," I stated, mostly to myself.

Drew snorted. "You've been here a lot of times. Go pick out a new set of wedding rings," he said looking down at the watch on his wrist. "We have to hurry."

"Where are the ones that I had?" I asked, not understanding.

"They cut them off of you in the wreck."

"Oh," that made sense.

I didn't care about the fancy diamonds, and picked the first set that my eyes landed on.

There weren't a lot of people at the party. I was glad of that. Right away I noticed the man in the wheelchair. I couldn't remember his name. He wheeled over to us with a smile. He took my hand and admired the wedding set.

"How are you doing, Morgan?" he asked.

"Better," I lied. I wasn't better at all, maybe physically, but certainly not emotionally or mentally.

"Well, you look radiant," he said.

"Thank you."

Derik's wife joined us next. She was said to have been my best friend there. I didn't think so. She didn't seem like someone that I would be friends with, but I didn't like a lot of things that seemed to be my life.

"It's so good to see you," Jena said.

"I'm sorry," I apologized.

"Jena," she offered. "I'm Derik's wife," she smiled.

Poor girl.

We were all led to a table and sat with the man in the wheelchair, his caretaker, Derik and Jena. I mostly listened to the conversation around the table. Everyone seemed fine with that except for the man in the wheelchair.

Callaway, yeah, that was his name.

For some reason, he was more concerned with my well-being than my husband was. He wanted to know what the doctor had said at my appointment that week. I wondered how he knew about that. I finally had to ask. I couldn't take it a second longer. Drew choked on the wine that he just sipped.

"How do we know each other?" I bluntly asked. I expected that he was going to tell me that he knew me through Drew.

"Let's just say that it has been a goal of mine ever since I found out about you, to make sure that you were always taken care of," he smiled.

I hadn't even seen Drew get up. The next thing I knew he was by my side. He held out his hand for me.

"Would you dance with me, Mrs. Kelley?" he asked.

"I don't think I know how to dance," I admitted, already taking his hand.

"He could be so charming and yet turn into such a dick when I least expected. I happen to know that you are a remarkable dancer," he smiled.

I could dance. How did I know how to waltz around the floor like that? I moved with Drew like we had done it a million times.

"I take it we have done this before?" I asked as he spun me back into his arms.

"Yes, you used to love to go out dancing."

"Drew."

"Yes, Mrs. Kelley?"

"I'm not sure that I am okay with what happened last night."

Drew looked down at me as though he was clueless.

"What do you mean," he asked.

"I just wasn't expecting our first time to be like that."

He snickered and pulled me closer to him. "It wasn't our first time, Morgan, and I was just trying to give you what you liked. You know? Hoping to jog your memory."

"I liked that?"

"I do miss that a lot," he admitted. "That was actually mild compared to what you normally like."

"It was?"

Oh, God. I was some sort of sex freak.

He laughed again. "Don't worry about it. I'll try to remember that your memories are gone. How's that."

"Maybe we should start by sleeping in the same bed together again," I suggested. I could have sworn that I felt him tense.

"I don't think you are ready for that just yet."

Who the hell was he to tell me what I was ready for?

I leaned in closer to his ear. "You don't think that I am ready to sleep in your bed, but I was ready for you to stick your dick in my ass?"

I know for a fact that he tensed that time.

Drew pulled me from the dance floor and back to the table. He never let go of my hand as he spoke to the other guests around the table.

"I think we are going to call it a night. Morgan's not feeling too well."

I pulled my hand from his. "Actually, I feel fine. I would love to try the pie," I spoke up, sitting back beside Mr. Callaway.

Mr. Callaway smiled and patted my hand. "That's my girl. The pecan pie here is to die for. I think I'll have one too," he smiled.

My girl? What did that mean? Drew took his seat in front of me and glared at me. I had just defied him in front of other people. I was sure that he wasn't okay with that.

Drew drove us home, and Derik left with his wife. I could tell that he was pissed. He wore a clenched jaw and his knuckles were white from gripping the steering wheel so tight.

"What the hell is wrong with you?" I asked. I didn't care. He was acting like some spoiled overgrown child.

"What's wrong? What's wrong? You just embarrassed the hell out of me in there, and you want to know what is wrong?"

"And how the hell do you think I did that? You shouldn't have lied and said I didn't feel well. Had I always let you talk for me and decide what I wanted?"

"Yeah, Morgan you did and when you didn't listen, you would be punished once we were home. Maybe I need to show you how we do things around here," he said through clenched teeth.

That scared the hell out of me. Punish me? What the hell did that mean? I wasn't backing down. I wasn't about to let him think I was intimidated by him for one second.

"Fuck you!" I yelled.

He grabbed me by my hair. "You need to stop. I'm warning you, Morgan. You don't want to do this."

I knew at that moment that he did hit me, and that vision of him backhanding me did happen. I had a feeling that it happened more often than not. I didn't care. I wasn't stopping.

"Take your hands off of me. Now!" I demanded through the same gritted teeth.

Drew let go. I was happy. I was no match for his muscular build, and I knew it. I also knew that I had to get away from him. I don't know who I was before my accident or what I allowed to happen to me, but I knew that I wasn't willing to let it happen again. I just didn't know what I was supposed to do about it. Where would I go?

I didn't wait for him to open my door. I stormed into the house and right up to my own room.

"Of course, no lock," I said out loud to the empty suite.

I took off the expensive dress, pulled the pins from my hair and pulled on my baggy flannel pants and simple white t-shirt. Drew didn't bother me, and I was glad. I went to bed thinking about him telling me that I needed to be punished. I wondered what kind of sex life we had. I didn't think that I liked it.

The pain pills allowed me to doze off. I slept solidly and sound. I was in deep sleep when I woke hours later with tears in my eyes. I sat up trying to remember what I had dreamt. I couldn't remember. The only thing that I had taken from my dream was the name Dawson. I didn't know who he was, but I knew that my heart ached for him, and I missed him. I hadn't heard the name Dawson at all. I wondered if Drew knew a Dawson. I decided not to ask him. Maybe he was someone that I had met in Florence. Maybe that was why I was there and not here with Drew.

I lay awake for a long time, trying to remember something, anything. I didn't care what it was. It's unexplainable to wake up and not know who you are or where you came from. There were so many questions that nobody could answer for me. I had talked to the lady that cooked for us, but she said that she hadn't been there that long, and didn't know me pre-accident. Why did it seem like Drew and Derik were the only two people that I was acquainted with?

I reached for the bottle of pills on my nightstand and took two of them. It was dark, and I didn't look at them, but they did seem to feel different in my hand. I rolled them around my finger and almost turned the light on to see if they had been replaced with something else.

Oh my God, Stop it, Morgan...

I dry swallowed the pills and was quickly dozing back to a comatose state. I could have sworn that Drew was standing in my room. I could see his shadow or maybe it was the pills that I had just taken. I didn't feel so good, and it felt like I was drifting down, down, down.

"Don't worry my little bad girl. You'll be out in no time. You won't remember any of this," Drew said. I was sure that he said it. I think.

I felt his hands slide up my shirt and squeeze both of my nipples. I know I felt it. I think.

He sat me up to remove my shirt, and I couldn't hold my head up. I was trying to move, but none of my limbs would work. I knew I was naked. I knew my legs were spread open, and I was being touched there, but I couldn't move.

"Where were you for two years, Morgan?" Drew asked, kissing and sucking on my breast. "Did you really think you were going to get away with it? Uh? Did you, Morgan?"

I was sure that I felt the sting of his hand on my bare ass, but I couldn't really tell. I thought it stung, but then again, I didn't really feel anything. Was I drugged? Was this just another bad dream? I had to think. I had to stay focused, but I couldn't. All I could do was lay there and drift in and out of what was going on. I knew I was being moved around like a rag doll, but no matter how hard I tried, I couldn't move.

"Open your mouth, bad girl," Drew said. I was lying on my side, and his fingers were trying to pry my mouth open. I wanted to bite down, but I couldn't do that either. My jaw muscles wouldn't work and only parted at his command as I felt his penis slide across my tongue and to the back of my throat.

"Yeah, baby. This is all that you are good for. You need to learn that real fast. I own you. You do what I want, when I want," I could hear the words. I knew what he was saying.

I felt him pull out and slide between my legs. He would pump in and out of me fast and hard and then slide back in and out of my mouth. I don't know how many times he kept up the routine, but I knew. I could taste myself every time he did it.

Drew said, "I brought your favorite toy, bad girl." I couldn't see it. I couldn't really see anything, and what I did see was distorted and distant. I could no doubt feel it. Whatever it was caused and instant orgasm, almost. Whatever he was touching me with would send some sort of current through my female parts, bring me to the peak of orgasm, and stop. If I had been able to speak, I would have been begging to come. It was that intense.

I don't know how long Drew played with the toy before he had me flipped over. I felt him drag my legs so they hung over the bed. He split me open, and I felt something being inserted into my ass. I didn't think it was him, but I wasn't sure and then I knew it wasn't when I felt the vibration. He moved it in and out, making lustful noises and saying perverted things as he did. I felt him smack my naked bottom more than once. I knew it was him shortly after, and he pounded hard and fast into my ass for I don't know how long. I knew it was over when I heard him moan loudly and steady himself deep inside of me.

The next morning I woke fully clothed, dressed the same as the night before. Did I dream all of that? Was it all just a nightmare? I tried to notice how I felt down below, but I couldn't assuredly tell. It felt a little off, but I didn't know if that was just me being paranoid or not. I grabbed the bottle of pills to see if they had been switched. They hadn't. It was the same little blue pills that I had been taking for over a month, the ones that Dr. Tharp had prescribed when he released me.

I showered and pulled on a pair of jeans and a knit shirt. I went into the kitchen, and Marta had eggs and toast ready for me sitting on the table in the kitchen.

Drew came in shortly after wearing a smile, dressed in his expensive suit.

"Good morning," he said, kissing the top of my head.

"Good morning," I replied. I didn't want to be a bitch if I had imagined the nightmare that I was almost sure took place the night before. I was trying like hell to convince myself that the incident in the car was just a fight, and to not dwell on that either.

Drew ate with me and then disappeared into his office. I needed out of that house. I needed to go someplace where I could think.

I walked right into his office, purposely not knocking. I got the same dirty look for barging in.

"Could you leave us please," I asked Derik, standing in the same stuffy clothes as Drew.

He blew out a puff of air as if he were saying, in your dreams.

"Go, Derik," Drew demanded.

He left, but gave me a look that I wasn't sure of. It was somewhere between a warning and a vengeful expression. I didn't care.

"I need a car today," I spit out. I thought Drew was going to fall off his chair.

"You need a car?"

"Yes. I have to get out of this house for a while before I go crazy. I did drive before, didn't I?"

"Not really. You were driven to where you wanted to go. Don't you remember what happened the last time you drove?"

"No, Drew. I don't. I don't remember any fucking thing," I smartly replied. How dare he?

"Where do you want to go? I will have Derik drive you."

"I don't even want to be in the same room with that man. I want to go alone. I do have a driver's license," I stated. I did have a license. My hair was blonde in them, and they were good until my next birthday.

"You don't like Derik? You liked him before," he reminded me. I rolled my eyes.

"Maybe I did, and maybe I didn't. I have a feeling that my whole life before the accident was nothing but a lie."

"What's that supposed to mean?"

"Nothing, Drew. Can I take your car or not."

"How long are you going to be gone? Where are you going?"

"I have no idea, but I'm not twelve. I think I will be fine."

"Why don't you go to Lennox Park?" he suggested and stood to take his keys from his pocket.

I knew where that was. I don't know how I knew, but I did.

Chapter 15

I knew I was being followed. I could not only see Derik but also Drew in the rearview mirror. I didn't care. They could follow me all they wanted. I had nowhere to go. I did take Drew's advice and went to the park. I walked the red brick path around the park and sat on a bench. I watched the kids play and run around. It felt good. I smiled at their innocent happiness as they ran and yelled.

I knew Drew and Derik were somewhere close, but I wasn't going to even look around for them. I didn't care. I needed to figure out what I was doing. I couldn't stay with him. Maybe I could talk to Mr. Callaway. He seemed to be genuinely concerned about me. That would be fine had I known where to find him or how to call him. My cell phone had one number in it, Drew's. Why didn't I have other friends? Why didn't I know anyone else? Why hadn't anyone come by to check on me?

"Dawson," I whispered out loud. Who was Dawson and why did I feel lost without him? I wasn't sure about anything, and sitting there amongst a bunch of strangers was doing nothing for my memory. I may as well give up and live with the cards that I have been dealt. I got up and started walking through the park again. I kept my head down. The red brick went in a big circle around the park, and I walked, following it back to where I started. If I could only follow the path back to where I remembered who the hell I was I would be a happy camper or would I. Something told me that I didn't want to know who I was before.

I stopped and looked up at the building across the road. 'Lennox Library,' I knew that building. Well maybe not knew, but it did seem to be ambiguously familiar. I walked off the path and onto the drought infested lawn. I could hear the crunch beneath my sneakers as I walked across the dry grass.

I pushed the crosswalk button and waited for the sign to tell me that it was my turn to cross. I went into the building, and for some reason I knew to go to the second floor of the massive library. I didn't know what was on the second floor, but I knew I had been there.

"Can I help you find something?" a lady asked from behind a desk after I just stood there.

"Do you know who I am?" I asked. It was a dumb question but worth a shot.

"Excuse me?" she asked as if she hadn't heard me.

"Never mind," I said and walked to the nonfiction section. I had read so many of those books, and I knew that I had gotten them from right there in that library.

Why does it even matter Morgan? It's not like you're going to remember anything of any importance anyway. Who cares if you used to check out books there? Wait... I had an e-reader. I remembered Drew taking it away from me. Why would I come to the library if I had access to millions of books right at my fingertips? I took a deep breath and ran my hands over my face and pinched the bridge of my nose. I had a horrible headache that seemed to be getting worse the more I tried to figure out my life.

I was just exiting the building when my cell phone rang.

"Are you okay?" Drew asked. Who else would it be? I only had one number.

"Yes. I'm fine. I'm heading back now."

"Did you have a nice time?"

"Yeah. I'll see you in a little bit," I replied, agitated as hell.

Drew must have believed me and knew that I was coming home. The car that I was sure they had followed me in was parked in front of the house.

Once again I barged right into his office. I tossed his keys and left without a word. I pretended not to notice the screen on his computer and walked in and right back out. I had a headache from hell, and couldn't process what I had seen just yet. I went right to my bed and lay across it holding my head. I wasn't about to touch the bottle of pills again. I would deal with the pain.

The sound of the white phone on the nightstand was deafening and echoed through my head. I was annoyed that I had to move to answer it.

"What?" I answered. I didn't know who it was. I didn't care.

"Are you okay?" Drew asked.

"Fine, I just have a horrible headache and want to rest awhile."

"Why don't you take a pain pill and sleep a little."

"I am never taking those pills again," I assured him and myself.

"Why?" he asked. I didn't know if I had imagined the whole thing the night before or not. I really didn't know, but I wasn't taking the chance.

"Because they make me have horrible nightmares," I retorted, hung up and lay my head back into my hands.

When I woke a couple hours later, my head did feel better. The headache wasn't entirely gone, but at least it wasn't pounding like it had before I fell asleep. I didn't move. I lay in the same position that I had for the past couple of hours with my face buried in my hands.

I knew that I had to revisit what I had seen in Drew's office. I knew that there were cameras in this room. I didn't get a close look, but I knew this room was on that screen. I wondered if my bathroom was under surveillance, as well. I had a good feeling that it was. That was how he knew that I couldn't get out of the tub that first day that I was home. That was how he knew to come and take the e-reader from me, but why? What was on it that he didn't want me to see? That was how he knew that I was pleasing myself the other night. Why was I on constant surveillance? Were there always cameras in here or was it just since my accident and he wanted to be able to see that I was okay?

For some reason, and I wasn't sure what about the reason. I knew that this had always been my room, and Drew and I never had slept together. What the hell was going on? Why couldn't I just remember? Dammit, I just wanted to remember. I needed to remember.

I pretended to stay asleep when Drew opened the door and sat on the side of my bed. He ran his hand up my arm and shoulder.

"Morgan," he softly spoke.

I moaned and removed my hands from my head.

"Feel better?" he asked. His hand brushed across my breast and my stomach as I rolled over. I ignored it.

"Yeah, I think so. Sorry, I was a little testy earlier. It wasn't you. I just had a horrible headache, probably too much sun." I had no idea what my plan was, but I knew I had to keep Drew at bay, at least until I knew whether my fears were real or not.

"It's okay. You've been sleeping for quite a while. Why don't you come down and get something to eat."

I smiled and sat up. I wrapped my arms around his neck and his wrapped around my waist. I could tell he was taken aback. That was what I was going for.

"Do you love me, Drew?" I asked, running my fingers through the back of his hair and along his neck.

"What kind of question is that? Of course, I love you. You're my wife."

"You never tell me," I said, pulling away and touching his bottom lip with my finger. That took him by surprise too.

"I guess we've just never had that kind of relationship. You have never been one to say it either, but we both know."

He moved my finger away from his lip. He didn't like the intimacy. Hmm… I pondered.

I kissed him next. I mean; I seriously kissed him, holding the sides of his face and shoving my tongue into his mouth. I pulled myself up to my knees, forcing my body closer to his. He pushed me away and looked at me totally stunned. I had just knocked the wind out of him, rendering him speechless. I couldn't let it stop me. I didn't know what I was doing. I had no plan, but I knew something wasn't right. I didn't belong with him. Something was missing. I knew that he didn't operate this way. I could feel it.

He didn't speak, even when I brought my bare feet to the floor and stood directly in front of him. I don't think he was able to. I wrapped my arms around his neck once again, and his stayed on the knees of his dress pants. I softly kissed his lips and moved down his neck. I didn't really mean to become aroused. I was only trying to take charge, something that I was sure I never did before. I don't know how I knew that. I just did. I was, however, becoming aroused. His expensive cologne and sexy physique was undoubtedly causing me to become instantly wet.

I moved my hands to the top button of his dress shirt and slowly worked my way down while my tongue and lips teased his neck and occasionally his lips. By the time I got to the third button his hands were on mine.

"What are you doing, Morgan?" he asked, trying to regain the control. I wasn't having it.

I pulled my hands out of his, not taking my eyes from his. I liked being over him. I felt like I had a little more power with him having to look up to me. My heart and nerves would have argued. There was such a rush of epinephrine pumping through my veins; I had a difficult time hiding it. I moved my hands to my jeans, ignoring his question. He watched my hands unbutton my jeans and slide down the zipper. I lifted my shirt over my head and slowly and seductively removed my bra. I moved my hands back to the buttons on his shirt, and he didn't stop me. He took my breast into his mouth, and I moaned. Dammit. I didn't want to do that.

I ran my hands over his strong chest, and he flipped me over so that he was now towering over me. I didn't want that either. I needed to stay in control. Think Riley. Think. I froze. Who the hell was Riley? The question remained, but I did manage to move it to the back of my mind while I figured out how to seduce my husband. I raised my hips and slid out of my jeans and panties. I could feel the protrusion grind into my hip as he kissed me. He pulled his lips away from mine and looked down my body, hungrily. Yes. That was what I wanted.

What I did next not only took him by surprise, but me, as well.

"Go down on me, Drew," I whispered in a pant. His eyes shot back to mine. I didn't let it phase me and tilted my bent knee, exposing myself for him. I moved his hand from my bare hip to the wet folds between my legs. I moaned as I felt his fingers slide up me. I did mean to do it that time.

"Taste me," I whispered again. He wasn't moving. He was stoned stupid. I moved up to the pillow so his head was at a level playing field with my throbbing sex.

"Morgan?" he muttered. I had totally dumbfounded him, and he didn't know how to react. I was sure that I was never the one to give the orders, but I was, and he wasn't sure how to respond.

I bucked my hips and ran my own fingers between my folds, beckoning him to do as he was told. He moved in and licked me once, almost like he wasn't sure what to do. I took his hair in my hand and kept his head there while he stroked me with his tongue.

"Hmm, yes Drew," I moaned. It must have been turning him on, and my plan, whatever that was, was working. I came as soon as he inserted two fingers into me. I came hard and clenched his hair in my fist. As soon as I was coherent enough to regulate my breathing, I moved him to his back and released his erection into my hand. He still couldn't speak. I bent to his lips and moaned as I inserted my tongue into his mouth, tasting myself on his lips. He raised his hips and helped me slide him out of his clothes. I ran my hands up his strong pecks as I slid him into me. I rode him hard, as fast and hard as I could. As soon as I called out in agonizing pleasure, he thrust deep, holding my hips into him. He came just as hard. I could feel him convulsing beneath me.

I smiled down to him as he dropped back to the bed. I moved his hand from my hip and kissed his fingertips before removing myself.

"I'm going to shower. I'll be down to eat with you in a little bit." I left him lying on my bed staring after me I was sure. I knew that had I turned around he would have been wearing that dazed, confused look that he had when I demanded that he go down on me.

I showered, and while I was rinsing the soap from my hair, I knew that I could see the camera lens around the ring of the shower head. I didn't stare at it and pretended not to see it. I showered as normal, wrapped myself in a towel and walked out to my room to dress. I opened the closet and pulled a pair of jeans and a knit shirt from the closet. I knew Drew hated me not wearing the designer clothes right at my fingertips. I loved to defy his wishes. I even went a step further and omitted the socks.

I walked down to where he was waiting and smiled with narrowed eyes in a flirtatious manner. I brushed my hands across his broad shoulders and let my fingers dance in the back of his hair before taking my seat beside him.

"What's gotten into you, and where are your socks?" he asked from the head of the table.

"I didn't want socks, and what do you mean, what has gotten into me? I don't remember anything, so if I am acting in a different way than I normally did, you have to tell me what I am doing wrong. I'm just trying to make sense of everything and be your wife. Did I do something wrong?" I asked, feeding him right out of my hand.

"No, you've just never been the um," he stopped, trying to think of the word, "aggressive, you have never been the aggressive type before."

I leaned in for a kiss. He hesitated but leaned in and kissed me. "I think I might like being aggressive," I smiled as Marta brought our food. I wanted to keep him talking. I just didn't know what to talk about. I didn't want to ask about anything that would throw up any of his defenses. I was determined to bring him down a few levels. Why? I wasn't sure yet, but I was working on it.

We ate our salads in silence, looking at each other every now and then. I decided to go for the pity party.

"Drew," I quietly said his name.

"Hmm?" he replied with food in his mouth, looking over to me.

"What if I never remember? What if I never remember the day we met, or our wedding day, what if I never remember how much we mean to each other?"

"I think you will. Don't worry about that. I think you are trying too hard. Just let it come on its own."

"You said that we have been married for almost eight years."

"Yes. We will be married eight years in June. Why?"

"June what?" I asked. I really did want to know that.

"June 4th."

"My birthday is June 4th. That means that we got married the day that I turned eighteen, right?"

He smiled a nervous smile and nodded.

"Where did we meet?"

"I came to your school when you were seventeen and did a seminar on success, and I donated some money. You were the prettiest girl in that school," he smiled. "I told you then that I was going to marry you. I would sneak back there, and we would spend weekends together and as soon as you graduated and turned eighteen I came and took you away."

"We got married the same day?"

"Yes, but that was all your idea. I had nothing to do with it. I think you wanted to make sure that no one else claimed me."

"How old are you?" I kept the conversation going. Some of it I wanted to know and some of it was irrelevant.

"Thirty-one, what's with all the questions?"

I took a deep breath and pushed my half eaten salad away. "I don't know. You just have no idea what it's like, not to know who you are or where you came from. I remember some things but don't know why I remember them.

"Like what?" Drew wanted to know.

"Like my birthday. I know when I was born, but not when I got married. I remember books that I have read and songs. You said that I would have never been caught dead dressed like this. Did my personality change too?"

"Your personality did change from what I remember too."

"Like how?"

"Well, like I said before. You would have never been as bold as you were earlier today. You didn't wear flannel pants or go barefoot. You would have never barged into my office the way you do now, which, by the way, I do not like."

I smiled even though I knew he was serious. I placed my hand on his forearm, and he looked down at it, almost confused.

"Thank you for being here for me," I said, looking at him with half a grin.

He didn't answer and only smiled.

Drew excused himself to go finish up some work after supper. I was working on a plan. I didn't know why. Maybe because I wanted him to come back to my room and do to me what he had earlier. He was rather good at it, and I felt myself throb at the thought of it.

I walked around outside until almost dark, thinking and contemplating my life. I wondered why I had called myself Riley earlier. Who the hell was Riley? It was someone that I knew at some point. I was sure of it, but was it me? Why did I think that? Did Riley have something to do with Dawson? Why couldn't I just remember?

There were cameras in my room, I wasn't sure where they were, but I was sure they were there. I didn't look for them and undressed, trying to do it as I always did, not wanting Drew to think that I was onto him. I took off my jeans, my shirt and my bra and left my panties. I walked over to the window and moved the curtain. I stood looking out, pretending to be lost in an unknown world. I was, but that wasn't what I was thinking about at the time. I was thinking about trying to get Drew to come to my room. I wanted to make sure my intuitions were right although I was pretty sure they were.

I ran my finger along my back and lightly through the lace of my panties. I could picture Drew sitting at his desk watching me. I closed my eyes and leaned against the frame of the window, running my fingers over my stomach and up to my breast. I could feel my panties becoming damp. I knew that it was the fascination of Drew watching me. I must be a sick individual. Did I have some sort of sex fetish? I didn't care at that time. I had a goal to achieve.

As I slid my fingers through the lace of my panties and to the wet creases of my sex, I wondered about something else.

When did I start shaving down there? Had I always kept it smooth? I moaned and knew that whether Drew appeared or not, I was going to climax. I brought my left leg up to the chair in front of me and moaned as I inserted one finger, dragging it back to my swollen clitoris.

I turned my head toward the door when it opened, smiling inside, but keeping a somber face as I saw the shocked expression on Drew's face. I would have loved to know what was going through his mind seeing me with my legged cocked on the chair with my fingers in my panties.

"What are you doing?" he asked in a husky tone, walking toward me.

I dropped my leg and turned my back to him. "Don't you ever knock?" I asked, using his words.

"Had I known what I was walking into, I would have."

Lying son of a bitch...

He was close. I could feel the heat from his body. I could smell him, but I didn't turn around. I did stop the movement of my hand but didn't remove it. I gasped when I felt his hands slide down my hips, removing my panties. He ran his hands over my bare ass.

I tilted my head, beckoning him to kiss my neck. He did. His hot breath on my neck and shoulder sent an exciting chill straight to my vagina.

"Do you remember me spanking you?" he rasped. "You used to beg for me to do that."

"I did," I asked. I *was* a sick individual.

"You did. Do you know what else you liked?" he asked as his fingers traveled to my wet folds from behind, stopping at my puckering anus.

"I have a feeling I know the answer to that one," I admitted as I felt his finger penetrate me.

"Do you want me to spank you, Morgan?" he asked.

"Yes," I replied, barely above a whisper. I would have done anything the man told me to do at that moment.

I watched as Drew removed his clothes. He was hard as iron, and I wanted to taste him.

"Come here, Morgan," he demanded, and like a puppet on a string, I walked to him.

"Bend over the bed, my bad girl," he coaxed, moving my arm to guide me.

I didn't like the bad girl comment, and for some reason panic was setting in, and I was afraid of him. He rubbed my bare ass softly right before I felt the first sting of his hand. I jumped.

"Don't move, Morgan," he warned. I didn't like the dark tone, but I was afraid to move. I suddenly didn't think my idea was so great anymore. After four, blows, he was done with that and was spreading me open. I felt the head of him on my anus, but he didn't penetrate me. I was no longer in control; he had taken it back, and I had let him. Dammit. He knew I was afraid. It's what he wanted, what he thrived on.

If I didn't act soon, I was going to lose the battle that I had been working on. All of a sudden the nerve came from somewhere. I wasn't sure where, I was just sure I needed to act on it before I lost it. I rolled over and dropped to my knees in front of him and took his hard shaft to the back of my throat. I couldn't see the look on his face, but the rapid stiff posture told me what it said. I moaned as I took him in and out of my mouth. I looked up to him as he placed his hands over his head and let me have my way with him. I kept it up until I could tell he was losing control. I wasn't about to let him come in my mouth.

I kissed him up his body, and lightly tugged his nipple between my teeth. I circled his naked body, catching a glimpse of the baffled expression as I kissed his strong shoulders and back.

"Do you know what I think, Drew?" I said in a low tone. I had the power. I was now calling the shots.

"Hmm?" he managed to moan. I was sure that was all that he could come up with in his state.

"I think that you are the one that liked for me to take it up the ass. Do you want to put your dick in my ass, Drew?" I asked, still standing behind him as my lips and hands explored his back.

His head snapped back toward me. I was almost scared again when I saw the vengeful look on his face. Maybe I went a bit too far.

I ignored it and walked in front of him, keeping my back to him. I couldn't let him see the fear. I took his hand and guided it between my legs and bent over in front of him, giving him permission to take me. I breathed a sigh of relief as I placed my hands on the mattress and felt him slide his dick inside of my wet pussy before moving it to where he wanted it to be. I squeezed my eyes shut as I felt the head slide in. He hissed as he moved in a little more. I didn't let him stop rubbing my clitoris. I needed to keep my mind on achieving orgasm and not what I was doing to him.

I moaned once he was pumping in and out of me. His fingers on my swollen core kept the same rhythm of his cock sliding in and out.

"Don't come, Morgan," He demanded.

Fuck that...

I did come. I came so hard that I had to drop to the bed as he continued to thrust frantically and finally dropping with me.

"I told you not to come," he said with the angry tone again.

I didn't care. I had won. I wasn't afraid that time. I laughed, which I am sure wasn't the reaction he was hoping for.

I turned over, forcing him to slide out of me. I kissed his lips softly, and then shoved my tongue into his mouth. "I guess you'll just have to spank me again for being a bad girl," I smirked.

"Come with me," I requested, taking his hand and leading him to the bathroom.

"What are you doing now?" he asked as I started the shower water.

I turned and kissed him again. "Stop asking questions that you already know the answer to."

"I have my own shower," he protested.

"Shut up and get in here with me," I demanded. I would have loved to hear the voices going crazy in his head. I pulled him in with me and leaned my back into his front. He was so out of his realm it was dangerous, probably more dangerous for me than him.

I washed my hair and bathed while he stood watching me, not knowing what to do. When I turned to face him to rinse the soap from my hair, he surprised me. He pressed our wet bodies together and crushed his lips to mine. I felt weak and almost faint. I didn't want those feelings. It was a game, and I was winning. He couldn't make it about feelings, but there was so much passion in his kiss that was exactly what he was doing.

I got out and dressed, letting him shower. I was sitting in bed with the covers pulled down wearing a midnight blue nighty with matching panties. I had one bare leg brought to my chest, and the other one folded under it while I brushed my hair. He stopped in his tracks when he saw me, almost like he realized for the first time that I was beautiful or something.

"Come here," I softly spoke, and just like I was now controlling his strings, he walked toward me. I actually felt a twinge between my legs again, looking at his damp body wrapped in a towel around his waist. I touched his chest with the back of my hand and looked up, urging him to kiss me. He did.

"Stay with me tonight," I requested softly to his lips.

Snap. Just like that, he was grabbing his clothes and getting far away from me. Too much intimacy. "I can't, I still have work to do. You should get some rest."

Drew left, and I lay down. I stared out to the dark Nevada sky as my mind began to wonder once again. I wasn't sure if I had made things worse or better. I was more confused than ever. Maybe he wasn't the bad guy. Maybe the vision of him hitting me was nothing more than a vision. Maybe we really could have a life together. But who was Riley? Who was Dawson? I still had so many questions, and now I had feelings for Drew.

Stupid brain injury.

I didn't want to wake up. I wanted the dream to be real. I was sick. I was in bed, and somebody was making me drink chicken broth. He kissed my head and told me that he loved me over and over. He rubbed my naked back with his strong hands and kissed my heat fevered flesh with tiny, tender kisses. He loved me, and I loved him, but it wasn't Drew. I couldn't see a face. Who was taking care of me? I could hear waves. They were so close. I sat straight up squeezing the satin of my nighty in two fists on my chest. I was panting and sucking in air that wasn't there.

"Drew," I said in desperation as soon as I saw him enter my dark room. He was watching me sleep. I knew it. I could picture him sitting at his desk watching the camera in my room as I slept.

He hesitated and stood by my bed, not sure how to handle me. I grabbed for his t-shirt and pulled him to me. He sat down and wrapped his arms around me. Was he afraid that I was dreaming about something that he had done?

I couldn't get close enough to him. I needed to feel secure, but I wasn't feeling it with him. Why?

"Tell me why you were screaming," he pleaded.

I wasn't screaming. I knew I never screamed. It wasn't that kind of dream. He was watching me. He saw me sit up and suck in the unavailable air. I never screamed.

"I was screaming?" I asked, burying my face into the crook of his neck.

"Yes. How else would I have known you were having a bad dream?"

"Lay with me, Drew," I requested. He paused but did.

I didn't give him a choice but to hold me. I pressed my back to his front and took his arm, wrapping it around my body myself.

"What was your dream about?" he asked.

"I was sick. Somebody was taking care of me. He was making me drink chicken broth and kissing my back. I could hear waves. I was so sick, and then he left me. Was that you, Drew? Did you take care of me when I was sick? Did you leave me?"

"I am sure that I took care of you when you were sick a time or two. Shhhh, you're okay. Go to sleep."

"Drew."

"Hmm?"

"Don't leave me," I pleaded.

He didn't answer, and only took a deep breath. I wanted him to kiss my hair, and tell me that he loved me the way the man in my dream did. He didn't. He lay very still with me in his arms.

I was awake when Drew woke in the morning. I didn't let him know that I was awake, and stayed still, lying on his chest with both of his arms securely around me. I knew he was awake when he moved his arms from me, almost like he was afraid of me or afraid of the feelings that he had for me. I felt his head move and look down at me sleeping on his chest. I wished I could have seen his face. He tried to slide from beneath me. I reached for him before he could leave.

"You said you wouldn't leave," I said opening my eyes, holding onto his wrist.

He smiled back at me. "I have to work," he said and tried to get up. I held his wrist.

"Kiss me," I demanded before he left.

He looked at me with a look that I hadn't seen from him. It wasn't the startled, afraid of me, baffled look. It was more as if all of a sudden he was terrified of me. I knew that he didn't do intimacy. I don't know how I knew that. I just did.

I sat up and pulled myself across his lap, wrapping my arms around his neck. His right hand went to the satin on my back, and his left hand rested on my thigh. I dropped my head to his forehead and smiled at him, landing a small kiss on the corner of his lips.

"I don't know who you are anymore, Morgan," he admitted.

I smiled. "That's okay, I don't know who you are either." He smiled and laughed a short laugh.

"I have to get ready. Derik is going to be here wondering where I am."

"Tell him you were making love to your wife," I offered, getting another smile, but no response to my request.

I moved off him, and he thought that I was going to let him up. I didn't and brought one leg over, straddling his waist. I took matters into my own hands and kissed him. He kissed me back with a moan. I won again. He flipped me over and took me quickly in the normal missionary style.

"Now can I go work?" he asked, looking down at me once we were both spent.

I traced his lips with my finger. "Yes, you can go work. Can I take your car today?" I asked as he rolled off of me.

I could tell that he didn't like it, but I had to get him to trust me. I had to make him know that I would come back to him every time. I would come back. I would come back unless I found out that the dark Drew that I once knew wasn't anything more than a figment of my imagination.

"Where are you going?"

"I don't know, shopping maybe, maybe to the park and to that little Bistro café for lunch."

"Promise me that you will stay on this side of the city? I don't want you in all the chaos of the strip."

"I promise," I said and got up. I kissed him, and let him leave.

I showered and felt good that morning. I blow dried my hair, parted it on the side and added loose curls. I did my makeup, my nails and toenails. I looked in the closet at the mass of clothing. I found an outfit with tags still hanging from the band. It was a short outfit that was a little fancy for my taste, well for my post brain injury taste. I didn't know what my taste was before that. It was black satin shorts with a black sleeveless top. The shorts fit exceptionally well, and the sleeveless top was cut low in the front with bright blue trim bringing the focus to my cleavage. The front of the top was cut at a point, and the back was shorter showing a little midriff. I thought I looked hot. I smiled. I put on a pair of dangling silver earrings and a wide silver and gold bracelet. I wondered where I had gotten them and wondered if Drew had bought them for me. He didn't have to buy them. He owned them. I remembered.

I walked down the stairs wearing a pair of black heels with a delicate strap wrapping around my ankle twice. I opened Drew's office door, without knocking, of course. He and Derik both were going over some charts strewn about his desk.

Derik looked annoyed. Drew's jaw dropped when he saw me.

"I need your keys," I said walking over to him.

He fumbled for his keys in his pocket.

"What the hell are you doing, Drew?" Derik asked. He didn't want me to leave alone for some reason.

I shot him a dirty look. Who the hell did he think he was?

Drew placed his keys in my hand, and I kissed him. I was sure that wasn't something that I did before either. Derik was the one picking his jaw up next.

I started out of the office and then turned back. "Drew?"

"Yeah?"

"I need some money," I stated, remembering that I had an expired credit card in my purse, and that was it.

He smiled and took his wallet from the inside of his suit jacket. I walked back to him and took it from his hand. I looked up at him with a smile, and he leaned in and kissed me. He did it. I never even moved toward him for that. He did it all on his own. I smiled a victorious smile inside.

I left but purposely didn't let the door close all the way. I wanted to hear what Derik had to say.

"What the fuck is wrong with you?" Derik asked.

"Nothing. Don't worry about it."

"I thought you said that you would have her back to being your little sex slave in no time. You're letting her dictate you. What the fuck, Drew? You're going to ruin everything."

"I'm not going to ruin anything. I would rather she trust me and not run again."

"I saw the way you looked at her, Drew. You're playing with fire. You're going to get us both burned. You need to reel her back in, like right now. I've got almost ten years invested in your get rich scheme. You're not going to ruin this for me. What are you going to do when she wakes up and remembers how you used to beat the fuck out of her and torment her with your sick sex games?"

"Drop it, Derik," Drew warned.

"Leave me alone with her for a week. I'll make her remember why she is here. What about Skyler? Do you remember her?"

"I haven't talked to Skyler in months. I'm over that. Get back to work."

"We need to stick to the plan here, Drew, better yet, we need to go kill off the old man and do away with her before she ruins it all."

My heart sank as I quietly walked away from the door. What the hell are those two up to? I ran? Where did I go? How did I get back here? Where was I? How long was I gone? I had so many questions and couldn't answer a one of them.

Chapter 16

I sat on the bench at the park in my fancy clothes, feeling sorry for myself. He did hit me. He did do sadistic sex acts on me. All of my insights were right, all but one which I didn't understand. Why did the mention of another woman make me jealous? Drew didn't love me. He never did. He was in love with Skyler, whoever that was. I sat staring blankly at the dry, cracked ground for over an hour. I had to snap out of it. I had to stick to the plan.

What fucking plan, Riley?

I did it again. Who the hell is Riley, and why did I keep referring to her as me?

Okay. Morgan, you can either sit here and have a pity party all day or you can keep doing what you've been doing. What if they were planning on killing me? I heard Derik say that they needed to get rid of me. Why? I didn't have anything that they could want.

Stop it, Morgan. Let's just think for a minute. Maybe I should run. I did it before apparently. Maybe I was Riley when I did. I couldn't run. Where would I run to? I didn't even know who I was. I got up from the bench and went about my planned day. I had lunch at the little café, went to a book store and bought two magazines and a romance novel. Why the romance novel, I didn't know. I didn't think it was my type of book, but it looked interesting.

I knew I had lost my mind when I walked into the next store. Well, I really did lose my mind. I had an excuse. I was in a corner store with every kind of sex toy imaginable. What the hell was I doing?

The store was fairly empty. I was glad of that. The older woman running the place paid me no mind as I walked around looking at the different objects. I shook my head, not believing I was about to do what I was about to do. I bought my two items with Drew's credit card and left with my head down. I stopped at the little café again before heading back to the mansion. I bought Drew one of the Danish's that I had. They were mouthwatering, delicious. I bought him some sort of fancy coffee with whipped cream and chocolate swirled on the top.

Once again I didn't knock. Derik looked pissed. I didn't care. I was pissed.

"Can you leave us for a few," I asked him.

He huffed. "No," he point blank replied.

"Go, Derik," Drew demanded.

He gave me a dirty look and stormed out. I should probably watch my back.

"You have got to stop doing that. I am trying to work here."

"Why don't you go to work like normal people?" I asked, and caught his half grin.

"What can I do for you, Mrs. Kelley?" he smirked.

"You mean now or later?" I asked with a serious expression.

"Now."

I gave him the bag with the pastry and opened the lid on his coffee. "I brought you something," I said. He looked surprised. I must have never brought him anything before.

"You didn't bring Derik any?"

I glared at him with narrowed eyes. "I don't like him."

"Why?"

"I don't know. I think he hurt me before."

"What do you mean?" Drew asked with a peculiar look.

"I don't know. It's probably nothing, just a feeling I get around him. Forget it."

"I'm not sure I want to forget it," Drew was defensive over me, maybe this wasn't such a lost cause after all.

"I bought you something else too," I said with a sexy look, wanting to forget about Derik.

Drew sipped his coffee. "Why are you buying me stuff?" he asked.

I moved in front of him and leaned against his desk right between his legs. I slid my hand into the brown paper sack and pulled out the anal beads with a smile. His eyes widened, but he couldn't control his lip curling up a little.

"You are a bad girl," he smiled.

I pulled out the next toy, one that I was certain he would enjoy trying out. It was a metal ring that went around the base of his shaft with two rods sticking out in different directions. When he moved into me, the silver balls would move in and out of my ass. The other rod would hit my clit with every thrust.

"You're crazy," he smiled.

"But you like it, right?"

"I do," he admitted.

"Good. Now stand up and kiss me so you can get back to work."

Drew did exactly what I told him to do. He stood, spreading my legs with his and kissed me. He even went as far to wrap his arms around my back and grind into me. I moaned into his mouth.

"I thought you had work to do," I exclaimed, placing my hand on his chest.

"I do. Get out of here," he said with a quick peck on my lips and a swat to my behind as I walked away.

Derik glared at me right outside the door. I knew that he couldn't believe my audacity, but I didn't care. I couldn't believe his.

I went upstairs and changed. I only wore the fancy duds to impress Drew. I think I succeeded. I hated them. I was done impressing him. I changed into a pair of white stretch shorts with a blue stripe running down both legs and a blue camisole.

I walked to the kitchen barefoot, and Marta was putting away the sack of groceries that I had brought home. I didn't know how I knew, but somehow I knew that I liked to cook.

"I've got this. Mr. Kelley said to tell you that you could go for the night."

"He said that I was only to leave if he told me to go," she countered, afraid of losing her job.

"I would kind of like to have Mr. Kelley to myself tonight," I smiled. "I want to cook for him myself. I promise you won't be in any trouble."

She smiled, knowing why I wanted my husband alone. "I see. Well, I wouldn't want to stand in the way of romance," she stated, drying her hands on a towel before leaving for the day.

I got right to work with my salad. I almost bought stuff to make spaghetti, but for some reason, I knew that Drew hated spaghetti. I didn't know how I knew that, but I did or at least I thought so anyway, maybe I would ask him.

It was almost six o'clock. I was starting to wonder if Drew and Derik were going to stay in his office all night. My Swiss steak had been simmering for over an hour, not that it would hurt anything. They were actually better the longer they simmered. It was the mashed potatoes warming in the oven that I was concerned about.

Derik walked into the kitchen and took a bottle of water from the refrigerator. He twisted the cap and scanned my body with his eyes. I self-consciously pulled down on my cami.

"You're treading on thin ice," he boldly stated.

I didn't have time to respond when Drew was right there.

"Derik," he reprimanded.

Derik toasted his bottle of water toward me and left. "I'll see you in the morning."

"What are you doing?" Drew asked.

"Cooking. What did he mean by that Drew," I asked.

"Don't worry about it, Morgan. Just ignore him. Why are you cooking? Where is Marta?"

"I sent her home. I like to cook. Don't I," I decided to ask. "Did I cook for us before?" I wondered out loud.

"Yeah, sometimes. Marta left?" he asked. I could tell he didn't like it.

"I told her to, Drew. She didn't want to go because she said she was told not to leave unless you told her to. I just wanted us to have the house to ourselves for once. It seems like there is always someone here."

Drew walked closer to me. "There is. This house is huge. Did you forget that too? Where are your shoes?"

I was still feeling extremely apprehensive about the overheard conversation. I wanted to lean into him and make him touch me, but I didn't. I couldn't quite read his mood, and I was afraid to.

"I know how big the house is, my shoes are upstairs, and I don't like people always around here. Why can't I do the cooking?"

"You don't belong in the kitchen. I'm going to shower," he said, turning to leave.

"Drew."

He turned without speaking. "Hurry, I'm going to set the table."

He smiled. Yes… he smiled. It might have been a small victory, but at least it was something.

My jaw dropped when I watched Drew stroll into the dining room. He was wearing jeans with a knit shirt that had three buttons at the top, all unbuttoned. I had never seen him in anything but suits. Well, not that I remembered anyway. He was hot. Sex appeal was dripping off him, causing me to feel like I might drip a little too.

"Earth to Morgan," he said.

I shook my head trying to come out of the trance. "Sorry, you just, never mind," I said. There was no way that I could say anything without it sounding ridiculous.

"What?" he asked, taking the head of the table with a smirk.

"Do you hate spaghetti?" I asked.

You idiot. You should have just commented on the jeans.

"What?" he laughed.

"I was just wondering. When I was trying to decide what to cook, I thought about making spaghetti, but for some reason I knew, well I thought, you didn't like it."

"You remembered right. I do hate spaghetti."

Drew praised my cooking, but then we ate in silence. I don't think either of us knew what to talk about. I was fighting with what I had overheard, and trying not to be afraid of him. I could tell that he was fighting something too. I had a good hunch that it was his new found attraction to me. I was sure that

271

we hadn't had that before. I also had a pretty good feeling that I was a weak, pathetic, sad human being when I was there before. Before I ran away to God only knew where.

"I have to leave tomorrow for a few days," Drew finally said, breaking the stillness between us.

"Where are you going?" I asked, and I thought I caught a hint of irritation for asking, but he quickly replaced it.

"Montreal, I have a very lucrative prospect there that could turn into a major purchase."

"Is Derik going?"

"No. Why do you ask?"

"What if he comes here while you are gone? I don't trust him."

"He won't come here. I promise."

"But what if he does? How would you know?"

"I would know. Don't worry about Derik. He won't come here."

"Take me with you," I threw out. I didn't know why. I didn't even know that I was thinking it.

He snickered. "You can't fly yet. Remember? Dr. Tharp doesn't want you in the higher altitude for six months."

"Let's clean up," I said, looking away from him. I felt sad. I didn't want him to leave me, and I was terrified of Derik even though I was sure that Drew was telling me that he would know if he was there because he had cameras in every room of this house. What the hell was wrong with me? I was sure that when I overhead Derik saying that they should stick to the plan and get rid of me that he was talking about killing me. Why? I didn't know. That was why I had to continue to get inside of Drew's head. I was just having a difficult time controlling my feelings for him.

"Clean up? You're joking," Drew said in a disbelieving tone.

"Why? Because, you don't belong in the kitchen either?"

"Exactly, let's leave it for Marta."

"You get off of that chair and help me clear this table. We're not leaving it for Marta," I demanded. He listened. He made some sort of disapproving growling noise, but he got up and started carrying dishes to the kitchen. I smiled to myself.

Steady now, Morgan. Reel'em in slow.

I rinsed and handed the dishes for Drew to deposit into the dishwasher. I wiped off the counter once we were done and turned to him staring as I dried my hands.

"I like you in jeans," I said.

"You do?" he asked with a flirty grin.

"Yeah, I think you're sexy as hell in jeans."

He smiled a sexy smile and took a step toward me. My heart fluttered at his closeness; my hands became clammy, and the emotional desirability was almost unbearable. I grasped his shirt in my hand and leaned into him. He fisted my hair and pulled my head back, forcing me to look at him as he hungrily took my mouth with his.

Whoa vagina.

I turned my head, beckoning him to take my neck. He did and ran his hand up my ribs and back. I thought I was going to faint. I needed to be lying down in bed with my legs wrapped around his waist.

Before I knew what was happening I was naked, standing in the kitchen while his hands explored every part of my body except the one part that was begging for him to touch. He avoided that area as his hands discovered my body. It was a little strange, almost like he had never touched me before, and he was trying to entrench my body in his mind.

Drew fiercely turned me and forced me onto the bar. It scared me. He had an aggressiveness going on that I wasn't sure about. I quickly hid my fear and stopped him. I held his hands so he couldn't move them on me anymore. He looked up at me.

"Easy, Drew," I whispered, and just like magic he went from hostile to gentle.

I never even asked. He spread me open in front of him on the bar and ran his tongue up my wet pussy. I dropped my head and moaned. I think he liked tasting me. We never got the chance to try out the new toys, and once I was yelling out, and I mean yelling, he pulled me up and down his body. He took me on the kitchen floor, and it was the most glorious love making I had ever had in my life, not that I could remember any other ones, but still.

"Was our sex life always this good?" I asked, running my nails down his back.

He rose up and looked down at me with a remorseful look. I didn't understand it. I ran my fingers gently over his bottom lip.

"No. Morgan. It wasn't always like this," he softly spoke.

"How was it?" I asked, afraid of the answer.

I didn't get one. He pulled out of me and lifted me to my feet.

"It doesn't matter," he demanded. He was distant. He let go of my hand and gathered his clothing, leaving me staring after him, alone in the kitchen.

Well. Okay then.

I didn't want him to leave me. I didn't want to go to the room upstairs that left me feeling, feeling; I wasn't sure what it was. I just got a bad sensation in that room, and I hated it. I wanted to go for a walk with him or maybe watch some television with him, and fall asleep in his arms. That wasn't going to happen, and he had shut me out when he shut his bedroom door behind him.

It was still pretty early, not even nine thirty yet. I ran a tub of water and sank into it, trying to decipher the thoughts running through my mind. I knew I was being watched. I sensed it. I could see Drew sitting on his bed with his laptop staring at me. I didn't care. I felt hurt, rejected and alone.

I didn't put on one of the sexy nighties or stringy panties. I pulled on a comfortable t-shirt and a pair of plain cotton panties. I crawled into bed and was surprised at how tired I felt, emotionally drained, more like it. I rolled over to my side and pulled my hair out, sprawling it behind me on my pillow. I was emotionally drained and fell asleep in no time.

It was cold, and I was dressed in jeans and a hoodie. I was on the beach, laughing. I was with friends, and we were playing football. Somebody grabbed me around the waist and playfully tackled me to the sand. I loved him. I felt it. I tried to see his face, but I never could. He kissed me and told me that he loved me. I squirmed away from him and yelled to the strawberry blonde girl to throw me the ball. I knew her. She was my friend. I woke straight up out of bed when I saw Drew there too. He hit me, and dragged me away from my friends and the man that I loved.

I was crying and breathing heavy when Drew was once again right there. He was watching me sleep, something that I was sure he did every night. I once again clung to him, but something was different. He did make me feel safe as he stroked my hair and calmed me down.

"Come on, come with me," he finally said, taking my hand.

"Come with you where, Drew?"

"To my bed, maybe it will help with the nightmares."

Drew never asked what it was about. I think he was afraid of me remembering something that he didn't want me to remember.

He walked in before me and quickly closed his laptop, not wanting me to see the image of my bed; I was sure. He lifted the covers, and I crawled into his bed. I hated feeling weak. I may have been that person before my accident, but for whatever reason, I didn't want to be that person anymore.

Drew's legs tangled with mine, feeling like they belonged there. "Did you remember something?" he asked to the back of my head.

"I hope the hell not. I was being chased by monkeys." I lied. I have no idea how that story just popped into my head, but it did. I turned my face toward him, and he kissed my eye. "Was I ever chased by monkeys?"

He snorted. "I'm pretty sure that was just a nightmare. Go to sleep."

I did sleep. I slept so sound, and when I woke, I was alone in Drew's bed. I wondered if he left for his trip already. He hadn't.

I turned the knob to his office door, and it wasn't locked. He was on the phone. I was glad Derik wasn't there. I walked around his desk, still wearing my t-shirt and no shoes. I leaned in front of him on his desk, and he looked at me with a look that I could read. I could read it like a book. He ran his hand up my bare leg, not looking at my face. I was getting to him, and he couldn't get enough of me.

"Um… She's doing much better. She's actually sitting here in front of me," he spoke.

I watched him with a peculiar look as he stared at me. Who was he talking to that would have been asking about me?

"Sure, just a second," he said, handing me the desk phone.

"Hello," I cautiously spoke.

"Morgan, dear, how are you?"

I knew that it was Mr. Callaway. I smiled at Drew as both his hands glided up my legs, lifting my shirt higher. "I am doing well sir, much better."

"Good, that makes me very happy. Is Drew taking care of you?"

"Drew has taken very good care of me," I said as my fingers went through his hair. He wrapped his arms around my waist and laid his head on my lap with closed eyes. I wished I knew what he was thinking. "But he's leaving me today. I'm not real happy about that," I admitted. Drew looked up with a crooked grin.

"Tell him to take you with him," he demanded.

"I'm not allowed to fly yet, something about the altitude and my injury not getting along with each other."

"Well, if you need anything while he is away. You call me. Is your nurse still with you?"

"No, only on Tuesdays and Thursdays for therapy, I don't really need her anymore, but Marta will be here with me."

"Good. You tell Drew to hurry home."

"I will. Thank you."

Drew stood and crushed my mouth with his lips. I kept my hands on the sides of his face.

Jesus vagina. Did you get a brain injury too?

Drew lifted my shirt and trailed kisses down my chest, landing on my erect nipple. I moaned. What else was I supposed to do? He slid me out of my panties and released himself from his dress pants.

I moaned again as he slid into me. There was so much passion between us that it was almost excruciating. I was almost sure that I had never felt that way in my life.

"Drew," I called out, dropping my head. It was a little strange, almost like I was asking permission to come or something.

"Yes, you can come, baby," he answered, giving me permission. I blew it off. I had other things brewing that took precedence over my investigating mind at the time. Drew thrust deep into me; I let go with him feeling every ounce of passion between us.

"How long are you going to be gone?" I asked once we were back to normal breathing. He was still inside of me and pulled me close to him.

"Two days, three at the most."

"Make it two," I demanded, and he smiled.

"I'll do my best," he said to my lips as he delicately brought my feet to the floor.

"Can I have your keys?"

His head snapped up. He didn't like it.

"Stay here until I get back."

I didn't like his tone, but I didn't falter. "Drew, you can't make me stay in this house for two days without you. I'll be bananas by the time you get back, and I *will* have monkeys chasing me. I'll make Marta go with me."

He smiled at the monkey comment. He was giving in. I could see it.

"Promise me you will not go to the strip, and you'll stay at this end of town."

Yes… Triumph.

"I promise," I said, wrapping my arms around his neck. He kissed me and swatted me on the butt.

"Fine, get out of here so that I can be on my way, and stop running around the house like that," he demanded, playfully. "And keep your cell phone on you," he added. I winked at him and left him alone.

I didn't go out of the house that day. I really didn't need to. I hung out with Marta most of the day. I liked Marta. She wasn't much older than me. We sat by the pool until the heat was ridiculous and then made chocolate chip cookies. I knew that wherever Drew was he was connected to what was going on in the house. Every time Marta and I would be talking about him, my accident, or trying to remember anything, he would call, interrupting our serious conversation.

We did leave around seven that evening, picked up a pizza and two chick flicks. I had fun with Marta, and we both put on comfortable, sloppy clothes and ate pizza and watched a movie in front of the television.

Drew called around eleven, and I told Marta that I was going to bed.

"How was your day?" he asked. I knew that he already knew how my day was, but I played along anyway.

"It was good. How was your day? Did you get your big deal?"

"Not quite, but I'm pretty sure that it's in the bag."

"Good, does that mean that you will be home tomorrow?"

"Probably not until the next day," he replied.

Drew and I stayed on the phone talking about unimportant things for almost an hour until I yawned.

"You get some rest, and I'll talk to you tomorrow," he said, and we said goodnight.

I woke around three in the morning, drenched in my own sweat. I was sure I was suffocating, and I didn't have Drew there to show up and rescue me. It was so vivid, and I wondered if it actually happened or was it just a nightmare. It wasn't about the no faced Dawson or Drew. It was Derik. We were in the backseat of a limo, and he was doing horrible things to me. I knew there was a reason I hated him, and now wondered had he hurt me before. I wished to God I could remember pre-accident.

I got up. I couldn't go back to sleep after that. I was afraid to go back to sleep. I ran a tub of lukewarm water. I wished Drew would call. I knew that if he were awake he would know that I was up, but then again that would blow his cover and I would know that he was watching my every move. I lay awake for a long time after that, not really thinking about anything, just afraid to close my eyes. I finally dozed back off some time in the early morning. I slept until Marta woke me after nine. She was afraid something was wrong because I had slept in later than normal.

The next couple of days I spent getting to know not only Marta better, but also myself. I was happy and felt content for the first time since my accident. I couldn't believe how much I missed Drew and couldn't wait for him to be home.

Marta and I did go out the next day. We went to the park and walked around, ate at my new favorite little café, and then came home. It was too hot to stay outdoors for very long. I did go out alone after dark, once it cooled down some. I walked around barefoot along the property line. The grass there wasn't dried up and crispy the way it was in the park. There was a timed sprinkler system that kept the grass healthy. If felt funny between my toes as I walked.

I answered my cell phone, already knowing who it was. "Hello," I answered, smiling.

"Where are you?" Drew asked. He had a tone, but I didn't let it phase me. I was learning how to handle his hard attitude.

"Lying in bed naked, where are you?" I asked. I knew that he knew that I wasn't in bed or inside the house.

He chuckled. "You're such a liar."

"I was just walking around outside a little. It's actually a nice night."

"I would rather you be inside this time of night," he countered.

"I'm going. I'm going," I replied. I could see his smile through the phone.

I stayed on the phone with him as I walked into my suite, and started the bath water. He asked what I had done that day, and I told him what Marta and I had done.

"Why don't you go down and sleep in my bed tonight?" Drew asked before we said goodnight. I knew it was because of the nightmare the night before, and he wasn't here for me.

"Why?" I asked, feigning ignorance.

"Because I want you to," was the only answer he gave me. I wondered if there were cameras in his room. I doubted it, but then again, I didn't think he would be asking if he couldn't see me.

"Well, okay, being that you have a good reason and all," I teased.

I did sleep better in Drew's bed. I could smell his scent on his pillow. I felt safer there. I never woke up once, and when I did, I felt rested, relaxed, and excited for Drew to be home.

I took special care to look nice. I curled my hair, put on makeup, and a spritz of perfume. I tried; I really did. I tried to put on one of the expensive outfits from my closet. I just couldn't do it. I settled on jean shorts, and a nice tight white shirt that was low cut and showed the skin around my waist.

Marta made supper, and I sent her away. I wanted the house left to just Drew and me.

I excitedly went to the door when I heard it open, but it wasn't Drew. It was Derik. We both stopped dead in our tracks.

"You don't live here. Do you think maybe you could knock on the door?" I protested. I didn't want him there. Drew would be there any minute, and I wanted him to leave.

He smirked, and walked toward me as my heart picked up about twenty extra beats. He didn't speak, and I knew it was because he knew that Drew could hear anything that he said. Instead, he walked around me. I jerked and shoved his hand when he brushed his thumb over my nipple. I knew my nightmare hadn't been a nightmare at all, and he had hurt me.

I'm not sure if my accident had given me a new sense of heroism or what, but I shoved him as hard as I could. He did stumble back a couple of steps, but I was no match for his muscular physique. He hit me so hard I flew clear across the room. I think I may have even blacked out for a second because when I opened my eyes he was on top of me, and then he wasn't.

Drew threw him off me and had him on the floor.

"What the fuck are you doing?" he screamed at him.

Derik came to his feet. "What the fuck are you doing?" he retaliated. "She's trailer park trash. You're going to let her ruin everything."

"Shut the fuck up, Derik," he demanded.

"What the fuck is wrong with you, Drew? She's nothing; she's a piece of meat, and you know it. Put the little bitch back in her place and open your fucking eyes before you blow everything."

"Get the fuck out of here, Derik," Drew demanded, forcefully moving him toward the door by his jacket.

I wasn't excited to see Drew anymore. What did Derik mean? Drew hurt me too. I knew it. I'd known it from the beginning.

Drew helped me up after slamming the door in Derik's face.

"Are you okay?" he asked, running his thumb over my battered lip.

"What the hell was that, Drew? What did he mean by all of that?" I asked, pulling away from him. He didn't feel so safe and secure anymore.

"What happened? Why did he hit you?" he asked, ignoring my question.

"Because I shoved him after he grabbed my boob," I said, angrily.

"He did what?" Drew asked. I could see the veins popping in his neck.

"I'm almost certain that wasn't the first time. I think he did other things before."

"Why do you think that?" he asked. He seemed like he really wanted to know, and I almost felt like he was defending me.

"I keep having nightmares about it, but I don't really think they are nightmares at all."

I had a new plan. Derik was going to be out of the picture one way or another. I didn't know how, but I would figure something out. I wanted him dead. I had a good idea of what I was going to do. It might get me killed, but I would take that chance.

"Where is Marta, have her get you some ice," Drew said. I had a feeling that he wasn't going to comment on my suspicions. He didn't.

"I sent her home."

He raised one eyebrow and looked down at me. "Why?"

"I didn't want her here, but now I guess I really don't care."

"What's that supposed to mean?"

"Nothing, Drew. I'm going to get some ice."

Drew let me walk away and he disappeared into his office. I wiped the blood from my lip but didn't use the ice. It wasn't as bad as it felt. I walked into Drew's office. He only shook his head at me for not knocking. I didn't bother him and sat on the sofa across from him while he led a conference call. I flipped through my new magazine. After almost an hour of him still being on the phone, I scooted down on the sofa and curled into a little ball. I wished I had a blanket. It was freezing in his office. I dozed off waiting for him to be done working.

I'm not sure how long I slept, but when I woke, I was covered with a soft, warm blanket, and Drew was on another call. I stared at him, and his eyes met with mine. He continued to talk, something about a new cut. I didn't care what he was saying. I cared about the feeling I got when he looked at me the way he was. I pulled my bottom lip between my teeth, feeling the puffiness from stupid Derik's knuckles.

I sat up and ran my fingers through my tangled hair that I had worked so hard on for him. I got up and walked over to him. He ran his hand up the back of my leg. I kissed the top of his head and left him.

Chapter 17

I went to the kitchen and got our plates ready for Marta's prepared meal. I didn't set the dining room table and set them on the bar in the kitchen. I set two wine glasses by our plates and took out a bottle of chilled wine.

I was just putting the food out when he joined me.

He picked up the wine and twisted the corkscrew into it.

"Do I like beer, Drew?"

"Excuse me?" he asked with a frown.

"Beer. Do I like beer? I was just thinking that I would like to have a cold beer, but there isn't any here. Did we drink beer?"

"No. We hate beer."

"Oh," I said, brushing it off. It was probably just my mental state. I didn't even know what it tasted like, so how could I be craving it?"

Drew poured our wine, and we ate quietly. I don't think either of us knew quite what to say after the Derik incident. He knew that I had questions, and I knew that I didn't want to know the answers. I was afraid of them.

I cleaned up the kitchen while Drew showered. I walked out to the yard, barefoot of course, and sat in the soft grass about half way out. I'm not sure why I jumped. I knew he would come out to find me, but I did. He laughed as he sat, moving in behind me. My hands went to his calves.

"Jeans," I said, and smiled.

"I figured I may as well dress down too. It's obvious that you're going to continue to do it," he said wrapping his arms around my waist. "What are you doing out here? It's hot."

"I don't think it's that bad now," I said, leaning into him. I sat back up and laughed.

"Are you laughing at me?"

"No, your shoes. Do you not own a pair of sneakers?" I asked, looking at the shiny brown leather.

"What do you think?"

I moved his foot to my lap and removed his shoes and socks. He didn't stop me or say a word. If I had eyes in the back of my head, I would have bet that he was smiling, amused at me.

"There, doesn't that feel better? Put your toes in the grass," I urged, and he did.

We sat that way while the Nevada sky changed to a midnight black, neither of us spoke and Drew every so often pulled me tight in his arms or kissed my neck and shoulder.

"Drew," I softly said. I was trying not to. I didn't want to ruin the moment, but it was weighing on my mind, and I needed to know.

"Please don't, Morgan."

He knew what I was going to say before I ever said it.

I sat up so I could turn to look at him. "I need to know, Drew," I begged.

"You don't need to know. You only need to know that you are fine now, and I am going to make sure that you stay that way. Please, just trust me."

I turned back around. "Am I different than I used to be?

"Yeah, in some ways I guess."

"Are you different, Drew?"

"I guess I am," he answered as if he were just realizing it for the first time.

"Look up," I said.

"What?" he asked surprised at my sudden train of thought. I didn't want to be serious, not that serious anyway.

"Look, there are a million stars out tonight," I said. There was. The sky danced with tiny little twinkles.

Drew leaned back a little and stared up at the sky. I pushed him back more and moved to his side. I lay in his arm with my leg thrown over his waist, gazing up at the star filled sky.

"I'm going to have to take another shower," he said, grazing his hand up the back of my leg.

I laughed at him. "It's grass. I think you'll be fine," I teased.

Drew tensed when I ran my hand up his shirt and along his contoured abs. I didn't stop. I moved it around to his ribs and shifted my weight so that I was above him. I ran the back of my other hand down his cheek as we stared longingly into each other's eyes. Drew raised his head a little. I accepted the invitation and kissed him. He moaned into my mouth and pulled my leg higher. I could feel his hardness right between my legs as he ground into me.

I screamed and tried to get away from him, but he wouldn't let me. I was soaked in about two seconds when the sprinkler system kicked on. He used me for a shield, laughing as hard as I have ever heard him laugh before. I had never heard him laugh other than a snicker or a snort here and there. This was a full-fledged laugh, and I loved it.

He flipped me over so that he was now towering over me, shielding me from the downpour. He moved a strand of wet hair from my face and ran his hand up my side and then to the snap on my shorts. I was the one to moan in his mouth next as soon as I felt his fingers slide up my wet slit.

He tugged on my shorts wanting me to raise my hips.

"Drew, what are you doing? Someone's going to see us," I protested, but not too much.

"We are twelve miles from the closest person. Spread your legs."

Okay... No problem...

I don't think I had ever experienced anything more erotic in my life. Yeah, yeah, I know. My memory only held four months of memories, but still. I pulled on Drew's shirt, and he slipped it over his head. The water falling from his strong shoulders onto me as we made love under the Nevada sky was incomprehensible. The beauty of his wet body over mine with only the light from the moon and stars was one of those special moments. You know the once in a lifetime kind. That moment would never be recreated.

I slept in Drew's room that night, and the next, and the next, and the next. I stayed with him a lot in his office too, just because I wanted to be close to him, and for another reason that I wasn't going to disclose to him, ever. I hung out with him and read while he tended to business, and it seemed as I always ended up taking a nap on his sofa. I couldn't help it. His business was so boring. The only time that I wasn't with him was when Derik was there, and then I got the hell out of the house. I didn't want to be anywhere near that bastard.

When I did drive into the city, it was on the north side. I didn't go against Drew's wishes and venture to the strip. I didn't really want to go there anyway. I liked the north end. I liked my little café, where the guys Timmy, Stan, and Jewels all knew me by name, and knew what I liked. I had graduated from the park and ventured to a nearby high school, where I would sit and watch the baseball games, track meets, and sometimes just the girls practicing their cheers. I enjoyed my time there. It made me happy.

I was watching a boy's baseball game one afternoon when Drew phoned. I didn't want to leave and groaned when I saw that it was him. I had been keeping up with the Scorpions, and they were 4 and 0. It was only the fourth inning, and it was going to be a close game. I didn't want to leave.

"Where are you?" he asked.

"Trinity High," I answered with a smile. I knew he had no idea what that was.

"I'm not even going to ask. Come home. I'm done working for the day and Derik left."

"Uh-uh, you come to me."

"Excuse me?"

"I'm watching a ballgame. You come here."

"Um, no. I'm good on that. I'll see you when you get home."

"Get out of that stuffy suit and come and join me. Please." I begged.

"I don't know the first thing about baseball."

"I didn't either, but I'm learning. Do you know where Trinity is?"

"Yes, but I never said I was coming."

"You are. I'll see you in a little bit." I hung up laughing to myself.

Drew was there in fifteen minutes, wearing his oh, so sexy jeans with a red t-shirt. I smiled when I saw that he was wearing the sneakers that I had bought him just the day before. I moved over on the bleacher, and he slid in beside me.

"I can't believe I let you talk me into this," he said.

"Shhhh, bases are loaded, and this kid who's getting ready to bat is remarkable. If he can get at least two of them home, it will tie the game."

"How do you know so much about baseball?"

"I learned by coming here watching when dick face Derik is in my house."

Drew laughed, and then looked at me like I had lost my mind when I jumped up with the rest of the Scorpion fans, screaming when the batter hit a home run bringing in all four players.

The other team was good too, and it was neck and neck all the way to the ninth inning.

"I thought there were only nine innings," Drew presumed. He was into the game as much as I was. I thought it was cute.

"There is. They're going into an extra inning because it's tied. We're the home team. If we score this time the game is over, and we win. If not, the other team gets another try," I explained.

The first batter got a hit. The second batter was tagged out, but the player on first made it to third. Everyone held their breath when the third batter was trying to beat the throw to first. He slid, and the umpire called out, but the guy on third beat the ball to home plate, and scored the winning point.

"That was kind of fun. When do they play again?" Drew asked. I took his hand as we walked back toward the school.

"Friday," I smiled.

"Where are you parked?"

"In the parking lot at the park, walk with me," I coaxed.

We walked through the park holding hands and then along the sidewalk of the different stores and restaurants.

"Let's go in this sports bar and eat barbeque for supper," I suggested.

He looked up at the sign and then back to me with a frown. "I don't think so. Have you been in this place?"

"No. Only because I knew you would throw a tantrum about it."

"I would. I will take you some place to eat if you want to go out. Not here."

I gave him the same frown and pulled his hand toward the door. "If you take me out, you're going to make us go home and change into stiff outfits. We will fit in just fine here."

Drew growled, but he caved and followed me in. We sat at a high table with bar stools.

"Country music? Are you kidding me?" he protested.

I laughed, and then got serious. Why did I know the words to this song? I was deep in thought when the waitress came to take our drink orders.

"Bud Light in a bottle," I spoke, unconsciously.

"The same," Drew said. He knew that I was remembering something.

"What's wrong, Morgan?"

"How did I know to order that? And why do I know this song?"

"Maybe from when you were in Florence," he suggested.

I gave him a look. I might regret it but here goes.

"I was never in Florence, Drew."

"What do you mean? Where do you think you were?"

"I don't know, but I heard Derik tell you that I was going to run away again. I think I ran from you, for whatever reason. I'm just not sure how I ended up back with you or why I left in the first place."

The waitress brought our beers, and I chugged half of mine in one drink. Damn that tasted good.

Drew reached for my hand. "Morgan, I would do anything in my power for you to never remember," he said.

"But, you're not going to tell me, are you?"

"I can't."

"Don't you think I have a right to know, Drew? Do you have any idea what it is like to wake up every day not knowing where you came from?"

"You have the right to know, but I don't want you to know."

"Because it would hurt me?" I asked, quietly.

"Yes, Morgan. It would."

I drank the rest of my beer in the next drink. "Then don't tell me," I said. I didn't want to know. I was afraid it would ruin what Drew and I had. I didn't want that.

The waitress came back, and I ordered for us.

"One basket of ribs, an order of jalapeno poppers, and two more beers," I said, handing her back the menu.

Drew only stared with a confused look. I knew he was fighting his own demons.

"Drew, let's just forget it, okay?" I said, trying to ease his trepidation.

"I'm afraid of losing you," he admitted. I smiled a warm smile.

"Don't be. I'm not going anywhere. Do you know why I'm not going anywhere?" I asked as our beers were brought to us. I waited for her to walk away. "Because I am so madly in love with you, I couldn't imagine not having you in my life."

He smiled. "You love me?"

"A little," I teased.

"Well, if it's any consolation, I love you a little too."

I laughed, even though I wasn't laughing on the inside. We had just said I love you to each other, sort of.

Drew ate seven of the ribs, I ate one of them. He loved it. We drove back the five miles to the house and picked up Marta to drive my car home. I tried to tell Drew I wasn't that drunk, and I would follow him, but he wouldn't hear of it. Marta rode with us and drove it home.

I was stripping clothes as soon as his *our* bedroom door was closed.

"I think I like you drunk," Drew teased, removing his own clothing.

"We have a new toy that we haven't tried out yet," I teased, kissing his chest and shoulder. He got serious, and I wasn't sure what it was about.

"We don't have to do that, Morgan. I'm happy just making love to you."

I shoved my tongue into his mouth. "You've had an obsession with my ass the whole four months that I remember knowing you, now all of a sudden you're not interested? I don't think so. Put it on," I demanded.

He smiled moving me back to the bed. I scooted up on my elbows and waited for him to come back with the contraption.

"Spread your legs," he whispered, in that damned sexy raspy voice as he toed off his sneakers and removed his jeans.

No… Problem…

I lay there exposed, propped on my elbows while I watched him figure out how to slide the device up his rock hard shaft. Drew never took his eyes from my unprotected body, lying on top of his covers. Once the new toy was securely in place, he stroked himself.

Holy mother fucker…

I thought I was going to orgasm just watching him.

"Slide to the edge of the bed," he rasped. I did.

He moved my legs up so he could watch and guide the knobby ruse into my ass. He was longer, and I felt him move into my wet pussy first, and then I felt the penetration sliding into my ass. I moaned as he held my arms to the bed. I moaned louder as he began to move in and out of me, and then ridiculously loud when the third part of the new toy came in contact with my clitoris with every thrust.

I didn't feel at all used or abused. It was hot as hell, something that we were sharing together. I had to keep my eyes focused on his face. Every time I closed my eyes I was taken to a dark Drew, one that was angry and made me do things that I didn't want to do. I didn't dwell on it. I wanted to stay right there in that moment with Drew. He didn't have that look on his face. It was pure rapture, like he was tuned into me and nothing else. The faster he went, the more I felt myself losing control.

"Drew, can I come?" I panted. He stopped.

"Don't you ever ask me that again. I am trying my damnedest to make you come."

I smiled, and he began to move again. I was spent and sent spiraling into a whirlwind orgasm. As soon as I was coherent Drew pulled out and removed the device. He lifted my legs higher and slid into my ass with a moan. He pumped hard in and out of me while his thumb kept my clitoris happy. We climaxed together, and he fell to my body, out of breath and panting.

I ran my hand up his damp back and sweaty hair.

"You're hot," I said.

"You're hot," he retorted, kissing my nose. "Let's go shower," he suggested.

"Let's not. Let's go get in the pool," I countered.

Drew started to protest, but didn't. He pulled me up and kissed me before turning to grab his shorts. I pulled them out of his hand.

"Not with clothes," I warned with a smile. I opened the door and walked out, down the long hall toward the pool.

"Morgan!" he called after my naked behind in a loud whisper. "Marta is here."

I didn't answer and only gave him a sexy smile as I flipped my hair.

I walked down the pool steps and had to laugh at Drew covering himself and speedily walking after me.

As soon as he was in the water, I had my arms and legs wrapped around him. He held me tight to him and walked us out to about four feet. I let go of my hold around his neck and laid back, dipping my hair in the water. He ran the palm of his hand down my chest and brushed my nipple with his thumb.

I pulled myself back up to him, and we kissed.

"I love you, Morgan," Drew whispered to my lips.

"I hope so, we've been married for eight years," I teased. He wasn't laughing.

"I mean it, Morgan. I love you more than I ever thought possible, and no matter what happens, I am telling you now, how sorry I am while you love me too."

"Don't, Drew." I begged. I wanted him to stop. I didn't want to know anymore. I didn't care about what I didn't remember. I hoped that I never remembered.

Drew had to go out of town the next morning, but surprised me Friday afternoon by showing up at the Scorpions baseball game with me. I loved watching him walk toward me knowing that he was mine. Our eyes locked with the same smile. He missed me when he was gone. I could tell.

We ate ribs again at the little sports bar because he said that he was in love with them. We only drank one beer because we had no Marta at the house to drive one of the cars home.

He flew me to Ubud, Indonesia for our eighth honeymoon and my birthday. It was already past both, but he decided that we needed to celebrate. I was game. I had to make an appointment with Dr. Tharp before he would tell me anything. I would have never thought Indonesia could have been so exotic. It was, and we had a blast. The food too was exotic, and I loved trying all of the different cuisines. I chose items that Drew had to pronounce and order for me. He loved it and laughed when I tried to say the names, as well.

He gave me a beautiful necklace for my birthday and a brand new wedding set that I was sure cost more than I cared to know. He took the set back that I'd been wearing. I almost ruined his moment when I stared blankly at him sliding the rings off of my finger. It was déjà vu. This happened before. Drew sensed it too.

"Morgan," he softly spoke, pulling my eyes from my fingers to his eyes.

"What's wrong with the rings that I have been wearing?" I asked, trying to recover.

"They were put there for the wrong reason. I think you know that. This set is truly from my heart, and I hope you will always wear them."

I smiled as he slipped them on my wedding finger. "I will try my best," I said, and he knew what I meant by that. "I love you," I said kissing him.

"Read the back of the necklace," Drew said.

"Please give me twenty more," I read, and I hoped that I could.

We spent seven days in Ubud. We had amazing food, watched some shows, joined in a street dance, and made love several times a day, including the plane ride home. It's a good thing we had a private jet, I was sure we would have been thrown to our deaths.

Other than hating Derik, my life was perfect, and I was working on that. I had finally gotten the number for Mr. Callaway one afternoon when Drew left me in his office while he got us something to drink. I had the yellow Post-it in my pocket, and when Drew left the next day I went to town with Marta. We walked around a pawn store for a little bit and then had lunch at my favorite café. That was where I was going to make the call to Mr. Callaway so that I didn't have to use my cell phone.

Marta and I were standing at the counter laughing with Timmy and Jewels when I heard my name.

"Riley?" I heard, and instantly turned my head.

Everything came crashing back to me like a tsunami. I stood frozen while my whole life flooded my brain, my home in West Virginia, my parents, my little lost brother, Drew... Oh God Drew. I thought I was going to throw up right there. My entire wretched life was being played out right before my eyes. My head hurt. It hurt horribly. Was it the flood of memories? Why did I have such an excruciating headache all of a sudden?

"Dawson," I managed to say.

"Morgan, I think you need to sit down," Marta said, concerned with my ghostly white complexion.

"Riley, please talk to me," Dawson begged.

Marta was right. I needed to sit down. My head felt as if it was going to explode and the sick feeling I had in the pit of my stomach was unbearable. Dawson, it was Dawson, my sheriff. I couldn't breathe. What was happening?

"I'm sorry, but you evidently have the wrong person," Marta told Dawson, but she knew something was up too, she had to. I didn't just have this reaction for no reason. She helped me slide into a booth while Timmy brought me water.

"Marta, could you leave us alone for a second please?" I asked.

"I don't think that's a good Idea, Morgan. You look like you're ready to pass out."

That's because I am…

"I'm okay. I'll just be a minute."

Marta walked back to the counter, and I knew all eyes were on Dawson and me.

He sat across from me and looked like he didn't understand. I didn't understand. What the hell just happened? What a sick fucking joke. Was life really this cruel?

"There's a high school two blocks north of here. I'll be there at six tonight. I can't talk to you here. Meet me there," I explained.

"Riley, I'm not sure what's going on here," he stated. He too looked white as a ghost.

"I can't talk to you here. Please just meet me over there," I got up and Marta followed me out. I needed air, not that the Nevada heat had much to offer, but I had to try. I didn't know if Dawson would show up or not. Hell, I didn't know if I would show up.

"What the hell, Morgan?" Marta asked as we walked to my car.

"You drive, Marta," I said, ignoring her and getting into the passenger side.

"Will you tell me what the hell that was all about?" she asked again as she pulled on her seatbelt. I didn't put mine on. I wanted to crash and burn.

"That was someone from my past, Marta. I remember him."

"You do! That's great. We should call Dr. Tharp."

"It's not great. He is someone Drew wouldn't understand," I snapped at her. I didn't mean to snap. I just didn't know what to think myself, and I wasn't about to explain it to her.

"Oh," Marta said. I could tell she thought that he was someone that I was cheating on Drew with. I didn't care. I wasn't even going to try. I knew her enough to know that she would mind her own business.

I went right to mine and Drew's bed and lay down. I couldn't take the pain in my head. I couldn't think about anything until it stopped. Marta brought me the water and pain pills that I asked her to bring to me.

My cell phone rang. I didn't want to answer it. I knew that he could tell something was wrong from wherever the hell he was. I didn't care. I didn't want his pity party at the moment.

"Hello," I almost yelled. Even my own voice echoed through my head.

"What's wrong, Morgan?" he asked concerned.

"I just have a headache from hell. I need to rest for a little bit. It was probably just the heat."

"I'm calling Dr. Tharp," he demanded.

"I don't need Dr. Tharp. I just need to rest for a few minutes. I'm fine."

"Okay. Go rest. I will call you in a couple hours to see how you're doing. I love you," he added.

I could only grunt as I felt the tears. No. I didn't want to cry.

I covered my head with a pillow, one I couldn't stand the light at the time, and two, I didn't want Drew to see me cry.

Dawson Bade, Lauren, Starlight, the coffee shop, my house, Misty Bay, my trip to Vegas, my wreck. I remembered it all. I was going to marry Dawson. We were to get married two months ago. I never fell asleep. I would probably never sleep again. I felt the love that I had for Dawson as soon as I saw him. It was real, and I knew that he loved me. Wait. He knew. He knew all about Drew. He knew what a monster he was. Why did he wait five months to come for me? How did he find me?

I let everything flood through my mind, everything but the one that was going to rip my heart out. I saved that for my last memory or memories. There were so many of them. Not one was good. Drew hit me. He called me names, humiliated me, and he did treat me like a piece of meat. Why Drew? Why did you buy me for cash if you never wanted me? How could you do those things to me? I hated him. I hated him with everything in me. What should I do? Should I just run away with Dawson? What if he didn't want me anymore?

I lay with my head covered for almost three hours while thoughts and memories flooded my mind. I finally sat up around four to see if my head felt better. The pain wasn't gone, but it did feel better. I guessed my head was just overloaded and needed time to funnel all of the abrupt information.

"Feel better?" Marta asked as I walked into the kitchen.

"Yes, thank you. Could you make me a sandwich or something before I head out," I asked, sitting at the table.

"Yes, but I'm not sure you should go to that game. You had a pretty bad spell this afternoon."

"It was just the heat. I'm fine now," I lied. I wasn't fine. I had no idea what to do.

"Maybe I should come with you."

"Marta," I warned with a look. "I'm fine. I just need something to eat."

I didn't shower, change, do my hair or put on makeup. I wasn't trying to impress anyone at the time. I wore the same jean shorts and red tank top. I had been looking forward to this game for three days, and now I knew I wouldn't even see it.

I saw him standing at the concession stand. My heart ached for him. He smiled a warm smile as I neared.

"Do you want something to drink?"

"Lemonade, please," I replied.

We didn't walk to the bleachers around the crowd of people. He followed me to a picnic table under a shade tree. He sat right beside me rather than across from me as I preferred him to. I hoped he would start. I didn't have a clue what to say. He didn't either.

"How did you find me?" I asked.

"You didn't make it easy. You lied about everything."

"No. I didn't. I only lied about things that would lead you to Drew, which would lead him to me."

"I don't understand, Riley."

That wasn't my name. I snorted. "How did you find me?" I asked again.

"I tried everything to find you with Starlight and Lauren's help. I was lying in bed the other night, and I just remembered you telling me about Drew coming to your high school and donating money. I went there and pretended to be investigating a fraud case. They told me that the money that was donated that year was from Callaway Jewels. You told me he was a software developer from Indiana. Did you leave me, Ry? Because, you could have just told me."

"Daw," I quietly said. How was I supposed to explain this? "I didn't leave you. I didn't know you."

"What do you mean?"

I took his hand and ran his finger over the L shaped scar down the whole right side of my head. "I was in a car accident before I got out of Vegas. I didn't remember anything until I saw you in that shop this afternoon. I remembered my whole life today, right at that moment. I have spent the last five months of my life not knowing who I was."

"But you were on the plane. The airline told me that you had departed and landed in Chicago."

"I did not get on the plane. I left the airport because Derik saw me. He chased me. I ran underneath the front of a bus. I was in an induced coma for five weeks."

"You are at his house?"

"Yes," I answered and then had to answer my phone.

Shit...

"I didn't think you would go to the game. How do you feel?" Drew asked

"I'm better. I told you I just had a headache."

"But, I worry about you when I'm not there."

"You shouldn't." I didn't want to say much. Dawson Bade was sitting right beside me, and my lying abusive husband was worried about me.

"Well, I do, and there is nothing you can do about it," he tried teasing. I wasn't in the mood.

"I'll call you when I get home, Drew. The game is getting ready to start."

"Okay. I love you."

I shook my head in disbelief. "Love you too," I replied, hanging up.

"Did he hurt you?"

"No. Dawson, he hasn't hurt me. He has been very good to me."

Dawson looked down at my wedding rings. "Are you staying with him, Ry?"

"No. I don't know what I am doing yet. There are too many things that I don't have answers to."

"Leave with me now. I can't leave you here, knowing what he is capable of."

"I'm not afraid of Drew."

"What do you mean you're not afraid of him? You're terrified of him."

"I was terrified before. I haven't been afraid of him since I didn't know who he or I was. I'm fine. I can't leave yet."

"Can I call you?"

"No. I have to lay low until I figure things out."

"What do you mean, figure things out. Ry? I'm not going to let you sneak around and play investigator. You're going to get yourself killed."

"Dawson. I have to do this. I will call you when I can."

"You need to call Lauren and Star. They have been beside themselves worried about you."

"I can't right now, Dawson. Just tell them that I love and miss them, and I will talk to them when I can."

"Am I just supposed to go home and do what, Ry? Are we still a couple?"

"I don't know, Dawson. I truly don't. I just remembered who I was four hours ago. I need time to process all of this."

"Have you been sleeping with Drew?"

"Dawson, don't do this. I didn't even know that you existed."

"Was it consensual?"

"I'm not going there with you right now. I can't," I pleaded. What the hell did he expect?

"You're in love with him aren't you?"

"Dawson, he's not the same man that he was then."

Dawson blew out a puff of air. I could read his face. It was calling me a dumb girl.

"You know where to find me when you figure it out," he said and stood. I stood with him.

"Dawson," I pleaded. He turned and crushed his mouth to mine.

God Dammit.

I kissed him back, and it was all there, all the love, understanding, care, him putting up with my hang ups. It all came flooding back. I loved this man.

"Please take care of yourself," he whispered to my lips and let me go.

I sank back to the bench and watched him go. What else was I going to do? The first thing I had to do was get Dawson out of my mind. I hated doing it to him, but he had to get put on the back burner for a while.

Chapter 18

Okay. This time I had a real plan. Well, sort of.

The guy at the pawnshop told me that it was a Smith and Weston semi-automatic, nine millimeter, five shot revolver. I used Drew's credit card and paid for it. It was small enough to fit in the back of my jean shorts so that he wouldn't see it. I turned just before I got out of the store and picked up a ball bat.

"I'm going to need this too," I told the clerk.

"I'm not gonna see you on the news later, am I?" The older black male with gray hair asked.

"Maybe," I replied tossing the bat in the air and catching it by the handle.

"Just take the bat," he offered. I smiled some kind of crazy person smile. I was crazy. There was no doubt about it.

I left both of my new weapons in Drew's car. I needed Marta out of the house before I did anything. I didn't want to put her in the middle.

I slept in Drew's bed as hard as it was. I talked to him on the phone like nothing was wrong and got up the following morning feeling like a super hero. Yeah, I know it was stupid, but I was going to get answers if it were the last thing that I did.

I walked out to the kitchen and said good morning to Marta.

"You can take off whenever you want. Drew is on his way. We're going to go away for a few days," I lied, pouring a cup of coffee. I didn't know where Drew was, but if he wasn't in a meeting, or in the air. He was listening to me. He was probably smiling, thinking that I was sending her away again because I wanted him to myself. I did.

Marta left shortly after, telling me to have a nice time, not suspecting anything. As soon as I knew that she was gone. I took a shower, pulled my hair back and walked out to Drew's car to retrieve my weapons. I stuck the pistol in the back of my jeans, and carried the bat in like I was Rambo or something. I started in the kitchen, smashing the tiny camera hidden in the handle of one of the cabinets. I turned and smashed the one in the light switch next.

My cell phone rang. I smiled.

"You don't need to call me you son of a bitch. You can hear every word I am saying. I smashed the last camera in the kitchen and started in the living room next. My phone wouldn't stop ringing. I was afraid to hear his voice. I was afraid that I would coward out. I didn't want to do that. I started to smash a black vase. I always hated that vase. It appeared to have a crack going in a jagged line and the artist had messed up at the top, and it dipped in on one side. I'm sure it was on purpose. I stopped the bat in midair. I knew it had to be expensive, and something told me that it was Mr. Callaway's money who had bought it and not Drew's at all, besides, I liked the idea of the screen in front of him going black from the contact of my wooden bat. I decided to stick with smashing cameras.

By the time I had finished smashing the cameras in the living room and hallway to Drew's office my cell phone had stopped ringing. I knew that he was in the air, or I thought anyway. I just didn't know where he was coming from this time. Would he be there in an hour, two, or ten? I didn't know. I couldn't remember where he told me that he was going.

I walked to the lavish painting hanging in the hallway and pulled the key, velcroed to the back from behind it. Yeah, I remembered where that was too. My heart started to beat faster as I unlocked his office door. I walked around and sat in his plush leather chair. I picked up the phone with trembling hands and dialed the number on my little sticky note. I had to hang up and redial three times before my shaky hands got it right.

"Can I talk to Mr. Callaway please?" I asked the lady who I was sure was his nurse.

"I'm sorry, but Mr. Callaway isn't feeling well today."

Shit… Now what?

"Who is it?" I heard Mr. Callaway grouchily say in the background.

"Tell him that it is Morgan," I said quickly before she had a chance to ask or say goodbye.

"Morgan, how are you?" he asked after demanding to talk to me.

"I've been a lot better sir," I lied. I had never been better, well, that's a lie too. I was better in Maine where I had friends and a man who loved me for all the right reasons. I would have to revisit that later.

"Is there something that I can do for you?" he asked sincerely.

"I hope so. I want Derik to go away. I need for Derik to go away."

"Derik Hastings," he asked.

I don't fucking know.

"The Derik that seems to always be around. Yes."

"Did he do something to upset you? Derik has been around almost as long as Drew has. I'm sure that whatever it was, a good old talking to from me would do the trick."

"He raped me," I blurted out. I didn't want him to have a talking to. I wanted him dead. The line was silent. I wasn't sure if he hung up or not.

"Does Drew know about this? When did this happen?"

"It's been a while ago before I went to Florence. I just remembered yesterday, and no, Drew doesn't know, and I would like to keep it that way for now. I am home alone, and I am afraid that he is coming here."

"Get Sal and Dillon over to the mansion... Now! Tell them I will call them on their way and to hurry." I heard him say to someone. I relaxed a little. I didn't know why, but for some reason this man would take care of me.

"Thank you," I said and I meant it.

"I think that you should stay on the phone with me until they arrive," he assured me.

"I can't right now, but I'm fine now. I promise. I just need him to go away."

"Oh, don't you worry about that. He is going away. You'll never have to worry about Derik again. Do you need some help, I mean like, coping or whatever it is that you do when you go through something like that?" he asked concerned.

I smiled. I had been raped so many times I couldn't even count them. "No. I'm fine Mr. Callaway."

My intuitions were right. Drew called Derik. I had to put my hand on my shaking knee to stop it or settle it anyway. I couldn't seem to stop the trembling going on in my body. I heard the door slam. I didn't think it had been long enough for the two men to show up, not that I knew where they were coming from. It could be hours before they got there.

"You little whore," Derik yelled with a look that I knew could kill me dead right there on the spot.

"What did I tell you about entering my house without knocking?" I said with my finger shaking on the trigger from my lap.

"You fucking little cunt, I'll…."

"You'll do what, Derik? Rape me again?" I asked, pulling the gun from my lap, and stopping him in his tracks.

"You're not going to ruin this for me," he demanded. "I have almost ten years of my life invested in this money. I will fucking kill you."

"No. No. Derik. I don't think so." I couldn't believe how cool my voice sounded. I sure wasn't feeling cool. I was shaking like a leaf. "Do you really think that I won't pull this trigger?" I asked. I knew that I didn't have to cock the gun. The old man at the pawn shop had already told me that it was ready. I only did it to add a little bit of excitement to my show, kind of like putting an exclamation mark behind it.

"You don't have the guts, you little pussy."

I could have shot him in the chest. I didn't know how to shoot a gun. I pulled the trigger and grazed his left arm. "Don't fuck with me," I said feeling, extremely cocky all of a sudden. "Have a seat."

His eyes were huge. Did I mention that it was priceless? He stumbled back, holding his arm and sat down.

I saw him debating on whether or not to lunge at me when my eyes darted and I jumped, startled from the ringing desk phone. I kept the gun pointed right at his head while I picked it up.

"Hello," I answered, having a pretty good sense of who it was.

"Morgan, please," I heard Drew's voice.

"I'm sorry, Drew. I can't talk to you at the moment. I'm a little busy, waiting for your friend to be picked up." That look was priceless too.

I hung up and then removed the phone from the receiver when it rang again.

It was a good thing that I had a gun. I was sure that the ten minutes for the two men to come and retrieve Derik would have given him plenty of time to stop my heartbeat.

They too entered without knocking. Derik looked at them confused while I laid the gun down on the desk, still pointing at him.

"Let's go, Derik," the enormously, huge bald man said.

"Me? Get her the fuck out of here. She's the psycho one," he demanded, still holding his arm.

The other big man with black as coal hair grabbed him by his suit jacket and yanked him up, shoving him out the door. I almost felt bad because of the terrified look on his face. No, not really.

"If you need anything else, you call this number," the bald man said, handing me his card.

"Thank you," I smiled, taking the card.

I hadn't realized that I had stopped breathing until I was once again alone. I sucked in every last bit of air from that room.

Now to take care of Drew. I was running on pure adrenaline. I could feel the blood dry up in my veins, and the adrenaline was the only thing keeping me alive.

If only I knew where Drew was, He could have been anywhere. I was sure he was in the air somewhere. I just wasn't sure where. Was he an hour away, two, four, or six? I had no clue. Why the hell hadn't I asked more questions last night? Oh, yeah, because my brain was overloaded and I couldn't think straight. I still couldn't think straight. What was I going to do when he got there?

I sat in the same spot for an hour and forty minutes with my thoughts a scrambled mess. I went from one memory to another. There were so many of them. It's the weirdest thing in the world to not know who you are or remember things that happened to you. It's even weirder to have them all come surging back like a lightning strike. I finally got up, taking my pistol with me.

I walked toward the north corridor and knew exactly why I had avoided that side of the mansion. I wouldn't even do my therapy in that room. I didn't know why at the time. I just knew that I couldn't go in there.

I opened the steel door to the still empty gym and looked straight across the room at my reflection in the mirror. I didn't know who I was looking at. It was like looking into the eyes of a ghost without a soul. I was empty.

As I looked over to the padded bench, the memories once again flooded my awareness. I felt everything Drew had done to me in that room. I felt the shame, the humiliation, the hurt and the neglect when the steel door would close, and I would be left alone in silence for days.

I dropped to my knees and sobbed. I cried for the little girl who lived in poverty. I cried for the girl whose little brother was ripped from her arms. I cried for the girl whose mother deserted her. I cried for the girl whose father sold her to a monster. I cried for Starlight and Lauren. I cried for the only man who had ever truly loved me, and I cried for the girl who was having a hard time believing that Drew was capable of what he had done.

"Morgan," I heard Drew, quietly say from behind me.

I didn't move. I stayed on my knees and kept my hands on my lap, covering the gun.

"Do you think it's still Stockholm syndrome when you fall in love with the Drew that you didn't know?" I asked.

"Morgan, please give me time to explain," he pleaded.

I saw him step toward me through the mirror. I spun around and came to my feet. I pointed the gun right at his head.

"Explain what, Drew? Explain how I remember every last thing that you ever did to me? Explain how you used me for your own personal toy or would you like to explain why you used me for your own personal punching bag?" The tears were falling. I knew they were, but I was too shook up to control them. I couldn't hold my husband at gunpoint and think about that too.

"Morgan. Put the God damn gun down and talk to me," he yelled in a tone that I remember scaring the hell out of me at one time. The thing was; it didn't scare me anymore. It pissed me off.

"Back up!" I yelled. I wasn't intimidated by his overly aggressive demeanor anymore. I was Charlie's Angels, Cagney and Lacey, GI Jane, okay, so I watched a lot of television. It was all that I had to do when I was a prisoner in this house.

"Morgan, it doesn't have to be this way. Haven't I let you come and go as you please?"

That pissed me off even more. "You let me? Fuck you! I don't need you to let me do shit."

"I didn't mean it that way. Please, put the gun down. Where is Derik?"

I knew he sent him to settle me down.

"Don't underestimate me. I shot him." Well, I did. It just barely scraped his arm, but I did shoot him.

"Morgan, I am so sorry. Please let me tell you the whole story. I love you."

"Back up!" I yelled again, when he tried to walk toward me. He took a step back, and I told him to keep going until he was on the far side of the room. I walked toward the door with the gun pointed right at his forehead.

I barely got the steel door locked when he crashed into it. I jumped, but knew he wasn't getting out of that room until I let him out. I slid down the door, sinking to the floor. I just knew that my heart was going to beat right out of my chest and be lying on the floor in front of me at any second. I thought I had an adrenaline rush before, but this was ridiculous.

I walked back to Drew's office and logged onto his computer. I remembered the first password with ease, but when I clicked the icon for the cameras, I had to try three different ones, but finally got it. I clicked on the gym camera and just like magic. There he was. He had removed his jacket and tie, and was pacing back and forth, running his fingers through his too long hair. I told him a week ago that he needed a haircut.

Okay, I could see and hear him. How did I make him hear me? Was there a button somewhere? Where the microphone? I looked around the desk for something to make him hear me. I couldn't find anything. I knew there was a way. He talked to me when I was locked in there. No, he didn't talk to me. He made me perform for him. I should make the bastard take all of his clothes off and do the same to him. I saw the little microphone in the corner of the screen and clicked it.

"Hello," well, that sounded stupid. I watched him look right into the camera.

"Morgan, open the door. You're not thinking straight."

"Have a seat, Drew. You're going to be there awhile."

"I can't fucking be here awhile. I have work to do."

"No. No. You don't. The only thing that you need to worry about is starving to death. How many days do you think it will take? I've heard that it can be anywhere from three days to six weeks. Did you eat today, Drew?" Wow, I was crazy.

"Morgan, what do you want from me?"

"I want answers. I want to know why you brought me here. I'm not buying the whole I wanted a virgin to train anymore. You didn't just pick a poverty stricken town and pick me. I want to know why?"

I watched Drew sit on the bench and run his hands through his hair. He took a deep breath and looked right at me.

Dammit, don't look at me like that...

"Mr. Callaway sent me there to get you."

"Why?" I had a hunch that he had something to do with it. He was too concerned about me.

Drew took another deep breath. He didn't want to tell me.

"Tell me, Drew" I coaxed.

"I have known Randal since I was thirteen. His son was going to marry my mom before he got cancer."

"Yeah."

"I would have inherited it all, millions of dollars. When Michael was on his death bed, losing his battle after six long years, he told Randal about you."

"What about me?"

"Michael Callaway was your father."

"What? How could that be? My father is Gary Willow."

"No, he isn't Morgan. Remember when I came to your school. We were sitting on the bleacher, and I picked a piece of fuzz from your sweater?"

I did remember that. "Yes, so?"

"It wasn't fuzz. It was a hair. You are no doubt a Callaway."

I needed time to process again. What the hell? I'm not sure what I was expecting, but it wasn't that.

"What did you buying me have to do with any of that?"

"Randal Callaway had a stroke three days after he buried his son. He was in bad shape. When I went to see him in the hospital and give him the DNA results he cried. He knew from the many pictures that I had taken how you lived. He felt horrible and changed his will the next day, leaving you every last penny. I was pissed. I was supposed to step into that role, not some stupid hillbilly from West Virginia."

"I'm not a stupid hillbilly."

Drew snorted and looked up to me again. "No. You're not, Morgan. You're a very strong independent, beautiful woman."

"Stop. Finish telling me how I ended up gracing your presence." I didn't want to hear compliments from Drew Kelley at the time.

"Callaway gave me an ultimatum. He wanted me to continue to run his companies, and I would always have his money, but I had to marry you, and promise to take care of you."

"You didn't take care of me, Drew," I sadly spoke. I didn't even mean to say it. It just came out.

"I know that, Morgan, and if I could go back and change it, I would. I didn't want you. I didn't want you to be my wife, and you were ruining everything. I was in love with a girl named Skyler. I wanted to share all of this with her, not you."

"You punished me for something I didn't know about?"

"I deserve to starve to death in here, uh?"

"Yeah, you do. I was here for almost six years before I ran away. Why didn't I ever know that Randal Callaway was my grandfather?"

"He didn't want you to know. He was ashamed of his son for leaving you there when he knew how you lived. You were his only grandchild. It wasn't supposed to be for that long. He was in awful shape. We didn't expect for him to be around very long. I figured you would be here for six months at the most."

"What were you going to do with me if he died?"

Drew looked down at the floor and buried his face in his hands.

"Were you going to kill me, Drew?"

"You were going to have an accident. That was the only way I would get what was rightfully mine."

I sunk in the chair. Wow, if Randal Callaway would have died. I would be dead right now.

"Morgan, I don't know how to make this right. I don't care about one rotten penny of that money. I care about you, and that's it. I hadn't planned on falling in love with you, but you changed, and I don't mean because you couldn't remember your name. You are stronger, beautiful, and so much fun to be around. I wished to God that I would have given you the chance to show me that in the beginning. I would walk away from all of it right now if you would forgive me."

"Drew, do you have any idea what you put me through? You hit me. You used me for a sex slave. You locked me in that room for days, and then, and then… you made me love you."

Drew dropped his head in shame.

"I'm sorry, Morgan."

"Where is my mom?"

"Randal paid her to go away."

"My mom sold me too?" I said it more as a statement than a question. It was a fact.

"You've been through hell."

"I'm still going through hell. What about my little brother. He's here in Vegas somewhere."

"How do you know that?" Drew looked up with a wondering look.

"Dawson found him for me."

"Who's Dawson?"

"Where is my brother?" I asked. I was asking the questions, not him. He didn't have that right.

"He was adopted by a client and good friend of Randal's. He wasn't about to leave him in the system, knowing how he'd turn out. He's in a good home with parents who love him very much. He lives in the suburbs on a cul-de-sac. He's doing very well."

"Mr. Callaway thinks that we are happily married, doesn't he?"

"Yes. That's why I got so mad when he insisted that you talk to him without me. I didn't want you to say anything to blow my cover, and I *have* been happily married these last few months."

"Derik was in on all of this too, wasn't he?"

"Yes. He knew."

"Did he know that you raped me?"

"Don't say it like that, Morgan."

"How would you like for me to phrase it? Did you know that he raped me too?"

Drew stood up. His face was instantly red. "Are you serious? When?"

"A bunch of times, every time he would drive me anywhere."

"I'll kill that motherfucker."

"You don't have to worry about him. I told Mr. Callaway what he did."

That got another shocked look right toward the camera.

"When?"

"Before you sent him here to kill me."

"I never sent him here to kill you. I sent him here to calm you down."

"He was going to kill me," I assured him.

"Who's Dawson," he asked again.

"My sheriff," I replied with a sad tone.

"Excuse me?"

"I was going to marry him until I ended back up here in your web."

"You were going to marry him?" he asked with an almost hurt tone. Good. I wanted him to hurt. "How were you going to do that? You're married to me."

"No. Morgan Kelley was married to you. I wasn't Morgan Kelley there. I had a whole new identity. A whole new life. I was happy there."

"Do you love him?"

"I loved him more than anything alive. He is the only one who has ever been there for me my entire life, and he loved me too. I do still love him, but I don't know if it's enough anymore."

"I'm sorry, Morgan. I should have let you get on that plane."

"Yeah. That would have made things easier," I said it, but I knew that I would have spent the rest of my life wondering the answers to all of these questions.

"Morgan, I know that it's selfish of me to even think, but I want you. I love you."

"That is pretty selfish. A leopard's spots never change, Drew."

"My spots started changing the first time you kissed me."

"You never kissed me before."

"I didn't want to be intimate with you. I wanted you to pay for messing everything up."

"How could I mess something up that I was unaware of?"

"You couldn't, Morgan. Your dad would be so disappointed in me," Drew said with his head down. He was ashamed of himself. I never thought I would see the day.

"How did he meet my mom?" I couldn't say my dad. I never knew the man existed. I thought that when I heard my dad from back home say that he raised another man's child that he was talking about Justin, not me.

"I don't know the answer to that. I didn't want to know any of the details."

"You said your mom was going to marry my dad. Where is your mom?"

"She shot herself in the head the day after Michael's funeral."

I gasped. "I'm sorry, Drew."

"Don't you dare apologize to me. Don't you ever apologize to me. I deserve to feel every bit of pain humanly possible," he said, getting angry.

"I have to go to Mr. Callaway."

Drew only nodded. He knew that I would.

"You're not really going to leave me in here to starve are you?"

"No," I said getting up, "but you are going to stay there awhile."

I didn't need an address. Mr. Callaway's address was programmed into the GPS on Drew's car. I had found it when I was sitting in his air-conditioned car one afternoon waiting for a game to start.

His house was just as extravagant, only newer. I wondered if that would be left to me too. The grounds were meticulously kept, and the blacktop drive looked like it was freshly laid. It wasn't quite as big as the house we lived in, but bigger than the normal mind could imagine.

I walked up to the massive door. I'd never seen anything like it. There was an arch built from stone, and the double doors were glass with etched tree branches galore. It was breathtaking. I rang the doorbell and all of a sudden felt sick.

The nurse that seemed always to be with Mr. Callaway answered and I wondered if she were the only one there. She smiled at me.

"He saw you walk up," she said, gesturing with her hand for me to enter.

Did this man have a camera fetish?

Holy shit…

The house was beyond astonishing. The ceilings looked like they could go on forever and I wanted to run my fingers across the vibrant marble floor. I followed the nurse as my eyes widely took in the surroundings. I was expecting to be taken to his bedroom, but I wasn't. She led me to a den of some sort. I waited while she opened the wood pocket doors.

Mr. Callaway must have been an avid hunter. There was every exotic animal on the planet in that room. I almost jumped when I saw the stuffed black panther beside me. It looked so real, and his eyes looked hungry.

I'd never seen Mr. Callaway look so bad. His eyes were sunk into his skull, and his lips were dry and cracked. The nurse pushed the button on his bed and he struggled to sit. I got an immediate cold chill. You could feel death lurking in the air. I didn't want him to die. I wanted to know him.

He put his hand out to me, palm side up, and I placed mine in his.

"How are you, Morgan?" he asked. I knew he was talking about Derik and what I had been through with him, and I was going to leave it at that. My intentions all along were to go there and expose Drew. I couldn't do it. I didn't want him to think that he took me out of a bad situation and put me in a worse one.

"I'm good Mr. Callaway. How are you?"

"I have never been better," he smiled.

My eyes couldn't seem to stop looking around the room at death. I'm sure if I would have counted, I would have counted close to fifty dead animals, including the paintings around the room. I couldn't help but look at the owl straight across from me hanging from a branch that miraculously grew from the wall. His big eyes never left the sight of me.

"You're a hunter," I stated the stupid fact.

"I used to be. Have you ever been to Africa?"

"No," I replied. I had only been out of the country once, and that was when Drew took me for our anniversary.

"You tell that boy I said to take you there, beautiful country," he assured me.

I dropped my head. I didn't mean to let him see the sadness, but he did. He read me like a book.

"What's wrong, Morgan?"

I looked into his cloying eyes. "I know who you are," I said.

He smiled a warm smile.

"Why didn't you tell me? Why didn't you give me time to know you?" I pleaded.

"I'm sorry, Morgan. I don't always make the best decisions; I guess," Mr. Callaway confessed.

"I need to know what you expect of me. I don't think Drew and I are going to stay together."

He looked shocked. "Are you two having problems? What did he do?"

"It's nothing like that. Drew is fine. I just need some time. I don't know how to process all of this," I lied. I should have thrown him under the bus right there. Anyone in their right mind would have wanted him to suffer a slow painful death. I wasn't blessed with a normal mind, whatever that was.

"Morgan, I don't know how much Drew has told you, but all of this is yours," he said, waving his weak hand around the room full of dead animals. "You will never want for anything for the rest of your life."

I knew that was a lie. Money couldn't buy what I needed.

"None of this will be Drew's without you. If he walks away now, he'll be homeless," he added.

"He's not the one who wants to walk away. I am. And I don't want that. Drew runs your company better than anyone could. He is good at it. He takes great pride in it," I stated, not having any idea what I was saying. Why wouldn't I render the bastard homeless? He deserved it.

He smiled at that. "He always did, even when he was still just a boy. What do you want, Morgan?"

"I don't know. I guess I just need some time to figure things out."

I went there with the intention of finding out how my mother became pregnant by his rich son. I wanted to know where she was, and what she was doing. It didn't seem to matter anymore. She was obviously one of the people who could be happy with money, and it was also apparent that she didn't need me.

I cried all the way back to Drew's, or my house I should say. I knew what I had to do, and the sooner, the better.

As I walked the north corridor and unlocked the door to hell, I didn't walk in, and stayed back as Drew slowly walked out. He stared at me cautiously, hands in his pockets.

"I don't want any of this," I said, crossing my arms. "I'm going back to my small town, my job, and my friends."

He nodded. "I'll have Felix fly you there," he said.

He took a step toward me, and my heart fluttered as I closed my eyes.

I tried not to feel anything when he placed his hands on my arms.

"Morgan, for whatever it's worth, I'm sorry."

"It's not worth anything, Drew," I replied looking up to him.

Dammit… Why did I have to go and look at him?

I was fine until he ran his hand up and held my face with his hand to keep me from looking away.

Drew said, "I know it's not worth anything, but I do love you, Morgan, and if I could take it all back, I would in a heartbeat."

I stepped away from him. I had to. I was having an emotional breakdown, and nobody in their right mind would forgive this man.

"I'm going to a hotel," I said. "I can't stay here."

He let me go with a nod as his hand slid back into his pockets.

◇◇()◇◇

I stayed locked in a hotel room for three days. I didn't shower, I barely ate, and I cried a lifetime of tears. Finally, on the third day I called Drew.

"Morgan?" he answered on the first ring.

"I would like to fly out this afternoon," I said.

"Okay, I will have Felix get things ready."

I hung up. I wasn't interested in carrying on a conversation with him.

I stopped and visited Mr. Callaway before going back to the house to pack. He looked a little better and talked more. I ate lunch with him, and for the first time in days, I felt like I was going to be okay. He hugged me and told me that I should stop by Desert Springs Hospital and say hello to my friend Derik.

I did do that. I felt the need for some reason. Call me a little malicious. I needed to rub it in.

The nurse directed me to his room. He was in a body cast, and his face was black and blue. He had a tube running down his throat and was hooked up to every machine possible. I didn't stay but just a minute because I knew that Jena was close by getting coffee, and I didn't want to run into her.

I bent close to his face. His eyes fluttered open with a look of pure terror.

"I told you not to fuck with me," I whispered with a honeyed voice. "Have fun shitting in a bag for the rest of your life."

Derik would never touch me or anyone else for that matter again, ever.

I didn't see Drew while I packed a few things. I knew that he was watching me from his office, but I paid no mind. I shook my head with a snort when I realized that I didn't need to pack anything. I was going home, home to my cozy little house in Misty Bay. I had everything there. Thinking about my little house in Maine gave me a warm, comfortable feeling.

Chapter 19

I thought about how things would be in Misty Bay as I stared out the small plane window. I knew that it wouldn't be the same. I was a different person than when I had left. I didn't know what was in store for Dawson and me, but I owed it to him to try.

Drew had arranged for a car to take me wherever I wanted to go once I had landed. That surprised me. I had the driver take me to my house. I needed time to myself to regroup before I let anyone know that I was home, wherever that was.

I smiled when I saw my old white Honda sitting in the drive. I hated that car so much; I loved it. It was beautiful there that time of year. I could hear the ocean screaming my name. I took a deep breath, savoring the warm summer, sea air.

I moved the flowerpot, hoping the key that I had kept hidden there was still there. It was and fell from the bottom of the pot, clinking when it hit the concrete porch. I opened the door and stepped in. I wasn't sure how I felt. I didn't feel how I had expected it to feel. I mean it still felt warm and inviting. It just didn't feel like mine anymore. I looked around and noticed the thick dust around the furniture.

Confused, I looked toward the table. I had a whole stack of mail. Some of it was opened, and someone had been paying my bills. I was sure that it was Dawson. I would figure it up and pay him back.

"I wanted to make sure that you had electricity when you got home," I heard Dawson say from my front door.

I smiled at him. He was so handsome in his uniform, and my heart ached for him. I couldn't imagine what he had been through for the last almost six months.

"Hey, sheriff," I quietly spoke. I walked toward him as he smiled back.

He wrapped me in his arms, and he felt so, so, I don't even know how to describe how he felt. I felt like I belonged there, and I missed him.

"Are you home?" he asked. I couldn't answer that. I didn't know where home was at the moment.

I didn't answer. I just looked up to him, and he kissed me, softly. "I missed you," he whispered to my lips.

"I missed you too. How did you know that I was here?"

"I didn't. I come by and check your mail every evening."

"Thank you."

"You're welcome. Does Lauren know you're here yet?"

"No. I didn't tell anyone. I just left."

"Did he let you leave?"

I didn't want to talk about Drew. I know it was stupid, and Dawson would never understand, not after what I had told him, but I didn't wish anything bad on Drew, and I knew that Dawson did.

"Riley!" Lauren screamed from the door.

I laughed. I loved that girl.

She squeezed me so hard that I thought my eyeballs would pop out.

"I can't believe that it's you. It is you, isn't it?" she teased.

I couldn't answer that either. I wasn't Riley Murphy. I was Morgan Kelley. I only smiled. "How are you?" I asked.

"Better now that we know that you're okay. Do you have any idea what you've put me through?" she asked, cocking her hip and resting a fist on the side.

I laughed. "I'm sorry. How can I make it up to you?"

"Well, after you get settled back in, you could cook for me," she joked.

"I would love to cook for you," I admitted. I realized at that moment the simple things in life. I did miss her waking me up at the butt crack of dawn, and her coming over and raiding my refrigerator for leftovers.

Lauren didn't stay long, knowing that I needed time with Dawson. I told her I would call her later and gave her my Las Vegas number.

Dawson ran back to town and brought us Mexican food while I showered. The refrigerator had been cleaned out, and there wasn't much to cook there.

I pulled on my Riley jean shorts and a t-shirt. My cell phone rang while I towel dried my hair and I had a feeling that it was Drew. I didn't think that Lauren would be calling already. It was Drew. I determined, looking down at the name.

"Hello," I answered.

"Hi, I just wanted to make sure you were okay."

"Yes. Drew. I'm fine."

"Are you with him?" he asked. I could hear the hurt in his voice.

"Yes and no. He went to get us something to eat. He should be back any minute."

"Oh," he replied.

"Drew, I don't know what you expect from me."

"I don't know that either, Morgan. I guess I was just hoping that you would see things differently."

"How could I ever forgive you?"

"I don't know that you could, but I sure would like for you to try," he softly spoke.

I closed my eyes and pinched the bridge of my nose. Why did this have to be so difficult? I should hate him. I should throw him out on the streets. That's what anyone else would have done. Why couldn't I?

"I have to go, Drew," I said hearing the car door from the driveway close.

"Because he is back?"

"Yes, and I have enough on my plate right now. He doesn't understand why I would talk to you."

"Did you tell him?" he asked. He didn't have to say anymore. I knew what he was asking.

"Yes, Drew, but I will tell you about it later. I have to go."

"I love you, Morgan."

"Drew," I said. I couldn't say it back. How could I?

"You don't have to say anything. Goodbye Morgan."

"Bye, Drew."

Dawson and I ate out on the deck. I loved my deck. I missed my deck and the views of the endless ocean. I wasn't as hungry as I had thought, and folded the wrapper over my half eaten burrito.

"Come here," Dawson requested, moving to the glider.

I went with him, and he wrapped his arms around me. I loved his smell, his protective feel, and the security that only his arms could give.

"We need to talk, Ry," he said, tracing my fingers with his.

I didn't feel right being called Riley anymore. I know that was what they all knew me by, but it seemed so superficial now, like a lie. It was a lie. That wasn't who I was.

"What do you want to know, Daw?" I asked. I owed it to him to tell him anything that he wanted to know. I just didn't know if I was ready to disclose it.

"I mostly want to know if I am losing you. I don't care about the rest. You have no idea how hard these last few months have been. All I could picture was you being hurt, and I couldn't find you."

"I don't know where we stand right now," I told him honestly. I was done with the lies, and I didn't know. I didn't know if we could go back to being Dawson and Riley. I wasn't Riley.

"You're not seriously thinking about going back to him, are you?"

I know that it shouldn't have. He had a right, but it pissed me off. "No, but I'm not going to lie and tell you that the feelings aren't there. They are Dawson, and I don't expect you to understand. I know that it sounds absurd, but I can't help it. He's not the same Drew that I ran away from."

"Why? What changed?"

"I don't know, Dawson. He was different. He cared."

"How can you say that, Ry? Six years. Six years he did horrendous things to you. You do remember that don't you?"

"I'll never forget, but people can change."

"A leopard doesn't change its spots," he stated. I snorted. I had told Drew that exact same thing.

I thought about telling him the whole story, about how it came that I would end up married to Drew Kelley and that I had more money than ten people could spend in a lifetime. I didn't. I'm not sure why. I guess I just didn't feel like we were there yet.

Dawson announced that he was going to head out around nine, and I was surprised, but glad. I thought for sure he planned on spending the night. I didn't really want him to, but I wasn't going to tell him no.

I walked him out to his car, and he leaned against it, pulling my hand to come to him. He traced his thumb along my jaw line, and then moved his finger, tracing my scar. I kept both my hands on his chest, but not opened, they were clenched, almost like I was afraid to touch him. I wondered if it was because I felt like I was betraying Drew.

"You're making this really awkward," I smiled up at him.

"Are you waiting for me to kiss you?" he asked with the boyish grin that I also loved about him.

"Well, since you were planning on it anyway, you may as well."

He leaned in, and I moved up on the tips of my toes. I wanted to kiss him, but I didn't, if that makes any sense at all. He held the back of my neck as his tongue parted my lips and entwined with mine. I couldn't help it. I moaned into his mouth after a moment or two. He felt so right. Was he though? He was before I forgot who I was. Why was it different now?

"I'll see you tomorrow," he whispered to my lips before pulling away. I didn't want him to let me go. I wanted to tell him not to go, but I didn't. I took a step back and slid my hands into the back pockets of my shorts.

I thought about calling Lauren, but decided against it. Why did it feel different? Why didn't I feel like I did before I left. I would have called Lauren anytime day or night, but now I felt like we weren't that good of friends and we had drifted apart or something. I don't know. It was probably just me. I guess I was reading more into it than I should have been.

I walked back into the house and right out the back door to the deck. I missed the beach. I hadn't walked along the shore in months. I made my way down the rocky terrain and sat down in the still warm sand. That too didn't feel the same. The ocean was more of an enigma, like it thought I didn't belong there, like I had abandoned it too. Why was I having such a hard time being there? This was my safe haven, the only place in my life that I felt wanted. I knew what it was. I just hated to admit it. It was Drew Kelley. I let him get into my mind, and even worse, my heart. I was such an idiot.

As the darkness took over the night sky, I stayed on the beach. I didn't feel any better sitting along the sands of the shore than I did in my house. I blindly made my way back up the rough terrain. It was dark; I mean really dark. I couldn't see one white sneaker in front of the other.

I showered and decided to dust and clean my forgotten, neglected house, trying to keep my mind busy. Hopefully, I could tire myself out so when I went to bed, I would sleep, rather than contemplate. I didn't want to think anymore. I just wanted it to stop. It wasn't going to work. I knew this when my cell phone rang. I debated before answering when I saw Drew flashing across my screen.

I took a deep breath and answered, plopping on the couch.

"Hey," I answered.

"Can you talk?"

"Do you mean am I alone?"

"Yeah, sort of. I hate the thought of you being in another man's arms or anyone else kissing your soft lips."

I blew out a short puff of air. This man was impossible. "I'm alone."

"What are you doing?"

"Cleaning house. What are you doing?"

"It's eleven o'clock, and you are a millionaire times a hundred or so. You don't have to clean house."

"I'm cleaning because I need to occupy my mind, and that's a lot of money, huh?"

He laughed. "Yeah, it is. What's on your mind?"

"Stupid you."

"You're thinking about me?"

"Not like you're hoping that I am," I lied. I *was* thinking those stupid thoughts. "I was just thinking about this place they call skid row in LA. It's the largest stable population of homeless people in the United States. I figure you could probably make a few friends."

Drew laughed even though I didn't say it lightly. That was exactly where I should have sent him.

"I heard that Derik was in pretty bad shape," he commented, changing the subject.

"Yeah, I went to see him before I left."

"You did?" he asked a little shocked.

"Yeah, I think that I may be just a little demented. I took great pleasure in seeing him in pain. Did you go see him?"

"No, I'm afraid that I would take great pleasure in that too."

"You did the same thing, Drew, only worse."

"How can I fix it, Morgan?"

"I'm not sure that you can. I don't know what to do. I have Dawson here, who loves me and has always treated me like I was a princess with the utmost respect. And then I have you, who for the life of me, I can't figure out why I would even second guess it, but I am."

"Are you in love with him?"

"I am, Drew, but it's different from the way that I am in love with you."

"What does that mean?"

"I don't know. I just feel different in his arms than yours."

"Don't make me picture that. Did you sleep with him?"

"Today?"

"Yes, I'm sure that you did when you were away for almost two years."

"I didn't sleep with him today. Did you sleep with Skyler?"

"Today?" he asked a stupid question.

"You're not funny."

He laughed anyway. "Yes, I did, but I haven't seen or talked to her in almost a year. The last I heard, she was engaged."

"Because she got tired of waiting for you to get rid of me?"

"Exactly that."

"Did you do the same things with her that you did with me?" I didn't know why it mattered, but I wanted to know.

"I'm not going to lie to you anymore, Morgan. No, I did not. It was just your normal boring sex, and even back then, I fantasized about getting back home to you. What about you? Did you and Dawson?" he asked, not saying any more than that. He knew that I knew what he was talking about.

"No, but do you want to hear something really messed up?"

"Probably not, but go ahead."

"I used to beg him to do those things to me. How fucked up is that?"

"Pretty fucked up. Did he?"

"No. He wouldn't dare. He cared too much. You never went down on me," I boldly stated for whatever reason.

"I know, and God do I wish I would have. Did he?"

I smiled at his comment. "Yes." That was all that I was going to say about that. I knew he didn't want that image.

"You know that night when you told me to do that. I almost shot my load before I ever touched you."

I laughed. "Stop talking about it. You're making me wet."

"Dammit, Morgan did you have to go and say that?"

"Sorry, let's stop talking about sex."

"What do you want to talk about?"

"I want to know why you couldn't love me before I didn't remember who you were."

"Because I am an idiot, and the old saying that money is the root of all evil is very true. That's what I wanted, and I felt like you were standing in my way."

"I was, but I didn't even know it at the time."

"I know, and you were nothing but an innocent victim who got pulled into a sticky situation."

"Why didn't you just pay me to keep your secret? There are so many other ways that you could have handled it. I would have been more than happy to leave my life in West Virginia."

"I was pissed, selfish, irritated as hell that you were screwing everything up. I don't know how to answer that, Morgan. I looked at you like worthless trash that was going to be handed everything that I worked so hard for."

"What about the whole virgin thing? Was that something that Mr. Callaway requested too?"

"No. That was my own sick way of humiliating you right from the beginning. I wanted you to know what your role was to be."

"Wow, Drew."

"I know Morgan. I don't deserve you anymore than I deserve to breathe, but I can't get you out of my head. I am so madly in love with you; I can't stand it."

"What about the whole baby thing? Why would you even think about bringing a baby into a mess like that?"

"Mr. Callaway," was all that he replied. It was enough. I could see Mr. Callaway demanding that he give him a grandbaby.

I took a deep breath. I didn't know what to say. I didn't know how I felt. I didn't know where I belonged. I was a fucked up mess, and there was no easier way to put it.

Drew and I talked until one in the morning. I told him that I wanted to know where my mother was and that I wanted to see her. He didn't try and talk me out of it and said that he would talk to Mr. Callaway and try to find out where she was for me. He told me that he loved me before saying goodnight, but I couldn't say it back.

I lay awake for the longest time. I could hear thunder in the distance and see the flashes of lightning. My bed felt good and comforting, and I thought about Dawson. He was always in my bed there. I thought about Drew too, wondering how it would feel to have him in my bed there in Maine. I knew that would never happen, he wouldn't be welcomed in Misty Bay, and would be lucky to make it out alive had he showed up there. I wondered how much Lauren and Star knew. Did Dawson tell them about my marriage to Drew?

I woke a couple hours later to an angry summer storm. The rain was beating against my window, and the wind sounded like it was going to rip the roof right off of my house. That wasn't what woke me though, well it may have helped, but I woke because of Drew. I was bent over his desk, and he was playing with me while he conducted business. He spanked me in between calls and would sensually dip his finger inside of my throbbing core every time he rubbed away the sting from his hands.

My eyes popped open with the loud crack of lightning, followed by the roar of thunder. I lay still for a few minutes, staring out at the blustering storm. I had my own storm going on and could feel the dampness in my panties.

Stupid vagina, never on my side.

I rolled to my back and slid my panties off. I figured if I were going to do it; I may as well do it right. I spread my legs and ran my finger through my slippery pussy. It *was* wet, and it wanted fucked. I moaned as I ground my hips into my fingers.

Aw fuck…

I rolled to my stomach and moved my hips up and down into my fingers until I was calling out in Drew pleasure. Why it had to be him, I didn't know. It just was. I know that it should have been Dawson. It wasn't that Dawson wasn't amazing in bed or that Drew was better, it was more of the chemistry that Drew and I shared that Dawson and I didn't. I couldn't explain it if I tried. That's just how it was.

I smiled when my old Honda started right up. I shouldn't have been surprised. I was sure that Dawson started it, and maybe even drove it to make sure that it was running when I got back.

"Good morning. Welcome to Reminiscent," the too chirpy young girl said from behind the counter. I had been replaced. "Would you like to try one of our new lemon muffins," she asked in an adenoidal voice that already annoyed the hell out of me.

"No, thanks, I'm here to see Star. Is she here?"

"Yes, she's in her office. I'll go get her for you."

"That's okay. I know the way," I smiled and walked past her.

Star was sitting at her desk painting her nails some tropical pineapple color. I smiled when I saw her. "Still hard at it, I see," I said leaning against the threshold and crossing my arms.

"Oh my God. It is true," she exclaimed, jumping up, and frantically blowing on her wet nails so that she could hug me.

I hugged Star as she put her arms around me, wet fingers, sticking straight up. "I can't believe you are here. Sit down. I have a million questions to ask you," she rattled off.

"How are you, Star?" I asked. It was good to see her. She looked exactly the same, not that she shouldn't. It hadn't been that long. It was just different, me being there and all. It just felt, I don't know, surreal I guess, kind of like I was a different person or something. I left there Riley Murphy, Riley Murphy, who hated Drew Kelley. I came back as Morgan Kelley, in love with her husband. What a fucked up situation. Star wore the same thick braid down her back, her free flowing skirt, a patchwork vest, and her customary Jesus shoes.

"Forget me. How the hell are you? Is it true that you lost your memory?"

"Yeah, it's true. It's so strange, Star. I thought I would gradually start to remember. It didn't happen that way at all. I saw Dawson, and it was all just there. I knew him, and everything else from the time I was around three."

"I can't even imagine."

"You couldn't. It was crazy. I don't know any other way to explain it."

"Dawson has been beside himself. He spent hours and hours on the phone or on the computer trying to find you."

"I feel horrible about that."

"It wasn't your fault. You didn't even know him let alone that he was looking for you."

"How much did he tell you, Star?" I wondered if he had told her about my abusive husband and that I had run from him."

"You know Dawson. He didn't say much at all. He would never say anything that you told him in private, but I have a pretty good idea. I have known all along that you were running or hiding from something. I witnessed one of your nightmares in the hotel, remember?"

"Yeah, I remember, but you never mentioned it."

Starlight shrugged her shoulders. "I figured if you wanted me to know, you would tell me. How are you and Dawson?"

I took a deep breath and slumped in my chair. "Stressed," I admitted. "I'm not really the same Riley that I left here as."

"What does that mean, Ry?"

I grunted and shook my head. "I'm kind of in love with my husband for the first time in our marriage. I'm so confused, Star. I am still in love with Dawson too, and I know that he is the one who makes the most sense. I just can't stop thinking about Drew, and it's really absurd. He wasn't the most pleasant husband." Boy was that ever putting it mildly.

"Are you staying?"

"I'm not sure yet. I kind of think I need to step away from both of them to be fair." That made absolutely no sense at all. Drew didn't deserve a second chance, let alone being fair to him. Dawson, however, did deserve all of my love. He had never been anything but good to me, and I knew that he loved me.

"What's fair to you, Riley?" Star asked with a warm expression. It felt good to talk about it with someone. I just didn't know how much I was willing to disclose.

"I honestly don't know." I didn't feel like I deserved to be happy. I felt like I cheated on Dawson, but then again, I felt like I cheated on Drew.

Star and I talked for over an hour until her new annoying help got busy and needed help with the lunch crowd. We talked about the shop, and the new girl, who I was sure, was fine. I guess I just felt a little replaced. I wasn't sure that I was going to come back anyway, although Star told me that I always had a job there. She really did appreciate all that I had done there, and the business that was established and making a good profit, thanks to me.

I walked out with her and said hello to a few of the locals. My friend, John, from the beach was there, and I visited with him for a while before heading out.

I walked across the street and the two blocks to the police department. I hesitated at the door.

What the hell are you doing, Morgan?

I quickly pushed open the glass door, before I turned and ran down the sidewalk like the maniac that I was. Matt the deputy was sitting across from Dawson's desk with his feet propped. He was laughing and telling Dawson a story about his son. Dawson stood up when he saw me. It freaking broke my heart. He looked at me as if I were the only thing in his life that mattered.

"Go write some parking tickets or something, Matt," Dawson demanded.

Matt said, "Hi, it's good to see you, Riley I'll just go bug Starlight for a while and eat some doughnuts. I'm too nice of a guy to write tickets," he teased, dismissing himself.

"Hi," Dawson said with a smile.

"Hey, sheriff, I smiled back.

"Are you hungry, want me to order some lunch?" he asked, always thinking about me.

"No, I had a pastry at Star's."

"Then how about supper?" He asked with that damned grin that melted my heart.

"You can come for supper, but I'll cook. I am going to the grocery store before I head back. I couldn't say home. What the hell?

"Normally, if you showed up here I would kiss you about five times," Dawson grinned.

"You can kiss me five times."

Dawson did just that. He kissed me with four quick pecks. I counted. His fifth contact with my lips wasn't just a peck. He rested his lips on mine and ran his tongue around the opening of my closed lips. I parted my lips, and he accepted the invitation. Damn was he ever a good kisser, of course my lady parts had to agree.

We kissed for, I don't know, two maybe three minutes before he left my lips and trailed my jaw line with his lips. His spellbinding hands found their way to the bare skin beneath my shirt as my head dropped back on its own accord. My breathing became shallow; my heart felt full, and my panties dampened.

"Jesus, Daw." I finally said pulling away. I was about ready to bend over his desk.

He snorted and kissed me one more time. "I'm sorry. I just can't get enough of you."

"I'm going to get out of here before I start taking my clothes off," I teased, stepping away from him. "I'll see you when you get off."

Lauren showed up while I was putting away my groceries. She pulled one of the bananas loose and sat at the table. I sat with her, and we talked about more than I had planned. She too knew that I was in love with two men, maybe I was just fishing for someone to make sense of all of it for me. I needed someone to tell me what to do. Unfortunately, she couldn't give me the magic answer either.

"Does Dawson know about Drew?" she asked.

"Yes, he knows. We don't really talk about it though. I think he is afraid of me not choosing him."

"You can't keep them both, Ry."

"I know, and Dawson makes the most sense, and I do love him."

"But?" Lauren said, knowing that there was a *but*.

"But, I don't know, Lauren. Drew and I are just different. It's so... I don't even know how to describe what we have."

"Intense?"

My eyebrows rose. "Yeah, that undeniably fits."

"Are you staying in Misty Bay?"

"I don't know that yet either. I want to find my mom and visit her, maybe just get away from everything for a few days."

Lauren was so easy to talk to, and I knew that what I said to her would go no further than that table. I didn't tell her everything. She knew that Drew was abusive to me before she knew that my mother left us, and I told her about how I was raised in poverty, but I didn't tell her about the money. I still didn't know how to process that one.

Lauren abruptly had to go when Dawson got there dressed in jeans looking way too fine for someone who hadn't had sex in almost two weeks. I wasn't sure about the look the two of them exchanged. Was it pity? Was it relief? I wasn't sure. I assumed that the two of them had spent a lot of time trying to find me.

Dawson grilled burgers outside, and I made roasted and garlic potatoes and corn on the cob. We sat on the back deck overlooking the immense ocean. We didn't talk about anything serious. I think he was avoiding it as much as I was, and we both spoke of nothing but trivial day to day events.

I wondered all night if he were planning on staying. I wanted him to, and I didn't want him to. That was the state of my fucked up mind. I wanted him to take me to bed and make slow passionate love to me, just like he would have before. I also wanted him to leave so that he didn't do just that.

I didn't have to worry about it when my cell phone rang, and Dawson looked down seeing Drew's name displayed on the screen.

I gave him an apologetic smile when I answered.

"Hey, can I call you back in a little bit," I answered.

"Why, Morgan?" Drew asked cautiously. He already knew why. He was just playing dumb or hoping that his intuitions were wrong.

"I have company right now."

"Yeah, that's what I thought. You do know that you are still my wife don't you?"

What a dick...

"Really, Drew?" I asked.

"I'm sorry, Morgan. Don't pay any attention to me. I just hate the thought of you in his arms."

"I'll talk to you later," I said hanging up. I didn't want him to tell me that he loved me with Dawson sitting there with his head down right in front of me.

I dropped my phone on the table and shook my head. This whole situation was unbelievable. Dawson stood and took me in his arms.

"You know that I love you, don't you, Riley?"

"Yes. Dawson. I do know that, and I love you too."

"I'm going to go," he said, shocking me a little. Was this how he was going to fight for me?

I looked up at him confused. His eyes looked just as mixed up as mine.

"I know that you are going through a tough time right now. I also know that it wouldn't be fair to you for me to beg you to choose me. I am trying my best to give you your space, and let you work through this, just know that I am right here, and I love you."

I smiled and kissed him. "Thank you, Dawson." I was glad that he was giving me my space. I don't think I could have handled two of them pleading their cases.

Dawson left me with a kiss, and I dialed Drew back.

"You know, you're kind of a dick," I said as soon as he said hello.

"Yes. I have been told that a time or two. Did your boyfriend leave?"

"Shut the hell up." I demanded. I almost said that he wasn't my boyfriend, but I really wasn't sure what he was. I left that part out.

This became my routine for the next nine days. I would spend my days with Star, and then Lauren when she got home, then Dawson, and Drew would call every night. I did have dinner with Dawson and his parents a couple of times, and once at his house. He never stayed at my house, and I didn't stay at his. He wasn't even trying to get past second base. I was sexually frustrated and was tired of taking care of things myself.

Dawson came over on Friday night, and we barbecued chicken with Lauren and Joel. I knew I had drunk too much beer, and was feeling it. I even sent Drew a text lying to him. I told him that I was going out with friends and would talk to him the next day, not wanting him to call with everyone there. I was getting laid. I needed to get laid, and the evening make out sessions with Dawson wasn't helping.

Lauren and Joel left around eleven, leaving Dawson and me alone on the deck. We stared attentively at each other while he sat at the table, and I leaned against the banister facing him.

"Take me to bed, Dawson," I said in a low raspy voice.

He came to me and took me in his arms. "Are you sure, Ry? I don't want to pressure you, but I would love nothing more than to do just that."

"I'm sure," I assured him shoving my tongue down his throat.

He led me to my room. I felt awkward around him, and wasn't sure what to do. Thank God he picked up on it and took matters into his own hands or took me into his hands, I should say. He lifted my shirt over my head, and I slid out of my bra. He kissed soft kisses around my chest and to my nipples giving them both much needed attention. I moaned as his hands slowly unzipped my jean shorts. I was with him one hundred percent. My mind was on nothing but the sensations he was causing throughout my entire body. That is until we were both naked in bed.

Dammit, why didn't I just turn my cell phone off? I knew it was Drew. Dawson looked over to my phone and then back to me with a lost look. I didn't answer it, and continued to kiss him, trying to regain the passion. It worked briefly until my phone rang again. Dawson knew that he had lost me, and the hunger along with it.

He rolled off me with a heavy sigh. I didn't stop him and lay beside him naked staring up at the ceiling.

"I'm sorry, Daw," I said. I didn't know what I was apologizing for, I guess everything. Mostly for making this so difficult for him, he didn't deserve any of it.

Dawson rolled over and kissed me. "Me too, Ry. Me too," he said and removed himself from my bed. "I'll talk to you tomorrow," he said, getting dressed and leaving me alone.

As soon as I heard the door close I grabbed my phone.

"What is your fucking problem?" I asked, angrily as soon as I heard Drew's voice.

"I can't sleep," he replied. I laughed. What else was there to do? It was funny. It was a funny sick fucking joke.

"Why?" I asked, pulling on my panties and a nightshirt.

"Because I haven't talked to you today. I needed to hear your voice. Were you in bed already? Why didn't you answer?"

"Which of the ten times are you referring to?" I asked, eluding the question.

"All of them. Is he there?"

"No. Drew, he's not here. You ran him off."

"Good. Did I run him off in time?"

"You're such a dick."

"And you are avoiding my questions. Did you sleep with him?" he asked, bluntly.

"No. Drew. I did not, thanks to you. Now I am going to have to take care of it myself."

"You know there was a time that I would have spanked you for that."

Are you serious? Stupid fucking vagina.

I didn't reply. I couldn't reply. I wanted him there doing just that. What the hell was wrong with me?

"You want that, don't you, Morgan?" he asked in that dominating tone. I have no idea what was conspiring in me, but my core throbbed like mad at the tone of his voice.

"Yes," I rasped a breathy reply.

"Come for me, baby."

My fingers had already found their way through the elastic of my panties, and I let the stupid bastard talk me through one hell of an orgasm. It was settled. I was surely losing my mind. I should have been put into a straitjacket and locked up.

Chapter 20

I called Dawson the next day and apologized again. I invited him over for supper and of course he accepted. That was just how Dawson was. He wasn't going to make me feel bad for my issues, and I loved him for that.

I had the salad chilling in the refrigerator. I had gone into town earlier to buy fresh vegetables from the local fruit market. My homemade spaghetti sauce was simmering on the stove, and I just had a shower. I did my hair, makeup and spritzed just a dab of perfume. I pulled on my nice fitting jeans and wore a white, V-neck shirt that showed my midriff. I looked hot, I decided, looking into the mirror behind my bedroom door. I smiled a big smile when I heard the knock. I was determined to have a good night with Dawson, and keep Drew in Las Vegas where he belonged.

Holy fuck...

He too was wearing nice fitting jeans that hung low on his hips, a tight knit shirt with the sexy as hell pecks peeking out from the three unbuttoned buttons on his chest. The only problem was that it wasn't Dawson. Drew stood at my door with a sexy smile and a dozen red roses.

Shit...

I was speechless. Dawson was going to be there any second. What the hell was he doing here?

"Drew?" was all that I could manage to get out in my shocked state. I looked over him toward the road searching for Dawson's police cruiser that would be in my drive at any time.

"Hey, beautiful," he said, holding out the flowers.

I took them and ushered him inside not wanting Dawson to see him on my porch, not that he wasn't going to pass the fancy black car backing out of my drive.

"What the hell are you doing here?" I asked, not leaving the door. I had to intercept Dawson.

"Is that any way to greet your husband?" he asked, and had me in his arms in a split second.

Son of a bitch...

"You could have warned me. I have company coming for supper."

"Do you want me to leave," he asked, kissing my forehead. Did I?

I didn't have time to answer his or my question when I heard the car pulling into the gravel drive.

"If I told you not to leave this house, would you listen?" I asked, shoving the roses back into his arms.

Dawson saw me coming and slid his hands into his jean pockets as he leaned against his car. I heard the door behind me open and close. "Of course not," I said turning to Drew on the porch.

"I guess I'm eating at Millie's tonight," Dawson said with a defeated smile.

"I'm sorry, Daw. I didn't know he was going to show up here."

"I'm fighting a losing battle here, Ry," he stated, looking down at me.

"No, you're not. I just need some time, Dawson. Don't give up on us just yet, please," I begged. I didn't want to lose Dawson. Why couldn't I just have him for everyday life and Drew at bedtime?"

Dawson leaned in and kissed the same spot that Drew had just kissed on my head. "Call me later and let me know that you're okay," he said.

"He's not going to hurt me, Dawson," I assured him.

"Call me," he demanded and got in his car and backed out.

"Your audacity is ridiculous," I called to Drew, leaned against the post with his arms crossed. I swear he had sex appeal dripping from his contoured body.

"What? I had to see what I was up against," he pleaded his case.

"What do you want?" I asked, taking the stones beneath my bare feet a little easier than I had when I walked out.

"You. Any more questions?"

"Yes. What the hell are you doing here?" I asked, walking past him and back into the house.

"I wanted to tell you that I found your mom."

"And you couldn't tell me that over the phone?" I asked, walking into the kitchen to stir my sauce.

"I could have done that. I didn't want to," he smirked, dipping his finger into my sauce.

"You hate spaghetti," I said, turning to him right in front of me.

"I do," he admitted, holding his finger out for me to lick the sauce. Dammit if I didn't do it. I sucked the sauce from his finger and of course the sensation went right to my groin. I swear if I could have traded this vagina for another one, I would have.

"You're eating spaghetti or you're starving," I assured him, stepping away from him. I had to. I was ready to forget the spaghetti, and have him for supper.

I put the roses in a vase, and he watched me finish supper. "So, where is my mom?" I asked, placing the uncooked spaghetti into the boiling water.

"Rodanthe, North Carolina. She's doing well. She runs a bed and breakfast out of her beach house. She's remarried and," he stopped.

"What, Drew?" I asked, sensing that he didn't want to tell me something.

"She has a seven-year-old daughter."

My eyes widened as my mouth dropped. What the hell? She just dumps her two kids that she already brought into a bad situation, and goes off and replaces us with a new life and family? It pissed me off, and I wasn't so sure that I wanted to find her anymore. I didn't reply to that. I didn't know what to say.

"Let's talk about something else," I stated. My mother needed to be placed on the pile of things that I needed time to process.

"Um, I'm interviewing for Derik's position. Do you want to be involved?"

I looked at him puzzled. "Why would I want to be involved with that?"

"You do own the company," he reminded me.

"I do not. Stop saying that."

"You do Morgan, whether you want to accept it or not. Your name, not mine is in that will."

"How is he?" I asked, needing to put that in my processing pile, as well.

"I went by yesterday. He didn't look good. His nurse told me that his kidneys were starting to shut down."

"He's dying?" I asked. I'm not sure why I asked that. He looked like he was half dead the last time saw him.

"Yes. He's been dying for quite some time, but I don't think it will be much longer. I don't think he will make it to the end of summer."

I couldn't process that either. I just found out that he was my grandfather. I hadn't even had the chance to get to know him.

"This is a nice little place you have here," Drew said, sensing my uneasiness.

I snorted. "Thanks. I almost said that I bought it with your money, but I guess it was mine, uh?"

"Yeah," he now snorted, "It is. I'm still not quite sure how you pulled that off. I could hear every word you said in that house anytime I wanted, and I could see you. How the hell did you get into my office without me finding out?"

"You probably shouldn't underestimate me. I'm not as dumb as you think I am."

"Oh, I have learned not to underestimate you, and I don't think you are dumb at all. How did you get in there?" he asked again.

"Rebecca shut the power off a couple of times, and I learned a lot from all those times that I spent bent over your desk. I knew all of your passwords, how to freeze the cameras, and how to move money so that you wouldn't notice."

"I did underestimate you. I'm glad I have you on my side."

"I'm not on your side."

"We'll see," he smirked.

We walked out to the back deck and Drew again commented on the view. My heart skipped a few beats when he walked behind me and trapped me between the railing and his dangerous body. I think I may have even stopped breathing when he kissed my ear and whispered.

"You do know that I plan on fucking you, don't you?"

Fuck...!

"And you know that I should throw you out of my house, don't you," I said with my eyes closed, trying not to think about what he had just said.

"Maybe, but you won't. Do you know why you won't, Morgan," he whispered with that same low whisper. I knew what he was insinuating, but I asked anyway.

"Why?"

"Because, you *want* me to fuck you."

"I do?" I asked the ridiculous question. Of course, I wanted him to do just that, and the sooner, the better.

"You do. I would bet that if I slipped my fingers inside of these nice fitting jeans right now that you're already wet, thinking about it," he said, grinding into my backside.

"Jesus Christ, Drew. Stop it," I demanded, turning to him. I was human after all, and being that my vagina seemed to have a mind all of its own, I was ready to spread my legs right there on the deck.

He laughed, knowing that he was getting to me. The mind games that he played oh so well were no competition to my throbbing need, and he knew it.

Drew ate my spaghetti without complaining. He didn't brag about it or go after seconds, but he ate it. I took him down to the beach after supper, and he did complain about that.

"Why didn't you buy a house by a real beach?" he asked as we made our way down the rocky cliff.

"I like this one, and besides, I had to make sure you couldn't find me. Stop being a pussy," I added with a smile that he couldn't see from behind.

"Did you just call me a pussy?'

"Yeah, I did. Stop being so domesticated."

I heard Drew laugh behind me, but he didn't comment. We walked along the beach not really talking about anything. I found a piece of sea glass which I wished I wouldn't have. We spent forever walking around so Drew could find one. I didn't want him stooped over looking for beach glass. I wanted him holding my hand and paying attention to me and my needy body.

"Drew, it's going to get dark on us, and we have to climb back up. I've done it in the dark. It's not fun."

"But I want to find a piece of that stuff too," he whined. I thought it was cute. I knew how he was with his jewels, and that was exactly what he had seen in my light green sea glass find.

"You can have mine," I offered, handing it over.

He took it and kissed me. "Thanks, but I still want to find my own. Can we come back tomorrow?"

"How long are you staying?" I asked, leading him back to the path.

"Are you trying to get rid of me?"

"No. I was just curious, and I have things to do tomorrow."

"I have to be in New York Monday afternoon. What do you have to do tomorrow?"

"I need to change the oil in my car and mow the yard."

"You're joking?" he asked, stepping around me and taking my hand to help me up a steep part of the bank.

"I'm not," I replied, kissing him quickly before stepping around him again.

"Why don't you pay someone to do that for you?"

"I'm not as rich as you. I made ten dollars an hour here. I can mow my own yard and change my own oil."

"Morgan, you are richer than me. I don't have a pot to piss in without you. How do you even know how to change your oil?"

"Dawson taught me."

Drew didn't reply, and I could tell that he didn't like the thought of Dawson and me changing the oil in anything.

We removed our muddy shoes on the deck before going in. I looked out the living room window to see if Lauren's car was home yet. It was not. I knew if she were home she would have barged in by now.

"Do you want a shower?" I said, turning to Drew, staring at me.

"Yeah, that would be nice."

"You can go first. I want to take a bath."

"How about you just shower with me?" he asked, taking my hand and spinning me in a dance.

I smiled at him. "I want to shave," I admitted, and he smiled next.

I warmed up a couple of strawberry and cream pastries from the shop after our showers and fixed us both a cup of Star's famous mocha coffee. We sat on the sofa and ate.

"Did you have sex with Dawson?" Drew asked.

I chewed the food in my mouth before answering. "I had sex with Dawson lots of times."

"That's not what I mean, and you know it."

"You mean, have I had sex with him since you decided that you loved me?"

"Yes."

"No. I haven't. I was going to tonight," I told him honestly, "and there were a couple of times that I almost did, but you seemed to always call at the perfect time."

"He hasn't spent the night here?"

"Not since I came back. He did before I was forced under a bus by Derik. We practically lived together."

"Do you love him, Morgan?"

I sat my Danish on the table. "Yes, Drew. I do love him, and he doesn't deserve any of this. I feel horrible for putting him through all of it."

Drew took the last bite of his pastry and set his plate beside mine. "I don't want you to love him," he spoke softly and took my hand.

I touched the side of his face and smiled at him. I didn't particularly want to love him right then either, but the truth is, I did. "I love you too, Drew, and I have no clue what I am supposed to do."

"Come home with me," he begged.

"I can't. I need to decide this on my own. I forgive you for everything, but I can't forget it, Drew. You have to understand that."

"I do understand that, and I know that I don't deserve you, but I love you so much, it hurts. I hate myself for wasting six years of trying to be..." He stopped, trying to think of a word.

"A prick, a bully, my master," I replied, helping him out. I didn't care if it stung a little. I wanted it to.

"Do you want me to leave you alone?" he asked in a hurtful tone. I didn't want to hurt him although that is what I should have wanted. Most people would think that I had lost my ever loving mind. Maybe I had, I don't know.

"Yes. Drew. I need to try and fix things with Dawson. I don't expect you to understand that, but I do."

"Are we getting a divorce?"

"I suppose we should. Don't you?"

Drew took a deep breath and leaned back on the sofa. This was not how I wanted to end our night. I quickly tried my best to recover the situation. I moved to his lap with one leg on each side of him. I held his face with my hands and our eyes collided. I looked into his gray eyes and realized for the first time that I had no idea who Drew Kelley even was. I knew nothing about his past, his family, did he have any family, where his father was nothing. Our entire eight year existence was based solely on sex.

"There are things that we need to discuss, Morgan," he stated, moving his hands to my hips.

"You mean business, right?"

"Yes. You have a multimillion dollar company to run."

"I'm not running shit. I want no part of that."

"Somebody has to run it."

"Yeah. You. Why would you not? You're the one that wants it. I don't care one iota about that, nor do I want to care."

"I have no problem with that, but I will not have my name on anything. You have a lot of things to work out."

"Like what?"

"Like my salary. Do you want the house? What you are going to do about your multiple assets."

I moved off Drew and lay at the other end of the couch with a deep sigh. What the hell? I didn't want any of this. I didn't know anything about being rich. I was a poor little hillbilly from West by God Virginia. How the hell was I supposed to know what to do?

"Let's go to bed," Drew requested, pulling me up with a groan. At least I could get my mind off of it for a little bit.

Or not...

Drew removed his jeans and climbed into his side of the bed. I stared down at his bare chest lying in my bed with hungry eyes. I wanted him. I didn't care how wrong it was. I needed him. I slowly unbuttoned the first two buttons on my night shirt.

Drew grabbed my wrist and pulled me in bed. "Stop taking your clothes off," he demanded.

What the fuck...?

"Why? Don't you remember what you said you were going to do me?"

"I remember, but I changed my mind. I just want to hold you in my arms. I want you to realize how much I love you and I don't need sex from you."

Um... Yes you do.

Drew moved close to my body, forcing me to turn away from him as he snuggled closer to me. I wasn't getting sex. Dammit I wasn't getting sex. I could tell shortly after lying there in his arms, still dumbfounded about not getting any that he was falling asleep when his breathing began to slow.

"Drew?" I quietly spoke.

"Hmm," he murmured.

"Where is your dad?"

"I don't know. I never knew him. He took off when my mother got pregnant."

"You know if your mother would have married my real dad, you would be my step brother."

Drew snorted. "I guess. I never thought about it, but they never married, so it's not incest if that's what you're worried about."

"Where did you grow up?"

"What's with all the questions?"

"I don't know. I just feel like there is only one part of you that I really know."

"I grew up in Vegas. My mother worked for your dad. She ran the store on the strip, you know the one that I used to take you to when I wanted to pretend you were my wife for the night?"

"Yeah, and then you would take the rings back after whatever function we were attending, take me home and…"

"Stop it. Morgan," Drew said with an angry tone, cutting me off. "I know what I did, and I don't want you to remind me. Go to sleep."

I let it go at that. It was obvious that he wasn't touching me, and I wasn't sure that I wanted him to anymore. I waited until I knew for sure that Drew had fallen asleep and slid from beneath his arm.

What the hell was I supposed to do with a multimillion dollar company? I quietly opened the door to the deck and walked out. I didn't understand my life, I mean come on, this doesn't happen. There are two things that I wished would have happened so that I wasn't in the place that I was. I wished that I had never gotten on that plane and left my safe little life in Misty Bay. Then again, I wished I would have never remembered who I was.

I thought about Dawson as I listened to the waves crashing below. I had been on the deck for at least twenty minutes. Drew was sound asleep. Dawson would have been out there by now. Did he really care more than Drew? I got my answer when I jumped as the door opened.

"You okay?" Drew asked, taking my hand and pulling me to him as he leaned against the banister.

"Yeah, just a lot on my mind," I said as my arms mechanically went around his neck.

"Anything I can do?" he asked, pulling me tight around the waist.

"Not unless you can make up my mind for me."

"You're in luck. I can do that. Choose me," he teased, sort of.

I smiled and kissed him. I took his hand and led him back to bed. He still didn't touch me, and I was beginning to think that I would starve from lack of sex. I would have, had it been possible. He whispered that he loved me before dozing off again.

"Drew."

"Hmm," he moaned, with closed eyes.

"Why are you not touching me?"

He snickered. I already told you why. I want you to know that I want you without the sex."

"You want me without sex?"

"No. I want the sex too. I want you to know that I love you, and it's not just about sex."

"I believe you, but I still want sex, like now." There I said it. I was either getting laid, or I wasn't, but at least he knew that I wanted it.

"What am I going to do with you," Drew laughed.

"You know exactly what you can do with me."

"If I do, will you promise me that you won't have sex with Dawson?"

Fuck...

"Forget it Drew, just go to sleep," I said, rolling away from him. He rolled with me.

"I take that as no," he rasped in my hair.

I couldn't help it. His cock was too close. I could feel it on my ass. I ignored his last statement and rubbed my ass against him.

"I'm beginning to think that somebody needs their ass beat," he softly spoke, licking my ear.

Fuck yeah, that's exactly what I needed. I did it again, egging him on. He rolled me over more so that I was flat on my stomach. He pushed the covers off, exposing my silk covered ass.

"Do you want me to spank you, Morgan?"

His sexy low tone had changed. He wasn't playfully asking anymore. He was being serious. He really wanted to know if I wanted him to spank me. I was a fucked up excuse for a human being. I did want it.

"Yes," I said with closed eyes, feeling my pussy throb and my panties become moist.

He slid my panties down and rubbed my backside as I waited for the first blow. I didn't care how fucked up I was, and I didn't care how society felt about our sexual cravings. I liked it. It turned me on like nothing else. I would worry about how I was supposed to be the next day. Right then all I cared about was getting Drew inside of me.

The sting from Drew's thick hand was instantly rubbed away.

Jesus vagina, calm the hell down, I'm working on it.

After the next sting, I raised my leg a little. Drew took the hint well, and once he had rubbed his soreness from the third blow he dipped his finger inside of me. I thought I was going to come off the bed.

"You're always so fucking wet, Morgan," he huskily said, sinking his fingers again. I moaned. Shit did I moan. I flipped my leg over him so I was lying on my back. My hips arched into his fingers all on their own accord. I had nothing to do with it. It was all my backstabbing pussy. It had a mind of its own, and made my mouth say words that I never even thought about. Like.

"Lick it."

Shit. Where the hell did that come from?

"Spread your legs," Drew replied to my outburst.

I did.

"More."

I did, and Holy Geez Louise. I was going to come. I was going to come fast. His tongue sliding up me was unbearable. He stopped a couple of times with his mouth but kept his fingers busy so that he could come to my mouth. His tongue would dive into my parted lips, forcing me to taste myself on him and then back to pleasing my core.

Drew thrust his middle finger as deep as he could when I called out. No, when I yelled out. Two of his other fingers, I wasn't sure which ones, penetrated my clit while another one penetrated my puckered nub in back. I knew that he could feel every last one of the convulsions from my wall contracting around his finger.

"Are you good?" he asked once I was able to release the sheet, squeezed tightly in my two fists. I opened one eye to see the proud grin on his face.

"No. I need you inside of me," I assured him that I was not done. Not even close.

"I need inside of your mouth," he countered.

"Then I suggest that you get out of those shorts."

He did. He lay back with his hands over his head. I took his steel rod in my hand, and then sank it balls deep into my throat. I devoured him. It had to be the most erotic blowjob in history. I know it was a bad time to be thinking about what was going on, but I did. I wondered if maybe I were more in lust with Drew then in love. He kind of ruined me in that department. I already knew how Dawson felt about my immoral, kinky shit. He would never in a million years spank me. It wasn't normal, not that I didn't enjoy making love to him. I did. It's just, I don't know. Sex with Drew was so intense, strong and powerful. It was the kind of sex that left me thinking about it for hours.

"Sit on me, Morgan," Drew demanded once he knew that he couldn't handle another second of my torturous mouth.

I slid onto him, and his head went back as his eyes closed with a moan. I slowly moved up and down on him, gradually picking up speed. I rocked my hips, frantically back and forth on his shaft, feeling myself reaching my peak once again. Drew waited until I was right there, and flipped me off him, onto my stomach. He pulled my leg over his thigh, dipping his hardness into me a couple of times before pulling it out. I didn't want him to remove himself. I wanted to come again. I needed to come again.

"Can I?" he asked as I felt the tip of him penetrating my ass.

"Yes," I moaned. God yes.

I squeezed my eyes closed, waiting for my body to relax and let him in.

"Do you have any KY?" he asked.

"No. I don't really need that here," I admitted. Dawson would have never done what he was doing to me.

I felt him move in a little more, and then a little more until my muscles had relaxed, and he easily took me from behind. He rubbed my throbbing clit as he thrust in and out of me until we were both spent, moaning in loud, breathy, whimpers.

"Now will you go to sleep?" Drew asked. I laughed. Okay, maybe I did love him for other than sex reasons.

"I'm making coffee! Get your lazy bones out of bed," I heard, opening my eyes.

Shit. Lauren.

I slid from under Drew's arm and wrapped the robe hanging from my door around me. I quietly opened and closed the door and went to the kitchen.

"Good morning, I thought for sure I would wake up to a police car in your driveway. He didn't stay?"

I sat on the bar stool and ran my fingers through my hair.

"No, Dawson didn't stay, but," I didn't get it out when Drew opened my bedroom door wearing nothing but his jeans as he walked toward the bathroom.

He didn't speak and only nodded.

"Holy fuck, Ry. Who the hell is that?"

"That would be Drew. He showed up here yesterday afternoon."

"You didn't tell me he looked like that," Lauren exclaimed.

I snickered. Talk about awkward.

Drew came out of the bathroom and started back toward the bedroom.

"Come here. I want you to meet my best friend," I called to him.

"Can I get a shirt?" he asked.

"You don't have to," Lauren giggled. He snickered and continued to get his shirt.

I scolded Lauren, "You idiot."

"You can't beat a girl for trying," she smiled.

"Lauren, this is Drew," I said, introducing my husband who calls me Morgan to my friend who knew me as Riley.

The three of us went out to the deck and had coffee. I was surprised at Lauren and Drew, hitting it off like they did. Then again, Lauren could make friends with the devil himself. She was just that bubbly. They were talking diamonds of all things. Lauren had traded a horse for a ring years before and wanted to know if he could tell her what it was worth, if anything. Of course, he said yes, and she planned to bring it over later.

Lauren left after about an hour, leaving Drew and me alone on the deck, overlooking the breathtaking, morning ocean.

"It's very tranquil here," he said, looking out to the endless sea.

"Yes, a lot more so than the desert," I replied.

"We don't have to live there, Morgan," he said with a serious expression.

I snorted. "Where would we live?"

"Wherever you want," he assured me.

I didn't reply. I didn't want to think about that at the time.

"Do you want to mow or change the oil first?" I asked instead.

"I'm pretty sure I have no clue how to do either," he admitted.

"You're such a girl," I teased.

"Are you calling me a pussy again?

I laughed. "Yes, but I was trying to be nice about it."

Chapter 21

Drew and I dressed and walked out to the back yard to retrieve the mower. The yard really wasn't that bad. Dawson had kept up on it throughout the summer. I primed the pump by pushing the little ball three times and had to explain to Drew why I did it.

"Where's the key?" He wanted to know. I couldn't help it. I laughed, really laughed. He couldn't be that domesticated. No man was that ignorant.

"That's it. We're not friends anymore," he determined and started walking away.

"I'm sorry. Come back. I promise not to laugh at you for the rest of the day."

He wrapped his arm around my back and kissed me. "If you do, I am going to bend you over my knee and beat your sexy little ass," he promised.

Okay, maybe I would laugh at him again.

"Pull the handle," I explained, pointing to the T-handle cord.

He pulled it gently and nothing happened. I had to bite my lip to keep from laughing again.

"You're asking for it," he warned.

"Pull it like you mean it," I coached, and held the handle to engage the blades. He did; it started right up. He grinned like he just passed a milestone or something. I know most women would have been turned off by his lack of manly mechanical ability, but I wasn't. I thought it was cute.

"You're ready," I called over the loud motor. "Just go in straight rows, up and back," I explained.

I watched as he made his first swipe. He had the biggest smile as he turned and mowed the next strip toward me.

"This is kind of fun," he said, stopping to kiss me.

"Pull back on the handle and lift the front wheels when you turn," I told him, still wrapped in one of his arms.

"Why?" he asked. That's when I noticed Dawson parked across the road, standing by his cruiser with Lauren, both looking right at us.

I self-consciously stepped away from Drew. "So that you get a clean straight line without the curves," I explained. He didn't catch my sudden retreat and did what I told him to do.

I smiled over at Dawson. He sort of smiled back. He was hurt, and it was killing him to see me with Drew. Lauren just had a pitiful look. She didn't like the hell that I was putting Dawson through.

I retrieved the weed eater from the shed and started doing the trimming while Drew mowed my yard. I wanted to walk across the road and go to Dawson, but I couldn't, not at the time. I wouldn't know what to say anyway.

Drew and I spent an hour in the yard, and then he helped me pull weeds from the flower bed, which surprised me. I was sure he had never in his life pulled a weed. I looked up to see Dawson backing out of Lauren's driveway. He had his hand on his chin, staring right at me.

Drew helped me carry the car ramps to the driveway next. I really didn't need them and wouldn't have even bothered had he been a little more mechanically inclined. I placed the ramps in front of both tires. He was afraid of running over them, so I had to pull the car up.

"I cannot believe that I am lying under a car in the gravel," he said.

Our heads were side by side, and our feet hung out the front of the car. I thought it was extremely sexy for some reason.

"What do we do now?" he asked, moving his lips to mine. He must have thought that it was pretty hot too. He kissed me for at least three minutes.

"Are we changing the oil or are we going to get it on?" I asked, ready to say the hell with the oil.

He smiled on my lips. "I'm changing the oil. Tell me what to do."

"This is the drain plug," I pointed. "You have to take it out and let the old oil drain into the pan." I had to tell him to back up before he got a face full of oil.

We stood by the car and waited for it to drain.

"Your friend left," he said, looking over to Lauren's.

"You noticed that?"

"Yes. I noticed, and I don't like the way he looks at you," he admitted.

"Will you buy me a new car so that I can drive to find my mother?" I asked, totally circumventing his comment.

He laughed. "No. I would rather you fly. I will get you a private flight."

"I don't want to fly. I want to drive. I drove all the way from Vegas to here in this car," I explained. I did want to drive. I wanted the alone time to think, and try to figure out what road I should take in my fucked up life.

"I don't like it, but, you don't need me to buy you a car. You have enough money to buy every car on the lot. I will go with you though. I'm definitely not letting you drive this thing."

"This has been the best car I have ever owned," I assured him.

He laughed again. "How many cars have you owned, Mrs. Kelley?" he asked with a kiss.

I didn't answer. It didn't need an answer. It only needed my tongue, dancing with his.

"I never imagined an oil change could make me wet," I said to his lips.

He took a step back. "You can't say stuff like that."

I laughed. "Why?"

"Because it makes me want to slide my fingers inside of those skimpy little shorts, and find out for myself."

"Jesus, Drew. You can't say stuff like that," I demanded, using the same words.

He smiled. "Okay, that's enough foreplay. Let's get back to the oil change. What do I do now?"

I took the wrench for the filter and explained that we had to change the filter. He got it off, and was damn proud of himself for the small task of removing the old and securing the new filter. He backed the car off of the ramps, and I showed him where to add the new oil. He closed the hood, and we put the ramps away.

"Now can we go look for more of those jewels?" he asked.

"I'm kind of hungry. Can we eat first?"

"I guess so," he whined.

We ate toasted cheese sandwiches with a jar of Starlight's homemade tomato soup. Nobody made tomato soup like Starlight. It was the best soup in the world, and I am not exaggerating when I say that either.

Drew and I walked down the rocky path toward the beach. I really hoped that he found a piece of sea glass. He was really excited about it, although I wasn't too optimistic that he would. It didn't get washed up very often.

I told him everything that John had told me about looking for it. We squatted at a gravel pile and carefully moved rocks looking for the dull glass. We had walked for quite a while, scavenging through the little rocks. He found a piece of shiny green glass with sharp edges. He was super excited. I hated to burst his bubble, but I had to.

"Yes!" he exclaimed wiping the dirt and grime away with sea water.

"That's junk Drew," I explained. "Throw it back and maybe someday it won't be."

"What do you mean is junk? It's pretty," he assured me.

"It's nothing but a broken bottle. It hasn't been ground or polished by sand and rock, and it doesn't have any erosion from the salt water."

He pouted with a long face and threw it back to the sea as hard as he could.

I was beginning to lose hope when we searched our seventh pile of graveling sand. I saw the black glass. My heart even started to pick up a few extra beats. I knew that the black glass was the rarest of all to find. I didn't want to point it out. I wanted him to find it. He was just too excited about it.

My sneaker tapped, nervously, waiting for him to see what I was seeing. Black glass was so hard to find because it looked so much like a normal pebble. This piece however, showed the frosting from time and condition. I almost pointed it out when he picked it up and brushed his thumb across it.

"How about this?" he asked, looking up to me.

I feigned ignorance and took it from his hand. "Yes. Do you have any idea what you just found?" I asked. He stood, curious as I held it to the sun.

"What is it?" he asked.

I handed it back. "Hold it to the sun and you will see that it's not actually black at all."

"It's purple," he said. "Do you know what it's from?"

"My guess is an old medicine bottle, at least a hundred years old." I explained how they were made with iron slag. Because of no refrigeration back then, they made the bottles stronger and more resistant to shattering and the harsh conditions of centuries past kept its contents from going bad.

"I found a rare piece?" he asked with a boyish grin.

"The rarest," I assured him. "That piece may have even come all the way from Italy."

"Wow. Really?" he asked, looking at his treasure through the sun again.

"Yup," I smiled at his excitement.

"I'm going to have a necklace made out of it."

"Are we done hunting sea glass?" I asked. We had been there for almost three hours. I was hot and needed something to drink.

"Yeah, but I kind of wanted to climb that rock," he said, pointing to the peak, where the sea only let you cross at a certain time of the day.

"You're joking," I said, hoping that he was.

"No. Come on," he said, placing his new treasure safely in his pocket, pulling my hand.

"Drew, we can't climb that rock. One of us is going to get hurt."

"I'm a doctor," he said, ignoring me.

I didn't laugh. This was not just a little rock. This was a cliff. There was no way we were going to make it to the top without breaking our necks.

I complained the whole walk back, protesting his mission. He won.

Drew made me go first, and I slowly and carefully chose where to put my fingers and toes. This was ridiculous. This was the type of rock that you wore harnesses and had security ropes for when you fell. We were going to fall. I was sure of it. There was no doubt in my mind. Maybe that was the plan. If I fell to my death rock climbing with my husband, he would inherit all of my fortunes. I started to panic, wondering if I was climbing my way to my death.

"Morgan?" Drew said, grunting from behind me, pulling himself higher up the sea cliff.

"What," I answered, pulling myself up the complex elevation.

"Thank you for this. This has been the best couple days of my life."

Okay, maybe he wasn't planning on murdering me. I smiled as I continued against my will to make my way to the top.

We finally made it, and my seldom used muscles quivered. Rock climbing was hard work. I couldn't believe it when we finally sat on the edge of the cliff. We were high, really high. Our feet dangled over the dangerous cliff. It was absolutely breathtaking.

"How are we getting down?" Drew asked with a laugh.

"We're not going down," I assured him. "We are going up." There was no way I was climbing back down.

He laughed. "Take your shorts off so that I can fuck you up here."

My first thought should have been no fucking way, but it wasn't. I looked around. There was absolutely no way anyone could see us up there, except maybe the sail boat, if they had binoculars.

"Drew?" I said in a question.

"What?" he mimicked my tone. "I will do all the work. You just get naked and lay back."

"You're serious?" I asked.

He unbuttoned his jeans and removed his half-staff cock. "Take your shorts off, Morgan," he demanded, stroking himself and letting me know that he was more than serious.

Of course, I did just that. What the hell else was I supposed to do? My vagina always seemed to be working against me.

I slid out of my shorts, hooking my panties with them and laid back. Drew stroked himself up my wet pussy a couple of times before sliding into me.

Fuck...

The sound of the waves below us, the sea salt breeze and the heat from the sun while Drew made love to me on top of the world was something that I am sure I will never experience again for the rest of my life. Drew took his time and made slow passionate love to me. He brought me to bliss not once but twice before he plunged deep into me, releasing himself.

He stayed inside of me for as long as I could stand the rock digging into my lower back.

"I love you, Morgan," he said, staring down at me.

"I love you too, Drew," I assured him. I did love him. I knew that I did. The problem was, I loved Dawson too. "You have to get up," I finally said.

"I don't want to," he admitted with a smile.

"I don't want you to either, but you see the thing is, I have this rock digging into my back and it hurts like hell."

He laughed and slid out of me. I pulled on my shorts, and he pulled me to my feet. We walked on up the cliff, through the woods and into a clearing that led to my road. He held my hand as we walked through the neighborhood back toward my house. I didn't want him to hold my hand. All of my neighbors knew that I was supposed to marry the town sheriff. I wasn't going to explain that to him though.

"When were you planning on going to North Carolina?" he asked, brushing his sea glass with his thumb.

"Next week."

"I really wish you would fly. I can arrange for a plane and a driver for you."

"I'm not going to fly, Drew."

"Yeah, I didn't think so. I think you should get a sports utility vehicle. There're safer."

Drew sat at my table and searched vehicles online while I started supper. I knew he would probably complain, but I was so hungry for sausage, eggs and gravy and biscuits.

I set our plates on the table. He gave his plate a strange look.

"Breakfast?" he asked the rhetorical question.

"Hmm, yes, I was hungry for it," I replied taking a bite of the scrumptious gravy and biscuits.

He raised his eyebrows and took a bite. "Hmm, this is good. Where did you learn to cook?"

"I cooked a lot growing up, and Rebecca taught me a lot."

"You cooked growing up?"

"I had too. I didn't have the best parents in the world."

"Mr. Callaway knew that. That is why he paid your mother to stay away from you both. He wanted you both to have better lives."

"But why wouldn't he want me to be with my brother?" I asked. I didn't understand that part. I loved Justin, and he loved me.

"That wasn't him, Morgan. That was all me. I talked him into doing it that way because I didn't want a kid getting in the way of my plans for you."

"That makes me want to hate you, Drew."

"You should hate me. I hate me for the things that I have done."

I could have very easily thrown him out of my house at that moment. I was pissed, but abstained from talking anymore about it. I knew that he was leaving the next morning, and I didn't want it to end in a fight. He admitted he was wrong and was trying with everything in him to make it right. Me, opening up old wounds wasn't going to solve anything.

"Did you find anything?" I asked about the car shopping instead.

"Yeah, a few things. What do you think of this?" he asked, sliding my laptop for me to see.

I looked at the BMW X6 M and swallowed the lump in my throat. "Starting at $92,000, Drew?" I asked. I drove a 1993 Honda Civic. I didn't need a car that cost that much, let alone one with 555 horsepower. "What the hell am I going to do with that much car?"

"Drive it, what else?"

"No. Thanks for your help. I think I will just go shopping myself tomorrow."

Drew helped me clean up and then went to the shower. I sat at the table with my laptop and opened up my email while I waited for my turn. I felt like the worst person on earth when I read Dawson's email.

"Hey, beautiful. I just wanted to see if you were okay. You didn't call or text me like I asked you to. I'm sure you're fine. You looked to be very happy when I saw you with your husband this morning. I can't do this, Ry. I love you, and I want you more than my own life, but I can't just keep waiting on the sidelines for you to decide what you want. You have a husband for Christ sake. I should step out and let you try to make it work. I don't want to. I hate the thought of you being with anyone, especially a man that I would love to stick my gun in his mouth, but I have to. It's breaking my heart, and I just need to distance myself. I love you, and if you ever need anything, you know where to find me.

Fuck...

I wanted to go to him right that second. That wasn't an option. Drew was in my shower.

I quickly emailed him back. "Don't you do this, Dawson. I have known my name for two weeks. You can't expect me to just go back to who I was. I love you too, and you know it. Don't give up on us, Daw. Please. Give me some time. I am going to North Carolina for a few days next week to try and make some sense-of this tangled mess. Give me that much, please. I don't want to lose you, Dawson."

I started to log off of my computer when I saw the, one new message, pop up in the corner. I didn't want to be talking to him when Drew came out. I had enough to deal with without adding him to it too.

"Is he still there?"

"Yes. He is leaving in the morning. Will you come over tomorrow night so that we can talk?"

"I can't tell you no. Yes. I will be there."

"Okay, I will see you tomorrow." I quickly replied and closed out of the email when I heard Drew open the bathroom door.

Of course, he was wearing his jeans low on his hips, no shirt and no shoes. He made me want to devour his sexy as hell body with kisses. His hair was uncombed, and only towel dried. Shit. Why did this have to be so hard? Why couldn't he be ugly? I'm sure it would have helped.

"Your turn," he said, pulling me from my wicked thoughts about him being naked.

I closed the laptop and grabbed a quick shower and shaved speedily, just in case.

I dressed in short white shorts, with a light pink cami, purposely pulling it up to show my midriff. I walked behind Drew sitting at the table and ran my hands down his sexy as hell, bare chest.

Fuck. Fuck. Fuck.

"Maybe I should be the one to step out," Drew said, moving my hand from his chest and standing.

Dawson's last message was displayed with the rest of them. "I love you, Riley."

"Maybe you shouldn't be reading my emails," I snapped.

"I give up Morgan or Riley, whatever the fuck your name is. That right there tells me that I don't have a chance in hell."

"Why, Drew? I never once lied to you about Dawson. You knew that I was supposed to marry him. I told you that I was in love with him. How was I supposed to know that you could be this person?" I said waving my arm around animatedly. "You're going to get pissed at me because I'm confused about whether I should choose the man that I know will always do right by me. Do you really think that it's that easy? What, Drew? Do you think I should choose the one that has hurt me more times than I can count?"

"No, Morgan. I think you should choose Robocop. It's obvious that you are going to hang over my head what I did, and bring it up every time you get pissed off."

"What the fuck do you expect, Drew? I have had a hell of a lot of shit dumped in my lap the past couple of weeks. Can you not get that?"

Drew turned and grabbed me by both of my arms, hard. He had the look that used to scare the hell out of me. My heart plummeted to my stomach. His eyes were dark and cold, the same eyes that I saw so many times, right before his hand came in direct contact with my face.

"I'm scared, Drew," I whimpered, trying to get him to calm down.

He eased up on his grip and pulled me into his arms. "Jesus Christ, Morgan. Don't be afraid of me."

I relaxed. "I'm sorry, Drew," I apologized. "I know this is hard for you too, but please try to see things from my eyes."

"I'm trying, baby, believe me I am. What I really want to do is force you to get on that plane with me tomorrow and keep you locked up forever, but I can't. I don't ever want you to run from me again. It's kind of like that old saying about if you love something let it go, if it comes back to you, it's yours forev…"

I laughed, stopping his stupid quote. "Drew, please don't say that. That is so lame." I couldn't help it. I always did hate that saying. I mean come on, If it comes back to you, it's yours forever if it doesn't it never was? Can you say puke in my mouth?

Drew sat on the sofa and pulled me into his lap. "I'm going to let you go, Morgan," he said, looking into my eyes.

"What does that mean, Drew?"

"It means that I am going to give you your space and let you spend the time you think you need with Dawson. I have no right not to let you."

"I don't want you to let me go, Drew. I want you to give me some time."

He looked sad. He moved his eyes from mine to my bare leg. He rubbed my leg and softly spoke.

"I have to let you go, Morgan. I can't turn my back while you're doing, what I know you will be doing with Dawson. I can't. You do what you need to do, and I will understand one way or the other."

I moved myself from his lap, walked over to the refrigerator, took out a beer and walked out to the deck. I had to. I was ready to explode on him. I put up with so much shit from that man, and he couldn't chill out long enough for me to figure things out? Bull shit.

Drew followed me out. He could tell that I was pissed.

"Morgan?"

"You remember one God damn thing, Drew. I didn't walk away. You let me go."

"How am I supposed to feel, Morgan?"

"You know what? I have no clue. I don't even know how I should feel. How the hell am I supposed to tell you how you feel?"

"I should just go. It's obvious that we need a time-out from each other."

"Yeah, you probably should, except there are no cabs, or phone call away, drivers around here," I coolly said crossing my arms. I was done. What the fuck? This man should be kneeling at my feet, giving me everything I ask for.

"I can take care of myself," he assured me.

Go for it...

"You do whatever you have to do," I demanded. I didn't mean it. I didn't think he would really leave. Where the hell did he think he was going to go in the middle of nowhere? I couldn't stop him. My proud ego refused to go after him. He would be back or call or something. I hoped.

He didn't come back. I wanted to call Lauren and tell her to get her ass over to my house and bring every alcoholic beverage she could find. I couldn't do that either. She got up with the chickens for work.

I went to the ringing doorbell after six beers. I laughed. I'm sure most of my humor was alcohol induced. It was still funny. Poor bastard probably never even left my front yard.

I opened the door with a smirk.

Fuckity, fuck, fuck, fuck.

"Hey," I managed to spit out.

"You okay?" Dawson asked.

"Yes. Why wouldn't I be?"

"Oh, I don't know. I just presumed that you and your husband must have had a fight or something."

I looked at him peculiarly. "Why would you presume that?"

"Can I come in?"

"Oh, sorry. Yes. Come in."

"I just picked him up and gave him a ride into town."

"You did?" I asked, stumbling a little.

"Are you drunk, Ry?"

"Yeah. I think maybe I am. Where was he going?"

"I don't know, but he was on the phone arranging for someone to pick him up. I can't imagine calling someone and telling them to send the plane, not just a plane. He said the plane, like he owned it or something."

"He kind of does," It wasn't a complete lie. He did kind of own it, as long as he was married to me.

"Did you guys have a fight?"

"Yes."

"About what?"

Kind of nosey, eh?

"You, he read my email while I was in the shower."

"Is he gone for good or just gone?"

"Dawson, please don't do this. I can't handle either one of you anymore. I'm ready to tell you both to go to hell," I said walking away.

"Jesus Christ, Riley. Did he hit you?"

"What? No." I said in disbelief. "Why would you say that?"

"How the hell did you get that enormous bruise on your back then?"

I didn't know that I had a bruise. I couldn't see my back, but I knew exactly what it was from.

Dawson lifted my shirt a little in the back. "Shit, Ry. What the hell did you do?"

"I fell on some rocks down by the beach," I lied.

"Do you want some ice?"

"No. I didn't even know that it was there. I'm fine."

"You can't feel that?"

"I can now that you pointed it out. Thanks a lot," I smiled at him.

He smiled back with his perfect white toothy smile. Son of a bitch. How can you be this in love with two men?

"Did Drew know who you were?"

"Oh, he knew alright. I made sure of it?"

"Oh God, Daw. What did you say to him?"

Dawson shrugged his shoulders and puckered his lips. Shit. Those damned lips. Okay. I was drunk, that had to be the beer talking, either that or I was seriously beginning to lose my mind.

"Not much, just that he didn't deserve you. I let him know that I knew all about his purchase, what he did to you. I made sure that he knew that I was the one there night after night when you woke screaming or crying because of him. And I told him that I love you and that I think that I am more stable and more of the man that you need."

"What did he say?"

Dawson scratched his head. "He's kind of weird. He said to give you a message and to tell you the quote, when you love something set it free if it comes back to you... you know the one."

I laughed. Oh, Drew, Drew, Drew. "Yeah, he is kind of weird," I agreed.

"He said he let you go so you could make a go of it with me. Is that true, Ry?"

I snorted. "Yeah, I guess so, that's what he says anyway."

"You don't sound like that is what you want."

"I don't know what I want, Dawson. I am in love with both of you. I want you both."

"Well, that's not going to happen. I'm not willing to share any more than he is."

"Yeah, that's kind of clear."

"I think that you need to talk to someone, Riley."

"You mean a shrink?"

"No, a professional that can help you with your feelings for him," he replied.

"My feelings for him?"

"I don't think your feelings for me are from Stockholm syndrome."

I laughed. I had to. I was now a case in Dawson's eyes. "Stockholm syndrome is when you fall in love with your abuser. I didn't fall in love with my abuser. I hated him. I fell in love with somebody totally different than that man."

"Ry, stop being so naïve. He did horrible, inhumanly things to you for six years. What makes you think that he isn't going to flip and do it again. It's obvious that the guy's a nut case."

"You know what, Dawson? Just stop. You know nothing about Drew Kelley."

"I know that you're getting pissed off and defending the bastard."

I shook my head, giving up. This whole thing was hopeless. "Did you come over for a reason?" I asked, annoyed.

Dawson grabbed me and kissed me. I was shocked. I wasn't quite sure where his abrupt behavior was coming from. His hands went up my back, and his lips dropped to my neck, my throat, my collarbone, and then my chest.

That's it. I'm getting a fucking vagina transplant.

I was acting like the same maniac that he was, pulling his tucked shirt from his pants, and unbuckling his belt. What the fuck was wrong with me? He lifted my shirt over my head, and I removed my shorts on my own. I swear my vagina overpowered my brain sometimes. Dawson pulled me to the back of the couch and entered me, sending my head back with some sort of preposterous whimper.

"Oh, God you feel so good," Dawson murmured. I couldn't reply. He felt good too, and I was going to come. Shit. I was going to come.

I came and went. Dawson was still driving in and out of me. What I mean by I went is, I wanted more. I wanted the kinky fuck that Dawson wasn't going to give me. I wanted him to bend me over the couch and finish in my ass. I didn't act on my sudden need. I let him finish, and we were finished, no, spanking, no oral, and no backdoor, just raw sex. It was good, don't get me wrong. Had it been six months ago I would have been satisfied with that. By the time I had landed back in Drew's tangled web, I was getting used to the love making with Dawson, and had stopped fantasizing about the fucked up sex that Drew and I had.

Dawson spent the night. We made love again after going to bed. I was gratified once again, and felt like I was right where I belonged as I lay naked in his arms. I didn't know whether I was coming or going. It felt right when I was with Drew, but dammit if Dawson didn't feel right too. I knew exactly what I was going to do. I was going to buy a car the next day and do some traveling. I was going to find my mother and lay that one to rest. I had so many questions for her. I wanted to see her and put that part of my life in the past. I knew that I would have one chance and one chance only. I would never see her again after this. I didn't want to ever see her again. I drifted off to sleep with soft kisses to my forehead from Dawson. He did love me, and I loved him.

I was just getting ready to have another amazing orgasm the next morning. Dawson should have been at work two hours ago. I wouldn't let him out of my bed. My amazing orgasm was interrupted by someone ringing my doorbell. It was only eight in the morning. Lauren was at work already, besides she would have just unlocked the door and walked in anyway.

I pulled on a pair of shorts, a bra, and a t-shirt. Dawson dressed and came out with me.

"I'm coming," I yelled at whoever was blowing up my doorbell.

"You would have been if you had stayed in bed with me," Dawson said behind me. I looked over my shoulder and smiled. I still planned on doing that.

My mouth dropped when I opened the door.

You have got to be kidding me.

There was a man holding a clipboard with a car waiting in my drive to pick him up. Just in front of his ride was my new ride, a beautiful BMW X6 M.

"I need you to sign for your new car, Mrs. Kelly," the man smiled. I was sure by the smile on his face that his Monday morning commission made his day.

"My car?" I asked. I knew it was a dumb question. I knew that Drew had arranged to have it delivered to me.

Dawson walked up behind me and looked out too. He didn't speak, and I am sure had I had eyes in the back of my head, I would see bulging eyeballs and an opened mouth.

"Yes, ma'am. The paper work is complete. I just need a signature that you have received it.

I signed the X on the clipboard.

"Riley!" Dawson scolded from behind me.

I turned and shrugged my shoulders. The man thanked me and asked if I would like a demonstration.

"No. Thank you."

I walked out to the car, hopping like a bunny as the sharp gravel penetrated my bare feet.

Holy fucking Hawaii.

This car was fucking hot. No, hot doesn't even come close to describing this car. It was sophisticated, striking, elegant, and I swear it had its own personality. I can't even describe the color of it. Its official name was Nightfire metallic red. That's what the window sticker said. It also had an MSRP of one hundred and twenty-two thousand dollars. The black porosus crocodile leather was the softest leather I had ever felt. It barely felt like leather at all. The dash looked like something from a Sci-Fi movie, and the GPS was outrageous.

Dawson sat in the passenger seat, still speechless as he looked over the window sticker at the massive amount of standard and available equipment that this thing had. It had it all.

"Ry, you can't accept this. Do you have any idea how much this guy spent on this thing?"

Yeah, not a penny, it's my money.

"Drew's not really the type to take back a gift," I said, running my hands over the indulgent steering wheel. I was in a luxury trance. I could so see me driving this car on my adventure.

"Riley, are you serious?"

"What Dawson? I told you that I was going to find my mother. He didn't want me driving the Civic that far."

"How far? Do you know where she is?"

"Yes. Drew found her for me."

"Oh, well thanks for discussing this with me."

"I just found out two days ago, Dawson. We haven't really discussed anything."

"Let me come with you. I will get the week off; we'll go see your mom, and spend the week together."

Um… that wasn't going to work.

"Dawson. I am going to get away from you and Drew. Can you give me that and try to understand?"

"Yeah, sure, Ry. I've got to go. I'll call you later."

"What? Now you're pissed off?"

"Not pissed off, fed up."

"What the hell, Daw?"

"Nothing Ry. You go wherever it is you're going since you think running away by yourself is going to fix your problems. Riley loves Dawson. Morgan loves Drew," he stated and slammed the door.

"Riley loves Dawson. Morgan loves Drew," I repeated his words out loud to my new car. He hit the nail right on the head. I was giving myself a split personality.

I jumped when the phone in the car rang. Where the hell was it coming from? How the hell did I answer it? I finally figured out that I only needed to push the little phone button on the steering wheel.

"Hello," I said, looking like an idiot trying to figure out where I was supposed to be talking.

"Do you love it?" Drew asked.

"No. I freaking hate it. You idiot."

Drew laughed which made me smile. I loved his laugh.

"You're such a liar. Tell me how you really feel."

"I love it. I can't believe that you did this. How did you pull this off so fast?"

"Money talks, baby."

"You're not supposed to be talking to me, remember?"

"Yeah, yeah. I won't talk to you tomorrow."

"Can I go in and make coffee and call you back?"

"Yes, but make sure you call me back. I want to hear if this car is as sleek as everything I have read about it."

"It is. I'll call you in a few."

Chapter 22

I started the coffee, went to the bathroom and brushed my teeth before calling Drew back. I know, I shouldn't have been calling either one of them, but I couldn't help myself. I missed him. I walked out to the deck with my coffee and cell phone.

"Hey gorgeous," Drew answered.

"Hey," I smiled.

"So? What do you think?"

"You already know what I think. It's amazing. I can't wait to take off in it."

"I knew you would love it. When are you leaving?"

"I was going to wait until Friday, but I think I need to go now."

"I met your boyfriend last night," he stated.

"Yeah, I heard. I'm kind of stunned by that. I would have loved to have been a fly on the dash of that car."

"It's fucking dark in Maine. I mean spooky ass dark. I was scared shitless. I was thankful to take the ride offer."

I laughed. I could just see Drew walking down my road looking over his shoulder for something to jump out at him.

"Where did you go?" I asked.

"To the airport. So let me guess. He came right to your house as soon as he dropped me off, didn't he?"

I ran my fingers through my long hair and looked up to the sun with closed eyes. Of course, we were going to go there. I give the fuck up. "Yeah, he stopped by," I tried.

"Did he spend the night or just stop by?"

"Does it really matter? You told me that you were going to step out of the picture so that I could see if it were him that I wanted. How am I supposed to do that if I'm not around him?"

"So he did spend the night. You fucked him too, didn't you?"

"Really Drew?"

"Yeah, that's what I thought. I won't bother you anymore. You drive safe, okay."

"Drew," was all that I was able to get out before I heard the silence and looked to see his name blinking on my phone.

Fuck...

I wasn't going to have to worry about choosing. They were both pissed off now. Fine, I was better off. I could go anywhere I wanted to go. I wouldn't live in Misty Bay or Vegas. They could both go to hell.

I went straight to my room, packed a bag, and got into my new car and headed south. I stopped at the coffee shop, had a cup of coffee and pastry with Starlight before heading out.

"I wish there was something that I could do to help. I hate it that you are going through this, Ry," Star said, sympathetically.

"I'll be fine, Star. I have had a life that tends to make you pretty strong. I'll get through it, one way or another."

Star hugged me and told me that if I needed anything to call.

I put in the address for Rodanthe, North Carolina. I didn't even groan when the robotic voice told me that I would be driving for almost fifteen hours. 1 was actually looking forward to it. I hoped that neither Drew nor Dawson called. I listened to Lauren and Levi on my satellite radio all the way until they signed off, and then changed it to an oldies rock station. It brought back memories of living in West Virginia.

I thought about my cousins that I hadn't seen in years, my dad, who wasn't my dad after all, and my grandma who passed away when I was only sixteen. I thought about my friends from school, which was really only Julie Waybright. She was as poor as me, and was just as much of an outcast. She got herself pregnant when she was fifteen and had two kids living on welfare by the time she was eighteen. I wondered how she was, and hoped that she wasn't another statistic, popping out kids and living with an alcoholic.

For some stupid reason, I reprogrammed my GPS and headed right to my old hometown. I wasn't sure why. It was going to add eight hours to my destination, but what the hell. I had time. I wouldn't stay. I just wanted to drive through, just for old times' sake, not that the old times were pleasant but still.

I stopped and got a hotel in New York around nine at night, taking a pizza with me. I know I said that I hoped that Drew or Dawson didn't call, but I was surprised that either of them hadn't. Weren't they worried about me or wondered where I was? Of course, they both did think that I wasn't leaving until the next day. I still couldn't believe that one of them hadn't called. They didn't, and when I checked my phone at seven the next morning, there was nothing from either of them. I know, I know, that's what I wanted. Whatever.

It only took me four hours to make it to my old roots. Not a lot had changed. It looked as poor and rundown as it had the day I was forced to leave. It almost made me happy that Drew had bought me. I bought me. I laughed, saying that out loud. I turned down the old dirt road to the trailer. It was abandoned. The aluminum had been ripped off, probably for scrap, and the windows were all broken out. I'm not sure why, but I parked my expensive car in the drive. I looked around, nervously. This wasn't the place for a female in a fancy car to be poking around. The closest house was barely visible from our old trailer. I didn't see anything that warned me not to go in, so I got out, locked the door with the two beeps, and walked up the old steps.

"Fuck," I called out when my foot went through the rotten plywood on the little porch. It hurt. I felt the burn up my calf from the wood scrape. Of course, my shoe had to fall underneath when I tried to pull it out of the hole. That should have been enough of a warning to get back in my car and get the hell out of there, but determined me had to go in. Once I retrieved my shoe, I walked along the edge of the porch so I didn't fall through again.

I pushed the door. It was hard to push because it was weathered and warped. It looked like some local kids had been using it for a party pad, but not recently, I didn't think. There were ashtrays running over, beer bottles, liquor bottles, decomposed food, and empty packs of condoms strung about.

The same table, couch, and wood stove were still there from when I had lived there. I walked into the kitchen and opened the cabinets. Our mismatched dishes were still in the cupboards. It was like my dad had just left and left everything behind. I wondered where he was. Did he die? Did he move? I walked back to mine and Justin's bedroom, and it too still had the same old mattress thrown on the floor. My old dresser that wasn't much of a dresser when I used it was still in the corner. I got excited when I saw it.

A couple of days before I was to leave with Drew Kelly, I placed a square tin in the back, underneath the bottom drawer. It was one of those tins that you get cookies in at Christmas. I think the local church had dropped it off for my brother and me one year. I slid the dresser out and screamed to the top of my lungs. A hiding cat jumped out with a squeal and darted right under my legs out the door.

Jesus H Christ...

My heart was now beating out of my chest. I swear it was. I held my hand on the corner of the nasty old dresser and held my chest, trying to regain my bearings. What the hell was I doing there? I pulled the thin sheet of wood from behind the dresser and there it was, just where I had left it. I picked it up and beat it on top of the dresser to knock the mice shit off of it.

"What the hell are you doing here?"

"Awwww," I let out a blood curdling scream. There went my heart again. I turned to see a big burly man with a beard clear down his chest. His head was wrapped in a rebel flag do-wrap, and I could tell that he had long hair in a ponytail hanging down his back. His arms were covered in raunchy girl tattoos that were clearly unprofessional.

"Bobby?" I asked.

"Morgan?" my first cousin, Bobby said, and then grabbed me up into a big bear hug.

"Where the hell you been chica?" he asked, grinning his missing teeth smile.

"Oh, around," I replied. "How the hell are you? You grew up," I stated. Bobbie must have been about fifteen when I had left. He was a scrawny little, pimple face kid the last time that I had seen him.

"Is that your fancy ass car out there?"

"No. I just borrowed it for a few days. I drive a 1993 piece of shit." It wasn't a complete lie, and with my cut off jean shorts and my ace of spades t-shirt, I thought that I could pull it off.

"It's sweet as hell," he exclaimed. "How long you in town for?"

"Just passing through, I'm not sure why I even came here to tell you the truth."

"Well, I'm glad you did," he smiled.

I talked to my cousin who really was no relation at all now that I knew that my dad wasn't my dad, but I wasn't about to tell him that. I hadn't been around him in years. I didn't trust him at all. We walked around the trailer poking around. There wasn't really anything there that I wanted. It was all pretty much trash. I did find a couple of pictures that had seen their better day. I took them and placed them on top of my tin box. I didn't open the box yet. I decided to wait until I was alone for that. I really couldn't even remember what was in it.

"Do you know where my dad is Bobby?" I asked, plundering through a drawer in my parent's room. There was nothing there, some old bills, a penknife, and a container of KY.

"He lives in town now, over top of the laundromat. He married Connie Patterson; you remember her?"

"Yeah, she worked with my mom," I replied. I knew exactly who she was. She was a truck stop whore. She'd broken the record for the most times being in the bunk of a semi-truck.

"Where's your mama?"

"She lives in North Carolina now. I don't talk to her much anymore." That wasn't a complete lie either. Okay, I was a liar.

"You gonna go see your pop?" Bobbie asked.

Fuck no... bastard sold me.

"Nah, we didn't really split on good terms," I smiled.

Bobby walked me out to my car, carrying my treasures.

"You sure you don't want to stay the night. We'll probably end up over at Booner's later on."

I had no clue who Booner even was, and there was no way in hell I was staying there.

"I'm meeting a friend. I can't, but thanks for the offer. It was good seeing you."

Please don't hug me.

"You come back and see me now, hear?" Bobby said with a big, brawny hug.

"I will. You take care."

I had decided before I backed out of my old drive that I wouldn't go all the way that day. I didn't think I would go far at all. I felt dirty, and was kind of grossed out from walking around my abandoned, childhood home. My head itched, too. I knew I was just being paranoid, but I wanted a shower. I was hungry and wasn't about to touch food until I could bathe.

I drove for eight hours. Not what I had planned on doing at all. I was so hungry I almost perished. I drove all the way to Point Harbor. All I needed to do was take the ferry to I-165, and I would be at my mother's. I got a room at a rather expensive hotel. There was no reason for it to be that expensive, except for the fact that it was a tourist trap. I knew I didn't need to be concerned with a hundred and seventy five dollars. I could drop that all day long and never put a dent in how much money I had. That part would probably never change. When you grow up on dented cans of donated baked beans, you tend to ration a little.

I used lots of antibacterial soap and washed the nastiness away from the tin. I smiled remembering the scene on the top and around the sides. I had sat on the couch with Justin when he was probably three or so. We were alone and trying to stay warm. We sat on the couch and ate the stale cookies as we observed the Norman Rockwell painting.

"And we'll live in this house, and play in the barn, and walk along the dirt road by the stream."

"And go pishen in dat pond," Justin explained, pointing his little finger to the painted pond.

I smiled running my fingers over the scene, the scene that his little fingers had touched. I could hear his little voice as plain as day. God, I missed that little man. I still hadn't opened the tin, and decided to shower and find some food before I really did perish.

I walked along the sidewalks and tourist trap vendors. I laughed when I saw the abundant amount of jewelry hanging from hooks from one of the street vendors. It was necklaces, bracelets, key chains; you name it, and anything that could be hung from a chain, this guy had it.

"Would you like a cheap piece of history," the guy asked.

"History?" I smirked.

"The finest sea glass around," he smiled.

I couldn't help myself. I had to do it. "Buddy, there is not one thing here that is real sea glass."

His expression changed. He knew that I knew my shit. "Well, it was found on the beach," he assured me.

"Yeah, from a spring break party maybe," I replied, and kept walking. I heard him ask the next naïve lady the same question. I looked over my shoulder and smiled, shaking my head when the lady pulled out her wallet.

Stupid lady.

I had the best shrimp and lobster I ever had in my life, sitting at a quay restaurant. I loved the ocean. I decided at that moment, wherever I ended up; it was going to be by the ocean. The ocean and I had become friends. We had an understanding, a bond that in some way counseled me. The sea was full of emotion. The ocean knew my moods. It could hate, love, it knew my dreams, my fears, my happiness. I told the ocean more secrets than I had ever told anyone in my life, without a word spoken, and it understood.

It was still pretty early, and I wasn't tired at all. I should have been after a long drive and the roller coaster ride from going back to my old roots, maybe I was tired and had too much on my mind to relax. I still hadn't opened my time capsule. I wasn't sure what I was waiting for. I knew there wasn't anything worth a damn in it. I still couldn't believe that neither one of my men had called to check on me. I hadn't talked to either one of them in two days.

I had to pry the tin lid off because it was so rusted around the edges. I broke a nail in the process. That pissed me off.

Mother fucker...

The first thing I saw brought a happy smile to my face. It was a faded green Christmas tree, cut from construction paper. Justin made it in kindergarten. It didn't say, I love mommy, or I love daddy. It said I love my sissy. I held my finger through the red piece of yarn. I then took out the love letter from Polecat. That wasn't his real name. His real name was Billy Sweeny. It seemed like everyone in the hills had a stupid nickname. It was dumb. I used to think that I was in love with Polecat. He was a tough guy, always in fights and drinking beer. He got his first amateur tattoo when he was only thirteen.

I read about two lines of the childish love note and tossed it to the paper can. A week after he wrote it, he broke up with me to go out with Missy Glass. She put out. I didn't. I picked up the picture of my Grandma Joyce next. She was sitting on her porch, where I pictured her the most. She always sat on that porch, rocking for hours.

I picked up the tarnished, cross necklace next. It had been a gift from my grandma. I think it was for my birthday or maybe Christmas. I was sure that it came from Avon. I used to sit on her porch and circle all the things that I wanted from the little catalogue. I had three tarnished rings, as well. I remember thinking how rich I felt when I had worn my little pink diamond to school, showing it off to my other poor friends. I kept the Christmas tree, the cheap jewelry, the two dollar bill, the picture of my grandma, and the newspaper obituary from Grandma Joyce. The rest I left in the tin and tossed it to the paper can.

I lay in bed, thinking about reconnecting with my mother. I should have kept my mind on that. I thought about how I would feel when I saw her. I was angry, and carried a lot of bitterness, not that I wasn't grateful for getting away from that hell hole. She sold me, just like my dad had. She let the almighty dollar come before her own flesh and blood. How could she just go off and start another family when she left us behind. Why didn't she take us with her? I already knew the answer to that. Randal Callaway was going to make sure that she disappeared. Money does talk, no matter who it hurts.

Thoughts of Dawson and Drew were next, wondering what the hell I was supposed to do about them. Maybe I really did need to start thinking about moving on without either of them, but I loved them. I loved both of them. Could I ever love like that again? I just had to go and think about having sex on the peak with Drew. I moved my hand to the small of my back. The bruise still felt a little sore when I pressed on it. I could almost feel him entering me as I closed my eyes and visualized our love making on top of the world. Of course, my vagina had to go and stick her nose in it too. I felt the throbbing between my legs.

I knew my body and my betraying female parts all too well. It wasn't going to shut the hell up until I gave it what it wanted. I moved my fingers between my wet folds. Talk about being fucked up. My mind went from Drew to Dawson. They were both fucking me as my fingers pleased my aching core. Dawson was on his back. I was on my hands and knees with Dawson in my mouth, and Drew was giving it to me up the ass. Maybe I did need therapy. I writhed beneath my fingers, frantically bringing myself to a much needed orgasm, shaking my head in disbelief at myself as I came down.

◇◇()◇◇

It was a very hot summer day. I was sticky from walking from my room to my car. I wore a sundress which let the ocean breeze braze my skin.

I was starting to get nervous as I drove to the ferry that would take me to my mother. What if she didn't want to see me? What if she told me to leave? What if her new family didn't know about me? It didn't matter. I had to do this. This was one of those parts of my life that would never be laid to rest if I didn't. I wouldn't stay long, just long enough to give her my two cents of what I thought about her and what she had done.

I stood outside my car and watched the waves swirl around the ferry as we crossed the bay. I was running on pure adrenaline, and my stomach was in knots. I realized that I had forgotten to go down to the continental breakfast like I had planned. Why the hell had I always forgotten to eat when I was anxious?

It took almost forty-five minutes to reach the dock, and then another forty-five from Kitty Hawk to Rodanthe.

"Shut the hell up," I yelled at the robotic GPS as I waited my turn to drive my car off the ferry. "If I turn right, you're fucking going swimming," I spoke to the car. I knew it was nerves.

The forty-five minute drive took five minutes. I swear I was there five minutes after I had gotten off the ferry. The road that I was driving on was something that you had to experience to even know what I am talking about. I had the ocean on both sides of me. It was almost surreal, and I felt as if the ocean were carrying me. I just wasn't sure what it was carrying me to. The ocean was its own god, its own boss. Nobody manipulated the ocean, and it could bring you the utmost peace or your worse wrath. I just hoped that we had gained enough respect from each other that it was taking me to a happy place and not the vehemence that was terrifying me as I drove over the top of it.

The gray beach house was beautiful with decks sticking out from all sides and angles. It was massive, almost as big as the mansion in Las Vegas. It was pretty secluded, and I could barely even see the closest house to it. I hated the house. I felt like it took the place of me and my little brother. It did.

I parked and walked up to the massive deck in the back of the house. I knocked on the door with my knees knocking louder, underneath my pale yellow sundress. Nobody came. I realized that I was supposed to open the door and walk into the lobby. I did, and stopped at the desk and rang the little bell on the counter.

Breathe, Morgan, breathe...

A nice looking middle-aged man walked out drying his hands on a white dish towel. He smiled at me.

"Morgan?" he asked.

I frowned. Who the hell was this guy, and how the hell did he know my name.

"Do I know you?" I managed to get out.

"No. You don't. I'm Jason, your mother's husband," he offered with his hand.

I cautiously took his hand. She talked about me. He knew who I was. I wasn't expecting this. I was expecting to hear that she never told him about me or Justin. How did he know from looking at me who I was? She must have pictures. I didn't speak. I couldn't speak. I was speechless. No words would come out.

"You have no idea how happy you are going to make your mother," he smiled.

"Is she here?" I managed.

"No, she had to take Caroline to the dentist this morning. She won't be long. Are you hungry? We were just getting ready to have brunch. Would you join me?"

"Sure." What else was I going to do? Sit outside and wait for her?

He led me to the front deck facing the ocean. There were two families, three other couples, and two tables with pairs of women. We sat at a table, and a lady wearing shorts with a palm tree on the right leg asked what we would like to drink. I'm not sure why I noticed the palm tree or why it was even significant. I just noticed. I asked for coffee. I hadn't had any yet. Jason got an iced tea.

"How did you know who I was?" I asked Jason. He smiled.

"I will show you after we eat," he answered.

We didn't talk about anything personal. Jason explained life at the beach house. He told me that they had eight rooms and were booked most of the year. He explained that they closed up for four weeks every year, two in the winter to celebrate the holidays without company, and two in late summer to vacation by themselves. I guessed that you would have to do that to keep your sanity, working where you lived twenty-four seven.

I had a delicious Reuben on toasted French bread with Jason. I hate to say it, but I liked him. He talked about seven year old Caroline. He was a proud pop, and I envied the little girl who had a family, a real family.

"She looks a lot like you," he said. "You can definitely tell that you two are sisters."

Sisters...

I hadn't thought about her like that, but she wasn't my real sister. We had different dads. Wait. Justin and I had different dads, and I couldn't imagine loving him anymore. That wasn't fair to Caroline.

Jason led me back into the house, and to a side of the house that I was sure was off limits to the guests. It was its own little house inside of a house. There was a small living room, opened to an eat-in kitchen with a small table. There were three other doors that I presumed were bedrooms and probably a bathroom. I was mesmerized when I looked around at the wall of fame. The whole wall was plastered with pictures of not only Caroline, but Justin and me, as well.

I watched my little brother grow up in pictures on the wall. I brushed my finger over one of him sitting in front of a birthday cake with seven candles and a happy, toothless smile. It made me smile, but made me wonder, as well. Every last picture of me on the wall lied. If you didn't know it, you would have thought that I too was the happiest girl on earth. Most of the pictures of me were when I was all fancied up and at one of Drew's functions. There were several of the two of us, and the one that I thought that I looked beautiful in brought back the after party memory. I had stayed locked in the empty gym, eating fruit, naked for three days.

I felt a little better when I moved to the next picture of Justin. He was just a little guy and riding on the shoulders of a man whom I presumed to be his dad. He was happy and the beautiful woman pushing him on the swing in the next one must have been his new mother.

"Morgan?" I heard my mother say. I knew that voice before I ever turned around. My heart took a plummet right to my stomach.

I cautiously turned to see her holding the hand of a seven year old mini me. I again was speechless, and couldn't think of one God damn word to say. She let go of Caroline's hand and embraced me. She cried. She really cried. She did miss me, and probably thought about me more than I had thought.

"Oh, my God, baby. I can't believe that you are here."

Baby? She never called me baby.

"Yeah." That was it. That was the only word that I could think of.

My mom let go of me and walked back to Caroline. She squatted to her level and held her hand out for me to come.

"Caroline, do you know who this is?" she asked as she took my hand. I squatted too. I didn't know what I was supposed to do.

"My sister," she smiled. I held out my hand and took her little hand into mine. "It's nice to meet you," she said.

I shook her little hand and smiled. "It's very nice to meet you too, Caroline." I fucking loved the kid, right off the bat. I fucking loved the little girl that I hated and resented just five minutes earlier.

"Come on kiddo, let's go batten down the hatches," Jason said to Caroline, wanting to give us some time.

"There's a big storm coming," Caroline informed me.

I only smiled. I didn't know what was wrong with me, but I suddenly had no words in my brain.

Jason kissed my mom before taking Caroline's hand and leaving us alone. She was happy, and I was happy that she was happy. I'm not sure why. I hadn't felt like that before I had gotten there. I hoped that she was miserable.

"Can you bring Morgan's things in?" she asked, kissing him back as she hooked his fingers with hers.

What? I'm not staying...

"Sure thing. Can I have your keys?" he asked.

I gave him my keys.

"Do you want to take a walk?" my mother asked.

I shrugged. "Sure."

This was strange. This was not the mother that I had grown up with for almost eighteen years. My mother was a loud mouth drunk with the vocabulary of a drunken sailor. This woman was soft spoken, well kept, and very loving. She was pretty with the same dark hair as mine, manicured nails, painted in a light pink to match the toes sticking out from her sandals. She looked healthy and in shape. My mother wore slutty clothes and didn't keep herself up at all.

She held my hand as we walked along the beach. We both laughed when we slid out of our shoes at the same time. We walked out to the end of the pier and sat down with our arms over the railing and our feet dangling from the side.

"You can ask me anything that you want Morgan. I am sure that you have a million questions," she started.

I couldn't hate her. I just couldn't do it. I loved her, no matter what she had done. I loved her, dammit.

"I want to know about my real dad. How did you meet a rich man from Vegas in the hills of West Virginia?"

My mom took a deep breath. I had just married your dad. We had been trying to get pregnant for about four months." She laughed. "I wanted to have a baby so that I could get a monthly state check, like everyone else. It just didn't happen. He decided to take off for the summer and follow the carnival across the south side of the United States. Michael was there on business, something about some diamonds that had been found while mining coal. I don't know a lot about that because he had told me that it was all hush, hush and he was there to retrieve them before anyone caught wind of the outrageous find.

"He was so young and good looking. He made me want out of there and make a better life for myself. I always knew that he wouldn't be my knight in shining armor and be the one to save me, but none the less I dreamt about it. I fell head over heels in love with Michael. We spent the entire two weeks that he was there together. We spent it in Charleston of course, in some fancy hotel. He wasn't the type to stay in the rent by the hour hotel back home. When your dad got tired of being a carney and came home after three months, I was almost two months pregnant."

"He beat the hell out of me but never told anyone that you belonged to another man. He would throw it up to me occasionally, but no one else knew."

"How did Michael find out about me?" I asked.

"He came back six years later for the same reason. That find didn't turn out to be the gold mine that he had hoped for. They were just some sort of crystals that weren't worth much. I was still waitressing at the truck stop. I spent the night with him and told him about you." She snorted. "I was hoping that he would take us away from there. He didn't, and he was gone before I woke up the next morning."

"I still don't understand. How did you end up here? How did my little brother end up adopted by a family in Vegas? How did I end up married to a man that I didn't even know?" I asked, not taking a breath from the never-ending questions.

"Is he good to you, Morgan?" she asked, moving my hair from the front of my shoulder to the back.

"Yes. He is very good to me," I said. That wasn't a lie. He was good to me. It just wasn't always like that. What was I supposed to do, tell her that he took me to be his lawfully fuckable sex mate? To fuck and to suck in various positions until his orgasm do we part? I had a good feeling that she had been through a lot herself, and this was harder for her than I had originally thought.

She smiled, content with my answer. "Mr. Callaway showed up at the truck stop when you were close to eighteen. He had a whole slew of pictures from a private investigator that had been spying on me. He made me feel like a piece of shit when he showed me the pictures of the trailer back home and the living conditions that I allowed my children to live in. He had pictures of the church bringing in food, you in a thin worn coat, trying to pry frozen wood apart, Justin with the same clothes, three days in a row. I didn't think I had a choice, Morgan. Please try to understand that I did this for you and Justin, not myself. I would have agreed had he not offered me one penny."

"He explained that he never knew about you until Michael was on his deathbed. I knew that you were going to marry Drew Kelley. I knew that Justin was going to be adopted by Hillary and Peter Dunn. They had tried to have kids for years and were not able to. I knew he would have a good home, and you would never want for anything."

I wanted for a lot of things, mostly love.

"But the welfare department came and took him away. I was there when they did," I assured her, still not understanding.

"That was only temporary. Mr. Callaway arranged that until the paper work was complete. He wasn't about to let him stay there. He didn't want to take you until you graduated because you were so close. I could have stayed until then too, but I couldn't stand the thought of being there without Justin and not being able to tell you what your future held."

"Where did you get all of the pictures?" I asked.

"That was the deal. I would only agree to walk away quietly if I was insured that I would always know that you guys were okay. I have actually talked to Justin's new mother. He was sick once, and she wanted to know about our family's medical history." My mom smiled. "She was so worried about him. They really do love him," she added, happy of the fact. I smiled too, knowing that he was with a good family made me glad that things worked out the way that they had, if only for him.

"I like your hair better your natural color. Blonde just isn't you," my mom said, playing with my hair again.

I snickered. "I did that for Drew," I replied. I did do it for him. I just didn't have a say in the matter.

"Tell me about him," she coaxed.

How was I supposed to do that? Oh, we have this amazing fucked up sex life.

"Well, he's busy. He works a lot." I couldn't do it. I couldn't think of anything to tell her that wasn't going to sound fucked up.

"So things are good with you two?"

I pondered for a second before speaking. "Not right at the moment. We are on a trial separation right now."

"But you're going to work it out, right?" she asked, almost desperately.

I shrugged my shoulders, and for the life of me, I don't know why I had just blurted out the rest.

"I'm kind of in love with someone else."

"Oh," she said, surprised. "Are you still in love with Drew?"

"I am so in love with Drew that I don't know which way is up, but I am in love with a simple sheriff with a simple life too."

My mom smiled. "Life is a fucked up mess, Morgan, but it always seems to find a way to work itself out."

I laughed at her choice of words. I knew I had picked up my foul mouth from her. I just didn't normally say it out loud. It was normally during conversations within in my own mind.

"Tell me about Jason. I like him," I said. She smiled. I could tell that she loved him.

"Jason is a good man and a good father. I wished that you and Justin would have had that."

"I think Justin does have that," I replied.

"Mr. Callaway let me choose anywhere in the world that I wanted to live. He told me to make it count because I was only getting one chance and would be cut off from his wallet. I didn't know where to go or what to do. I'd never even been out of the hills before. A week after our first meeting a man showed up with an envelope. Do you remember the man that I had left with the day that I told you goodbye?" she asked.

"Yes." Of course, I remembered that. I had nightmares about it.

"Mr. Callaway had done some homework himself, and thought that this place would give me a fresh start, and I would be able to run a business here and be able to take care of myself. I loved the pictures and the thought of living on the beach. The problem was; I knew nothing about bookkeeping, taxes, or how to run a business. He hired Jason to work with me for a few months to get me started. He and I stayed in this huge house alone for three months. I think I fell in love with him the first night. Of course I thought he was way out of my league, and I didn't have a chance," she added. I could see how she felt that way. I felt that way about Drew. I didn't think he could love a backyard, hillbilly like me.

"Jason and I had so much fun together those first few weeks. I was upfront and honest with him from the beginning. He knew about you and Justin. I swear if he hadn't been there during my many crying sprees I would have fed myself to the sharks."

"I was so mad when Drew told me that you were married and had a new family. I felt like you forgot us," I sadly told her how I felt.

"Oh, baby," she said hugging me tight. "I have not gone one day without thinking about you both. We even have birthday cake for both of you every year," she said into my hair.

"You do?" I asked, pulling away to look at her.

"Yes, we do. I know it's silly, but I kind of like being silly. It makes me happy."

"I'm happy for you, mom," I said. I was happy for her. This wasn't what I had in mind at all. It wasn't even close. I had planned on coming there for all of ten minutes, giving her a piece of my mind and spinning my tires out of there so fast. I was glad that my plan failed. I was glad that she had Jason and Caroline. I was glad that she was happy.

"Caroline reminds me a lot of me," I said with a smile.

"She reminds me of you every day," my mom assured me. "She is so smart, sometimes too smart for her own good," she added with a smile. "Guess what she loves," my mom persuaded.

I shrugged my shoulders with a big smile. I was happy. I really was.

"Peanut butter and pickles," she laughed.

I laughed too. That was my favorite food growing up. "I haven't had one of those in years," I said.

"Oh, don't worry. You will, just give it a day or two. How long are you staying?" she asked.

I shrugged again. "I don't have a deadline. I can leave whenever I want. I was supposed to be using this time to figure out what to do with these two difficult men in my life, but so far, I'm still at square one."

She smiled. "I hope it takes you a month," she squealed, happy that I didn't have to leave right away.

Chapter 23

"Amanda!" Jason yelled for my mom from the deck. We both turned to see him waving us toward the house.

We walked the beach and to the deck hand in hand.

"Someone must have known you were coming," Jason said, holding a brown wrapped package for me.

"Drew knew," I said, taking the package. I wondered if I should open it in front of them, but it was small, so I figured it was safe, probably diamond earrings or something.

I smiled when I pulled the black sea glass, dangling from a sterling silver chain. There was one diamond in the middle. I read his handwritten note.

"This was the best day of my life. I love you."

I know I was teary eyed. I couldn't help it. He was doing things that blew my mind lately which made my case even worse. I loved him. That was the bottom line. I loved the twisted bastard.

"Oh, my God!" Caroline squealed. "That is black. Where did you get that?" she asked, excited.

"On the beach in Maine," I replied, handing it to her to see.

She looked at it wide eyed and amazed. "This could have come all the way from Italy."

I smiled. The girl knew her sea glass.

"Do you hunt sea glass?" she asked, excited.

"Yeah, I do. I have nine pieces now," I told her.

"Do you want to see mine?"

"I would love to," I said, letting her take my hand and pull me to her bedroom.

I noticed my mother and Jason's reflection through the glass as I was being led away. He embraced her, and she wrapped her arms around his neck. It made me happy. A lot of things were making me happy that day.

My suitcase was on the twin size bed in Caroline's room. I was bunking with her. I know it sounds stupid, but I was giddy, thinking about sleeping in the twin size bed across from my little sister. I felt like we were having a slumber party.

Caroline took a shoe box from the shelf in the closet. I looked around her room while she retrieved it. What I wouldn't have done for a room like that when I was her age. The walls were pink. The two twin beds had matching pink quilts with dolphins. Her walls were covered with pictures of sea creatures and one of Justin Bieber. That one made me smile.

She sat on the bed beside me and explained to me each and every piece of her sea glass. She remembered where and when she had found each one. She even knew what they had probably come from.

"I still haven't found any black though," she said. "I can't believe you found black. Do you have any idea how rare that is?" she asked.

"Yes, I do. I can't believe I found it either."

"Hey, do you want to go with me in the morning? I'm getting up at six in the morning to go hunting. My dad said I had to wait until nine because he didn't want to get up that early. I don't want to wait that long. We're going to get a big storm later and right after a storm is the best time. I'm afraid someone else will walk by and find it before me."

"I would love to get up at six and go with you," I smiled at her. I just loved her to death. She hugged me.

"I think I like having a big sister," she said.

"I think I like having a little sister," I replied. She smiled the biggest smile ever.

Jason grilled burgers on their private deck off from their apartment away from the other guests. Caroline was showing me the sea glass that she wanted to find yet on her iPad. My mom was in the kitchen making side dishes. I asked her if she wanted help, but I think she was happy to see Caroline and me hitting it off so well. She even sat on my lap as her finger swiped the pages on her handheld computer.

Jason got on to her for not cleaning her plate and then made her get down from walking across the banister with her hands out, balancing herself. I was amused. This was what a real family was supposed to be like, and I hoped someday to have a little girl just like Caroline.

"Want a play a game?" Caroline asked, joining us back at the table.

"Let Morgan eat, Caroline," Jason scolded.

"It's not that kind of game dad. She can eat and talk, can't she?"

I laughed as I grabbed my napkin from being taken away from the wind. I knew too that there was a storm brewing. I could feel it.

"I can talk and eat," I said. I wanted to do whatever this little girl asked me to do.

"Okay, it's called the nosey game," she started to explain.

"No, Caroline," her dad insisted. I took it that he knew exactly what game she wanted to play.

"She can say, Nosey Rosy if she wants to," she exclaimed.

"It's fine," I assured him. He shook his head.

"Okay. So I ask you a question and you have to answer. If you don't want to answer you just say Nosey Rosy, but I get to pinch your cheeks," she explained.

"Caroline is an expert at making up games to figure people out," my mom said. I didn't mind. I thought it was cute.

"You can go first," she said, ignoring our mother.

"What grade are you in?" I asked.

"I'm going to be in second when school starts. What is your favorite color?" she asked.

"Pink. What is your favorite subject?" I saw her eyes light up when I said pink. I was sure that it was her favorite color too.

"I hate school, my favorite subject is art. What's your middle name?"

"Joyce, after my grandmother."

Her mouth plopped open. "Mine too, were we named after the same grandma, mom?" She asked, turning to our mother.

"Yes. You were both named after the same sweet lady," she smiled.

"Do you have a boyfriend?" she asked.

"I have a husband," I wasn't about to tell her that I had both. "Do you have a boyfriend?" I countered.

"Nosey Rosy," she giggled. We all laughed, and I pinched her cheeks.

We played the game until Jason said that was enough. The wind was really starting to get strong, and we needed to get things carried into the house.

We ate pie and had coffee later on with the guests in the dining room. The wind was howling, and we could hear thunder in the distance. It wasn't even close to being time for it to be dark yet, but the storm made it look as if it were ten o'clock at night.

"This is going to be a good one," Caroline said, standing in front of the glass doors.

"Get away from the glass, Caroline," Jason demanded.

She was like me. She couldn't stop staring out at the wicked weather. The lighting looked as it would strike the house at any second. The waves were massive, coming from an angry sea. The wind whipped through the house as if it was trying to carry it off, and the thunder set it all in stone. About ten minutes later, the lights flickered and then went out. I was a little scared. Caroline on the other hand, was excited. I assumed she had been through many storms, living that close to the ocean.

"I'll get the generator going," Jason said, excusing himself.

My mom ushered us all into the sitting area, and we played charades with the guests by the dimly lit generator lights. I laughed so hard at Caroline. She was quite the little ham and wasn't a bit shy.

The storm had quieted down, and everyone retreated to their rooms. Caroline had her own bathroom, and we both grabbed very quick showers in the dark. The lights still hadn't come on when Caroline and I crawled into our beds.

My mom came in as soon as we were in bed. "Are we reading tonight?" she asked.

"Oh, yeah," Caroline said, grabbing the hardback book from the nightstand between us. "Can we start over, so Morgan knows what's going on?" she asked.

"I guess since we are only on chapter three."

"Okay," she said, sitting up and crossing her legs Indian style. "We have to read three chapters, so Morgan can read too."

My mom smiled and rubbed her back. "Okay," she agreed. Caroline leaned into my mom's chest and began to read. I'm not even sure what she was reading. I was too busy reading into what I was witnessing. I didn't remember my mother ever reading a book to me or my brother.

"Tran, tranq, tranquility," Caroline paused, trying to sound out a word.

"Tranquility," my mom, said helping her out.

"What's that mean?" she asked, looking up to her.

"It means quiet, calmness, stillness," she answered.

"Oh, like peace. That makes sense," she decided and got back to her reading.

I loved the affectionate look in my mother's eyes as she stared at me. She really was happy that I was there. She read the next chapter and then I read the next. I had actually started getting into the book when my chapter was over. It was about a ten year old boy and an eight year old girl, lost on an island.

Caroline and I both lay down, and my mom tucked her and kissed her on the head.

"I love you," she said.

"Love you too, mom."

I wasn't sure how to react to my mother's affection when she did the same thing to me. She pulled my quilt up and kissed me on the head just like she had Caroline. She brushed my hair from my forehead and kissed me too.

"I love you, Morgan, and I am so glad you're here."

"Me too," I said. I couldn't make myself tell her that I loved her too. I could only remember her saying it once in my life, and that was when she left me. I wasn't ready to say that just yet.

I woke to Caroline shaking me in the morning.

"Morgan, come on. It's daylight," she said, trying to coax me out of bed.

I opened my eyes and realized where I was. I stumbled to the bathroom, brushed my teeth, pulled on a pair of shorts, and a tank top. She wasn't lying. It was daylight… barely. I slipped on my flip-flops and followed her out.

We walked way down the beach, at least a mile and a half. She wanted to start as far south as we could go and then slowly make our way back. We searched the many piles of pebbles, rocks and shells washed up from the previous night's storm. I found a piece right away. It was the most common, Kelly green, but it was still a nice piece. We were moving like a couple of snails, searching for our treasures. I still couldn't see the house, and I wanted coffee. Little Ms. Caroline on the other hand, was engrossed and wasn't about to pick up her dawdling pace. She was on a mission.

By the time Caroline finally found a piece, we were almost back to the house. I was so hoping that she did. She looked so bummed because she hadn't found anything. She found a rather rare piece. It was lime green, and I listened to her explain to me that it was probably from a soda bottle from the sixties. I already knew what she was telling me, but didn't dare put a damper on her enthusiasm.

Our mother was getting worried by the time we finally made it back to the house four hours later. I felt tired, and could have used a nap. She poured me a cup of coffee and had to make Caroline sit down long enough to eat something. One of the guests was surfing and wanted her to come. She didn't want to eat. She wanted to go play. She scarfed down the egg sandwich and was off.

Jason kissed my mom and left too. She explained that he always stayed near by without her knowing when she ran off to surf. He worried about her being in the hands of strangers, she explained with a smile.

My ten minute visit to tell my mother what I had thought about her leaving her kids to go create a better life for herself had turned into six weeks. I didn't want to leave. I liked bunking with Caroline, and we had started the second book in the Lost series. I still had not heard one word from Drew or Dawson. I liked being there, pretending that I was a little girl in a real family. I knew that I couldn't continue the charade for much longer, although I was sure that my mother and Caroline would have loved for me to do just that. I had to get back to life. My life, whatever that was.

It was looking like I would be finding a place to plant my roots alone. I was pretty sure that I was okay with that. I needed a fresh start. My mother's success had made me feel like it was okay not to choose either one of the men that I loved. Maybe I would find a man that loved me as much as Jason loved her, and I would eventually have a little girl as neat as Caroline.

I may be doing that sooner than planned. I was freaking out one evening, pacing back and forth on the deck.

"Hey, you okay?" my mom asked, coming to join me.

"I don't think that I am," I said running my fingers through my hair.

"Go play for a little bit, honey," my mom told Caroline when she came skipping around the other side.

"What's going on, Morgan?" she asked.

"I'm late," I stated.

"Oh, boy. How late are you?"

"Three days."

"That's not a lot," she tried to make me feel better.

"It is for me. I'm never later." This couldn't be happening right now. I was on the pill. I never missed a pill, and

I never missed a period. I would take my mother's advice and feed myself to the sharks if I was pregnant.

"Do you want to go into town and get a test?" she asked.

"No. That's going to make it real," I assured her.

She smiled. "Would this baby be Drew's or the sheriffs?"

I shook my head. My mother was going to deem me a cheating slut without ever knowing the truth. "I couldn't even begin to pinpoint it. I slept with Drew the Friday before I came here and Dawson the very next day."

"I'm not going to judge you, Morgan," she said as though she was reading my mind. "I had three kids from three different fathers. Caroline was the only one that was conceived with the man I was married to."

I snapped my head to her. "What do you mean?" I asked.

"The drunken, low life father that you grew up with isn't Justin's real dad either," she admitted.

"He isn't?"

She shook her head. "His dad was a trucker, Mad Dog," she added. I was sure she didn't know his real name. "I don't think your dad was able to have kids. You were seven by the time I had Justin, and I had never used any form of birth control. I slept with a trucker once and got pregnant."

"Did he know?"

"He suspected, but I never admitted to it."

"Oh God, mom. I can't be pregnant. What the hell am I going to do?"

"Let's go to town," she coaxed.

Caroline pouted because her dad told her she had to stay with him. I promised her that I would do something fun with her later. That satisfied her, but she still wanted to go along.

I rode with my head against the cool glass of my BMW. My mother drove. I didn't mind, I was having a nervous breakdown. I had a hard enough time reminding myself to breathe. My mother tried to console me, but it wasn't working. I knew with everything in me that I was pregnant. I just had a feeling. Going to buy a pregnancy test was pointless. I knew it with everything in me.

Jason took Caroline out to the beach to look for sea glass so that we could have some privacy. I knew my mother told him what was going on. I didn't mind. I was glad that she told him everything. That's the way it should be.

"What does the one line mean again?" I called out from the bathroom.

"It means you're not pregnant. A plus sign means that you are," my mom called back.

Fucking A...

I breathed the biggest sigh of relief when I saw the one negative line come into clear view of the little window. I don't think I had ever been so happy in my life. I opened the bathroom door and showed my mother the evidence. She hugged me, happy that I was happy. I wanted a baby. I just wanted to be living with its father and know who he was.

I spent the better part of the afternoon in the hot shed with Caroline and Jason. We made glass lit bottles to display our sea glass. I had to laugh at Caroline holding her iPad, giving her dad instructions from the pin that she found on Pinterest.

Our mother came to the door around six. Caroline and I were sitting at a workbench with our backs to the door, pushing the tiny strands of lights through the holes that Jason had drilled for us. I knew she would want us to come and eat soon.

"Morgan, you have a visitor," she spoke from the door.

I turned, seeing the most beautiful man in the entire world standing beside her. I wanted to throw myself at him. No. I wanted to fuck him. The sight of him sent a quivering sensation straight to my attention deficit disorder vagina.

"Well, come here," Drew finally said, pulling me from my frozen stool position. I smiled, slid off the stool and right into his arms.

"Hey, baby," he said into my hair. I could feel his smile.

"Hi," I said, pulling away, knowing that nosey Caroline was staring with her curious little eyes.

I introduced him to my mom and Jason, and Caroline took it upon herself to offer her name.

"I'm Caroline," she said offering her hand. "You must be Drew, I've heard a lot about you." What? Little liar, I never talked to her about Drew. I looked at her like she had two heads.

"You talk in your sleep…. a lot," she added. Shit… that could be bad.

"It's a pleasure to meet you, Ms. Caroline," Drew said with a smile, taking her little hand in his large one.

"Come, let's eat," my mother demanded.

"We're not finished yet," Caroline protested.

"We can finish them tomorrow," I assured her. I didn't want to play with Caroline anymore. I wanted to play with Drew.

We ate on the deck with the guests and were served by the help. We all had a glass of wine with our steaks. I wanted a cold beer. The wine tasted bitter to me. I didn't drink mine.

Drew and I stared across the table at each other, constantly.

"Did you just come for a visit," I asked, cutting into my too done steak.

"No. I came to take you back to Vegas with me."

My eyebrows rose. "Really?"

His face got serious. "Mr. Callaway passed away yesterday."

"Oh," I said. I wasn't sure what to say. I mean I was sad and grateful that he saw me as his only family and was leaving me all of his worldly possessions, but I really didn't know the guy.

"My car is here," I stated. I didn't know what else to say.

"We'll fly back and get it. We need to fly out tomorrow for the funeral."

There were no vacant rooms. Drew and I had to sleep on the pull out couch at my mom's place. I couldn't take it. Lying in his arms, fully clothed was killing me. I wanted him naked on top of my nakedness. I didn't dare though. I knew how thin the walls were. I had lain in bed many mornings, listening to my mom tell Jason how happy she was that I was there.

"I didn't think you were going to stay here for six months," Drew quietly said as his fingers tormented me. Not really. He was only tracing my arm with his fingers, but still. I wanted him tracing other parts of my body.

"I guess I was just trying to run away. Escape," I replied.

"How's that working out for you?"

"It was actually working out pretty damned good until you showed up."

"And Dawson?"

"I haven't talked to him either. We had a fight before I left. You both decided to give me my space at the same time."

"You had a fight? Why?"

"What do you think," I said, stating the obvious.

"Me?"

"Yup."

"We talked about you the night that he gave me a lift. I can see how you like him. He seems to be a good guy."

I snorted at him saying like. I didn't like Dawson. I loved him. Drew knew that. He just wasn't able to say it out loud.

Drew and I talked for a long time. I told him all about my mom, and everything that she had confessed to me. He already knew a lot of it, like the pictures that she was sent periodically.

Mother fucker. Fucking, lying son of a bitch.

I looked straight at my mom when I finally quit heaving enough to rejoin the rest of them for breakfast the following morning. She knew. She knew what I knew. The stupid little stick that I had pissed on, lied. I was pregnant. I knew I was. She knew it too and smiled a warm, motherly smile.

"You okay?" Drew asked as I sat beside of him, sipping my coffee.

"Yeah, I'm fine," I lied. I was far from okay. My stomach felt like it was going to regurgitate itself, and I was fucking pregnant. I was pregnant with a baby with two dads. No. I wasn't okay.

"When will you be back?" my mom asked. "We had a cancellation for next week. I'll keep that room open if you are going to be back in a few days," she offered.

I looked at Drew for the answer.

"We can come back in a few days. I hired a new assistant that is doing awesome. I can get away."

That wasn't my plan.

Drew and I weren't in the air twenty minutes before we were fighting.

"You don't have to fly back with me. I need to fly back, pick up my car and head home," I told him.

"Head home? So home is in Maine?" he asked.

"I don't know, Drew. What did you think I was going to do?"

"You know what, Morgan? I have no fucking idea what you are going to do, and I'm a little sick of trying to figure it out."

"Fuck you," I yelled. I was glad that we were on a private jet. I didn't say it quietly.

He turned on me, grabbing both of my arms, forcefully. "Is that what you need, Morgan? Do you need for me to fuck you?" he asked through gritted teeth.

Of course, my pussy was screaming and doing back flips, the stupid fucking mechanism, always taking over my brain.

"Yes," I rasped.

What the fuck? I didn't mean to say that.

Drew slid my sundress up and kissed me hard. I lost myself in a matter of seconds.

"Do you know what I really want to do to you, Morgan?" he asked, angrily taking my mouth, and not giving me time to respond, not that I had enough wits about me at that time to respond anyway.

"I would love to bend you over my knee and beat some sense into your naked ass."

Okay...

He didn't do that. He tossed me to the white leather seat, raising my skirt as his mouth did crazy things to my lips and neck.

"Get out!" Drew yelled, turning to the guy that had just walked into Drew being on top of me with my dress around my waist. I didn't look to see, but I could tell the guy got the hell out of there.

He undid his belt and pulled my panties to the side, forcefully entered me and fucked the hell out of me on the plush white leather seat. I lasted all of about three minutes before I was clawing his back and trying my best not to scream. I wanted to scream. I needed to scream. I hadn't had an orgasm in over a month, well, besides the couple that I gave myself in the shower.

Drew thrashed in and out of me, and I can't even begin to describe the look on his face. It was a mixture of the look right before he used to hit me, love, obsession and lust, all mixed together.

"Dammit, Drew," I scolded when he grabbed the fabric between my legs and tore it out of his way.

He ignored me with a shit eating grin. I was just getting ready to come again when he had to go and ruin it.

"I'm not letting you go, Morgan. I fucking love you."

What the fuck did that mean. He wasn't letting me go? I didn't reach my second high before Drew reached his. My mind relocated from what was being shoved inside of me to what Drew had just said. Should I be scared? Did he mean that I would be held against my will once again?

"What, Morgan?" he asked, seeing the confused look on my face.

"What do you mean what? I have to walk around in a dress with no panties now," I chastised. I didn't want to go there just yet, not with him still inside of my body.

He smiled and kissed me. "I have missed you like crazy," he said, biting my bottom lip.

"Why didn't you call me?" I asked.

"Why didn't you call me?" he countered.

"I didn't think you wanted to talk to me. You left pissed off, remember?"

"I always want to talk to you. Believe me, I had a hell of a time not calling you. I kept myself busy, trying to get this new assistant on board. I traveled every chance I got, and even filled the gym back up with equipment. Every time I couldn't get you out of my head and wanted to call, I would work out."

He slid out of me and took my hand, pulling me up.

"You need to go underneath the plane and get me a pair of panties," I said, removing what was left of mine. I didn't want to have a serious conversation with him just yet. I had other things on my mind, like what was growing inside of my uterus.

He smirked. "I love the idea of you walking around in this dress with no panties," he assured me, pulling my strap down and kissing my bare shoulder.

"You drive me crazy sometimes," I countered.

"You drive me crazy all the time," he assured me with a full blown tongue kiss.

◇◇()◇◇

"Drew, where are we going?" I asked when the driver took us in the wrong direction.

"We're having lunch with one of Randal's investors," he decided to tell me.

"Can't we go home first?" I asked; a little pissed off that he waited until we were on our way there to tell me.

"No. We don't have time. Why do you need to go home first?"

"You idiot. Where is my bag?"

"On its way to the house"

"I am not going to a restaurant with no panties in this thin dress," I demanded.

"Yes you are," he smirked. "You used to always wear dresses shorter than this with no panties."

"Because you made me!"

"And I walked around half the night with a hard on thinking about it," he smiled.

I crossed my arms and looked out the window, pouting. He was impossible. He would always be a manipulator, and there was nothing I could do to change that. I hoped the baby did turn out to be Dawson's he would be a much better father. I didn't want my kid to have any of Drew's hang-ups.

Drew held my hand as we were led to the waiting table. He introduced me as his wife to the man he called Mr. Rawlings, and then to the gorgeous blonde who stood to shake my hand. She was wearing a short black pencil skirt, white satin blouse, showing plenty of cleavage and three inch stilettos.

"This is Celeste, my new assistant," he offered.

Oh, fuck no!!!!

I shook her hand and tried to hide my shocked expression as best I could. Was he fucking crazy? I bet he already fucked her. Did he think that I was going to be okay with this perfect 10, being his assistant?

I paid no attention to the conversation going on around the table. They talked about stocks, and bonds, and moving money here to there, but my mind was reeling too much to stay focused. I was sure that I was pregnant with someone's baby, I was sitting there panty-less, and my husband just sprung his beautiful new assistant on me.

"Is that okay with you, Morgan?" Drew asked.

"What?"

"Morgan, you need to pay attention, this involves you too. You can have a say in anything thrown out."

"Why? I didn't get a say in anything else," I replied with narrowed eyes. He smiled. He knew exactly what I was talking about.

"That will be fine, Mr. Rawlings," Drew offered.

We stood on the sidewalk with Celeste waiting for our cars to be brought around. Drew asked her about some proposal. She said that it was finished and would bring it by later.

Of course, she was coming to our house. Why wouldn't she? Derik practically lived there when he was Drew's assistant.

"It was nice meeting you, Mrs. Kelley," Celeste said as her car was being pulled up.

I smiled and nodded as our driver pulled up, as well.

I didn't have time to light into Drew the way I had planned once we were in the car. Drew got a call and talked business the entire ride. I stared out the window while he conducted business. I did turn to him with a glare when he placed his hand on my upper thigh. I picked it up and moved it to his own leg. He smiled, shaking his head.

His conversation continued into the house and to his office. I followed him. We were having words. I was sure of it. He sat at his desk, and I sat in one of the wingback chairs across from him. Finally after another ten minutes of me patiently waiting, he ended his call.

"I'm all yours," he said, wearing the stupid little smirk that I wanted to slap right off his face.

"Are you sure about that?" I asked.

"What?" he asked with a confused expression.

"That you are all mine," I stated a fact.

"Come here," he demanded.

"No."

"No?"

"No, I am not coming to you. I can't believe that you hired someone like that to be your assistant. Did you not think that I might be a little pissed off about you traveling and working with someone who looks like that?"

"Excuse me. Would you like lunch, sir?"

"Hi, Marta," I smiled turning to the open door.

"Hi, Morgan. How are you?"

"I'm good; we had lunch, but I would love a cup of coffee," I requested.

"Me too," Drew said.

"Morgan, you should see this woman's track record. She knows her shit. I don't care what she looks like. You should see her negotiate, the woman's better at it than I am."

"Why didn't you ask my opinion about it first?" I asked. I'm not sure that I had the right to ask. We weren't even really talking but dammit all the way to hell and back.

"I think I did, Mrs. Kelly. I asked you if you wanted to be part of the interviewing process. You did not. Remember?"

Shit…

I stopped before saying anything else when Marta carried our coffee in on a tray.

"I'll come and see you in a little bit," I told her. I missed Marta. I really like her. She smiled and left us to get back to our argument.

"Come here," he requested again.

I stood and leaned against the corner of his desk with my arms crossed.

"If you tell me that you are going to stay right here with me, you never have to worry about another woman," he promised, looking up to me.

"I don't want you with other women if I don't stay," I assured him.

"And you think I want you to be with Dawson?"

Okay, he had a point.

"I have no reason to ever cheat on you, Morgan. I love you that much, and you are the hottest little thing that I have ever had between the sheets."

"You're just saying that because of our fucked up sex life. Any other woman would run away, screaming."

He picked up my leg and moved my foot between his legs. He ran his hand up my calf and straight to my already throbbing pussy. "I love our fucked up sex life," he said as his finger dipped inside of me.

Fucking hell.

I dropped my foot just as quick as he removed his hand from under my dress when Celeste cleared her throat from the door.

"Sorry to interrupt, Marta let me in," she said with her face as red as mine. She knew what she saw as well as I knew what I felt. That was twice in one day that we had been caught.

"I'm going to talk to Marta. I'll see you later," I told Drew, leaving him to his business. "Leave the door open," I whispered, kissing him just in front of his ear. I didn't look at Celeste as I walked out. I couldn't. I was too embarrassed.

I visited with Marta in the kitchen for a while, and then went to my old room for a needed shower. I thought about talking to Drew about being pregnant, but decided to wait until after the funeral the next day. I wasn't even sure that I really was pregnant. The test said that I wasn't, and I guessed that the morning sickness could have been just a bug or something.

Drew and I ate the evening meal that Marta prepared for us before leaving for the day. We sat at the table and talked. He asked me more about my stay in North Carolina, and I talked about Caroline a lot. I did love her like a sister and missed the little shit already.

"Morgan, there is a good possibility that Justin will be at the funeral tomorrow," Drew informed me. I wasn't sure how I felt about it. I mean I would be ecstatic if I did get to see him. I wondered if he would even recognize me. He was barely five the last time I saw him. I tried to remember when I was five. I remembered bits and pieces, like kindergarten, and my pet chicken that my dad had killed for supper. I wasn't sure if I would remember someone from when I was five. I barely recognized my cousin Bobby.

Drew and I went to bed pretty early. Of course we didn't go right to sleep, and had the most amazing fucked up sex ever. It consisted of the whole nine yards. Spankings, oral, anal, and I had even let him talk me into using one toy that I absolutely hated, the one that sent an electrical current to my clit, causing an immediate orgasm right before it stopped. It wasn't as bad as I had remembered. At least I knew that I would come, eventually.

Chapter 24

The next morning, Drew and I had another round of sex. No. It wasn't sex at all. He made slow passionate love to me while exploring my soul with his penetrating gaze into my eyes. It was great, unbelievable, and right on target with what I needed at the time.

I sat up, deciding whether or not I felt sick. I didn't. I pulled on a shirt and slid into my panties. As soon as my feet were planted on the plush carpet, I felt it and ran to the bathroom with my hand over my mouth.

Fucking, son of a bitch.

I turned to look at Drew between bouts of heaving into the toilet. He was staring at me with a bewildered look. He knew.

I looked at him through the mirror as I brushed away the nasty taste in my mouth. The toothpaste smell almost had me running back to the toilet. Drew never spoke. I swear he was in shock. I couldn't help it at the time. He didn't have to speak. I had to lie back down.

I brushed past him and sprawled across the bed with a groan.

"Morgan?" he questioned, sitting on the bed with me.

"Yes, Drew. I am pretty sure I am."

"Is it mine, Morgan?" he asked.

Fucking, shit... shit... shit...

"I don't know," I told him honestly.

He stood and paced the bedroom, running his fingers through his hair.

"I fucking knew it," he yelled.

Great...

"What did you know, Drew?" I asked, exasperated, already.

"I knew you fucked him. You don't fucking care any more about me now than you did before you left here."

Damn, he was pissed. I sat up. I was on the verge of being pissed myself.

"Really, Drew? You're going to go there?"

"Where the fuck would you like for me to go, Morgan?"

"To hell right now," I yelled. "What the hell, Drew? You don't get that right. You fucking raped me, beat the hell out of me, humiliated me, and I'll be God damned if you're going to stand here and fucking judge me for falling in love with another man. Fuck you!" I screamed.

Drew grabbed me by both of my arms.

"I have fucking apologized for the things that I did ten times over. I have tried everything I know to do, to make you realize how much I fucking love you. You don't have the right. You throw that shit up to me every time you get pissed off."

"I'm scared, Drew," I spit out. He had a cold dark glaze in his eyes. I was scared. I wanted him to let me go, and stop screaming in my face.

He let me go, and stormed out. He locked himself in his office until it was time to go.

We were both dressed in black and rode the back seat in total silence. He stared out the window, resting his chin on his fist. I didn't say a word. I didn't know what to say. I could understand his being upset, and I was trying to be mature about it and not just say fuck it and run away back to my mom's.

I walked to the coffin with my hand in Drew's. Mr. Callaway looked good. I thought his face looked a little sunken in, but overall he looked to be at peace.

"There aren't many people here," I whispered to Drew, looking at the empty chairs.

"Mr. Callaway wasn't the most admired man," he replied. I thought that it was sad, but could understand it. I had seen how he talked down to Drew the few times I'd seen them together. I looked around for Justin. I never saw him. His parents must not have been fond of Mr. Callaway either.

I thought there should have been more said at the funeral, but there really wasn't. It was a simple funeral with very few people. There wasn't even a graveside service, per Mr. Callaway's request.

Drew opened the door and held my wrist before I could slide in. "I'm sorry, Morgan. I'm trying my best to comprehend that my wife may be carrying another man's child," he said. I could understand that. I touched his cheek and smiled, letting him know that I understood.

"Can't you pinpoint the time frame? I can't stand not knowing," Drew said on the drive back to the house.

Fuck...

"No, Drew. I can't do that. I was with you three times in the two days that you were in Maine, and I was with him three times the following day."

Drew shook his head. He was angry again. I would be too; I guess.

I looked down at my phone and saw that I had a missed call from Dawson.

What the fuck? Neither of them had called the whole time I was at my moms. Not once did either of them call to see how I was, and now they both decide to pop back into my life at the same time.

Drew sent Marta home as soon as we were back. He went into his office, and I followed, removing my heels. I watched as he typed in the search.

"Can you have a paternity test while being pregnant?"

"Drew, I'm not even a hundred percent sure that I am pregnant," I protested.

"You're a week late, you have been sick for the past two mornings, but feel better shortly after. You are tired, and hungry. I'm no doctor, but I'm pretty sure you're pregnant."

"There!" he said, excited.

You could have a paternity test while being pregnant. I didn't know that fact.

"Yeah, read the rest. The court system needs to be involved before a physician will even do it. It's not safe for the baby," I said pointing to the article that he was reading.

"In rare cases," he pointed out. "How far along do you think you are? We have to do it before the fourteenth week."

"Drew, will you stop."

"No, Morgan. If we can do this, we are. I am not spending the next nine months waiting to see if this is my kid. I can't. I will end up hating you over it. How far along do you think you are?"

"Not very, six weeks maybe," I answered. I wasn't doing this before the baby. It was right there in plain English. There was a chance that it could harm the fetus.

Drew wasn't listening to me. He was on the phone calling his judge friend. The one who forced me to marry him, I was sure. I listened while he explained the situation, and of course the crooked judge agreed to sign whatever he needed to have signed.

He called Judith Bishop next; the gynecologist who used to come and give me my birth control shot every three months.

"She'll be here in about an hour," Drew exclaimed. I wanted to run away. He was going over my head and doing whatever Drew wanted to do. It pissed me off.

"Maybe, you could ask what I think before you make plans for me," I stated with an angry tone.

"It doesn't fucking matter what you think," he said just as angry. Okay, this was the Drew that I hated. This was the Drew who disregarded my feelings. I was secretly wishing the baby turned out to be Dawson's. Dawson would never treat me this way.

I stormed out of his office, and up to my own room. I wanted to call my mom, but I didn't because I knew that Drew had probably already turned his computer to my room. He was more than likely watching me through the cameras, and could hear every word that I said.

I took my funeral clothes off and pulled on a comfortable pair of shorts and a t-shirt. I lay across the bed, staring up at the ceiling for probably twenty minutes or so in the same position.

My cell phone rang, and after it quit I texted my mother and told her that I would call her back. It rang again a few minutes later. It was Dawson. I wanted to talk to him. I wanted Dawson. I needed Dawson. I wasn't sure what to do. I knew, or I had a pretty good suspicion that Drew would hear every word

I said. He hadn't called in weeks, if I ignored him he might think that I didn't want to talk to him. I did.

Fuck Drew...

"Hi," I answered, sitting up and crossing my legs.

"Hey, beautiful," he softly spoke. I closed my eyes and took a deep breath at the sound of his voice. I missed him. I wanted to be in his arms. And no, it wasn't because I was mad at Drew. I really missed him. I hadn't heard from him in almost a month.

"How are you?" I asked.

"Good, besides the fact that I miss you like crazy," he replied. "How are you?"

"I'm okay," I lied. I was never going to be okay. Every time I thought I was making progress, life decided to throw another curve ball.

"You don't sound okay. Where are you?"

"Vegas."

"Oh," he said with a hurt tone.

"I just got here yesterday. Mr. Callaway passed away, and I had to come here for the funeral. I'm leaving tomorrow." I hoped Drew heard that.

"Please tell me that you are coming home to me," he begged.

"I am coming there," I said.

"But not home to me, right?"

"I didn't say that."

"Are you any closer to deciding what you want than you were before you left?"

I snorted. Fuck no, I wasn't, and I had just gone and made things ten times more complicated.

"I haven't been doing what I left to do," I told him honestly. "I spent over a month at the beach with my mom and my little sister," I explained. I was happy that he dropped it and didn't try and pressure or badger me about it. He asked about my mom, my sister, and I told him about Jason. I talked to him for forty-five minutes. It felt good. I told him that I had to go when Drew knocked on the door with Judith.

"I love you, Ry."

"I love you too," I said it. I didn't care if Drew was standing right in front of me. I didn't even care about the hurt look on his face. He deserved it.

"How are you, Morgan?" Judith asked.

"Fine," I said with a bit of an attitude. I never did like her, and if I were pregnant she was not being my doctor.

"Do you think you can go to the bathroom?" she asked, halting the nice act. She picked up on my defiance right away.

"Do I have a choice?"

"Morgan," Drew chastised.

I took the cup from Judith's hand and stormed into the bathroom, slamming the door a little harder than I meant to.

I left the cup on the sink and walked out of the bathroom, right past the both of them and downstairs to the pool. I didn't want to know the results. I knew that I was pregnant, and I didn't want Judith fucking Bishop to be the one to tell me the fact that I already knew. Fuck both of them. I wished I had my car. I wanted to leave. I didn't want to be there for one more second.

I sat on the side of the pool, swirling my feet around the not so cool water. It was hot, very hot, but I didn't care. I didn't want to be in that evil house full of demons.

"What are you doing, Morgan?" Drew asked, in a calmer voice from the door.

"Nothing," I snapped.

"Come inside," he politely requested.

"Why?"

"So we can talk," he said with a little more annoyance.

"So we can talk or so you can tell me what I am doing?" I replied still sitting by the pool, not about to budge. I spent six years of my life listening to this man tell me when, where, how, what, and why, no not why, it was never any of my business, why. I wasn't about to bow down to him.

"Please come in the house. It's a hundred degrees out here."

I got up and walked past him and into the kitchen. He followed. Marta was preparing our supper. I took a bottle of water and sat at the island.

"Can you leave us, Marta?" he asked. She smiled and walked out.

Drew straddled the stool beside me. "Look at me," he softly spoke.

I turned my head to his, but I didn't look at him. I looked past his right shoulder at one of the replaced, tiny cameras that I had broken. What? Was he afraid someone was going to steal his food?

Stupid idiot. Stupid fucking idiot…

"Don't you want to know what the results are?"

I did look into his eyes with that, dead on with my cold, despicable glare. "I already know what they are."

"She can do a paternity test, and she can do the abortion if it turns out to be his."

Dammit, what the hell did I do with that gun?…

"One, Judith is not doing shit with any test. Two, Judith is not touching me. I will find my own physician, and three. What would ever give you the idea that I would even consider an abortion?"

"I knew you would say every bit of what you just said," he admitted.

"Then, why would you even suggest any of it?"

He shrugged his shoulders. "Wishful thinking, I guess. What do you want, Morgan?"

"Not you," I assured him. He snickered.

"You want to run back to your boring little life in Maine, back to your safe little sheriff," he replied with a tone. It wasn't a question, more of a statement.

"Boring? Let me explain to you what boring is. Boring is being trapped in this house for six, very long years. Boring is being allowed to leave the house escorted to go to one place and check out one book. Boring is being locked in a room with nothing in it for days, boring is…"

"Stop, Morgan. You want to leave? I'm not forcing you to stay. You're free to go whenever you want."

"Fine. I want to go now," I demanded.

"Where do you want to go?" he asked, I knew he wanted me to say back to my mom's. I kind of wanted to go there too, but I was pissed. My only goal in life at that moment was to hurt him.

"Maine," I spouted off with one word.

He took his cell phone from his pocket.

"I need the plane ready in an hour," he said into the phone glaring at me.

Fuck...

I didn't want to leave like that. I knew that he was trying to do what he thought was best. Hurting me wasn't his intention, but dammit, he couldn't just tell me what I was doing anymore. I felt like a real shit. I felt even worse when he kissed my lips softly and whispered that he loved me before he turned and walked away. Could somebody please explain how this got turned around? I wasn't the bitch here, was I?

I was just getting ready to go to him when Marta let Celeste in, Celeste in her long legs, short pencil skirt, and beautiful flowing blonde hair.

"Good afternoon, Mrs. Kelley," she smiled, carrying an armful of folders.

"Hello," I smiled back as she made her way to Drew's office.

I went upstairs and packed the clothes that I had taken to North Carolina with me. I didn't really need $2,000 dresses in Maine.

I walked past Drew's closed office door. I couldn't believe that he was going to let me go without a word. He never came out.

My face instantly turned red when I opened the door to see Gary. The same Gary who saw my legs wrapped around Drew's waist in the back of the plane.

He took my bag and said goodbye to Marta. Drew was really letting me leave without one word.

I was happy when we landed that Drew had arranged for me to have a ride. I really didn't want to call Dawson, and it was getting pretty late. I knew Lauren would be in bed already.

I smiled when I got out of the car at my mowed lawn, and then again at my stack of mail on the table. Dawson was still taking care of me even though I had been a fucked up mess around him during the last couple of months. No. I had always been a mess around him, from day one, and he was always there for me. I opened the sliding glass door, went around and opened windows, and sprayed a can of Lysol around the house. I guess the humidity from the hot days and the closed up house caused the musty smell.

As I soaked in a hot bath and ran my hand over my belly, I swear I could see a bump already.

"Oh, little baby, what a mess you are coming into," I said out loud.

I smiled, and got out of the tub when I heard Dawson.

"Ry?" he called.

I pulled on my musty-smelling robe from the hook behind the bathroom door. I made a mental note to throw it in the wash.

I'm such an idiot. I walked right into the man's arms. I had serious problems.

Dawson placed his hands on my back and pulled me to him with a smile and a kiss. I think maybe my vagina was on break, pissed off, or just not interested in making love to Dawson. It wasn't giving me fits like normal when one of these men touched me. I know it was because it wasn't what I needed. I needed someone to understand me, someone to confide in without being judged. Was Dawson that someone? I was about to find out. He had just as much right to know about the baby as Drew did.

"I'm going to get dressed. I'll be right back," I said, pulling away from him. I couldn't help but notice how our fingers seemed to linger as he let me go.

"Do you want a beer?" he called.

Hmmm. No alcohol for a while. "No, I think I'm just going to have tea," I called out.

Dawson had the tea kettle on the stove when I came out.

"I didn't think you'd be back this soon. How was the funeral?"

I didn't think I would be either. I shrugged my shoulders. "Fine, I guess. There weren't many people there, but it was nice."

"Do you want to sit outside?" he asked, pouring hot water over the tea bag.

"Yes."

I watched Dawson put the teaspoon of honey in my cup. I'd bet that Drew didn't even know how I liked my tea. Dawson got himself a beer and carried my cup. I slid the door open for him, and he paused. He moved his head and kissed me lightly with a smile. I smiled back. I could tell that he was happy to see me, and had missed me.

We sat at the table. Dawson didn't sit across from me. He slid his chair around so that we were both looking out to the endless sea.

"How did you know I was home?" I asked.

He smiled. "Lauren texted me."

I smiled too.

"You okay, Ry?" he asked, and for the life of me I don't know what happened. My guess was the hormones were a little wacky, but I started crying. I don't mean a tear escaped. I bawled like a baby. He held his arm around me, not speaking. I'm sure he had no idea what to say. He held me, kissed my head, and rubbed circles around my back.

Once I was able to stop sobbing like some sort of lunatic, I wiped my nose with the back of my hand and smiled up at him.

"I'm sorry," I apologized.

Dawson walked into the house and came back with a box of tissues. I pulled one from the box and blew my nose.

"What's going on, Ry?" he asked, taking my hand. I ran my hand over his light blue t-shirt where the blue was darker from my wet tears. He looked down.

"Don't worry about it. It's not the first time you cried on my shirt," he said.

"Why are you so good to me?" I asked. I didn't deserve him any more than a child molester deserved to keep their private parts. I had been so rotten to him, but couldn't really help it. I still didn't know what the hell to do. I loved Drew. There was no doubt in my mind. I loved Dawson too, and now I had to go and throw a baby in the middle. Fucked up, that's what it was.

"Because I love you," he quietly said.

"I'm pregnant, Daw." There, I said it. It was out. I was afraid to look at him. I was afraid that he was going to get up and walk out of my life, for good this time. It was really stupid of me. Dawson wasn't that man. Dawson would be right there for as long as I would let him. I knew he would. I heard him take a deep breath and looked down at his hand caressing mine.

"Is it mine, Ry?"

I felt a sudden sense of déjà vu. I had already had this conversation.

"I don't know, Dawson." I was honest with him. I was done lying to Dawson Bade. Whether we were together or not, I would tell him everything.

I spent the next two hours, pouring my heart out to him. He knew that I was worth more than Bill Gates. I told him about Drew and Derik's plan to dispose of me once Mr. Callaway had passed, and how they hadn't expected him to live but a few months. I told him about Drew being forced to marry me or be cut out of the will. He knew about my mother being paid off too. I told him everything, even the demand from Drew that I have this paternity test.

"I can't understand how you can love this guy, Ry. And don't take it the wrong way. I'm not trying to be a dick. I just don't understand. I want to go dig his grave right now."

I snorted and traced his fingers with mine. "He wanted me to have an abortion if the baby turns out to be yours."

"I'm afraid if you let him talk you into that, I would dig his grave."

I picked my ringing cell phone up from the table. I answered it. I wasn't hiding anything from either one of them anymore. If that sent them both running to the hills then so be it.

"I just wanted to make sure that you made it home okay," Drew said on the other end.

"Yes. I'm home." That's all I said. I didn't know what to say to him.

"Are you flying back to North Carolina, or do you want me to send for your car?"

"I'm staying here for a while, but you don't have to send someone to drive my car. I have my Honda. My mom said that it was fine there."

"You're not driving my baby around in that jalopy you call a car."

"My car is fine until I go out there. I promised Caroline I would come back before school started."

"I promised her I would go sea glass hunting with her next week. We were supposed to go spend a couple of days there, remember?"

"Yeah, I remember." I didn't say any more than that again. He picked up on it. He knew.

"He's there, isn't he?"

"Yes."

"That didn't take two minutes. I'll talk to you later, Morgan."

I didn't have a chance to say goodbye. My phone was blinking; call ended, two minutes, twelve seconds in my hand.

"You know what, Riley?" Dawson said, taking my hand and holding my knuckles to his lips.

Oh, boy. Here it comes.

"Hmm?"

"I think that you have been through enough shit for ten lifetimes. I think you should divorce *him*, marry me and let me take care of you and my baby for the rest of your life."

Shit, maybe I should just do the paternity test. I had a feeling that I would hear this from both fathers for nine months. I didn't respond and only smiled.

Dawson never left me that night. He didn't try anything that involved being naked, and I was glad. I think my vagina was on strike anyway; I never heard a peep. Dawson held me close all night, caressing my body and planting soft, sweet kisses on my forehead. I knew that Dawson made the most sense. I knew that Dawson would be the simpler of the two solutions if there were a simple solution.

I woke late to an empty bed. Dawson had gone to work. I lay in bed reviewing my options for a long time. For whatever reason, I decided at the moment that I was going to stop fretting over any of it. I wasn't going to try and decide anything. Whatever happened, happened. I really needed to clean the ceiling fan.

I got up, started the coffee and did just that. I cleaned the ceiling fan, drank coffee on my deck while listening to Lauren and Levi. I even laughed when Lauren told a caller that she was a black, Jewish girl from Kentucky. I went to town and had lunch at Millie's, stopped and visited with Star, and then walked along the beach.

It was easy to slowly settle back into my life in Maine. I had a man who adored me, friends that loved me, a house I treasured, and an ocean for solitude. Drew did have my car delivered to me, but I didn't drive it. I drove my old Honda. The BMW was a little out of place there, and I felt more like me in the Honda. I wasn't some rich girl who doted on the finer things of life, well technically I was a rich girl, but I didn't feel like one.

I hadn't heard from Drew for almost two weeks. I felt in my heart that I was doing the right thing. Dawson loved me, and I loved him. I had fun with Dawson, and yes we had sex. It wasn't anything like Drew and I had, not even close. Dawson was in it for the love making which was fine by me. He made sure my needs were met, and took his sweet, slow time. I didn't need the fucked up sex life that Drew and I shared. This was what I needed, right here in nowhere Maine, where life was simple.

Lauren took a week's vacation about a month after I was home and she and I spent a week with my mom on the beach. Lauren loved it. She was a bigger kid than Caroline and spent her days hunting sea glass, playing dumb little girl games, sitting on the beach with binoculars searching for dolphins, and shopping. Caroline loved her just as much as Lauren loved

Caroline. It was funny. I never pictured Lauren being good around little girls. She was.

My mom made sure that Lauren and I had a room so we didn't have to bunk with Caroline although Caroline camped with us all but two of the six nights we were there. It was mid-August, and one night Caroline insisted that we sleep on the beach and watch the meteor shower. It was the perfect night for it. We lay out on the beach, including my mom, on sleeping bags and watched the fireball sky. At last count there was somewhere in the ballpark of a hundred. Some of them were quick and small, and some felt like they were coming right at us. I had never watched a meteor shower before. It was amazing, and Caroline had so many wishes. It was comical. I made only one wish. I wished that the baby growing inside of me would be Dawson's.

On the fifth day Drew called. We were eating breakfast on the private deck, goofing off with Caroline. My heart sank when I saw his name. What the fuck. I needed him not to call. I needed to stay as far away from him as possible, and I sure as hell didn't need to hear his voice right now.

"Hello," I cautiously answered.

"Hey, where are you?" he asked, no hey beautiful, I miss you, nothing, just a cold tone. I should have been happy that he wasn't being nice. It should have made it easier, but it didn't. I wanted him to want me. It was dumb, but it was what I wanted.

"I'm at my mom's with Lauren. Why?"

"I'm flying there so that you can sign a power of attorney," he said.

"For what?"

"So I can work. I have a stack of shit on my desk that needs your signature. I need you to sign a power of attorney so I don't have to rely on you to take care of it."

"Okay," I replied. I didn't care about that. I wouldn't know what I was signing anyway. "When are you coming?"

"I should be there by three."

"Today?!?" I asked shocked. I didn't mean to sound so surprised. It just came out that way.

"Is that a problem?"

420

"No. That will be fine," I answered. It wasn't fine. I didn't want to see Drew. I couldn't see Drew.

"See ya later then," he replied and hung up.

I called Dawson and told him that he was coming. I wasn't going to feel guilty for him being there and hiding it from him. I was done with that. Dawson was okay with it. He trusted me.

Stupid boy...

The only thing that Dawson was concerned with was me signing something that was going to leave me with nothing and I would give it all to Drew. I didn't care. I didn't want any of it. I had a $4,000 a month trust fund for the rest of my life without having anything to do with diamonds, stores, stocks, negotiations, or conference calls. That was more money than I ever had in my life and more than enough to live on.

I was a nervous wreck the entire afternoon. I'm not sure why. I had a feeling he would pop in and out. I bet that he didn't mention the baby or anything else about us. I was right.

I was in a bedroom Lauren and I shared, taking a shower and getting ready. I knew it was stupid, but I wanted to look nice for him. I pulled on blue short shorts and a pink cami that made my breasts look bigger than they actually were. Well, maybe they were a little bigger. I was just finishing up with my makeup when I heard a tap on the door. I thought it was Caroline. It wasn't even two yet.

"It's open," I called, spritzing a dab of perfume on.

I froze. I wasn't expecting to see Drew.

Really vagina?

I hadn't had that response in quite some time, and I had almost forgotten all about the arguments I'd with my own sex. He looked good. I mean really good. He was in jeans that looked delicious on him, a tight gray t-shirt that showed that he was ripped. He'd been using the new equipment in the gym. I smirked a little. I knew he dressed for me too. He had a thin beard almost in a line along his jaw line. It was sexy as hell.

His eyes scanned my body and then back to my eyes. He closed the door, and my heart started to beat out of my chest.

Fuck fuck and fuck...

He walked to me with half a smile while I still stood like some sort of stupid, destitute derelict. He picked up the black sea glass hanging from around my neck and smiled as if he were saying, I own you. Jesus H. Christ he smelled good. What happened next probably bought me a one-way ticket straight to hell. He kissed me. I kissed him back. I still hadn't spoken when he turned to lock the door.

Shit.

He lifted his shirt over his head, and I swear I felt an orgasm coming on. I don't think my clitoris had ever throbbed like that from the sight of anything, ever.

"Take your clothes off," he demanded in a low ass sexy tone.

I did just that. I stood in front of the bastard and undressed as his hungry eyes watched.

He walked behind me and moved my hair off of my shoulder, lightly kissing the crook of my neck. "I want to spank you, Morgan. Do you want me to spank you?" he whispered in my ear. My eyes closed as I felt his warm words on my tender skin.

"Yes," I managed to get out.

"Yes?!?! Are you fucking kidding me?

I felt him smile on my skin. He moved away from me and sat on my bed. He nodded, and I knew what to do. I positioned myself across his lap placing my upper body on the bed. I swear I wasn't thinking about one God damned thing, not how ludicrous this was, not Dawson who trusted me, and not that this man hadn't even spoken to me in almost a month. I knew one thing and one thing only. I knew that I wanted him to fuck me and was only aware of my wet pussy throbbing after every blow and then the sensual massage calming the sting.

After exactly five tantalizing, sexually frustrating smacks to my bare ass, Drew dipped his finger inside of me. I wanted to come. I wanted to come right that second. He slid from beneath me and told me to spread my legs.

No problem...

I rolled to my back and did just that. I think I made it all of about three strokes from his twisted tongue strokes before I was writhing beneath his mouth. He stopped when I started to call out in heavenly agony.

Dammit, I hated when he did that.

"Shhhh," he said, taking my mouth. I could taste my juices as his tongue entwined with mine. "I'm going to fuck you now," he whispered to my lips as he released himself from the constricting jeans. He drove himself into me. There was nothing slow about it. It almost sent me over the edge again. He knew it. He was playing his fucked up mind games. He wasn't letting me come.

"You want me to fuck you up the ass, don't you, Morgan?" he asked, staring down at me.

"Yes."

What the fuck? Who the hell keeps speaking for me?

He moved my leg to the side. He did go slower with that. Inch by inch, he pushed into my tight ass as his fingers penetrated my nub. Once I was relaxed and accepted him, he fucked me, I mean really fucked me. I had to scream into the comforter as I was sent into a mind blowing, fucked up as hell, orgasm. I was ordained to hell, no doubt about it.

Drew pulled me up, and we got dressed. "Let's go, Celeste is waiting downstairs with the paperwork," he said, opening the door.

"You brought Celeste?" I asked pissed off as hell. "Did you fuck her on the plane before you popped in to fuck me?"

"I didn't pop in to fuck you. I had no intentions of fucking you and no; I didn't fuck Celeste on the plane. If I did, do you really have room to talk?" he asked as we walked out.

Good point...

Lauren knew. She fucking knew. She stood on the far side of the deck with her arms crossed, glaring at me. I sat with Celeste, and she went over everything, but I had no clue what she was talking about. I just signed the X's that she told me to sign. Drew never took his eyes from me. Dammit all the way to hell.

I walked out to their waiting car and Drew pulled me close to him. "Take care of my baby," he said.

"It was good seeing you again," Celeste said, smiling. Okay, she was nice, and I may or may not have liked her had she not been spending so much time with my husband, looking like that.

Chapter 25

I was pretty sure I had just fucked everything up once again. Lauren was pissed at me and barely spoke during our last two days at my mother's. I betrayed Dawson and told him that Drew was gone within an hour. He was. I just didn't tell him that forty minutes of it were spent fucking me. My mother had lectured me about leading both of them on and needing to decide my future. Like I wasn't aware that I had a baby to think about now, she felt the need to remind me of that fact too. She pointed out that I couldn't be Riley when I was with Dawson and Morgan while I was with Drew.

She still didn't know the reason behind the whole name change. I had forgotten to mention it until Lauren called me Riley our first day there. She was under the assumption that I pretended to be Riley in order to pull off the affair with Dawson. I was a horrible person, but I wasn't about to tell her that I ran away from Drew because he had beaten and used me for sex. It would kill her to know that she agreed to walk away from me, knowing what I had been through, so I let her think I was a rotten, cheating soul.

Lauren finally broke on our flight home.

"What are you going to do, Riley?"

I glared at her. It kind of pissed me off. I was pretty sure that it was none of her business.

"Don't look at me like that. Dawson is my friend and he doesn't deserve this," she stated.

Great, now my best friend thought that I was a poor excuse for mankind, as well.

"I don't expect you to understand, Lauren. I don't even understand it myself. I need them both. They both give me things that I need."

"You can't have them both."

No shit...

"I know that. It's just hard. Drew is in Las Vegas, and I am going back to Dawson, aren't I?"

"You may be going back to him, but the first chance you get, you'll end up fucking him again. You know it, and I know it."

"Shhhh," I demanded, looking around the plane.

"You need to tell Dawson what you did, and let him decide."

"I can't, Lauren. I can't hurt him any more than I already have."

Lauren shook her head. She was disgusted with me, and I felt for the first time that she was looking down on me. I hated that our fun week ended this way. I hated myself for jumping in bed with Drew. I didn't jump, I freaking dove. I lost all hope as soon as I saw him. Bottom line, I was pathetic.

◇◇()◇◇

Dawson was there through my first trimester. He went to all three appointments with me. I truly did hope that he turned out to be the father. He was so excited. I was almost tempted to tell Drew that I did have the paternity test, and the DNA was a perfect match to Dawson's. Dawson would have raised it as his own, no matter what the outcome was. I knew he would. I didn't do that, however. I may be crazy, but I wasn't quite that crazy---Yet.

Lauren had forgiven me and was back to waking me up too early and helping herself to my food. Dawson pretty much lived at my house, and Drew had probably moved onto Celeste. I didn't care. Yes, I did. No, no, I didn't. It was better if he had. I knew that we needed to talk and start the divorce procedures. I was procrastinating. I guess I felt like once I did that, it was done, which should have been what I wanted, but it wasn't.

I hadn't spoken to Drew for almost three months other than the occasional emails that he sent about business that I didn't know anything about. I emailed him more than once and told him to do what he wanted, and that was why I had signed the power of attorney.

Dawson was raking leaves one evening when I was about five months pregnant. When I answered the cell phone, I walked back in the house to talk to Drew. Dawson knew who it was and gave me a look, but continued to rake while I disappeared into the house.

"I need you to fly to Kingston," he blurted without so much as a hello, how are you, how's the baby?

"Kingston? Kingston what?" I asked.

"Canada. I just purchased a very prestigious jewelry store there, and I need you to sign some papers."

"I'm not flying to Canada, Drew. Why can't you do it? And furthermore, what the hell are you doing buying more stores? Don't you have enough already?"

"I couldn't pass it up. I can't do it. I need your signature on this."

"Drew. I can't just pick up and fly to Canada."

"Why?"

"Because, I have a life too." Geesh.

"Morgan, I need you to do this. You can fly in and right back out. I will send a plane for you."

"When, Drew?" I asked annoyed.

"Next Thursday."

"I'm going to have to call you back and let you know."

"Why do you need to let me know? Do you need permission?"

"Fuck you, Drew. I don't think you want to talk about asking permission." How dare him. I had to ask his fucking permission to go to the library. I wasn't about to take his shit, not for one second.

"There will be a driver to pick you up next Thursday. I will email you the details."

"I'm not going to Canada, Drew," I demanded to myself. He was gone, and his name was blinking across my screen.

"Well, what did he want now?" Dawson asked, coming in.

I was still standing there with my blank face, trying to make heads or tails out of Drew's demands.

"He needs me to fly to Canada and sign for a new property."

"No."

"No?" I asked, now annoyed with him. Why the hell couldn't people realize that I was twenty-seven fucking years old?

"I'm not letting you go there alone, Morgan," he demanded.

"Then go with me."

What the fuck? I didn't want him to go with me. Where the hell did that come from?

"When?" he asked.

"Next Thursday."

"I can't. Matt is taking next week off. Reschedule it for the next week and I will."

I knew that wouldn't work. Drew didn't wait on anyone. It was always on his terms.

"I'll see what I can do," I lied. I wasn't even going to mention it to him.

I checked my email religiously for the next five days, and every day there was nothing. I had even told Dawson that he must have changed his mind.

I got the email late Wednesday night. Dawson was in the shower, and I checked it for about the hundredth time since I had last spoken to him.

"Driver will be there at nine in the morning."

"Really Drew? You expect me to just jump on a plane with a twelve hour notice?" I emailed right back.

"You had five days' notice."

"You're such an egotistical idiot. I'm not coming."

"LOL." That was his last message in big bold letters. He wouldn't answer me back when I told him that I was being serious. Now, I either had to really defy him or fight with Dawson. Like an idiot, I chose to fight with Dawson.

"I'm dead serious, Riley. I don't want you to go there alone. I'm begging you not to go there alone," Dawson pleaded when I told him.

"It's a two hour flight, Daw. I will be back by like three or four in the afternoon."

"I don't like it," he said.

Well duh, I knew that.

I wrapped my arms around his neck. "Stop worrying about me. I will be fine," I promised.

He laughed when the little one kicked him. My belly had really grown. It seemed like I woke up one morning, and it was there.

"There and back?" he asked, giving in. I was hoping he didn't stay mad. I needed him to control my raging hormones and hoped that they stayed intact until I got back. I didn't need to be screwing up and screwing Drew again.

◇◇()◇◇

Evidently Gary hadn't gotten the memo that I was pregnant. His eyes darted straight to my stomach when I answered the door the following morning.

"Um, do you have a bag?" he stuttered.

"No. I'm not staying overnight," I replied, retrieving my purse. I should have known right that second that I wasn't coming home that night. The look that Gary gave me told me that I wouldn't be returning that night.

It was a pretty quick flight, and I was driven to a five-star hotel in Kingston and then escorted up to the penthouse suite. After tipping the bellhop, the only thing I could do was laugh. The room was as romantic as I had ever seen. A black sleek evening dress lay across the bed with beautiful shoes to match. I picked up the note and laughed again.

"No panties."

Fuck. He was planning on seducing me. My stupid vagina just happened to wake from the dead. How fucking convenient.

I dialed his number right away.

"I'm not staying here, Drew," I demanded as soon as he said hello.

"Yes you are," he replied. I was sure if I could see through the phone that he was grinning from ear to ear.

"No. I'm not. Where am I supposed to go sign these papers? And what the hell am I supposed to do with this dress?" I yelled.

"Yes you are, the papers will be signed tonight, and you are supposed to put it on and meet me downstairs for dinner at six," he rattled off, answering every one of my firing questions.

"Why did I need to be here at eleven in the morning? Where are you planning on staying? Why didn't you tell me you were planning on me staying, and if you would have been around me over the last few months you would know that my five months pregnant belly is not going to fit in that dress."

"Look at the tag. Yes, it will. I have to go wrap a few things up. I'll see you at six."

"Don't you dare hang up on me," I yelled a second too late.

"Grrrrr," I moaned, slamming my phone to the bed.

What the hell was I supposed to do now? I was stuck in a romantic hotel room. Dawson was going to be pissed.

"I'm coming after you," he yelled into the phone.

Yup. He's pissed.

"No, you're not. I'm fine. He said the papers would be ready in the morning, and I will be home by noon," I lied to him once again thanks to Drew Fucking Kelley.

"How the hell am I supposed to know that he's not going to take you away someplace, and I can't find you?"

"He's not going to do that, Daw. If that were his plan, he would have already done it. I'm not afraid of Drew. I promise; I am fine, and I will see you tomorrow."

Dawson groaned through the phone. "Tell me you love me."

I smiled. "I love you. Don't worry about me."

"Take care of my baby."

"I will. I'll call you later."

I was a nervous freaking wreck sitting around that room all day. I sat out on the balcony overlooking the city for a while, but it was cold. I mostly just paced, waiting for six o'clock.

This was a mind game. This was just another one of Drew's sick jokes. He knew I would go nuts with anticipation.

Someone knocked on my door at four o'clock. I opened it to find two women and a cart.

"We're here to help you get ready, Mrs. Kelley," the younger of the two said.

I never said a word. I just snorted and let them in.

"Would you like a shower first?" the same girl asked.

I didn't know why I said yes. I'd just showered that morning, but I did want to freshen up my legs. Yes. I was already thinking about the night ahead with Drew. I was still going to be strong, and refuse to let him stay with me, but I knew how un-resilient I seemed to be around him so just in case, I showered.

The ladies blow dried my hair, curled it, did my nails, toes and fingers, my makeup and then helped me with my dress. I thanked them and waited another thirty minutes to meet Drew in the dining room. I looked in the full length mirror, and for a fat chick, I looked hot.

I knew how anal Drew was about punctuality and decided to make him wait. I smiled down at my phone when I was being escorted to his table, fifteen minutes late. He lowered his when he saw me.

"You are stunning," he said, standing and kissing my cheek.

Fuck fuck, fuck, fuck, fuck.

Drew wasn't wearing his sexy jeans or his customary suit. He was in gray dress slacks with a black cashmere sweater with the sleeves pushed up on his arms. He was sporting a neatly trimmed five o'clock shadow, and I was no longer hungry, not for food anyway. I wanted to fucking devour him right there.

"Flying solo," I asked, trying to keep cool.

He smiled. He knew exactly what I was hinting at. "Yes. She's in Vegas."

"Where's the paperwork?"

"We're not signing it until tomorrow morning."

Other than the fact that I didn't really lie to Dawson, I was pissed. I didn't want to be Drew's pawn.

I stood up. I would meet him the next morning for the important business that he insisted that I had to be there twenty-four hours early.

He lightly took my wrist. "Sit down, Morgan," he demanded. I didn't want to sit down. I wanted to tell him to fuck off and make a scene right there. I couldn't. His spellbinding stare forced me to sit; besides he rented out the whole fucking room. We were the only ones there.

He smiled. "How's my baby?" he asked.

You have got to be kidding me.

"My baby is doing great," I smartly said.

He grinned. "You might want to watch the tone. I have been waiting for three months to bend you over my knee."

Stupid fucking vagina. You do remember that we are panty-less?"

"What do you want Drew?" I asked, exasperated.

He stood and took my hand. "Let's dance."

Huge mistake, being in Drew's arms, smelling him, touching him, feeling his heartbeat, did something to me. I can't explain that either. It just did. There was chemistry between us that Dawson and I didn't have. We never did. This understanding between Drew and me was something that had always been there, even when I hated him, and it confused the hell out of me. But I also knew what Drew, and I had been about... passion and that passion was in the bedroom. Drew wouldn't be the man that I wanted to help raise my baby.

"Are you wearing panties," he asked.

Drew had a one track mind, and it was focused right between my thighs.

I shook my head. "No," I answered, looking up to his accomplished smile.

He lowered his hand to the side of my belly and his lips to mine, and I freaking parted them for him. I even moaned into his mouth. I was doomed.

"You need to come, don't you?" he whispered, kissing my neck as I moved it back and to the side giving him full access.

"Yes," I whispered back.

Drew slid his hand between my legs, raising just the front of my dress. I grabbed his hand and regained my equanimity.

"I didn't mean right now," I protested.

"Move your hand," he demanded.

What the fuck? I looked around at the empty room and moved my hand. I thought for sure I would fall when I felt his fingers glide slowly up my throbbing, betraying, wet pussy.

"Fuck, Morgan," he rasped in the crook of my neck as his fingers did forbidding things in a public setting. I could only respond with a moan.

I was going to fucking come. I was going to let go right there on the empty dance floor. He ground into me, and I could feel his rock hard rod on my stomach. I wanted him. I wanted him inside of me right that second. I would have lain spread eagle right there on the marble dance floor. I didn't care who saw. I actually felt a little excitement at the thought of being watched.

"Shit, Drew," I whimpered.

"Come to me, baby," he whispered. I did. We shared a moan in each other's mouth as my walls constricted around his fingers.

"I hate you," I panted.

Drew laughed and removed his fingers from me. I looked around once again at the empty room. It was one of those times when you felt as though you were being watched. Whether we were or not, I didn't know, but it sure felt as there were eyes staring at us.

"I love you, and I love you," he said, bending and kissing my belly.

Great...

Drew led me back to the table, and I knew for sure we were being watched during our public, well my public orgasm, I should say. As soon as we were seated, we were served our

433

meals. I wasn't surprised that Drew had already ordered. He was known for ordering for me. I didn't mind. He always did okay.

"You can't stay with me," I told Drew matter-of-fact. He couldn't. I was trying my best to be true to Dawson. If I let him come anywhere close to me where there was an accessible bed, I was finished. Hell, I had just let him finger me on the freaking dance floor for God's sake.

"Yes I can," he said, twirling the noodles around his fork.

"Drew, what the hell are you trying to do here?"

"I'm trying to get my wife to understand that I intend to fuck her senseless tonight and then she's going to fall asleep naked in my arms. You're a pretty smart girl. I don't think you need a comprehensive walk-through."

"Jesus Christ, Drew. I haven't even talked to you in almost three months. What the hell makes you think that you can just insist that I fly here, have dinner with you, and then go to bed with you? You're crazy, and I mean that literally. I don't want to sleep with you." I demanded. Of course, he smiled that stupid sexy smile that went straight to my groin again.

"Let me stay with you, and I promise I won't touch you unless you tell me to."

Like I could do that. I shook my head and pushed my almost finished plate away. I was having sex with this man. It was inevitable.

"Tell me how the doctor appointments are going," he coaxed, stabbing my half eaten steak with his fork and placing it on his plate. My hand automatically went to my stomach. I rubbed in circles as I looked up to this beautiful man, defeated.

"They're going fine. Dawson thinks I need help. He thinks I have Stockholm syndrome."

What? Where the fuck did that come from?

Drew laughed. "Are you saying that you are in love with me?"

"You're so stupid sometimes."

"And I think this pregnancy is making you a little cranky, eh?"

"You make me cranky. You think I am just supposed to bow down and do whatever you want, when you want."

"If you did everything that I wanted, you would be home with me, in my bed."

"We need to start divorce procedures."

That would piss him off.

"I'm not giving you a divorce," he stated matter-of-fact.

I laughed that time. "You're not?"

"Nope. Do you want dessert?"

"No. What do you mean you're not giving me a divorce?"

"I mean that I'm not giving you a divorce," he repeated.

"Why?"

"Because I love you and I want you to be my wife, and you want to be my wife. The sooner you realize that, and quit trying to play house with Robo-cop in a small town, the better off we'll both be."

"I'm not trying to play house with anyone." I was getting pissed. The nerve of this man.

"Let's go," he said, standing and taking my hand.

"Go where?"

"To our room," he replied, pulling me close and kissing my lips. I kept my lips still in a straight line. I wasn't kissing him back. He needed to grow up and realize that the world didn't spin just because he was on it.

I knew that I wasn't going to win. I knew that I would be sleeping between the luxurious Egyptian sheets with Drew. I didn't have to do anything with him though. I would stay away from him. I had just started a good book on my iPad. I would read and ignore him.

"Drew, I have to call Dawson, and you can't make a sound," I demanded once we were back in the room.

He tightened his lips and pretended to zip them. I slipped out of the heels and stared at him lying across the bed.

Shit. How the hell was I supposed to talk to Dawson with him sprawled out looking like that?

"Hey sweetie," Dawson answered on the first ring.

"Hi," I said, sitting in one of the ornamental wing back chairs, staring directly at Drew, who wasn't taking his eyes off of me.

"How was dinner?"

"It was okay," I lied. It was far from okay. It still wasn't okay. Drew was undressing me with his eyes. I had to cross my legs to calm the quivering. It didn't help.

"How were things between you and Drew?"

"Intense," that was the only word to describe Drew.

"Did you mention the divorce?"

"I did, but we weren't alone, so I didn't go too much into it."

"You are going to tell him before you leave, right?"

"Yes, Dawson."

"Does that make you mad, Ry?" he asked, catching my tone. "I thought we talked about this."

"We did. No. I'm not mad, just tired. I will talk to you in the morning, okay?"

"Okay, get some rest and take care of my baby. I love you."

"Love you too," I quickly said.

I dropped my phone on the table and crossed my arms over my growing midsection.

"You're such a liar," Drew smirked.

"Shut the hell up," I shot back. I was so frustrated.

"Why do you feel the need to lie to him, but you make sure that I am very aware of what's going on in Misty Bay?"

"I don't make you aware of anything. You're just a nosey son of a bitch."

"But you don't lie to me about Dawson. I know you're fucking him. He has no clue that you are fucking me, does he?"

"He doesn't know because I am not fucking you, and furthermore, you and I are not together."

"So you're going to go home and tell him that I stayed here with you even if I don't touch you?"

"No."

"Thought so."

"I thought you told me that you were going to leave me alone."

"I did. I haven't talked to you in almost three months."

"Then what the hell is this, Drew?"

"I really did need you to come and sign these papers. I just figured I may as well kidnap you for a night. I'm starting to go through Morgan withdrawal."

I smiled at that, shaking my head. What I did next not only surprised him, but me also. I got up and went to him, pushing him back on the bed and straddling him.

"You know that I hate you, don't you?" I asked.

His hands went up my bare legs. I knew that I was flashing him, and to my surprise he never looked. He was looking into my eyes with a hungry, adoring, loving, and indulgent look.

"That's a shame because I love you more than life, and I love this," he said, running his hand over my round belly.

"You know, one of you is going to be wrong."

"It's mine. I know it," he said, knowing exactly what I was talking about.

I slowly moved my lips to his and kissed him like I never wanted to let him go. I didn't want to let him go. I just wanted Dawson too. I needed Dawson to keep some normality in my life.

Drew rolled me over not letting our lips lose contact. I wasn't sure where this Drew was coming from, but he took his good old sweet time with me. He kissed and sucked all over my upper body while he made slow passionate love to me. I felt like I was floating. There was none of his dominating sex hang ups, just pure making love. I didn't like it. I mean I did, but I didn't. This wasn't the fucked up Drew. This was the Drew that loved me and was showing me just how much.

We watched a movie after our love making session. He kept his hand on my naked belly, and I lay curled up in his arms. I was doing nothing but torturing myself. I belonged there, but I belonged in Dawson's arms too. What the hell was I supposed to do with these two men? Most women would be flattered to have two men chasing after them, not me. Maybe had I not loved them both it could have been flattering, but it was agony. I knew that if this baby turned out to be Drew's, Dawson wouldn't leave me, but Drew would never let me go. I wasn't sure how things would go if it turned out to be Dawson's. Would Drew let me go then? Maybe that would put an end to all of this madness. Maybe I just needed to let this little baby decide.

I woke to Drew's fingers between my legs sometime in the middle of the night. That session was beyond slow love making. That was the dark Drew that had me doing every kinky thing imaginable. Including getting off of the bed to place my hands on the side, and like a good little submissive, I did everything he told me to do. I was as sick as him. I loved it, and I'm not sure that I had ever had so many orgasms in one night.

I woke naked and wrapped securely in Drew's arms. His hand was on the side of my baby belly. I looked up to see if he was still sleeping. He wasn't. He bent and kissed me.

"This little guy is going crazy," he smiled.

"He always does first thing in the morning, and he is wreaking havoc on my bladder right now," I replied and got up to go to the bathroom.

"Come right back to me," Drew requested. I smiled.

I didn't come right back. I relieved myself and dug through my purse for the small tube of toothpaste and my toothbrush. I brushed my teeth, rinsed my mouth and looked at my reflection in the mirror.

"Drew!" I screamed. I really screamed. Had I been able to see through the wall I was sure that he was lying there with a big smirky smile.

"You fucking idiot," I ranted.

"What?" he asked, feigning stupidity.

"I can't believe you did this. What the hell?" I asked as he pulled me back to his naked body.

He towered over me with a smile. "I like it, I think it looks good on you," he stated looking at my breasts.

"You did that on purpose. You're animal marking your territory, and I don't find it a bit funny." It was huge. The bite mark was as big as a fifty cent piece, just above my right breast.

How the hell was I supposed to keep Dawson from seeing that? He wanted Dawson to see it. What the hell did I see in this idiot?

"How about I make a matching one right here?" he asked, kissing and sucking on my breast.

"Don't you dare," I demanded, grabbing his hair and pulling him off me. I'm not sure what the hell happened next. He looked up at me with a stare that entranced our vision. I couldn't see anything but him in my life, and I was sure he was seeing the same thing.

"I love you, Morgan," he whispered.

Fuck, fuck, fuck.

This trip did nothing but screw everything up again. I loved that he loved me, and I loved him beyond belief. Drew kissed me and then moved between my legs and made slow obsessive love to me.

We showered together, and I had to wear the clothes that I had arrived in. I didn't bring one thing. I hadn't planned on staying overnight. I didn't mind. It was only a two hour flight. At least I had my toothbrush.

I signed Drew's papers, and he signed just below my name. We ate a late breakfast together, and I had to get mad at him, before he stopped begging me to go home with him. I wanted to. Believe me, I wanted to, but I couldn't. Dawson was waiting for me, and I had to go home to him. I had spent the last three months trying my damnedest to make things the way they had been before with him. We were doing well, and I couldn't jeopardize screwing that up. Drew was not the type of man I wanted to help raise my child. He just wasn't.

"You are going to call me Wednesday, right?" he asked.

I sipped my decaffeinated coffee and tried to think of why I would be calling him on Wednesday.

"You're calling me as soon as you find out the sex of my baby. Remember?"

"Oh, yes. I will call," I promised, remembering the conversation the night before.

We stood outside on the blacktop for what seemed like forever. He wouldn't let me get on the plane.

"Drew, I'm freezing. I have to go."

"Can I call you?"

Yes. He could call. I wanted him to call. The only problem with that was Dawson. He was with me every night.

"Will you call during the day?" I asked.

He kissed me and let me go. "Probably not. I don't much care what your boyfriend thinks." I didn't know if that meant that he wouldn't call at all, or he would call in the evening while Dawson was there.

I spent my short flight, trying to figure out what the hell I was supposed to do. I knew what made sense. I knew what the safer choice was. I knew life would be a lot simpler in Misty Bay. I knew what choice people in their right mind would make. I wasn't in my right mind, far from it.

Gary dropped me off at my house around two in the afternoon. I did an online search on how to get rid of my new love bite from Drew. I tried toothpaste, ice, witch hazel, heat, and brushing a comb over the area. Nothing worked. I had no choice but to not let Dawson see me without a shirt until the stupid thing went away.

Chapter 26

I fell right back into the comfortable routine with Dawson. He worked, came to my house for supper and slept in my bed. I had sidestepped the shower request my first night back. We made love in the pitch dark, and by the third day the bite mark was starting to fade. I was home free.

Dawson traded shifts with Matt the following Wednesday so he could go to the doctor's appointment with me. I stared out the window on the ride back to my house. I'm not sure how to describe the wave of emotions. Don't get me wrong, I was happy. Once again, I was just confused.

Dawson reached for my hand after nudging me with his. I looked down and placed my hand in his.

"Are you disappointed?" he asked with a warm smile.

"No. Not at all. Why would I be disappointed?"

"I don't know. You seem distracted. Were you hoping for a girl?"

"No, not really. I'm fine with a little boy."

Dawson's smile reached his beautiful green eyes. "I am ecstatic for a little boy. I can't wait to take him fishing," he said, excited.

I couldn't help but smile too. I could just see the three of us walking along the beach with a brown haired little boy riding on Dawson's shoulders.

"Have you thought about names?" he asked.

"Not really. The only thing that I knew for sure was if it was a girl, her middle name was going to be Joyce like mine and Caroline's."

"Wait. I thought your middle name was Michelle," he stated, confused.

I smiled an uncertain smile." Riley's middle name is Michelle. Morgan's middle name is Joyce."

Dawson didn't reply right away. He contemplated what I had just said, briefly before responding. "I can't call you Morgan, Ry."

I kind of giggled. "I don't want you to call me Morgan." I didn't. I wasn't Morgan with him. I was Morgan with Drew, and I wanted to keep the two separated.

We stopped at Star's on the way through town and had one of her new club sandwiches. She now had two girls working for her plus the one that I had l already met. The place was hopping. Of course, she had to let her new help know that they were working there because of me. I believed that myself though. I know that it wouldn't have been more than the run down coffee shop, had I not taken it upon myself to turn it into something unique.

By the time we made it back, I was tired and ready for my daily nap. I never realized how much being pregnant took out of me. I was tired all the time.

Dawson stopped me just inside the door. He kissed me and told me that he loved me. He was as proud as an Olympian wearing a gold medal.

"I love you too," I smiled up at him kissing him.

"I suppose you are heading straight to the couch," he mused.

"That is exactly where I am heading," I assured him. What I really wanted to do was call Drew. I told him that I would call as soon as I found out. I wondered if he even remembered. Maybe I wouldn't call him. Yes. I would. The bastard asked if he could call and hadn't called one time in almost a week.

I sat on the sofa and started to call my mom.

"Who are you calling?" Dawson asked.

"My mom. I told her I would call after we found out."

Dawson knelt in front of me and kissed me again. "I'm going to my house for a bit and then to work. I'll see you tonight," he said.

"Okay, I'm going to lie on this couch and fall asleep to some tacky soap opera."

He smiled and kissed me. "I'll call you later. I love you."

"I love you too."

I had just gotten on the phone with my mom when my phone beeped. It was Drew. Of course, I had to take it right that second.

"I'll call you back in a few minutes, mom. Drew is beeping."

"Why? I thought you and Dawson were an item now. Have you filed for divorce?"

Okay. My mom and I hadn't talked for years. I didn't think she had the right to go there.

"We are. I will call you back," I said. I wanted to get to Drew before he hung up.

"Hello," I answered Drew.

"I'm having a boy aren't I?"

"You're an ass. I thought you were going to call me."

"You told me I had to call during the day while Columbo was at work."

"Who?"

"Never mind. You're too young to know who that is."

"I'm four years younger than you," I reminded him, "and you didn't call at all."

"That's because I don't work that way. I have to have everything under my terms."

"That's why you're an ass."

Drew laughed. God I missed him.

"Are you going to tell me what I am having or not."

"It's a boy."

"YES!" he exclaimed. "I knew it."

I smiled. He was just as excited as Dawson was. I couldn't help but wonder which one was going to be disappointed.

"Would you like a picture of him?"

"You mean an ultrasound picture?"

"Yes. It's 3D and neat as hell. You can actually see his little tongue sticking out."

"Hell yeah, I want to see. Do it now," he demanded.

I laughed and went into the small office, scanned the picture, and sent it to his email.

"I just sent it," I said.

"Got it. Holy shit, Morgan. That's a real baby in there," he stated the obvious.

"Um, yeah. What did you think was in there?" I asked, entertained by him.

"You can't tell me that this kid isn't mine. He looks just like me."

I laughed. Although the picture was very vivid, you really couldn't tell that yet. I tried.

"Fly home and spend a couple of days with me," Drew requested.

"I am home," I assured him.

"No. No, you're not home. This is your home. I wish you would hurry up and realize that so I could stop missing you."

I smiled. I would love to jump on a plane and go spend a few days with him, but I couldn't do that. I had already had sex with him on two different occasions while Dawson patiently waited for me to come back to him.

I liked the fact that he missed me. Why? I didn't know. I just wove tangled webs for myself. I seemed to be an expert at that.

"I'm sure Celeste is keeping you occupied," I stated.

"It really bothers you to think that I am having sex with Celeste, doesn't it? What bothers you Morgan? Is it the image of her bent over my knee or is it the thought of me giving it to her up the ass?"

"You're a son of a bitch. Are you doing those things with her?" I had to ask.

He laughed. "Are you doing those things with Dawson?" he answered my question with a question.

I had to laugh at that. "Um… No. Dawson isn't that type."

"So you still just have a boring sex life. I thought for sure you would have taught him a thing or two by now. What do you do, just the plain old missionary position?"

"This baby doesn't quite let us do that," I stated. I didn't want to talk about my sex life with Dawson. I wanted to know what he was doing with Celeste. "Answer my question."

"No. I'm going to let you think whatever you want, and I will continue to think whatever I want about you having boring sex with Dawson, and don't call me an ass or a son of a bitch either," he added. He wasn't going to tell me. That told me that he was doing it with Celeste. Bitch.

I stayed on the phone for over an hour with Drew. It soon became the norm. He would call every day around ten in the morning. I would email or text him when I knew that Dawson was off and would be at my house. Believe it or not, he didn't call when he was there. This went on for almost a month until I couldn't take it a second longer. I had to see him. I did feel bad for betraying Dawson, but in all honesty I had been betraying him all along. He wouldn't have liked my daily conversations with Drew.

My plan almost didn't work. I told him that I was going to visit my mom for a few days. He wanted to come with me.

"I want you there," I lied. "I just don't think I should give that impression to Caroline. She has already met Drew, and she knows that he is my husband," I explained.

"Are you ever going to divorce him, Ry?" he asked. I could tell that he was getting annoyed with the whole concept of me not filing for divorce yet. I was getting annoyed with him for constantly bringing it up.

I rolled my eyes and removed my legs strung across his on the sofa.

"I take that as a no," he called to my back as I walked away.

"We have this same conversation over and over. I've told you that I intend to divorce him. I don't see what the big deal is. I'm here with you, aren't I?"

"The big deal is; I don't want to continue to go to bed with someone that has another man's name, and I sure as hell don't want that son of a bitch's name on my son's birth certificate."

"You know, Daw, he might not be your son." Shit. I didn't want to say that out loud.

"Is that what you're waiting on, Ry? Do you need to see if he comes out looking like him before you commit to me?"

"No. I didn't mean it that way. Can we just go to bed?" I asked, not wanting to discuss this for the one hundredth time.

"Yeah, sure," he unemotionally replied.

I was a nervous wreck waiting for Gary to pick me up. I didn't want Dawson to run by my house, which he often did during the day, just to check on me. I was terrified that he was going to show up while Gary was picking me up. I had told him that Star was driving me to the airport. She agreed to go along with me if Dawson asked, but refused to listen to any of the details. She didn't want to know what I was doing, but at least she didn't judge me the way Lauren did. Lauren and I had an understanding. She didn't like the fact that I kept Drew at arm's length, and I didn't give her any unneeded information. I would have loved to have been able to talk to her, but I knew how she felt. She felt the same way that everyone felt. I had no one to talk to about it, so I kept my little secret a secret.

I slept during most of the flight. I did that quite a bit lately.

The warm weather was refreshing. I loved this time of year in Vegas. Unlike Maine, November in Las Vegas was comfortable. It had been forty-one degrees when I got on the plane. The seventy-four degree temperature when I stepped off the plane felt like a breath of fresh air.

I was a little mad that Drew wasn't there to pick me up himself, after begging me for a month to come and see him. Gary drove me to the house. I was even madder when he wasn't at the house either. Marta had a snack waiting when I arrived. I ate about half of the sandwich and texted him.

"Where the hell are you?"

"Calm down. I'm almost there. I had an unexpected meeting. Don't go upstairs until I get there."

"Why?"

"Because I said so."

I couldn't even finish my sandwich. For one thing I wanted to know why I couldn't go upstairs, and I could hardly wait to see him. I walked out to the front and sat down on the concrete step. I know that I only waited for about five minutes, but it seemed like at least an hour.

Drew got out wearing the grin that I loved. He was wearing his customary expensive suit and tie, but damn did he ever look hot. We weren't even supposed to be together. I was in a relationship with Dawson, and I presumed that he was doing Celeste. I didn't care at that moment. I wanted in his arms.

"Hey gorgeous," he said, taking me in his arms.

"Hi. Why can't I go upstairs?"

Drew laughed. I lost my happy smile when I saw Celeste standing behind the car carrying a stack of folders. She smiled at me, and I gave her a fake smile back.

"Why is she here?" I quietly asked.

"She's got work to do. Stop it," he demanded, kissing me on my forehead. I grumbled a quiet throat noise.

Drew pulled me inside. We went into his office with Celeste first. I sat there with my arms crossed while he went over some numbers that were throwing a red flag or something. I was trying not to pay attention. I didn't care. He was explaining what he wanted her to do when I got up to walk out. I didn't come all that way to listen to him conduct business. Drew grabbed my arm before I had a chance to escape, giving me a look to be still. He stood behind Celeste and pointed to some sort of graph on the computer. His eyes were boring into me. I wanted her to leave so that I could get him naked. He was already driving me crazy, and I had just arrived.

"I've got it. Go spend some time with your wife," Celeste animatedly told him, waving him out.

"Okay. Show me what you bought me," I demanded once he shut the office door.

"I didn't buy you anything," he assured me as he turned me to the wall. He held my hands above my head and kissed me like he really missed me.

"Damn. What was that for?" I panted.

"That was for making me miss you like crazy."

He took my hand, and I followed him upstairs. I didn't quite know what to say when he opened the door to a rarely used bedroom. It was the room right beside mine; only my room wasn't there anymore. The wall had been knocked out, and the massive room had been remodeled into a beautiful master suite. My private bath had been transformed into a luxurious retreat. The new tan stone flowed from the floor into the walk-in shower with six shower heads, full size bench and a full length mirror.

The king size platform bed was sleek with black and gold satin bedding. I walked over and moved the matching curtains to a full walk-out deck with comfortable chairs. It was absolutely gorgeous. I just wasn't sure what he expected me to say. I had Dawson.

"Open the pocket doors," he excitedly told me.

I'm sure my face was blank. I was so confused. What the hell had he done? I opened the pocket doors to the most beautiful nursery that I'd ever seen. The crib itself must have cost a fortune. It was custom made to look like a tree house. The branches came out for practical uses. One branch held the changing table to the right of the crib, another branch was full of newborn baby boy's clothing. The third branch had an automatic baby swing, and the last one came over the top of the crib and held a mobile, which I was sure was also custom made. It held diamonds that sent a sparkle across the walls and ceiling when Drew wound it up. The whole room was decorated like an enchanted forest. The hand-painted mural on one of the walls showed a vibrant forest with baby monkeys in a couple of the trees.

"Drew?" I quietly said. What did he want me to say?

"You love it, don't you?" he smiled.

"I do. I'm just not sure what to say. You do remember that this baby may not be yours. Right?"

"No. I don't believe that for a second," he replied, taking me in his arms. "I believe one hundred percent that this is my son," he said, placing his hand on my stomach. "And I believe that you are going to wake up and realize that I love you, and I want to wake up to the smell of your peach smelling hair every morning."

Shit...

Drew led me back to what he believed would be our master bedroom and made slow passionate love to me. It was just what I needed. I needed a distraction. Something bad was going to happen. I could feel it. I had to hurt someone, and for the love of God, I didn't know who that someone was going to be.

We lay naked, entwined in each other's arms in the middle of the day. Drew told me details about the construction project he'd worked on during the past couple of months. He explained the hours he'd spent picking out the bed and décor for the baby's room. I thought it was the sweetest thing ever.

"Have you thought about what we're going to call this little guy?" Drew asked.

"Not really. Dawson likes Brady." Dammit. I didn't want to say that. It just fell out of my mouth.

"Brady is a sissy name, and he doesn't have a say in what my son's name is going to be." He said it with a little bit of attitude.

"Did you have something in mind?" I asked, trying to smooth over my idiotic statement.

"I kind of like Nicholas. Nicholas Andrew Kelley," he replied.

"I like it, but why Nicholas?"

"I know I'm supposed to tell you some off the wall story about Nicholas being my hero or some shit, but I don't have one. I just like the name."

I smiled and rolled over to my side so I could kiss him.

"Tell me that you love me," he said to my lips.

"I do love you, Drew," I said to him.

"Then come home. I'm begging you."

I wanted to tell him yes that I would, but I just couldn't do it. I had Dawson, who was under the assumption that I was visiting my mother on the other side of the United States. Maybe coming here wasn't such a good idea after all. All it did was confuse me even more.

"I'm working on it, but I can't just say yes right this second." That was the best answer I had at the moment.

"You're waiting to see who the father is, aren't you?"

Was that what I was doing?

"You don't have to answer that. I know you have a lot going on, and I want you to know that I am not pressuring you. I want you to do what you want, and what you think is best for you, but you remember one thing. I want you more than I have ever wanted anything in my life. I want to spend the rest of my life making up for our first six years together."

"They weren't all bad," I replied.

"Tell me when it was good," he countered.

I couldn't do that. Drew was a monster then. He never treated me with dignity or respect. He loved to humiliate me and treat me like a piece of meat. What the hell was I doing in bed with this maniac? I should be at home getting ready to have supper with Dawson. I had to get up. I wanted away from Drew at that moment. I needed to stop remembering the past or this trip was going to turn into remorse and guilt, more than it already was.

"I'm going to take a shower," I said not answering his question.

He let me go. I stood in front of the mirror looking shamefully at my reflection. I wondered if there were cameras in the newly remodeled shower. What the hell was I doing? What in the world was I thinking? I stayed in the hot shower for as long as I could, trying to wash away my shame. It didn't work.

Drew was gone when I came out. I walked around the beautiful transformed room and then back to the baby's room. I took in every little detail. He had really gone above and beyond. The room was a mother's dream room. I sat in the gliding rocker and imagined myself holding my son as I rocked back and forth. I hadn't even realized that I had fallen asleep until Drew woke me for supper.

I opened my eyes to sweet kisses on my eyelids and then my lips. I smiled. One minute I hated this man and the next, I couldn't get enough of him. I wished there was a magic pill, a pill that would miraculously guide me in the right direction.

"You're the most beautiful mother to be on earth," he whispered.

"I fell asleep, didn't I?"

"You did. I like the idea of you falling asleep rocking my son."

"I was rocking him, wasn't I?" I smiled, realizing that I was indeed rocking my son. I couldn't say our son. I didn't know whose son I was rocking. I didn't know if I was rocking Brady Aaron Bade or Nicholas Andrew Kelly. I wasn't sure that I could keep this up for three more months. I wished I knew.

"Are you hungry," Drew asked, pulling me from my thoughts.

"I'm always hungry," I assured him.

◇◇()◇◇

I spent four days being in total love with my husband. We laughed, went for walks, watched a football game at the nearby high school, made love countless times, and fell asleep naked in each other's arms. I talked to Dawson every day, and he never suspected a thing. I was supposed to stay for two more days, but Drew had to fly to New York. He begged me to go with him, but I didn't. I didn't want to be stuck in a hotel while he was out taking care of business. We made plans to meet at my mother's in two weeks.

The last night I spent wrapped in his arms, dreading the thought of leaving him. Two weeks seemed like so far away. I drifted off to sleep after making love for the last time. I slept so soundly. I didn't even know that I was dreaming. When I finally realized what was going on Drew had me in his arms, trying to wake me.

"Shhhh, you're okay, I've got you," he said, brushing my damp hair from my forehead.

"Dawson?" I whimpered, still incoherent. I felt him stiffen and then move off the bed.

Shit. It wasn't Dawson.

"Drew?" I said to his dark silhouette.

He sat on the side of the bed and placed his head in his hands. I touched his arm, and he took my hand and brought it to his lips.

"You feel protected with him, don't you?"

What? What the hell did I say?

"I feel protected with you too," I tried.

"No, you don't. You have no idea how it makes me feel when you wake up like that."

"What did I say?"

He shook his head and breathed a deep breath.

"Tell me, Drew," I demanded.

"You were begging me not to hit you again. You were promising not to be a bad girl and telling me that you would do what I wanted" he confessed.

Shit. Stupid nightmares.

"Drew, don't, its okay."

He jumped up. "It's not okay, Morgan! I don't deserve you. I don't deserve this baby. You don't deserve me. You deserve someone like Dawson, someone who is going to respect and take care of you."

"You know what, Drew? You are absolutely right," I was getting angry with him. I didn't want him to act like this when I knew that he was leaving me in a couple of hours. His head snapped toward me. "You don't want me to bring up the past, than you're not allowed to either. I love you, dammit. I wouldn't be here if I didn't."

"Why?"

"I have no idea why. I have asked myself that same question a million times. I love you and I don't want to lose you."

"But you don't want to lose Dawson either, right?" he asked, coming back to me. I didn't want to lose Dawson. I loved him too. He was my safety net.

I didn't answer. I couldn't answer him. I didn't know what to say. Nothing I could have said would have made any sense, not to him and not to me. I needed them both.

"You need to decide, Morgan. If you don't want me, then tell me. Stop keeping me at bay. Either be with me or don't. I can't wait any longer. I have tried my best to give you time. I've given you almost six months. You have to choose, Morgan."

I knew I had to choose. I didn't want to choose. I wanted to keep them both in my life until I figured out who this baby's dad was. Drew would never understand that. Dawson would never understand that. No matter what I decided, someone was going to get hurt. Why didn't I just do the stupid paternity test?

"I can't give you an answer right this second, Drew," I said. I couldn't. I knew that as soon as I was back in Dawson's arms, I would be right back to thinking I needed him as much as I was feeling like I needed Drew when I was with him.

Drew lay back down and pulled me in his arms with a heavy sigh.

"I love you, Morgan," he whispered.

"I love you too, Drew. I really do."

Drew was gone when I woke. I knew he left before daylight. I didn't like it. I felt alone, sad, hurt, confused. I wanted him back. I wanted to be everywhere he was. I wanted Drew. I decided at that moment that I wanted Drew.

I walked up to our new master bedroom again before showering and getting ready to head back home to Maine, to Dawson. I smiled when I opened the baby's room. I thumbed through the tiny infant clothing and wondered if Drew had picked them out. There was no way a baby would ever wear all of those clothes. There were at least twenty little sleepers. I picked up the tiny little tuxedo and smiled at the embroidery that read 'Daddy's little assistant.'

"Oh, Drew what am I going to do?" I said out loud to the empty room.

I smiled again when I read Drew's text.

"You could start with coming home to me."

There were cameras. I looked around the room and answered my phone.

"Where are you?" I asked as soon as I saw that it was Drew.

"Waiting for a client. You look good in there."

"I can't believe you put cameras in here."

"You didn't really think I was going to leave my baby in there all alone without being able to look at him whenever I wanted, did you?"

"No. I guess not," I replied. Why did I feel so raw, so torn and undone?

"There is one right above the mobile. I can see him sleeping from anywhere."

I smiled and looked around the room for a camera. "I'm going to take a shower. By any chance are there cameras in there too?" I asked.

"Of course," he replied. I didn't mind. I laughed and shook my head.

"Will you call me later?"

"You call me when you land."

"I will. I love you, Drew."

"I love you too, baby."

I thought about calling Dawson, but changed my mind. One, I didn't want Drew to know that I was calling him, and two, I wanted to surprise him. He wasn't expecting me for two more days. I knew it would be later when I got home. I thought I would just show up at his house.

I showered and walked downstairs to wait for Gary. I opened Drew's office door, and Celeste was sitting at Drew's desk. I wasn't expecting to see her there. I had assumed she was with Drew. She was on the phone barking orders. I thought she sounded a lot like Drew. I felt sorry for the person on the other end. She smiled and waved me inside. I didn't really want to talk to her. I was just going to leave Drew a little note on his desk.

She talked. I listened.

"I don't care. If I wanted your excuses, I would have asked for them. You take care of this, and you take care of it now. Do I make myself clear?"

Wow, she was beautiful and powerful. Was she doing my husband? That was the question that I wanted answered. I was sure that she was. She was gorgeous, strong, and proud. She was a female version of Drew.

"Sorry about that," she smiled and sat in his chair once she hung up.

"Um, it's okay. I was just going to leave Drew a note. I didn't know you were here. I will just text him." I wasn't sure why, but I was intimidated by this woman.

"Sit down, let's talk."

What the fuck? I didn't want to talk to her. I didn't even like her, and I sure as hell didn't like her spending more time with my husband than I did.

I sat. Just like I would have had Drew told me to. I didn't speak. I wasn't about to speak first. I had no idea what to say to her. We had never even spoken before, other than a polite, hello, how are you?

"How's the pregnancy coming?" she asked.

"Oh, moving right along," I awkwardly replied.

She smiled. "Morgan, I hope you don't think that there is anything going on between Drew and me."

What the hell? Did I make it obvious? I decided to be honest.

"I do worry about the two of you traveling and spending so much time together. Things happen," I point blank told her. She laughed. The bitch laughed. I mean really laughed. She thought I was being silly. I could tell.

She stood and took her purse from the hook on the closet door. I wondered what she was doing when she pulled out a picture of the cutest little blonde haired boy ever.

"This is my son, Vincent," she said. I smiled at the little guy. He was adorable and had her blonde hair and emerald green eyes. She was married. I hoped she was happily married, but still, even married people slipped.

"This is my companion," she said handing me another picture of her, the little boy and another beautiful dark haired female.

Oh my God. She's gay.

I looked up to her smiling down at me.

"I promise, nothing would ever happen between your husband and me. He's not really my type," she teased.

I smiled. That made me feel so much better.

"Does Drew know?"

"Yes, he knows. I told him on the very first interview."

That bastard.

After talking to Celeste for almost an hour, I decided that I liked her. She even made me feel important when she answered the phone and told three different people that she was busy and would get back with them.

She didn't ask too many questions, but I was sure that she was aware of our situation. She had to know. She knew that I was never around. I wondered how much Drew had disclosed. Did they talk? Did he confide in her?

Marta knocked on the door letting me know that Gary was there for me.

"Here, give me your phone," Celeste, requested, standing.

I handed her my phone, and she programmed her number." If you ever need anything, you give me a call. I am here if you need to talk."

Not knowing how to respond, I smiled and thanked her. I was a little shocked. I couldn't believe that Celeste was gay. It was a load off of my mind, nonetheless. I hoped that she didn't say anything to Drew about our talk. I was going to keep letting him think that I thought he was doing her.

Chapter 27

I wasn't too excited about surprising Dawson anymore. It was almost eight before I was finally dropped off at my door. I was exhausted; my feet were killing me, and I was freezing. I wanted a hot bath and my bed. I would show up at the station the next day and surprise him. The only surprise that I cared about was how good my bed was going to feel.

I stepped out of the shower, when my best, annoying friend came popping into the bathroom, calling my name.

I wrapped myself in a towel just in time.

"I thought you weren't getting home until Friday," Lauren said, dropping her flannel pants and pissing in my toilet.

"I decided to come home early," I couldn't even be mad at her. I missed her audacity. Only Lauren would unlock my door, burst into the bathroom while I was naked, and drop her pants in front of me.

"What?" I asked, wondering what the glare was all about.

"You were with Drew," she demanded, following me out.

"What the hell are you talking about?" I asked, sliding on a pair of panties and night shirt.

"You're an idiot, Ry. You have no idea how much that man loves you," she stated.

"Yes. I'm sure I have a pretty good idea. What is your problem?"

"Did Drew give you a hickey?"

"What?" I hadn't seen a hickey and had even showered in front of a full length mirror. It was all steamed over, but still.

"Yeah, right below your collarbone."

I pulled my shirt out to look.

Fuck. Shit. Fuck. I'm going to kill him.

"Lauren, you can't say anything to Dawson," I all but begged.

"I can't believe you, Riley. If you don't want him, tell him. Stop letting him think that you are going to marry him, and he's going to live happily ever after."

"I do want that, Lauren," I assured her.

"So, you're going to divorce Drew now?"

Shit.

"Lauren, you have no idea what this is like for me."

"Yeah, that's what I thought. You're right, Ry. I have no idea how hard it must be for you to keep two good looking men going. You poor little thing."

"Don't do this, Lauren. This is really none of your business."

"You are absolutely right, Riley or Morgan or whatever the hell your name is. It is none of my business, but it is Dawson's. Are you planning on telling him that you just spent the last three days fucking your husband?"

"Really, Lauren?" I was speechless. I didn't know what to say. She was pissed.

"Yeah, Ry. Really?" she replied and left me standing dumbstruck in my room.

I pulled my covers back and crawled into bed with my cell phone.

"You stupid son of a bitch," I yelled as soon as Drew answered.

"Why am I a stupid son of a bitch now?" he asked.

"You know why. I can't believe you did this again. My best friend just stormed out of here pissed as hell because you had to go and leave your mark again. What the hell is wrong with you?"

"You didn't mind last night while I was doing it."

"I hate you, Drew Kelly," I stated. I did hate him. I was sick of him swooping in and out of my life and screwing everything up.

"That's too bad because I love the shit out of you."

"It's not funny, Drew," I pouted.

"I'm sorry."

"You are not, you're... whoa," I stopped when the baby's foot almost came out of my stomach.

"What's wrong, Morgan?" Drew asked alarmed.

"Nothing, the baby just kicked me."

"That's because he is pissed off at you."

"No. He's pissed off at you for upsetting me."

"No. He's pissed off at you because you are making me miss it all. You should be in my bed, and my hand should be right there."

Well, shit...

I was at my wit's end. I couldn't take either one of these men anymore. I needed to get away. I needed a break. My daily talks with Drew, sneaking off to meet him, lying to Dawson, Lauren thinking any of it was her business, I couldn't take it. I was going to lose my mind if I didn't decide on one of my men soon.

I stayed on the phone with Drew until almost eleven. I couldn't hold my eyes open for one more second when I finally told him I was falling asleep and would talk to him the next day.

Although I did sleep well, I felt like a horrible person when I woke. I felt bad for betraying Dawson, I felt bad for leading Drew on, I felt bad for being a bad friend to Lauren and I felt bad for having Star lie for me.

I got up, dressed, and headed into town. My first stop was to see Star. I needed to talk to someone who wasn't going to judge me.

We took our coffee and headed to her office.

"Talk to me," Star said. She knew something was up.

"Star. Help me. I don't know what to do, and I don't know how much longer I can keep this up."

She sipped her coffee and peered over her cup. I couldn't read her. Was she mad at me too? She sighed and sat her cup down.

"What's your heart telling you, Ry?"

"I don't know," I whined. I had decided just the day before that I wanted Drew, but now that I was back in Misty Bay, I wanted Dawson.

Star took a sheet of paper and drew a line down the middle. I snickered a little. I had watched Drew do this same

Ben Franklin so many times on different prospects. I knew what she was doing.

"This is Dawson, and this is Drew," she explained, writing their names at the top. "Only pluses first," she said. "Tell me one reason why you love Dawson," she persuaded with her pen ready to begin.

I went through a long list of whys. He was sweet; he loved me, he could read me like a book, he knew how I liked my tea; he was there for me when I needed him, he had never made me feel beneath him, I went on and on. Star had the whole side of the page filled. I could have probably thought of a few more, but I figured that was enough. She moved her pen just below Drew's name and looked up to me waiting to start.

I snorted and sucked in a deep breath.

"Drew is so damn good in bed," I said. Star smiled and wrote, great lover. "I can't fill up a whole page with Drew, Star." I told her honestly. "Drew drives me insane. Drew can push every button that I have. Drew makes me laugh when I feel like I am ready to fall apart, the sad part is, he doesn't mean to. His scent, his lips, his eyes, his touch, they all drive me crazy. I wouldn't say that is love, just something about him. Drew makes me want to swim with sharks. Dawson makes me realize the safer alternative."

"Like what?" Star asked; she had stopped writing and was just listening now.

"Like feeding goldfish," I laughed. It was the truth. Dawson made me rationalize before I did stupid things. Drew lived in the moment. Dawson would have never climbed up that rock wall, let alone had sex in the open universe.

"Can you talk to one more than the other?" she asked, tapping her pen on the desk in a slow tap, tap, tap, motion.

I thought for a second. "Not really. I mean; I guess I tend to keep silent more with Daw, I feel like I care about hurting his feeling more so than Drew. I don't have a bit of a problem telling Drew where to go. I don't really talk to Dawson like that. He would never talk to me like that."

"I see," she replied.

"You see what?"

Star sat back and crossed her arms. "I think you know who you want to be with. I think you've known all along, and I think you are afraid that the one person who could fix the pain is the one who caused it."

"You think I should choose Drew?"

"I think you already have," she spoke, honestly.

Fuck...

"But what if this baby turns out to be Dawson's? It's a very good possibility."

"Cross that bridge when it gets here. I'm going to miss you," Star said, like she knew that I was going to leave. I couldn't speak. I didn't know what to say. "You need to talk to Dawson, Ry."

"I know," I admitted. I just hated the thought of it. "I don't want to hurt him, Star."

"You're hurting him more by sneaking around with your husband."

"Maybe, if he knew, that is."

"He knows Ry."

"What do you mean?"

"He talks to me. I shouldn't say that he knows. He speculates."

"You think he knows that I have been with Drew?"

Star nodded. I wanted to get back on the plane and get the hell out of dodge. I didn't want to face him. Shit. He knew. What the hell was I supposed to say to him?

I hung around with Star until almost two. I knew that Dawson took his lunch from two to three and I had planned on meeting him and maybe going to Millie's for lunch. I felt my nerves stand on end with every tick of the Indian wall clock above my head.

Star hugged me and told me to call her. I thanked her for being my friend and not judging me the way my so-called best friend, Lauren, had.

I pulled over to the curb when I saw Dawson walking down the sidewalk. I smiled a sad smile at the sight of him. I really didn't want to hurt him any more than I had. I couldn't believe that he knew that I wasn't at my mom's. He never mentioned it when I had talked to him the day before. I lost my smile pretty quick.

What the fuck?

I watched Lauren run up behind him and jump on his back. He carried her for a few steps before she slid off. They were laughing and flirting. Was this why Lauren was so interested in my plans with Dawson? I watched Dawson hold the door open at Millie's for her. I couldn't help but notice the look between the two as she passed.

Dawson didn't have lunch with Lauren. They never hung out. I sat dumbfounded for a few minutes, trying to process what if anything was going on. How did I feel about it? That was when I knew exactly whom I belonged with. I thought about how it made me feel to think of Dawson with someone else. I smiled and shook my head. I was okay with it. I thought about Drew being with someone else and how I wanted to scratch Celeste's eyeballs out when I thought they were being intimate. I couldn't handle the thought of Drew being with someone, but I was okay with Dawson being with my best friend.

I wondered about Joel although I knew that Lauren had said she would never be serious with him. I really didn't know that Lauren had feelings for Dawson. I guess I should have. She was very insistent on me not hurting him.

What should I do? Should I walk in? Should I wait until later? What did Lauren tell him about our fight? I wasn't sure what I should do. I didn't want to embarrass either one of them. I decided to wait until later in the evening. I wanted to talk to Lauren first. I could very well just be an innocent lunch, and I was reading more into it than I should have been.

Staring out the window, I patiently waited for Lauren to get home. She pulled into her drive five hours later. I knew she wouldn't come over like she normally did. She was pissed at me.

I took a deep breath and slid my arms through my coat. I didn't even know what I was going to say. Was Lauren really seeing Dawson behind my back?

Lauren opened the door before I had a chance to knock.

"Can we talk?" I asked.

She stepped aside and gestured for me to come in.

"I just made coffee, want some?"

"Sure," I said, sitting at the table. "Lauren, I'm sorry," I blurted out even though I didn't know what I was apologizing to her for.

"Me too, Ry. I just don't want you to hurt Dawson. He is so in love with you."

Hmm. How do I respond to that? She wasn't going to mention having lunch with him. Should I? I decided to let it slide and pretend that I didn't know.

"Why don't you and Joel come over tonight?" I asked. I didn't want her to come over with Joel. I wanted to spend the evening alone, talking to Dawson. I was just fishing for information.

"Joel and I broke up almost a month ago," she stated.

"What happened? Why didn't you tell me?" I asked, playing the concerned friend.

"I came over to talk to you last night. We didn't really talk."

"Why did you break up?"

She shrugged her shoulders. "I don't know. I guess I have decided lately that I wasn't getting any younger. Joel's not really the settling down type. I want to be in love and start a family."

"Got anyone in mind?"

She thought briefly before answering. "No, not really."

She wasn't going to tell me that she went to lunch with Dawson, and she wasn't going to tell me whom she had in mind, but I could tell there was someone, and I had a good feeling that it was Dawson.

I answered my phone when I saw that it was Dawson.

"Where are you? I brought supper."

"How did you know that I was home?" I asked. I knew Lauren had told him. I just wanted to see what his answer was.

"ESP, baby. Get over here. I'm hungry, and I miss you."

I smiled. He wasn't telling me either. "I'm coming."

I stood up and took Lauren's hand. "Come, let's go eat."

"No. I think I am just going to hang out here. You go ahead," she said pulling her hand from mine.

"I thought you said you weren't mad at me."

"I'm not. I'm just not hungry. I had a big lunch."

"Please," I begged.

She groaned and got up. We walked across the yard, arm in arm. I knew I was being sly, but I couldn't help it. I had to know.

Dawson was setting plates out on the table and getting spoons for the carton of mashed potatoes and corn. I went to the kitchen and got Lauren a plate and the butter for the biscuits. I watched the two of them exchange a glance. It was not my imagination. I know what I saw, and I know that Lauren quickly redirected her eyes.

I placed the utensils on the table and decided to try something else. I wrapped my arms around Dawson's neck and kissed him.

"Hi," I said as his hands moved around by ever growing body.

"Hi," he said, and I kissed him again.

"I think I will just leave you two alone," Lauren tried.

"No. I'm done. I promise," I said, playing it off. "Sit."

We ate the chicken, and I purposely touched Dawson every chance I got, just to observe Lauren's reaction. It was obvious. She didn't want me touching him. There *was* something going on. I knew it.

Lauren helped clean up the trash. I could tell that she wanted out of there. I kissed Dawson again in the kitchen, and that was it. She was gone.

"I'll see you guys later," she stated, not looking back.

"What's her problem?" I asked Dawson.

He shrugged one shoulder. "She's your friend," he accused, like I should know better than him.

"Did you miss me?" I asked, moving into his arms. I don't know what the hell I was doing. I guess I felt a little rejected or some shit. I had planned on telling him that I didn't want to be with him and that I was going home to my husband.

I didn't feel that way anymore. I wanted Dawson, especially after realizing that Lauren wanted him too.

"Of course I missed you," he assured me, pulling me into his arms. "How's your family?"

Was he now fishing for information? "Good, I'm going back down in a couple of weeks. Caroline is in a school play, and I promised her I would come and watch."

I'm pretty sure he bought it. He kissed me, parting my lips with his tongue. I kissed him back and ran my hands along his ribs and to his strong back. I wanted him. I wanted him right that second. What the hell was wrong with me? I needed professional help for sure.

Dawson tried to lift my shirt over my head. I stopped him. I hadn't forgotten about the nice little surprise that Drew had left for me.

"I need a shower," I whispered to his lips.

He placed his forehead on mine and took a deep breath. "Then you better get away from me and go," he assured me.

I kissed him again and left.

I prayed that he didn't come into the bathroom. I think I showered quicker than I ever had in my life. I even dressed in record time.

Dawson was in my room emptying his pockets when I came out. He took clothes from his dedicated drawers and kissed me as he headed to the shower next.

Dammit he was staying. We were going to have sex. This was not the plan… at all.

I slipped on a pair of socks and eyed his cell phone, trying to tell myself not to do it. I had never looked through his phone. I never had a reason to. I jumped up and practically ran to it. I opened it up and went right to the messages. Fifty-seven of them were to and from Lauren. I scanned them quickly, listening for the shower to shut off.

Most of them were just quick little texts. Like, good morning, good night, how is your day going? And then I read where they were meeting. He knew that I was home the night before. Lauren had texted him and told him not to come over because I was home.

Why was I so pissed about Dawson and Lauren? It wasn't like I hadn't just lied to him and spent the last few days with Drew. I was furious. I was reading one from Lauren, telling Dawson that she missed his lips and couldn't wait until she could kiss him. I didn't hear the water shut off, and I didn't hear Dawson walk in.

I don't know how I knew that he was standing there. I guess I just sensed his presence. I turned to see his tight lipped face staring right at me, going through his phone.

"Dawson?" I said. I needed to know. Screw the private investigator crap. I wanted to know, and he was going to tell me.

"I've wanted to tell you, Riley."

"Tell me what?"

He didn't speak. I could feel my heart beating. I could feel the blood pumping through my veins. I was ticked. I wanted to pick his gun up and shoot him in the head. I was literally seeing little light prisms. I was so freaking mad. I couldn't see straight. Why, I wasn't sure. I really had no right, but God dammit, this hit me like a ton of bricks. I wasn't expecting this. I could have never seen this coming, not in a million years.

"How long has this been going on, Dawson?" I asked. I was trying my best to keep my cool. Never mind the fact that I was planning on dumping him that very night.

"Riley, come here," he tried. Fuck that. He wasn't touching me, ever.

"Just fucking tell me, Dawson," I demanded, still trying not to yell.

"Come out here and sit down. I will put on some tea, and we'll talk."

I stormed past him shoving his phone in his chest. I didn't want to sit. I couldn't sit. I walked out into the cold November chill in my sock feet. I needed air. I needed the brisk cold sea air. I felt that I was suffocating, and didn't know why.

Dawson left me alone while he heated water. It was probably best that he did. When I finally cooled off, I walked back in and sat at the table. I shivered, freezing from the cold air.

"Do you love her?" I asked, looking down at the table. I didn't want to see his face when I got my answer.

"I don't know, Ry. Lauren has been there for me through all of this. We spent hours together when you were missing."

"How sweet," I smartly, replied.

"Not like that. We spent hours looking for you. You were gone almost five months before anything ever happened. We were only intimate twice before I found you."

"Why didn't you just leave me lost?"

"Because I love you. I still love you."

"Do you want Lauren?"

"I don't know how to answer that right now. I guess that is up to you."

"Why would it be up to me?" I asked, turning to look at him.

He brought our teacups to the table and sat in front of me.

"If I thought for one second that you were going to divorce Drew and marry me and raise our family together, I wouldn't want Lauren."

"So, you are doing to her, what I have done to you."

"What do you mean?"

"I mean, you are putting her second because you feel obligated to make things work with me."

"Is that what you have been doing, Riley?"

"Not on purpose, but I guess so. It's always been Drew, Daw. I didn't always realize that, but it's a fact. We could have been happy had things not have happened the way they did. If I wouldn't have forgotten who I was and fallen in love with my husband for the first time, things may have been different. I do love you. You have been my safety blanket from day one."

"You want out too, don't you?"

"Yes. I didn't go to my mother's. I have been with Drew."

"I kind of figured as much, and it wasn't the first time. Was it"

I shook my head.

"What about the baby, Riley. If this is my kid, I want to be part of his life."

I smiled at him. I couldn't help it. "I know, and I would never keep you from that. I would actually be a little relieved if I knew that Lauren was going to be the other female in his life."

He smiled too. I think at that point we were both praying that this little boy wasn't his.

"I'm glad I had the opportunity to know and love you," Dawson, quietly said.

I don't know why that bothered me, but it did. I think because I knew he was at the place where he was telling me goodbye. I quickly swiped the escaped tear.

"Riley?" Dawson said, sadly, wanting me to look at him.

"I'm not Riley, Dawson. I'm Morgan."

He smiled a weak smile. "Are you going to be okay?"

"Yes. I'll be fine. I've been through worse. I'll manage."

"Yes, you have, and I hope the rest of your life is full of nothing but happiness."

I stood and walked toward the front door. I'd had enough for one night. I wanted Dawson to leave. "You can come and get your stuff whenever you want," I said, placing my hand on the door knob.

Dawson removed my hand and pulled me toward him. He held me tight, and I was trying with all of my might not to cry. It didn't work, and I let go. I cried into Dawson's shirt for the last time.

He pulled away after a bit and held my face with his hands. He bent a little so that we were at level eye contact. "I love you, Riley, and don't you ever think that I didn't."

"I love you too, Dawson. I swear I do."

I closed the door behind him, feeling as I was closing the door on that fragment of my life. I knew it was over for good this time, and I was hurt. I wasn't surprised, but I was definitely hurting. I wanted Drew. I didn't call him though. I needed time first. Instead, I called my mom and cried to her for over an hour.

She didn't speak and only listened until I was done sobbing and had cried out the last of my tears.

"Now that you are done, I think I should tell you something," she finally spoke.

"No, Mom. I can't deal with any more tonight. I'm coming out there tomorrow. I can't stay here. Save it for another day, please," I begged. She didn't.

"I understand Morgan," she began, ignoring my request. "Drew flew here when they picked your car up to bring to you. I know everything, Morgan. I know how you spent your first six years. I know that you ran from him and acquired a new identity. I know that he took you from the hospital with the same intentions as the day he picked you up when you were eighteen."

Drew told her everything. I was speechless. I couldn't believe it. Why would he do that?

"I know that he hit you and God knows what else happened. I know what his assistant did to you, and I know it was all for money. He was angry that he worked so hard on making sure that he was on that will, and you just happened to pop up out of the blue as the only living heir. But, you know what else, Morgan?"

I still couldn't speak. I shook my head, like she could see.

"I know that man loves you more than his own life. I have never seen a grown man cry as much as he did when he confessed all of his sins to me. I can't even judge him for putting a dollar before the happiness of another human being. I did the same thing. Maybe with different intentions, but nonetheless, I did the same thing."

Drew cried? Drew didn't cry. Drew wasn't capable of crying.

"Why didn't you tell me?"

"He made me promise not to. He said that he was going to step aside and let you decide on your own."

I snickered. "He never stepped aside. The longest he ever made it was almost three weeks. He couldn't stand not emailing, calling, or texting."

"That's because he loves you, baby."

"What if our past always haunts us?"

"Are you afraid of him?"

"No. Not at all."

"Then don't let the past haunt you. Leave it in the past and move forward."

"If this baby turns out to be Dawson's it will undoubtedly complicate things."

"I don't think so. We talked about that too. He actually told me that he was glad that Dawson was there for you and that if it is his baby, he couldn't have handpicked a better father figure."

I couldn't believe that it was almost midnight.

"I will let you go, mom. I'm sorry. I didn't realize it was so late."

"I've got all night, sweetie."

"Thanks for listening, Mom."

"You're welcome, honey. I am always here for you, and I am so glad that you are back in my life, even if you are making me a grandma," she teased. "I love you, Morgan."

"I love you too." I hadn't said that to my mother in years. It felt good, and it felt good to talk to her. I was so thankful she was there.

"Can I tell Caroline that you will be here tomorrow?"

I smiled. "Yes. I can't wait to see her."

"Goodnight, Morgan."

"Goodnight, Mom."

I lay awake for hours, thinking about my life. I was leaving Misty Bay. I couldn't stay there. It would be too awkward, and not fair to Dawson and Lauren. Wow. Dawson and Lauren. I still couldn't believe it. I had to talk to Lauren. I had to let her know that I wasn't mad. I was happy that Dawson would have her, and I hoped that they lived happily ever after. I needed to get hold of a realtor. No. I should wait. If this was

Dawson's son, I would want to be close by when he was visiting there. I might need to keep my house.

I'm not sure what time the exhaustion finally took over, and I slept, but I didn't wake until almost nine. I got up and started packing right away. I had wanted to be on the road by seven. I was brushing my teeth when I heard my cell phone and ran to the kitchen to grab it.

"Shit!" I yelled when my pinky toe came in full contact with the wooden bar stool leg.

"Hello," I danced around answering Drew's call.

"What's wrong? Are you in labor?"

"No, you moron. I stubbed my toe trying to get to the phone, but it feels like labor."

"I'm afraid you're in for a rude awakening my love."

I chuckled and sat on the stool, massaging my aching toe. "Are you home?"

"Not yet, getting ready to fly out. What are you doing? How's my boy?"

"Your boy is fine, and I am packing to go to my mom's."

That was the first time that I ever said "your boy." I had always rotated it back to my son and not either one of the two possible dads.

"I thought we were waiting a couple of weeks. You can't have the plane until tomorrow."

"I don't want the plane. I have a very expensive BMW, sitting in my driveway."

"Oh no, Morgan. Don't you even think about it. You're not driving all the way to your mother's in your condition."

"Drew, I'm pregnant, not crippled."

"You're not driving, Morgan."

"Yeah, okay."

"I mean it dammit. Listen to me for once in your life."

I had to bite my tongue.

"Did you call me to tell me what I can and can't do?"

"Yes. Now listen to me, would you?"

"Yes." I replied. I would just wait until we were off the phone and leave.

"I don't think your sheriff is as smart as you think he is. I can't believe he is going to let you get in your car and drive to North Carolina."

"Dawson doesn't tell me what to do. Only you do that."

"If you take off in that car, I am going to beat your pregnant ass, and that's a promise."

"Hmm, I'm positively doing it now," I teased.

"You're a sick individual, Morgan Kelley."

"You made me that way. Drew can I call you back in a little bit? Lauren is at my door."

"Doesn't Lauren just use her key and walk in?"

"We kind of had a fight."

"About what?"

"I will call you when she leaves."

"Okay, but don't you dare take off in that car."

"I'll call you back," I replied, opening the door to Lauren's weak smile.

I would call him back, just not until I was on the road.

"You're not at work," I stated the obvious.

"Nah, I'm sick," Lauren smiled. I stepped aside so that she could come in.

"You look sick," I teased. "Do you want coffee?"

"You know I do."

We were silent for a few minutes. Neither of us knew quite what to say.

I sat across from her, and it felt the exact same way as the night before, when Dawson was sitting in her chair. I guess I wasn't as mad, but I could sense the conversation we were about to have.

"Dawson told me that he told you everything last night."

"Actually he didn't. I figured it out on my own. I saw the two of you going into Millie's yesterday. I knew right away. I have never seen you two like that together."

"Riley, I'm so sorry. I never meant to fall in love with Dawson. You were gone. I didn't think you would ever be back after all of those months. I thought you ran away again."

I could see how she would think that. I had done it before, and she didn't know the details behind it. For all she knew I was running from Dawson, after all we were about to be married.

"I'm not mad anymore, Lauren. I'm still shocked; I never saw this coming."

"I almost left Misty Bay when you came back. I couldn't stand seeing him with you anymore."

"But you had Joel," I said trying to understand.

"I did, but I never loved Joel. Joel was just a distraction."

"You love Dawson?"

She nodded, spinning her cup in circles. "He had a really hard time when you disappeared, Ry. We spent hours looking for you. By the fifth month, we had gotten pretty close. We had pizza and beer one night, and I guess we were both a little tipsy. Dawson kissed me and…"

"I don't want to hear the details, Lauren," I said cutting her off. I didn't.

She nodded. "I was with him the night when he sat straight up in bed, remembering you telling him about Drew donating money to your school. I'm a horrible friend, Ry. I didn't want him to find you by then."

I smiled. "You're not a horrible friend. You fell in love. And to a good man. I fell in love too, but it wasn't with Dawson. I mean I loved Dawson. I still love Dawson, but it's not the same kind of love that I feel for Drew. I was actually going to break his heart last night. I'm glad that he has you, Lauren, and if this baby turns out to be his, I'm glad that you will be the other female in his life."

"You're going back to Drew?"

"Eventually, I'm going to my mom's for a while. I think I might have the baby there. She's been out of my life for a good many years. I want to make up for that."

"I'm going to miss you like crazy."

I smiled. "I would say that you and Dawson can come and visit, but that might be a little too awkward."

"Yeah, no doubt," she agreed.

Lauren and I talked for two hours and drank a whole pot of coffee. I felt good after all the cards were laid out. I was surprised that Dawson hadn't told her about why I had run from Drew the first time. Well, she didn't reveal that she knew anyway. I was hugging her at the door when my unbelievable husband pulled up. I should have expected it. He was only in New York, extremely close to Maine when you owned a private jet.

Lauren and Drew exchanged greetings, and she headed across the yard, back to her own dwellings. I stared after her, sadly. I was going to miss her waking me up, and eating my food. She turned and smiled at me before disappearing into her house. I turned my attention to Drew.

"What's going on?" Drew wanted to know, sensing the thick air.

"I was about to ask you the same thing," I said, sliding into his arms. I missed him; I loved him, and I wanted to spend the rest of my life being his wife.

"I had to come and drive my obtuse wife to North Carolina because she is so damned hardheaded and difficult, and the most beautiful woman on earth," he explained.

"You have to work," I reminded him.

"Not really. I own the company, and I have a really good assistant."

"I own the company, you kind of work for me," I teased.

"In that case, may I please have a few days off so that I can spend the next fifteen hours trapped in a car with my wife?"

"Hmm, most definitely," I replied, kissing him.

Chapter 28

We didn't get on the road until later in the afternoon. I wanted to stop and say goodbye to Starlight. I didn't know when I would see her again. Drew drank coffee and ate a pastry while she and I chatted in her office. I was surprised that she had known about Dawson and Lauren. She never mentioned it. I even poured my heart out to her. She had the perfect chance, and didn't say a word. I shouldn't have been surprised. She was Lauren and Dawson's friend too. She was just that kind of friend. I was going to miss her.

"Why do I get the feeling that something is going on that you're not telling me?" Drew asked when we were finally on the road.

I didn't want to talk about it yet. I was sad, and needed time to deal with the fact that I had just said goodbye to a man that I loved dearly, my friends, and my home.

I smiled over at him, and he took my hand. He was learning. He knew that I needed a moment and he let me have it. Well, he actually let me have three hours. I stared out the window thinking about what lay ahead while he conducted business on his Bluetooth. I have no idea what he was talking about and only picked up bits and pieces of his conversation. I knew that he talked to Celeste several times; some guy named Patrick with security in Chicago, and Felix the pilot.

He answered another call from Celeste two minutes after hanging up from his last call. I didn't want him to work anymore. I was done feeling sorry for myself, and I wanted his attention.

"Dammit, Celeste. I forgot about that. Can you fly them out to North Carolina? I will go over them there, sign them, and you can get them back to Mr. Richfield."

I picked up his smart phone resting in the cup holder without him realizing it. I switched off his Bluetooth and picked up the conversation. He looked at me like I'd lost my mind when he could no longer hear her, and I took over.

"Hi, Celeste. How are you?" I asked, looking at Drew.

"Why don't you bring your little guy and Alicia and spend the weekend on the beach?"

I watched Drew's bottom lip curl a little, amused.

"I'm sure it will be fine with Drew. My mom has a bed and breakfast there. I will see if there are any empty rooms if not there are nearby hotels."

"Don't worry about him. I can handle Drew, bring your family and relax for a couple of days."

"Okay. We'll see you tomorrow. I will call and let you know about the room."

I hung up and tossed the phone to the back seat.

"I need that," Drew smirked.

"No. You don't. You need me."

"I do need you, baby," he confessed. "How did you know about Celeste's family? You're supposed to think that I am doing her."

I laughed. "You're not really her type."

"You're kind of deviant."

"I learned from the best."

He smiled. "Do you want to talk to me now?"

I nodded. "Dawson and I called it off last night."

"Jesus, Drew!" I screamed when the tires hit the gravel, swerving off of the pavement.

"Sorry. What do you mean, you called it off."

"Keep your eyes on the road. I mean; I am coming home to you."

"Are you serious, Morgan?"

"Yes, I am very serious."

Drew hit the brakes and swerved to the side of the two lane road, causing a horn to blow past us.

"Oh, my God. We're not even going to have to worry about it. You're going to get us killed," I yelled, still holding the dash.

"You're not fucking with me right now? Please tell me this is real," he begged.

"It's real, Drew," I smiled. I didn't expect him to be as excited as he was.

He smiled the biggest toothy smile he could muster, not on purpose, I was sure. He couldn't help it.

"I am going to spend the rest of my life loving you," he assured me.

"And I am going to spend the rest of my life, loving you back. I am never going to bring up the past, and you can't go all dark on me if it comes up in my sleep." I knew it would. I hoped that eventually it wouldn't, but for now, it was inevitable.

"You're leaving Maine?"

I laughed. "I can't come home to you if I stay in Maine, now can I?" He had a hard time believing what I was saying. "I'm not going to sell the house just yet. I need to wait until this baby is born. If he has to go to Maine for visitations, I want to be close to him."

"He's not going to any visitations in Maine. He will be at home with his daddy, no doubt in my mind. There never has been."

I didn't tell him he could flip a coin. That was his chances of being the father. He was too excited. I didn't want to ruin that for him.

"Drive," I demanded.

He leaned over and kissed me. I placed my hand on the side of his face and let my tongue dance with his.

Down vagina, not now.

Our kiss was interrupted by the ringing of his phone in the back seat.

"You know this will drive me crazy, don't you?"

"Yes. I am aware of that," I said but didn't retrieve the phone for him.

Drew and I drove all the way to Pennsylvania before stopping for the night. We ordered Chinese delivered to our room, and I let him have his phone while I showered.

He was talking to Celeste when I came out. I shoved him back on the bed and straddled his waist while he talked. He smiled up at me with the eyes full of love. I couldn't have been happier. It may be crazy, but I was actually even happy for

Dawson and Lauren. I think it made it a little easier for me, knowing that he wasn't alone.

I unbuttoned Drew's dress pants and slid down the zipper.

"I have to go Celeste. My wife is demanding that I give her some attention."

He dropped his phone to the bed and raised his hips, helping me to slide them off.

He was already at full mast. I stroked him in my hand while our eyes stayed entranced.

"What are you doing, Mrs. Kelley?" he rasped in a sexy as hell voice.

"I need fucked," I rasped right back.

I hated my ginormous stomach at the time. I wanted to be wild and kinky with my husband, but I knew that he would be the one to control how far that went, knowing it wasn't going to be very far. He rolled me over and lifted my shirt, kissing our baby. I hoped it was our baby, anyway.

I moaned when his fingers slid between the elastic around my leg. Only Drew's fingers could do that. He slid me out of my panties and rolled me to my side a little. I guess he thought that was the easiest way to keep my round stomach out of the way. I didn't mind, especially when I felt him slide in me. I was almost embarrassed by the fact that I made it all of five strokes before I was grabbing the hotel sheets and calling out in pure ecstasy. That in turn, turned him on even more, and he thrust fast and hard into me.

"Yes, fuck me," I moaned once I felt the second wave.

That was too much for Drew. He thrust deep inside of me and released himself.

"Dammit, Morgan. You just had to go and say that, didn't you?"

I laughed and turned to face him. If somebody had told me a year ago that I was going to love this man as much as I did, I would have deemed them crazy, and possibly shot them in the head.

Drew and I lay naked, tangled in each other's bodies, talking for a long time before drifting off to sleep. I told him about Dawson and Lauren. I told him about deciding after my heart-to-heart with Star that I wanted him, and how I had dreaded telling Dawson. I told him that I found out about the two before the serious conversation. I sure am glad I did. It did make it easier to break his heart. I told him about the conversation with my mom, and let him know that I was proud of him for confessing his sins to her. I'm not sure what got into me, but I talked and talked. Drew lay silent beside me caressing my stomach. He would stop me and ask a question here and there, but for the most part, listened.

Drew stood behind me, trapping me in his arms as we floated across the ocean on the ferry. It was Friday, and I promised Caroline that we would be there before she got out of school. We barely made it. Our late night before had caused us to sleep in later than normal. I threatened to throw Drew's phone away twice already. I knew he was going to work. He couldn't help it. That stupid phone was a permanent part of his body. At least I would be with my mom and Caroline.

We did luck out and get an empty room, but Celeste wasn't going to be as lucky. They were booked unless someone didn't show, which I was hoping. I suddenly liked her and couldn't wait to meet her little boy.

My mom hugged us both at the door. We had no sooner gotten our things carried upstairs when Caroline came boring around the corner, coming to a screeching stop at our door. I smiled. She ran to me and wrapped her arms around my neck.

"That baby is getting really big," she stated.

"He is, and I can't wait for him to meet his Aunt Caroline."

"I'm going to be his aunt?"

"You sure are, and he is going to love you."

"But, I'm only seven and three quarters."

"That is the perfect age to be an aunt," Drew offered, smiling at me.

"I'm mad at you," she stated, cocking her hip and resting her fist on its side. "You said you were coming to hunt sea glass with me, you didn't show up."

"I'm here now. Let's go."

"Wait for Vincent," I told Drew, wanting Celeste's little boy to have fun too.

"Who's Vincent?" Caroline wanted to know.

"His mom works for Drew. He's seven too," I explained.

"I better go get my homework done," she stated and started off.

"Wait. It's Friday. You do homework on Friday?" Drew asked.

Caroline rolled her eyes. "My dad, he won't let me put off 'till tomorrow what I can do today," she said mimicking her dad's tone. We laughed at her and followed her out.

We sat in the guest dining room and drank coffee while Caroline did her homework. My mom smiled at me as we both observed Drew calling out spelling words to Caroline. He was going to be a good daddy, maybe not as cautious as Dawson would have been, but nonetheless, he was going to be fine.

"Dinner," Drew said.

"D-i-n-e-r," Caroline called out.

"Almost, that is diner like in a restaurant. This is a dinner, like what's for dinner, Mom? Just remember you need two plates for dinner. That will help you remember you need two N's as well."

"Oh," Caroline relied, liking his instructions.

"I have good news," Jason called, walking in to join us.

"Our newlywed couple just got into a fight and left. It looks like your friends just got a room for the weekend."

"It's good news that someone had a fight, Dad?" Caroline asked.

"No, simple Simon. It's good news that we have an extra room for Morgan and Drew's friends."

"Oh," she smiled.

We were just sitting down to eat when Celeste, Alicia and Vincent arrived. I swear I have never seen such a cute kid in all my life. I was surprised to see Celeste in jeans. I had never seen her in anything but expensive pantsuits and fancy skirts. Her girlfriend, Alicia, just as beautiful, but with light brown hair, also wore jeans. I assumed that Celeste had been the one to give birth to Vincent by the blonde hair, but he could have been adopted. I found myself curious about the couple, and wanted to ask Celeste about their relationship.

Vincent was shy at first, but my busy little sister didn't let that last too long. She insisted on him coming out of his shell. She was explaining sea glass to him, and they were both scarfing their plates, ready to head to the beach.

"Can I go now, Mom?" Vincent asked, leaving a little on his plate.

Celeste told him to let Drew eat first. Alicia told him to eat two more bites.

"Wait, which one is your mom?" nosey little Caroline asked.

"I have two moms," he replied proudly.

"Oh," she replied.

I just knew she was going to have a million questions with that one. I did. I had never had a gay friend. She didn't though. I was more inquisitive about it than she was. I was under the assumption that one always played the male role. That wasn't the case at all. Alicia was just as feminine as Celeste was. Her hair was perfect; her nails were manicured, and she was just as pretty as Celeste.

"My friend, Marissa has two moms too," Caroline explained.

"Let's go munchkins," Drew said, probably wanting to stop the conversation, as well.

We all made our way out to the massive deck once Drew, and Jason took off with the two little ones.

It was nice in North Carolina, not summer nice, but a lot warmer than it was when we left Maine. We all had on thin jackets or sweatshirts. I smiled when I watched Vincent reach up and take Drew's hand.

"Mom, come here," I exclaimed.

I placed her hand right on the side of my belly. Her face lit up. Of course, Celeste and Alicia had to feel it too.

"It seems like so long ago when Vincent was doing this," Alicia remarked. I couldn't help it. I had to ask.

"Did you carry him?"

"No. Celeste did. Can't you tell by the blonde hair?" she added. "She was not the most pleasant person to be around when she was pregnant. I swear I have never seen anyone cry as much as she did. I was ready to kill her."

I laughed. I couldn't see Celeste crying over anything. She was too strong, powerful and full of herself.

"Alicia gets to carry the next one," Celeste assured us.

"Are you trying?" I asked a little too excited.

"We're always trying," Celeste teased. They really were just like a normal couple.

"Shut up," Alicia badgered back.

Celeste laughed. "She starts her first round of in vitro the week after Thanksgiving."

"We are still talking about that," Alicia stated with a stern look right to her mate. "Celeste seems to want to do nothing but work all the time now. I'm not interested in doing this alone."

"I have a feeling my husband has something to do with that," I confessed. "But don't you worry, I will make sure you are spending the time with your family that you should be. You start the process Alicia. I promise she will be home more."

"Yeah because he fired me," Celeste said, not entirely joking.

"He would never fire you. You should hear how he talks about you. He is overly impressed."

"He is?" Celeste asked hopeful.

"Absolutely, but I'm not going to let you neglect your family to please Drew," I assured her.

My mom and Alicia got to talking about crocheting of all things. Before we knew it Celeste and I were alone on the deck while they were off looking at the new baby blanket that my mom was making for the baby.

"I can't thank you enough for this, Morgan," Celeste said, sipping her hot tea.

"You don't have to thank me. I'm glad you're here, and I love Alicia."

"Me too," she smiled. "We really did need this."

"How long have you two been together?"

"Nine years in March. How long have you been with Drew?"

"On and off for about ten years, on again for a day," I smiled.

"You are coming back to Vegas for good?"

I shrugged my shoulders. "We never really talked about it, but I am sure that is his plan. I told him that I needed to live by the beach, but he went and did all the new remodeling and the baby's room and all. I hate to disappoint him now."

Celeste laughed. "You should have seen him trying to do all of that. I couldn't help but be amused by him. He handpicked every piece of clothing in that room."

"He did?" I asked surprised. "I figured he had you do all of that."

"He had me going into every store in New York City with him, but he did all of the shopping."

I smiled out to the four figures, searching through sand and pebbles.

"I hope you know how much he loves you, Morgan," Celeste said.

I turned to look at her with narrowed eyes. "What has he told you?" I asked. I would be so embarrassed if she knew everything.

"He doesn't have to say anything. Nothing exists in his eyes when you are around. He will walk out of an important meeting to answer your call, and I have never seen any man more excited about this baby than he is."

"Are you aware that he might not be this baby's father?" I asked. Maybe I shouldn't have, but I did.

She smiled at me. "He never told me, but I had a feeling something was up."

"It's going to make things a lot more difficult if he turns out to be another man's child. Please don't tell him that I told you," I begged.

"Not a chance," she smiled as my mother and Alicia joined us again.

Jason was the only one to find any treasure, and of course he gave it to Caroline to put in her lighted bottle. We watched a movie with the two little ones on the big screen with a few other guests. Drew and I slipped off and went to our room around nine. We both showered and lay down in the, oh so comfortable bed. I hadn't realized I was as tired as I was.

"Drew," I whispered, lying in his arms.

"What, baby?"

"I'm very happy right now."

I felt Drew smile on my ear. "That makes me very happy. I love you."

"I love you too."

My mother walked out onto the deck to a full blown argument the following morning.

"No, Morgan. I want you home with me."

I didn't reply when I saw my mother; instead I brought her in the middle.

"Would you tell my husband how important it is to me for you to be there when this baby is born and that I should just stay here and get established with a doctor?"

"No. I can't tell him that. I think you need to be home with him. This is your first baby. I have time to fly out there."

"I love you," Drew said, kissing my mother smack on the lips.

I crossed my arms, pouting. She was supposed to take my side.

"You will be here in a couple of weeks for Thanksgiving and then again for Christmas. I think you should be with Drew," my mother informed me while standing behind me, playing with my hair.

Was I afraid of that? Was that why I was so insistent on only being with him for short periods of time? We had never lived together as a couple, other than when I didn't know who I was.

"Let's eat, I'm starving," Drew said with a big smile, rubbing in his victory. "I have a date with two little kids. We're going on a treasure hunt."

"We're going shopping," I stated.

Drew and Jason kept the kids occupied hunting for sea glass for the biggest part of the day. My mom, Celeste, Alicia, and I spent the day shopping. We were home by four and everyone dressed to go out for dinner. We had seafood by the ocean and then visited an aquarium. Drew and I couldn't keep our hands or eyes off each other. I had fallen asleep lying on him the night before, and we spent the evening flirting and undressing each other with our eyes. I had the best time ever with my family, my husband, and our new friends.

Drew and I went right to bed once we were home. We were undressing each other as soon as the door was closed. Dammit I wanted this baby out of me. I wanted all of Drew. I wanted him to do everything that I had despised at one time. It was a hopeless case. He wasn't about to do anything but make love to me. I knew. I had already tried. All I got was a promise that once I wasn't pregnant, he would take care of all of my deep, dark fantasies. That was almost three months away.

The five of us flew out on the private jet the next day, heading back to Las Vegas. I slept most of the way and Drew and Celeste worked, making up for the last three days.

We did fly back, all of us, for Thanksgiving and Christmas. I loved Celeste and Alicia. I hated to admit it, but Lauren had been replaced. Dawson called every week to find out how his baby was doing. He was still calling him his baby, and I didn't stop him. I just prayed that it wasn't his.

We never did send for my car. Drew liked having it there when we were at my mom's. I didn't really need it anyway. He didn't let me leave without him much.

Right after we had exchanged gifts on Christmas morning, Drew insisted that we had to go somewhere. I should have known that everyone was in on it. They all insisted on going, and we piled into two different cars. Drew couldn't contain his excitement. I was going crazy, trying to figure out what the hell he was up to. Celeste wouldn't tell me either. Caroline had to ride with her dad. She was dying to tell me.

We only drove maybe a mile up the shore and pulled into a driveway. I knew. I knew exactly what he was up to.

"You bought this house, didn't you?" I accused.

"You told me that you needed to live by the beach. I figured this way we could fly here when we wanted and would have our own space. If you look up that way, you can see your mom's house."

"I freaking love you," I exclaimed, getting out of the car.

The house was perfect. It wasn't anything extravagant like the one in Vegas. It was simple. Four bedrooms, two baths, an eat-in kitchen, and a magnificent deck, overlooking the ocean.

"I thought maybe you would want to decorate this nursery," Drew said as I checked out the best Christmas present I had ever received.

I loved the idea of decorating the nursery. Drew and Celeste had to fly to Europe for over a week. The newly pregnant Alicia, Vincent, and I stayed at the beach until Vincent had to be back to school after break.

I spent more money that week than I ever had in my life, furnishing our new home. There were delivery trucks coming and going for three days in a row. I even made Alicia pick out the furnishing and décor for the two bedrooms on the other side of the house. I figured they would be the ones using them anyway.

Vincent's room was done in surf décor and his bed was a floating bed in the shape of a surfboard. He was so excited about it. He stood on it moving his legs and holding out his arms, riding the waves painted on the wall that Alicia had done for him. I didn't know until that day that she was the one who had painted the enchanted forest in my baby's room back home.

I chose subtle for this nursery. It was painted light blue with pictures of Caroline, my mom, Jason, Drew, Celeste, Alicia and Vincent all framed in white. Justin's framed picture hung in the center of them all.

Alicia and I had a blast. We stayed up too late talking, fed our pregnant bellies too much ice cream and shopped until we literally dropped.

I didn't want to leave when Celeste and Drew came back to retrieve us. They loved the house and what we had done in such a short time. I was happy. I was so happy. I loved my new house close to my mom and Caroline. I loved Vincent. I loved Celeste and Alicia, and I loved Drew. My cup runneth over.

◇◇()◇◇

"Drew," I called to him, sleeping beside me.

"Hmm," he moaned, rolling over.

"My water broke."

He jumped out of bed wide eyed and nervous as hell. "Are you sure?"

I gave him a look and then looked down at the soaked bed.

"I'll call Dr. Long," he stated.

"Drew," I called before he got out of our room.

"What?"

"Where are you going? Your phone is right there."

"Oh," he said, realizing the obvious. He called Doctor Long, my mother and the one dreaded call to Dawson. That one caused an argument more than once, but I had promised I would call before I ever left. I hoped that he didn't come, but I was still going to hold true to my word.

I was only two centimeters dilated when we arrived. It was going to be a while. I wasn't even allowed to have an epidural yet because they said that it was too early. The contractions weren't too bad, and I was tolerating them okay.

By ten in the morning, my visitors started to arrive. Celeste and Alicia were there first, and then my mom. I couldn't believe she got there so quick. I wasn't looking for her until early evening, of course my husband had a hand in on that and got her a private flight out right away.

I had been in labor for nine hours, and the contractions were starting to come stronger and more frequent. Drew was great. He held my hand and talked me through every one of them. I finally got the epidural around three in the afternoon. It helped a lot, but the pain was still there, and I was feeling a lot of pressure. My visitors except for my mom and Drew stepped out to wait for the news.

At exactly five pm, after many bouts of nausea, sweats, and downright demon behavior, I finally felt like I needed to push.

Drew stepped out for just a second to tell our waiting party that it was time. I knew as soon as he came back that Dawson was there. I could tell by the look on his face. Dammit. I didn't want him there. Why couldn't he just wait and see if Drew was the father before he flew all the way there.

"Is Lauren with him?" I asked Drew.

"With who?" he asked, trying to feign ignorance. I gave him a look.

"Yes, she and Star are both here," he answered.

"Star's here?" I was so excited that Star was there. Dawson, not so much, and I wasn't sure how I felt about Lauren being there. I mean; I forgave her, and I was glad that she was with Dawson, but I still felt a little betrayed. I wasn't about to let it ruin my day. I was finally going to meet this baby that I had been waiting months for. I couldn't wait.

I pushed for forty-five minutes, and it just wasn't happening. The baby would crown, and that was it. He wasn't coming out. I would have said at that moment he was no doubt Drew's baby, being was stubborn as his daddy. Doctor Long explained that he wasn't going to let me go much longer. He was going to have an operating room set up for a C-section. I didn't want that. I wanted him to be born natural, and although I didn't think I had one more push in me. I tried. I tried like hell, over and over until his head was finally out. Drew never left my side and my mother was the best birthing coach ever. Had it not been for her I'm sure I would have passed out at least ten times from hyperventilating.

Finally, at seven twelve in the evening, baby Nicholas was born. He came out screaming, and I couldn't have been happier. It was no wonder he had such a hard time coming into the world. He weighed in at nine pounds, seven ounces and was twenty two inches long. He was a big boy.

Drew was the proudest papa ever, although after they lay him on my stomach I was scared. I swear he looked just like Dawson. Drew wasn't seeing it. He was seeing his son, and that was it. His hands were as bloody as the baby. He couldn't keep his hands off of him. He kissed me and told me that he loved me at least ten times before they took baby Nick to clean him up. Drew washed his hands and went out to give the good news.

"Drew," I called for him before he got out the door.

He was by my side, kissing me again in a split second. I couldn't help but laugh at him.

"I want to see Star," I said.

"You've got it, baby," he said with another kiss.

My mom left the room with him. Ten minutes later, Star came in alone with a big smile.

"I can't believe you're here, Star," I said as she wrapped her arms around me and hugged me.

"I wouldn't have missed this for the world," she said, walking over to the baby. The nurse held him up so that she could see him. She looked straight back to me. Dammit, she saw it too.

"He's just lucky I was going to be here in a couple of days anyway for the swap meet," she teased, coming back to me.

"How are you?" I asked.

"Me? How are you? You're the one who just gave birth to a football player."

"He is a little football player," I said, smiling down at him as the nurse placed him swaddled in a blanket back in my arms. I loved him already.

"How's Dawson been?" I asked not taking my eyes from my bundle of joy.

"He's been good. I told you before. Things tend to work themselves out."

"Yes, you have. I still can't believe him and Lauren though. It's so hard to picture the two of them together."

Star didn't know what to say. They were both her friends as much as I was. I respected her for that, and knew that she would stay loyal to both sides. That's just how Starlight was.

Drew came in, still smiling, of course. He kissed me, and then took the baby from my arms. He held him like he had done it a million times before. Celeste and Alicia came in next. They made as big of a fuss over him as my mom and Drew.

Everyone had been in except for Dawson and Lauren, and once Drew and I were alone again, I brought it up.

"Drew, you have to let him see the baby," I said

"I know. I was just hoping to wait until we got the test results back."

"That could be two or three days."

"Not when you just donated a quarter of a million dollars to the hospital," he grinned.

"Drew, what did you do?"

"I didn't do anything, just wrote a check and let them swab the inside of my jaw."

"There're doing it now?"

"Yup, four hours, tops," he said, staring down at sleeping Nicholas. "There is no way I was going to wait for two or three days. I want this behind us, today."

"Drew," I started to say. He stopped me.

"Don't, Morgan. We're not even going to discuss it."

I could tell that he was scared shitless that baby Nick was going to be Dawson's and not his.

"Okay, Mom and Dad. What are we putting on the birth certificate for this little guy's middle name?" the nurse interrupted.

Drew and I looked at each other. Why the hell didn't we talk about any of this before now? We couldn't give him Drew's name yet. Dawson would never let him have Drew's last name.

"We're waiting on a paternity test for that," I was the one to say. There was no easier way to say it. I was glad that she didn't ask any more questions.

"I'm going to take him to the nursery for his newborn screening, and then I will bring him back. Do you want to carry him to the nursery?" she asked Drew, no longer calling him dad.

"Yes, absolutely."

"Drew," I called.

He turned and smiled a warm, scared, smile. "I'll send him in," he said, knowing what I wanted.

Dawson walked in without Lauren. I was glad. I wasn't sure if I wanted to see her. He was wearing the same sacred smile. I wondered if he was now hoping that the baby wasn't his.

"Hi," I said.

"Hi," he said, kissing my cheek. "I think this has been the longest day of my life. How are you?"

I snickered a little. "I'm good. Happy. Scared."

"I bet. You look good," he smiled.

"Thank you. How are you?" I wanted to know if he was happy. It meant a lot to me that he was.

"I have been good, nervously waiting for you to have this baby."

That was the first time I had ever heard him not say his baby.

"Did you see him?"

"No, but Star said he looks just like me."

I looked down. I didn't want him to look like Dawson. I wanted him to look like Drew. I wasn't sure what to say. "Drew put a rush on the test. We'll know before the night's out."

He nodded. He already knew that.

We shared an awkward silence. Neither of us knew what to say.

"Lauren wants to see you," he said, kind of in a question.

I smiled and nodded. He left. I never thought that I would see the day when Dawson and I couldn't talk. It was sad.

Lauren on the other hand, acted as we were still best friends. She hugged me with a big smile.

"Congratulations," she said. "I just saw him through the window. He is beautiful, Ry."

"Thanks, how are you?"

She held up her left hand.

"Engaged!?" I said, shocked. Wow. That didn't take long. "Are you pregnant, Lauren?" I just spit it out. Why else would he be jumping into that again already?

"Dawson proposed on Christmas Eve, and yes, Ry. I'm pregnant."

"Oh, my God." I squealed, grabbing her and hugging her. I was ecstatic for her. It was weird. I felt no bitterness toward her whatsoever. "I'm so happy for you, and I'm sorry I am making things so difficult for you guys."

"You stop that. This is a happy day for you. It will all work out, besides if the baby is Dawson's, we'll have to stay friends forever," she stated.

I smiled. I really was happy that she was there. I could see me back in my little house in Maine while my son was across the street with her and Dawson. Maybe it wouldn't be so bad. It would take Drew some time, but I knew he would love him as if he were his own. Maybe I was just trying to place a little sunshine on a bad situation, but in the meantime, it seemed to be working.

Drew came in carrying our baby with a happier smile than he had left with.

"Do you want to hold him?" I asked Lauren.

"Yes, of course."

She held him, playing with his little fingers. "Ry, he is beautiful."

I was trying to read her face. Was she seeing Dawson in him too? If she was, she hid it well.

She talked about the shop, the radio station, Star dating John, my beach friend. I was glad she was talking like nothing had ever happened between us. I laughed when she said she had to take up cooking and how the first time she tried to make Dawson a nice meal, it all had turned out to be a nightmare. They ended up going to Millie's for supper.

She handed me my baby when he started to fuss. The nurse came in with a bottle, and Lauren hugged me.

"I'll see you later," she said.

"Geesh, I didn't think she was ever going to leave," Drew stated, kissing me.

"I'm glad she came," I said, watching my little man take his bottle.

"Yeah, but I have been dying to tell you something, and she wouldn't shut up," he exclaimed.

I laughed. "What?"

"Let me see my baby," he said, taking him and laying him over my legs.

"What are you doing?" I asked. Nicholas was mad. He was enjoying that bottle, and he didn't want to be unwrapped.

"Drew?" I asked again as he took the tiny diaper off.

He smiled and held him up, showing me the exact same strawberry birth mark that Drew had on the same left butt cheek. "My mom told me that my dad also had it."

I knew that a birthmark didn't prove paternity, but Drew sure did, and I was a little more hopeful.

The fifteen hour delivery was nothing compared to the wait on that stupid test. My visitors all left except, Dawson, Lauren and of course Drew. My mom made me promise her that I would call as soon as we found out. She had gone home with Celeste and Alicia because she didn't want to stay in our home alone for the first time. I think she was a little intimidated by it.

Finally at exactly ten twenty one, a man that I hadn't seen before entered with a clipboard. My heart sank. Finally, it was over. One way or another it was finally going to be out.

The man stood beside me with Drew on the other side. Drew took my hand as the man begun to explain the results.

I looked down the chart with ten lines, all saying marker 1 through 10 with numbers that I didn't understand. I didn't care. I just wanted the results.

"Based on the testing results obtained from analyses of the DNA, the probability of Drew Kelley being the father is 99.99%."

"It's Drew?!?" I asked. I was shocked. I had already set myself up for the bad news.

"Yes!" Drew yelled.

"You're sure?" I had to ask.

He flipped the page and showed me the results saying that Dawson had a 0% chance of being the father. That was a pretty low chance.

Drew kissed me and then his sleeping baby in my arms. His sleeping baby. I was ecstatic and sad at the same time. I knew that set it in stone and my life in Maine was over. I would sell the house and probably never visit there again.

Drew, of course, had to drag the technician out to Dawson. He didn't want him there, and wanted him to know that he was free to go with no further contact needed.

I didn't see Dawson again. He left without so much as a goodbye. I knew we had already done that. I still felt a little hurt that he didn't see me before he left. Lauren did come in and say goodbye with a hug. She too knew that we probably wouldn't stay friends. She hugged me with tears in her eyes.

I listened to Drew making the calls with the good news. I was suddenly exhausted. I had been up since five in the morning and endured a hell of a long labor. I had been running on adrenaline all day, waiting for the results. I couldn't have slept had I tried.

The last thing that I remembered was Drew on the phone with my mom. I was out of it.

I didn't wake again until around three in the morning. I heard Nicholas cry and opened my eyes to see Drew feeding him a bottle in a nearby chair. I smiled and watched him talk and hum to his baby. He was so proud. There wasn't an ounce of doubt left in me about the kind of father he would be. He was so in love with that little man.

Epilogue

I would have never in a million years dreamed that Drew would be so hands on with our new baby. He woke to midnight feedings, diaper changes, and a postpartum crying wife. I think I had more of an adjustment melt down than he did. It took almost three weeks before I was done with the crying sprees for no apparent reason.

Alicia spent a lot of time at the house with me. Celeste was there so much it was the only way they got to spend any time together. She was my new Lauren, and I loved her.

Drew made Alicia and Vincent come and spend the night with me five weeks after returning home. It was the first time that he had to leave since Nicholas was born. We had argued more than once about a nanny. I didn't want a nanny. Just because I was rich didn't mean that I was going to pay someone to raise my son.

I'm not sure how he got any work done at all. He called at least five times a day. He talked to Nick every one of those times. It was cute, but annoying as hell. Alicia and I had a good time though and after Nick and Vincent were down for the night we sat by the pool and drank a couple of beers, well, I did anyway. She had hot tea. I was so happy that she was pregnant and not me. I wouldn't be going through that again anytime soon.

I could have consumed more had Drew been there to take care of Nick. Alicia tried to tell me that she would take care of him, but I quit after two. The alcohol wasn't doing anything for my sex life anyway. I hadn't had sex in over two months, and dammit did I ever want it. I had one more week to go, and I couldn't wait.

We called it a night when Nicholas demanded my attention through the baby monitor.

I changed him and talked to him as I did. He was so handsome, and he no doubt looked like his daddy now. I loved the little cooing noises that he made and the way he stretched his little arms and legs like a cat. I knew his daddy was watching and as soon as I sat in the rocking chair with him he would be calling. It had become his routine if he wasn't home at bedtime.

I had just gotten the bottle in his mouth when my cell phone rang. I smiled, answering it.

"You are the hottest little mama on earth," Drew said.

"Do you know how hard it is to hold the phone, your son and his bottle at the same time?" I asked, teasing.

"Yes, but I need to tell him goodnight."

I smiled and placed the phone by his ear. I could hear him telling him that he loved him, and daddy would see him tomorrow. I loved that man.

"Let me get him down and grab a shower, and I'll call you back."

"You're going to make me watch you shower?" he asked.

I laughed. "No, you don't have to watch. You're the one who put the stupid cameras in the shower."

"I'm watching," he assured me.

"Okay. I love you. I'll talk to you in a little bit."

"I love you too, baby. Give my little man a kiss for me."

I kissed sleeping Nick, once for me and once for his daddy.

I tried to hide my sneaky smile as I undressed and got in the shower. I was no longer self-conscious about Drew watching me in the shower. It kind of turned me on. I seductively bathed for him and then placed my left hand on the tiled wall as my fingers made their way to my throbbing core. I made it show half, moaning and twisting my hips into my fingers. I heard my cell phone ring from the bathroom sink. I ignored it which I was sure he expected. I couldn't have gotten out and answered it had I wanted to. I was going to come, and he was going to watch. I did come. I came hard and called out in much needed pleasure.

I hadn't even gotten dried off when my phone rang again. I smiled and answered it.

"I'm going to freaking kill you," Drew promised.

"What's wrong, baby?" I asked, smartly.

"I can't believe you did that. Do you have any idea how long it's been? Do you really think I can handle that right now?"

"You didn't like the show?"

"If you could see how hard I am right now, you would know that I loved it."

"Dammit, Drew," I said. I didn't want to picture that. I wanted that inside of me.

"How much longer do we have?" he asked.

"One week, and we are staying in bed for a whole week."

Drew laughed and decided that we needed to talk about something else. We did. We talked about our baby boy, and going to our beach house with Celeste, Alicia and Vincent. Drew had an office built onto the house so that he and Celeste could work while we were there. Alicia and I would spend a lot of time together while the two work-a-holics did their thing. We didn't mind. She loved the beach house as much as I did, and Vincent wanted to move there. He and Caroline had treasure to find.

Alicia and I were eating lunch when Drew and Celeste arrived back home the following day. Marta brought them both a plate. Alicia and I rolled our eyes at each other because they couldn't shut up about a new merger during our meal.

I eyed Drew like I wanted to devour him. He sensed it and kept giving me the eye to stop it. I didn't. I waited until Nicholas was down for a nap and Alicia had to leave to pick Vincent up from school and went into his office.

"Alicia is leaving to get Vincent. Go with her. You're done here," I told Celeste point blank.

"I can't leave yet. I have to get this done," she stated, keeping her eyes on the laptop in front of her.

I closed her laptop. She had to move her fingers to keep me from closing them in her computer. She looked up the same time as Drew, both with shocked expressions.

"Go home," I demanded. She didn't even look at Drew for permission. She knew I was serious. She gathered her things and left.

"What are you doing?" Drew asked as I came to him.

I didn't answer. I walked around his chair and loosened his tie from behind. He didn't speak as I continued to unbutton his shirt.

"Morgan?" he questioned. I still didn't answer.

I bent and kissed his ear and sucked on his neck. That was all that it took. He was up, and I was in his arms as his mouth devoured mine.

"You can't do this yet," he panted to my lips.

"I have to," I assured him, sliding out of my pants. He helped me out of my shirt and ran his fingers between my legs.

"Jesus Christ, Morgan," he exclaimed as he felt my wetness. I moaned at his touch.

I stepped around him and bent over his desk, brushing his steel rod as I did. I thought I was going to come unglued just seeing the protrusion lying erect to the left side of his dress pants.

"What do you want?" he asked in a panty, raspy tone.

"I need for you to spank me," I instructed.

I knew I was being crazy and erratic. I didn't care. We hadn't had rough sex in so long. I was beginning to forget what it was like.

I felt the first painful, pleasure and moaned as he rubbed away the sting, dipping his finger inside of me. I could have endured the painful pleasure for an hour.

I heard him open a desk drawer. I knew what he was doing. I wanted him to do it. I felt his finger at the pucker of my ass. He moved his finger in slowly until he was easily taking in and out.

"Is this what you want, baby?" he asked.

"Yes," I panted. I wanted it there, and I wanted it right that second. I needed to come.

I heard his zipper and moaned when I felt him enter me. Drew didn't worry about going easy. That wasn't the sensitive hole. He took me rough, fast and hard, and it was just what I needed. I grabbed the side of the desk when his fingers, frantically went at it on my clit. I screamed out in pleasure which sent him spiraling into a mind blowing orgasm with me.

He stayed inside of me, panting and trying to regain control while we both came down.

Once I was finally able to breathe, I turned to him, sliding him out of me.

"I fucking love you," he said to my lips.

"Good, I love you too and thank you. I needed that."

"I'm more than happy to assist," he smiled.

"Stop working for the day," I begged.

"Can I have twenty minutes?" he asked.

I groaned but gave in, knowing that his twenty minutes were going to be at least an hour.

It was, and I was sitting by the pool with Nick when he came to find us. He took him and sat beside me on the glider.

Marta brought us coffee, and we sat hand in hand with our baby, talking about our trip to the beach house. I smiled as he explained to Nick about treasure hunting, and how the two of them would find him the best sea glass collection ever.

For the first time in my life, I was happy. I was where I was supposed to be, and I couldn't have asked for a better life. I loved my husband more than life itself, and my baby was the most important thing in my life. I loved Celeste, Alicia, Vincent, my mom, Caroline and even Jason. I don't think there was anything more in life that could have made me happier.

My nightmares had become few and far between, and when they did creep up, Drew was right there, holding me in his safe, secure arms. Even when he was gone he was always with me. I didn't even care that wherever he was, he could always see me. He even called in the middle of the night the two times that he had to be away, when I woke panicked, sweating and trying to suck in air. He talked me through both nightmares, and I was glad that he was always there.

"I love you, Drew," I whispered contently.

"I love you, Morgan," he replied with a soft sweet kiss to my hair.

The End

You can find more about Jettie Woodruff at
http://www.jettiewoodruff.com

Also, be sure to check out her other great book:

This Too Shall Pass
Starburst
Stardust
Falling Stars
Plausibility

7121089R00280

Printed in Great Britain
by Amazon.co.uk, Ltd.,
Marston Gate.